✦ Northern Lights Series ✦

IN THE LAND OF
White Nights

✦ Northern Lights Series ✦

IN THE LAND OF

White Nights

BONNIE LEON

THOMAS NELSON PUBLISHERS
Nashville • Atlanta • London • Vancouver

Copyright © 1996 by Bonnie Leon

Published in Nashville, Tennessee, by Thomas Nelson, Inc., Publishers, and distributed in Canada by Word Communications, Ltd., Richmond, British Columbia, and in the United Kingdom by Word (UK), Ltd., Milton Keynes, England.

Scripture quotations are from the NEW KING JAMES VERSION of the Bible. Copyright © 1979, 1980, 1982, 1990, Thomas Nelson, Inc., Publishers.

Library of Congress Cataloging-in-Publication Data

Leon, Bonnie.
   In the land of white nights
     p. cm. — (Northern lights ; bk. 2)
   ISBN 0-7852-7668-8 (pbk.)
    I. Title. II. Series: Leon, Bonnie. Northern lights series ; bk. 2.
PS3562.E533I5 1996
813'.54—dc20   95-19643
                                             CIP

Printed in the United States of America
1 2 3 4 5 6 7 - 02 01 00 99 98 97 96

Acknowledgments

Greg, you have displayed the kind of love God asks of husbands, and you always gave it willingly. From the beginning, before any promise of success, you believed in me. Your prayers and your trust in a God who is able to do all things have seen me through. I love you and will be forever grateful for your faith in me.

Paul, Kristi, and Sarah—I thank you for your loving patience. Your understanding and graciousness have not gone unnoticed. Even when writing this book meant long hours cloistered in my office, you understood my dedication to God and his claim on my life. It is said, "Children are a gift from God and his reward," and you have truly been that.

Ed Underwood, my pastor and teacher—thank you. It has been your devotion to God's word and your commitment to teach a pure and simple doctrine of grace that has brought me into a deeper understanding of God and his plans for me.

And praise to my Lord who does more than I can dare to hope or even dream.

Chapter 1

*A*nna's feet had barely touched the wooden decking of the sturdy little clipper ship when the captain's orders to sail sent the crew into a frenzy of activity. They clambered over the riggings, pulling on lines and climbing up the masts to unfurl the sails. Each knew his duty.

The rush of activity fascinated the young and inexperienced Anna. She'd never seen anything like it. As the sails expanded and the ship moved beneath her feet, she smiled and turned her face into the wind. The air smelled good. She smiled down at her young sister, Iya, and squeezed her hand, then hugged baby Luba close as she stifled an impulse to laugh. Her fears of the unknown momentarily faded as she delighted in being on the sea once more.

She took a slow, deep breath and looked up at her betrothed. Erik had his eyes fastened on the swelling sails. He seemed aware of nothing but the billowing white canvas that flapped in the wind. He smiled, and his blue eyes sparkled with anticipation as he gripped the railing tightly, as if by doing so he might hurry the ship along.

Anna felt his excitement. At last, they were on their way.

With its sails full, the clipper creaked as it edged forward and gradually picked up speed until they plunged toward the open sea. The small swells gave little resistance, and the boat skimmed across the waves.

Shouts and cheers came from the people standing along the shore. Anna answered their spirited good-byes with an enthusiastic wave until the well-wishers and the village gradually grew smaller and she was unable to distinguish them from the beach. Finally the cove blended into the shoreline and was lost.

"We will see them again?" Iya asked.

Anna thought a moment. "I do not know, Iya. Maybe one day we will come back." She turned and found Erik watching her. His eyes looked moist. *Do his eyes fill with tears or are they only wet from the cold and wind?* she wondered. He smiled at her, then quickly looked away, focusing his attention on the broad expanse of water stretching out before them.

Anna followed his gaze. She could see only sky and sea. Turning her face into the wind, she closed her eyes and took a deep breath, allowing the salty sea and the excitement of adventure to wash over her, thoughts of Erik and the children momentarily forgotten. The world, with its promise of rich experiences, awaited her. Her new life had begun! So much to take in, so many sensations—joy, expectation, caution. Before when she had considered her uncertain future, she had been afraid, but no longer. She knew she wasn't alone. She had Erik, Iya, and Luba, and she knew Erik's God watched over them all. *It will be a good life,* Anna told herself.

Erik leaned against the railing and gently placed his hand on Anna's arm. With her eyes still closed, she whispered, "Thank you, God." The wind whisked away her words as she looked into Erik's warm blue eyes. "This is right. It is good," she said and squeezed his hand. "I will never be afraid when you are with me."

Luba whimpered and squirmed. Anna lifted the infant up and peered into her round, flushed face. The little girl's eyes teared in the wind, and her nose ran from the cold. "Luba, would you like to go to a new home?" Anna asked brightly. Luba smiled, kicked her feet in the air, and swung her fists at the sound of Anna's voice.

Erik put his arm around Anna's shoulders and hugged her to him. "I think she likes it fine," he said and patted the little girl on the fanny. He turned to Iya and asked, "How about you? Are you ready to make a new home?"

Grinning broadly, Iya nodded. "I am glad to go to a new land. You say it is good. I know it is so." She leaned on the railing, tipped forward, and watched the waves wash against the side of the ship.

"Iya, no!" Anna cried and yanked the little girl back from the balustrade. Iya lost her footing and landed on the deck with a bewildered expression.

"I am sorry," Anna apologized, realizing her reckless reaction had only caused more trouble. "It is not safe there. You could fall.

You stay away from the railing. Until we are on land, you stay with me or Erik always."

"She's all right," Erik said as he lifted Iya to her feet. Spotting the captain he added, "I suppose we should find our rooms and get our gear stored." He headed toward the commander. "I'll talk to him. He ought to know where we belong."

Anna watched as he approached a paunchy, friendly looking man who had a pipe in his mouth and a small black cap pulled down over his unruly, brown hair.

"My name's Erik Engstrom," Erik said and extended his hand in greeting.

The captain bit down on his pipe and shook Erik's hand. "I'm Captain Bradley," he said with a warm smile. "Good to have you aboard."

"Thank you. I was wondering if you could tell me where my friends and I might find our cabins."

The captain peeked at Anna and the children, cocked one eyebrow, then looked back at Erik. He cleared his throat and said, "Certainly." He called to his first mate. "Show these passengers to their cabins."

The sailor bobbed his head. "Aye, Captain." He turned to Erik. "Your names?"

"Engstrom."

The man consulted a list. "Two rooms?"

"That's right," Erik said.

"Follow me," the sailor said curtly as he strode toward the companionway.

Erik set his jaw as Anna had seen him do many times before. She knew he was irritated, that something about the young man angered him, but he said nothing as he gathered their belongings and followed. Anna hoisted Luba onto her hip, took Iya's hand, and trailed along behind.

After following the seaman down a flight of stairs, they entered a narrow passageway. The sailor stopped outside a small wooden door.

"This one be yours, sir," the crewman said as he unlocked the door and handed Erik the key. Then he proceeded to the next doorway and, without looking at Anna, said in an unpleasant tone, "This one's for you three." He dropped the key in Anna's hand, quickly retraced his steps, and disappeared up the stairwell.

For a moment, Anna stared at the door to her room. She glanced at Erik. *We still do not share a bed?* She fumed. *At the beach Erik refused to share a hut, but why now?* She hadn't understood his reasons then but had accepted his wishes, thinking it would be different when they headed south. Her eyes filled with hot tears of humiliation. *Maybe Erik does not love me?*

Clenching her jaws and trying to hide her tears, she asked, "Why do you stay there?"

Erik blushed and looked at the key in his palm. He passed it from one hand to the other while he thought. When he looked up, he wore a crooked smile. Clearing his throat, he said, "Anna, I explained that back at the beach. We can't live together until we're married."

Anna quickly wiped at her tears and glared at him before looking away. Her anger slowly subsided, and she finally asked quietly, "Why? It makes no sense. You say you love me but do not wish to share a bed?" She hesitated. "You do not love me?" Erik moved closer to Anna and gently placed his hands on her shoulders. He cupped her chin in his hand and lifted her eyes to his. "No, Anna, that's not it. I love you very much."

Anna let out a deep sigh as he enfolded her in his arms. Of course he loved her. She snuggled close to him. "Why are we not husband and wife?"

"We will be as soon as I can find a minister to marry us. It's not right to live as one until God joins us and we are legally wed. I know it's hard for you to understand, but God wouldn't be happy with me if I disobeyed him in this. Please be patient. I'm sure there's someone in Sitka who can marry us." He hugged her tighter and added, "I can't wait to be your husband. It's what I want more than anything else in the world. Please believe me."

Anna nodded and managed a small smile. "We wait as you say." Anna felt reassured of his love. She could endure the delay.

Erik unlocked her door and carried her bag inside. The room was tiny, with two bunk beds on one wall and a washstand on the other. At the end of the room a round window let in a dim light, and next to that a cabinet was tucked into the corner. On the opposite corner stood an ugly, black coal stove. Anna unlatched the door and peered inside.

"What is this?" she asked as she backed away from the blackened interior, coughing at the dust she had raised when she opened the door.

"That's a coal stove. It's for heat. I'll show you how to use it later."

Iya studied the bunk beds. "What are these?"

"Beds," Erik explained. "You sleep on them."

Iya smiled and climbed onto the top bunk. "I will sleep here," she announced.

Anna set Luba on the floor and plopped down on the lower bed, exhaustion suddenly pulling at her.

"I'll get settled in my room while you put your things away and rest. I'll meet you on deck later," Erik said as he stepped out and closed the door behind him.

With Erik gone, the tiny room seemed empty. Anna's earlier enthusiasm vanished, and all she wanted to do was curl up and sleep.

Luba started fussing, forestalling any nap Anna might have hoped for. She scooped the infant up from the floor and settled back on the hard bunk to nurse her while Iya kept herself busy exploring the cabin. A mirror over the vanity brought a delightful exclamation from Iya as she stopped to examine her reflection. "This is better than Mother's tiny glass. Much better!"

Anna couldn't resist the temptation to look, and, as Luba was momentarily satisfied, she joined Iya. Standing behind the little girl, she gazed at her own reflection. Gold, almond-shaped eyes stared back at her. Although Anna had known for some time she was a woman, she was surprised to find the girl she remembered had grown up. She pulled her dark brown hair back from her face, exposing a smudge of dirt on her cheek. She scrubbed at it, frowning when it didn't come off. Holding Luba in one arm, she poured water from the pitcher on the washstand into a bowl, took the rough towel hanging from the bar, dipped it in the water, and scrubbed at the dirt once more. This time it submitted to her efforts and Anna smiled. "This is good," she said as she bent to wash Iya's face. Iya grimaced and pulled away, quickly finding something new to investigate. She peered beneath the bunks, reached into the dark recess, and pulled out a small pot. She removed the lid and tipped it one way then another. Unable to make sense of it, she asked, "What is this?"

Anna shrugged her shoulders. "You ask Erik. He will know." She sat down on a wobbly, wooden chair and finished nursing Luba. The movement of the ship made her uncomfortable in the close quarters, and Anna was anxious to return to the open decks above. As soon as Luba finished, she put away their few belongings. When the room looked tidy, she said, "We will go meet Erik now." With Luba strapped to her back and Iya hanging on to her hand, she slipped out the door and headed for the stairway.

They found Erik leaning on the rail, contentedly watching the shoreline. When he spotted them, he asked, "Is your room all right? You get everything put away?"

Iya cut in, "Erik, there is a big glass where I see myself!"

"I have one too," Erik said with a smile.

"There is something under our bed I do not know. It is like a bowl."

Erik thought a moment, then a blush rose in his face. He chuckled. "That's a chamber pot."

"What is a chamber pot?"

"It's there in case you have to relieve yourself," he tried to explain.

Iya's expression remained perplexed.

"You know, when you have to go in the weeds?"

Understanding dawned on Iya's face and she smiled. "That is good to have," she said matter-of-factly.

Anna turned her attention toward the sea. It felt wonderful to stand on the gently rocking deck. The ship moved differently from their small umiak; it rolled with the waves. Anna liked the rhythm. The gulls screamed overhead and dived between the sails and rigging, looking for tidbits a sailor might have carelessly tossed aside.

The ship cut through the water at an astonishing pace, and Anna felt certain it would only be a matter of days before they pulled into Sitka harbor. She felt uneasy at the thought, for that's when their new life would really begin. *What will it be like?* she wondered. Erik had warned her it might be hard, that some of the white people didn't trust Indians. She tried to reassure herself that it would not be difficult for her and the children, but she couldn't deny the fact that most of the other passengers had already made it clear they didn't associate with Indians. They kept their distance, as if afraid of contact with Anna. *I will show them. They will see we are good,* she reasoned. But despite her efforts to be nonchalant about the changes, fear pricked her and attempted to wrap itself about her heart. She closed her eyes and tried to block out her negative thoughts, focusing instead on the sensation of sailing. The wind rippled through the sails as the ship rolled, creaking and groaning, through the waves.

So much had happened so quickly. It was hard to believe only a few weeks had passed since she and Erik had acknowledged their love for each other. And although Erik wouldn't allow them to live as husband and wife now, Anna knew it would happen soon. She studied Erik and smiled. He kept his eyes trained on the great expanse of water, unaware of her scrutiny. He had seemed so different, even frightening, in the beginning. At their first meeting on the beach, she hadn't noticed how handsome he was. She had only seen a tall, white man with a wild bush of blond hair and piercing blue eyes. She hadn't noticed the ever-present smile in his eyes or known how gentle he could be. He had frightened her then, but now she couldn't imagine life without him.

A sharp, sneering voice broke through her reverie. "Looks like he's got hisself a fine bed warmer," one of the sailors jeered. "Wonder if he'd mind sharin' her with a poor, lonely mate."

Erik turned about sharply and faced the man. Neither one said anything as their eyes locked and they challenged each other.

The sailor finally conceded. "Ah, she don't look like much,

anyway. Not enough meat on her bones," he said as he returned to his work.

Anna looked at Erik. He said nothing, but Anna understood the apology in his eyes. He had warned her there would be trouble. Still, she could see it hurt him to have others mock her.

"It is all right, Erik. It does not matter," she tried to reassure him.

"It does matter," he answered between clenched teeth, but he said nothing more.

Several days passed without mishap. The weather remained calm, and Anna found the time on board pleasant. Her only company was that of the children and Erik, although the captain occasionally stopped to chat. The few women avoided Anna, so she filled the long hours fashioning hides into winter garments. She loved to spend time on deck, but the unsavory comments from the sailors kept her below much of the time. She didn't really mind their taunts but knew they upset Erik, and she worried about what he might do. Iya didn't feel the brunt of the sailors' animosity, so she most often could be found at Erik's heels.

One afternoon, the warm, sunny weather enticed Anna to journey onto the upper deck. With Luba and Iya napping, she enjoyed the freedom of roaming about with no encumbrances. She stood near the railing and watched the shoreline. Large spruce and pine replaced the small scrub trees she had grown accustomed to in the Aleutians. Dense brush and moss spread out beneath the giant trees that stretched over the water as if wishing to be part of both worlds—earth and sea.

Anna was so engrossed in the scenery she didn't notice that one of the sailors watched her. Not until he grabbed her waist and pulled her against his rough, fishy-smelling overcoat did she even know of his presence.

"Gotcha!" he said in a rough voice, his stale breath washing over her.

Anna tried to pry his arms free. "No. Go away!" she ordered.

"Ah, come on, just a little kiss for a poor, lonely mate," he sneered, as he pulled her closer.

Anna fought to free herself, but his arms only held her tighter "No!" she screamed.

Anna's battling didn't put the man off, and he nuzzled her neck, his beard scratching her soft skin.

Unexpectedly, Anna felt his arm drop as he was yanked away from her. If she hadn't been so frightened, she would have laughed at his surprised expression, but rage quickly replaced his shock as he recognized his adversary. He jerked free of Erik's grasp and swung at him.

Erik ducked and easily avoided the intended punch as he threw one of his own. He struck the sailor squarely on the jaw, sending the man sprawling across the weathered planking. The seaman rolled over and crouched close to the deck, then catapulted himself at Erik, managing to strike a sharp blow to Erik's chin.

Momentarily dazed, Erik didn't see the sharp blade the sailor pulled from his boot.

"Erik! He has a knife!" Anna screamed.

With a sick grin, the seaman swiped at Erik but missed.

Seemingly out of nowhere, a black whip slithered across the deck, wrapped itself about the mariner's ankles, and swept him off his feet.

Several sailors had stood cheering on their mate, but as they watched their friend fall, they saw the one who had bested him and stood mute.

"What's going on here?" Captain Bradley bellowed as he recoiled his whip.

The sailor pushed himself to his feet, his anger dissipating as he faced the master of the ship. He glanced at the deck and wiped away the sweat that dripped down his cheek, unwilling to meet the accusing eyes of his captain.

Captain Bradley waited. "Well?"

Forced to defend himself or confess his offense, the crewman finally said, "Ain't nothin' goin' on. He took a punch at me, and I wasn't gonna put up with nothin' from a bloody Laplander."

The captain turned to Erik and asked, "Is that what happened?"

Before Erik could say anything, Anna spoke. "That is not true. He, he . . . grabbed me. Erik only stopped him."

The captain's face darkened. He seemed to grow in stature as he turned his attention back to the frightened mariner. "You bothered the lady?" he growled.

"Lady? She ain't no lady. She's nothin' but a bloody Injun."

In two quick steps, Captain Bradley crossed the short distance to the sailor. Before the younger man knew what was happening, the captain had his hand clasped about his throat and, with his face only inches away, snarled, "To you and every man on this ship, she's a lady." When there was no reply, he tightened his grip and asked, "Do you understand?"

The sailor bobbed his head up and down.

"As long as you're on my ship, you'll do as you're told. Or would you rather swim for shore?"

The sailor only stared, his eyes bulging as he fought to breathe.

For a moment, the captain took his eyes from the crewman and glanced at the faces of the other men, then he thrust the man away from him.

"I want an apology from you." The man didn't move. "Now!" Bradley commanded.

Quickly shedding his hat, the sailor glowered at his mates, but quietly said, "I'm sorry ma'am. Didn't mean no harm."

Captain Bradley looked at his crew. "If any of you so much as touches a hair on her head, I'll have you thrown in the brig!" With that he turned to Anna and removed his hat. "I apologize for the behavior of my men. I hope there'll be no more trouble. Let me know if there is," he added with a sideways glance at his crew.

Thankful for Captain Bradley's fair-mindedness and over-whelmed by what had transpired, Anna could only nod politely before allowing Erik to usher her to her cabin.

As Erik closed the door, Anna turned to examine his wounded chin. She touched it gently, and Erik winced. She dipped one of the cotton cloths in cool water and dabbed at the swollen, red spot. "You will have a bad bruise tomorrow."

"Don't worry, it's nothing," Erik said, his eyes filled with concern. "Are you all right?"

"I am fine. You cannot fight for me."

Erik didn't say anything.

"Promise?" Anna insisted.

"I can't promise," Erik said shortly.

"There is a better way?"

Hesitantly, Erik answered, "Yeah."

"What?"

Erik grinned. "Talking is usually a first step." He paused. "I didn't do a very good job of it. I guess I wasn't much of a Christian. God says we're supposed to love our enemies."

"Love our enemies?" Anna asked incredulously.

"Yes, but it's not always easy. I really don't know what I could have done different this time. I don't think tact would have worked with that fellow." A pained expression crossed his face. Quietly he said, "Anna, I knew it would be hard for you and the girls. Most white folks just don't understand about Indians. I'm sorry. I never should have brought you."

"You should not be sorry. It is not your fault. I know it is hard. I come anyway." Anna smiled and stroked his cheek. "Nothing could be worse than to be without you."

Erik took Anna's hand and kissed her palm. "I love you. I'll do everything I can to make a good life for you and the girls. I promise." He glanced toward the door. "I better get going before we give those jack-tars something else to talk about."

Anna watched as Erik sauntered down the corridor and up the stairway. She closed the door and considered what had happened. Her stomach churned as she realized this "new life" she had chosen would be harder than she could have imagined.

Chapter 2

*I*n the days that followed, Anna met with little trouble from the crew. There was an occasional scowl thrown her way to intimidate her, but the men dared do nothing more. She knew many passengers on board mistrusted her. Their stares and rude behavior hurt and often stirred her anger. As much as possible, she tried to ignore them and the disquieted feeling that sat in her stomach like a lump of heavy bread. She stayed below decks much of the time. It was easier. And she knew instinctively that there was nothing she could do to change their way of thinking. She remembered her own mistrust of those from the outside and understood it would take more than a few weeks to dispel deeply rooted prejudices.

Despite it all, she began to enjoy the quiet routine of life at sea. It brought a sense of peace and contentment and provided her with long hours to work on her sewing and spend time with the children. Thoughts of her yet untracked future sometimes threatened to rob her of her peace of mind, but she pushed her doubts aside and forced herself to think about the promises of a new land.

Anna's greatest concern was for Erik. He seemed restless, uneasy, and distracted; his forehead was often creased with worry. She tried not to interfere. *He knows what he is doing,* she told herself more than once. But as time moved on and his disposition remained unchanged, she decided she must discover what troubled him.

One morning, she pushed aside her partially eaten breakfast, took a sip of coffee, and quietly watched him. He seemed in good humor, so gathering her courage, she took a deep breath and asked, "Erik, are you all right?"

"Yeah, I'm fine. Why do you ask?" Erik answered nonchalantly.

"I watch you. You do not seem like yourself. You seem . . . in knots. Is something wrong?"

Erik took a deep breath, clasped his hands behind his head, and leaned back in his chair as he thought about Anna's question. He didn't answer for a long time, and Anna waited patiently as he pulled his hat a little further down onto his forehead. Finally he said, "You're right. I haven't been myself lately. Thought I was doing a better job of hiding it. Should have known I couldn't keep anything from you. I'm anxious to start our life together, but that's only part of it. There is something else . . ." He sipped his coffee and glanced out the window. "The truth of it is, I'm nervous about getting to Sitka in time. To file a claim that is. There's only so much gold. If I don't get there soon, the good claims will be taken."

"This claim is important?"

"Yeah, real important. Without it we have nothing. Each man has the right to a small piece of land where he can dig and pan for gold. No one else can take it from him. That is, after he's filed for the ground. Latecomers end up empty-handed. There are only so many good places along a river, and when they're gone, that's it."

Anna felt uneasy. She tipped her cup on its edge, careful not to spill the contents, and without looking up, asked quietly, "Gold is important?"

Erik didn't answer at first. Instead he got up, walked across the room to the coffee pot, and refilled his cup. When he returned, he straddled his chair and rested his forearms on the table. Clutching his cup between his hands, he stared down into the hot, steaming brew. He cleared his throat and began, "Gold isn't everything, Anna. It's just a mineral that rests in the earth, waiting to be discovered . . . or left alone," he added with a shrug. "I don't know what God intended when he created it, but it's always been worth a lot." He took another sip of coffee. "In the big picture, I guess you could say it's not very important, but it can sure make life easier." He looked up at Anna, his eyes lively now and his voice animated. "If I strike it big, we'll never want for anything. I'll be able to buy you and the girls whatever you need or desire."

Anna studied Erik's face. Something seemed wrong. When he spoke of this gold, his voice sounded too passionate—his eyes looked too bright. Troubled, Anna stared down at her hands. Quietly, she said, "I do not want gold. I only need you."

Erik's exuberance washed away her words as if she'd never said them. He covered Anna's hands with his and continued, "I know you would be happy to go on living just the way you always have, but I want more for you." He gazed into her eyes. "This is important to me."

Anna could only manage a small smile as fear prickled up her spine. *When Erik talks of gold, he is not the same,* she thought. *Will gold and the new land change him?* The thought frightened her. She didn't want Erik to change. Would she be able to love a different Erik? Their new life loomed before her: a time and place of contrasts and disorder, always unpredictable. What would it be like to live among the whites and to be immersed in a culture she knew nothing about? For a moment, she felt smothered by the image and longed for the simple, predictable life of the beach. But even as she contemplated the possibility, her eyes wandered back to Erik and she knew it could never be. She could not return. Instead she would learn to live in the new land—she must. She longed to share her thoughts, but pride stopped her. What if Erik didn't understand?

"Captain says we're only a few days out of Sitka," Erik said, interrupting Anna's musings.

She nodded, but said nothing more.

After breakfast, they all took a stroll along the deck. Erik seemed his old self; Iya walked between them, clasping their hands in hers, while Luba gazed happily about from her perch on her mother's back. *All will be well,* Anna told herself. *Erik will not change. We will be happy always.* She leaned against the railing and looked at the sea. "The ocean looks different," she said as she studied the foreboding expanse of water.

Erik followed her gaze toward the murky waves. "It does look a little angry."

Anna shivered and pulled her cloak tighter. "It is cold. We go in now."

As the day progressed, dark gray clouds hung on the horizon, and the ship rode unevenly as the wind whipped whitecaps across the top of the waves. Large swells began to pile up, and an occasional, mountainous surge of water broke against the side of the ship.

Anna and the children spent most of the day working in their cabin, but late in the afternoon Anna felt the need to stretch her legs and went back on deck. She couldn't help but notice the men's uneasiness. Instead of their usual banter, they worked silently, their eyes repeatedly searching the sea. Anna followed their gaze and understood their anxiety. Dark clouds hung above large, threatening waves. Her stomach tightened into a knot of fear as she realized they were heading into a dangerous storm with no place to hide. Anna swallowed hard and, as if to say, "I am stronger than you, storm," turned and faced the oncoming gale, tilted her chin in the air, and stared hard at the angry clouds. She decided she would not yield to her fear and felt better.

That evening the ship rolled from side to side as they climbed into bed. Anna prayed to her newfound God for protection. She slept fitfully as the turbulent rocking disturbed her dreams. Partially asleep, she thought the movement was part of a nightmare, but as she came fully awake, she realized it was no sleep-induced illusion. The room actually pitched from side to side, and the sound of wind and waves thundered against the ship.

Iya whimpered softly and climbed down from her bunk to snuggle next to Anna. Anna hugged the little girl close, trying to comfort her. In the faded light of the oil lantern, she felt her own fear mount as she watched the pitcher on the washstand threaten to fall from its perch. Above, the mirror cast misshapen images of dark and light as it swayed on the wall.

Anna slipped away from Iya's grasp and out of bed. The little girl protested but Anna shushed her. "I will be back." Bracing herself against the unnatural roll of the floor, she slowly crossed to the teetering basin set and secured the bowl and pitcher inside the cabinet.

"That is better. They will not fall and break now," she said as lightheartedly as she could and climbed back into bed. Shivering, she snuggled close to Iya. "It is cold."

"I am afraid," Iya whispered.

Anna held her young sister close and stroked her shiny black hair. "Do not fear. The ship is strong and the captain is good."

A rapping came at the door. The noise of the storm nearly drowned out the sound, and Anna was uncertain she had heard anything until Erik poked his head inside. "You three all right?"

"Yes," Anna answered, trying to keep her voice from shaking.

"Good. The captain said we're in for a rough night and to stay in our rooms. It's too dangerous to roam about, especially on deck."

"Does the captain think it will get worse?" Anna asked, fearful of Erik's answer.

"Don't know. He didn't say. Just have to wait and see. I don't think we're in any real danger. Captain Bradley seems to know his stuff. I'm sure we'll be fine."

They looked at each other. Both knew how unpredictable the sea could be. Anything could happen.

Anna broke the silence. "You come in?"

"No time now. I might be needed up top. I'll stop by later and check on you." He allowed his eyes to rest on Anna for a moment before pulling the door closed.

He was gone. The pitching of the ship and the roar of the wind and waves seemed more intense. Anna wished he had stayed. She tried to think of something other than the tempest outside, tried to relax and rest, but she couldn't manage either. Somehow, in spite of the assault upon the ship, Iya slept, cradled in Anna's arms. Unaware of the danger, Luba slumbered peacefully, curled against the cabin wall.

The cutter groaned in protest against the battering of the storm, and Anna did her best to shut out the violent invasion. Frightened, she tried praying once more. She closed her eyes, as she had seen Erik do, folded her hands, and tentatively began, "Lord, I am scared. Erik says you can do anything. I believe you are most powerful. Will you quiet the storm? Bring peace? Please, protect the children. Amen." She looked up, but the storm hadn't quieted. It still raged. However, as she glanced at Iya and Luba, a sense of peace settled over her, replacing the fear that had oppressed her only moments before. She lay down, snuggled against Iya, and slept.

Murky light filtering through the small window of her cabin greeted Anna the following morning. The storm still buffeted the ship. Her first thought was of Erik. Why hadn't he returned? Frightening pictures filled her mind. She couldn't wait. She must find him! Pulling on her cloak, she shook Iya awake. "Iya, you watch Luba. I will find Erik," she told the sleepy youngster.

Fighting to maintain her balance, she staggered out of the room and, leaning against the corridor wall, edged her way to Erik's cabin. She knocked on his door and waited; her anxiety grew when there was no answer. She tried the knob. It was unlocked, so she pushed the door open and glanced inside. She found an empty room nearly identical to her own. Hesitantly she stepped inside and peered about, hoping Erik would appear from some unseen corner in the near darkness. But she remained alone and now didn't know what to do. Should she return to her cabin or go and look for him?

She glanced about at his things and longed to stay. His presence seemed everywhere. His duffel bag lay against the far wall, and his old coffee pot rested on its side where it had tipped over on the small stove. The stale smell of coffee still hung in the air. She sat on his bed and ran her hand over a coarse woolen blanket that had been carelessly tossed there. As she thought of him, she momentarily forgot the gale that assailed them until a large wave tossed the ship erratically, reminding Anna of her mission. She forced herself up and stepped back out into the hallway, pulling the door closed behind her.

Struggling to maintain her footing as the ship rode the spasmodic waves, Anna lurched her way down the narrow corridor. More than once she was thrown against the wall. Still Anna continued. When she reached the stairway, she stopped to catch her breath. She looked up the steps as she stood gripping the handrail. What had seemed so simple the day before now seemed an impossible task. She took a deep breath, firmly clutched the railing in her hands, and slowly began her climb. *Erik, where are you?* she worried.

After several minutes of battling the tossing ship's efforts to throw her to the bottom of the stairs, she reached the companionway and peered through the small window in the door. What she saw sent shivers of fear through her. The rain and wind pelted the small ship, while seawater washed over the sides and swept across the wooden decking. Pieces of rope, tools, and other debris sloshed across the floor. As water drained over the sides, the ship nosed into another monstrous wave and more seawater crashed aboard.

Anna considered turning back but after coming this far couldn't bring herself to give up. Determined to find Erik, she pushed against the door, which the wind thrust back against her shoulder. Finally forcing it open, she quickly stepped through the doorway before the wind slammed it shut behind her. She grasped the handrail, leaned into the gale, and inched her way toward the stern of the cutter. Through rain-sodden hair, she scanned the ship. Erik wasn't anywhere.

She knew calling for him would be useless. He'd never hear her above the shrieking wind. A large, wooden block slammed into the wall in front of her, nearly knocking Anna off her feet. Swallowing a sob, she decided she'd have to turn back. It was no use. She would never find Erik this way. Discouraged, she took one last look about and headed back toward the companionway.

Anna hadn't been in her cabin long when cries from the crew filtered down from above and someone pounded on her door. Before she could answer, Erik pushed it open. He braced himself in the doorway and at first could say nothing as he struggled to catch his breath. His clothes were soaked; his face was lined with fatigue and worry.

Anna shuddered. She could see more than simple concern in Erik's eyes. Panic surged through her, and she took a deep breath in an effort to suppress it. Her heart pounded so hard she feared it might burst. "What is wrong?" she finally asked, unable to keep her voice from shaking.

"The storm's pushing us toward the rocks. The captain says there's nothing to worry about, but to be on the safe side he wants everyone to put on a life jacket."

"Life jacket?"

"They're stowed here above the beds," Erik yelled above the storm's pounding as he worked his way across the room to the tiny cabinet and yanked it open. He pulled several unusual-looking pieces of gear from the shelf. "Put one on," he ordered as he lifted Iya out of bed and slipped the strange apparel over her head.

Anna watched and tried to imitate what he did, but ended up helplessly entangled. In frustration she raised her hands in the air and lamented, "I do not know how."

"You've got it on upside down," Erik chuckled nervously. Quickly he slipped the cumbersome flotation device off and placed it right side up over Anna's head. "That's better," he said as he pulled the laces tight.

"Why do we wear this?" Anna asked.

Erik hesitated and glanced down at Iya before answering. "If something happens to the ship, these will keep you afloat until help comes or you're washed ashore."

Anna nodded as she scooped her crying daughter off the bed. "What about Luba?"

For a moment, Erik looked blankly at Anna, unable to answer her question. Finally he said, "Just pray we won't have to worry about that. Strap her to you. If we abandon ship, I'll make sure you and the girls are the first into a boat. Now, everybody up on deck!"

Shocked, Anna stared at him. She'd just been there and knew what the conditions were. "We will not go. It is too dangerous."

"It's more dangerous here if the ship goes down. You need to be where you can hear the captain's orders, especially if he calls for us to abandon ship. We have to be up top. There's no other choice. Just stay away from the rail and keep close to the walls."

Erik didn't allow any more time for discussion. He took Iya in his arms and headed down the passageway and up the stairs. Anna followed, with Luba strapped to her chest. She tried to maintain her footing as the storm tossed them up each mountainous wave then dropped them down the other side of it.

When they left the protection of the companionway, the wind and cold rain hit Anna like a frozen fist, sucking away her breath and dousing her in frigid saltwater. She pushed her soaked hair aside and tried to blink away the rivulets of water that washed into her eyes. The storm had grown even more horrifying. Howling through the rigging and canvas sails, the wind threatened to pull them from their restraints and blow them out to sea. Rain fell in huge drops, adding to the seawater that flooded the decks.

Erik took a piece of rope and lashed Iya to the handrail along the wall. Then he looped another cord through Anna's belt, tying her alongside Iya. "Hang on," he yelled. "I'll go see where the captain wants us. Stay put until I get back." Before Anna could reply, he moved aft and out of earshot.

With Luba strapped across her chest and holding Iya tightly alongside her, Anna crouched against the wall and helplessly watched the frantic activity about them. Wet and half-frozen sailors wrestled with the wild and unresponsive rigging to keep the ship headed into the waves. Others worked to lash down gear that had broken loose, trying to keep it from dangerously tumbling about. Their faces were lined with exhaustion as they fought relentlessly against a power they couldn't possibly overcome. But they couldn't stop. Giving up would mean certain death.

As Anna watched, she gained a new respect for these men who embraced the challenge and danger of the sea. These were not ordinary men. No common man would choose such a life. Her thoughts lasted only a moment as Iya's fearful cries brought her back to their own peril. She'd never felt so vulnerable. At the beach, their homes had always provided protection from the storms, and even in the small umiak she'd felt a sense of control . . . not this helplessness.

Iya clutched at her older sister. "Make it stop!" the little girl cried, as tears ran down her face and mixed with the seawater. The wind bellowed, nearly drowning out her words before tossing them aside.

"Don't worry, everything will be all right," Anna yelled over the raging storm. "We can pray." She turned her eyes upward and called to the Creator of the universe above the discordant symphony swirling about them. "God! I know you are there. You are a powerful God. Stop the wind. Please carry our boat into safe water." To herself, she whispered, *"And if we die today, take us into your heaven."*

She pulled Iya closer and continued praying quietly, beseeching God for mercy. Glancing up at the deckhouse, she caught sight of Captain Bradley at the wheel. Even from this distance, she could see the fatigue on his face, but surprisingly, no fear. He stood fixed and immovable as he piloted his ship and barked orders to his men. His confidence stirred assurance in Anna, renewing her hope.

The minutes passed slowly as she waited for Erik's return. *Where is he?* she wondered. *He should be back. God, protect him.* Once more, fear began to gnaw at her as frightening possibilities played through her mind. She hummed an ancient chant and tried to push her dread aside. Closing her eyes, thoughts of her family filled her—Inoki, her mother and father. She blinked back her tears as she remembered her people. If not for the tsunami, she would still be there with them, raising Kinauquak's child. Even in the midst of such turbulence, her memories still brought intense pain. She almost welcomed a pounding wave as it washed across the deck and yanked her back to the present—away from a time and place she could never retrieve.

Drenched and shivering with the cold, Anna longed for their warm, dry room. She tried to draw the girls closer to warm them, but the wet and cold had already penetrated and chilled them. They were no match for such a storm. Trembling, the three huddled close together, drawing strength from each other as they waited for the chaos to abate.

As the sea's onslaught continued, Anna searched desperately for shelter. She scanned the deck, but the only protected place seemed to be the small companionway. *We will wait just inside. There is room for us,* she reasoned. *We will watch.* She glanced down at Iya. The child's lips were tinged with blue. *Out here we will die.* Her decision made, she moved to untie their bindings.

A scream ripped through the air as a strong gust of wind whipped across the deck followed by another surge of seawater. Anna glanced up just as a young sailor plummeted from the rigging. He landed only a few feet from her, and did not move. She stared at him, not knowing what to do. She couldn't leave Iya and Luba nor could she take them with her while she went to his aid. He lay frighteningly still. Anna looked about for help, and an older, whiskered sailor rushed to the young man's side.

"Johnny! Johnny!" he called. "Can you hear me?" Johnny moaned.

The older man slipped his arms beneath his friend and gently lifted him from the deck. He staggered momentarily beneath his burden and swayed with the pitching ship. At last, worry etched across his face, he found his footing and carried the young man to the companionway and out of sight.

Anna let out her breath, only now aware she had been holding it. She had begun to believe Erik's world lacked love and compassion, but as she watched the sailor care for his friend, she saw these characteristics in the man and felt comforted and hopeful.

A powerful wave hit the ship, worse than any before. She felt the floor slide out from under her as the small clipper tilted at a sharp angle. *The boat tips over!* her mind shrieked. She suppressed a scream.

Unexpectedly Erik's arm was about her. "The captain's trying to turn the ship about. It'll mean some rough going for a while. Just hang on!" he shouted and hugged her close. Anna clung to him, trying not to burst into tears.

With Iya and Luba protected between them, Erik and Anna huddled into the companionway and clung to the wall railing for what seemed like hours. Exhausted, Anna relaxed against Erik. In a half-sleep, she sensed a change in the ship's movement. The sway seemed less violent, and the wind no longer sounded as loud in the rigging and sails. At first she thought she had simply grown used to the feel and sound of the storm, but the sensation persisted and she opened her eyes.

"Sounds like things are improving," Erik announced cheerfully. He shivered. "I doubt there's any chance of having to abandon ship now."

Anna nodded and gratefully followed him inside. She sank to the floor and leaned against the wall. The smell of damp cloth and skins filled their small hideaway. Stiff and weary, she longed for a warm bath and her bed. She rubbed her neck and stretched, trying to work out some of her cramped muscles.

Iya continued to sleep, while Luba nuzzled against her mother's body, grateful for a meal. Anna breathed a sigh of relief and smiled at Erik. "Sleep will be good."

Groaning with fatigue, Erik pushed himself up from his crouching position. "Can't think of anything I'd rather do. I'll check with the captain to see if it's safe to return to our cabins." He headed back out into the storm, pulling the door closed behind him and shutting out the gale.

Anna slumped against the wall and, holding Iya and Luba close to her, thanked God for his mercy. She had no doubts that he had saved them.

She dozed off, and the next thing she knew Erik was shaking her awake. He wore a triumphant smile. "Captain says we're through the worst of it, and we're no longer in danger of washing onto the rocks. We can return to our cabins!"

Anna only looked at him, too tired to fully comprehend the good news. Erik pulled her to her feet, lifted Iya in his arms, and carried the sleeping child down the stairway. Anna followed quietly, trying not to awaken Luba.

Erik pushed open the door to Anna's room and settled Iya in her bed. Gratefully, Anna fell into hers, too tired to even bother removing her dirty, saturated clothing. Erik gently covered her with a quilt, and she was asleep before he left the room.

Several hours later, she slowly became aware of the sounds and smells about her. Opening her eyes, she found the sun slanting in through their small window. She smiled. The floor no longer swayed perilously, and the wind had ceased its howling. The smell of frying bacon and fresh bread made Anna's mouth water in anticipation of a long overdue meal. Iya still slept, but Luba's hunger had awakened her, and she insisted on being fed. Anna put the infant to her breast and settled back to enjoy the peace that saturated the small compartment. She found it hard to imagine that only a few hours before, their lives had nearly been extinguished by a deadly storm. She dozed a little, and after Luba had satisfied her hunger, Anna yawned and stretched lazily before leaving her bed.

The water basin was empty so Anna took her bucket, filled it from the barrel at the end of the companionway, and returned to her room. Her clothing had grown stiff while she slept, and the salt and dirt grated against her skin. Curling her lip in disgust, she carefully pulled the offensive tunic over her head, shivering in the chilly air. No heat came from their tiny coal stove, so Anna shoveled fuel into the small box and lit it. She quickly washed, donned fresh clothing, and combed her hair into a tight braid. With this done, she scrubbed her filthy garments and hung them near the stove to dry.

"Is the storm gone?" Iya asked as she sat up and swung her legs over the side of her bed.

"Yes, gone," Anna answered as she patted the little girl's leg.

"I am hungry."

"You need to wash and change your tunic before eating."

Iya pouted a moment before catapulting off the bunk. Knowing she had no choice, she stripped off her tunic and held the soiled clothing out to Anna. "This smells bad."

Anna nodded and smiled as she took the sealskin dress. With disdain, she looked at the filthy water in the tub. One washing was all it was good for, but nothing could be done about it, so she plunged the soiled garment into the bucket and scrubbed it as best she could. Pointing at the water pitcher, she told Iya, "You wash." The little girl obeyed without argument.

"After we eat we will get more water."

A quiet tapping came at the door. Anna finished squeezing out Iya's tunic, hung it alongside her own, and went to answer the knock. Opening the door, she found a weary but cheerful-looking Erik standing in the hallway.

"I thought I heard voices in here. You look a sight better than the last time I saw you."

"Did I sleep a long time?"

"Yep. We all did," Erik said with a laugh. "Captain said we can get something to eat anytime we're ready. They're keeping the galley open so people can come and go as they want. I think everybody slept the day away."

"We are hungry!" Iya announced as she pulled a clean dress over her head.

"Well, let's go, then," Erik said.

"Wait. I need to clean and change Luba first," Anna said.

Iya pulled impatiently on Erik's hand and leaned out the door as they waited. When Anna and Luba were finally ready, she giggled and headed down the corridor, yanking on Erik's arm to hurry him along.

Once on deck, Anna found it hard to believe a storm had pummeled the ship only hours before. Wisps of white clouds adorned a dazzling blue sky and cast moving shadows on deck. The cold, sharp breeze raised small whitecaps on the crest of the ocean swells, but no hint of the brutal wind remained.

Anna stopped along the railing and took a slow, deep breath. The air smelled clean and fresh. The ship no longer hugged the shore and, as Anna gazed out at the distant coastline, the heavy forests looked tiny. Mists hovered along the beach, making the coastal peaks seem to float above the drifting haze as they reached into the sky.

"It is beautiful," Anna whispered to Erik.

"It is that, all right. We're close to Sitka now. I think you'll like it there. It looks a lot like this."

"I will like it then."

"I want to eat," Iya whined.

"I'm more than due for a meal," Erik agreed.

The coastal beauty momentarily forgotten, the travelers headed for the galley.

Chapter 3

*E*arly morning light filtered through the doorway of the nearly empty saloon, illuminating the dust and smoke that hung stagnant in the air. Three men sat at a table tucked into a dark corner. One peered at the cards in his hands over the spectacles that perched on his nose, while a large native sat across from him chewing on the end of a cigar, his face partially hidden behind his cards. The native broke into a smug smile and slid several coins across the table. "I'll raise ya two bucks."

The third man had the look of an eagle, and said nothing, only studied his hand.

The man with the glasses slapped his cards down on the table and said, "I'm out. That's it. I'm done in." He scratched at his scraggly goatee, nudged his glasses back up on his nose, and pushed himself away from the table. "Enough's enough," he mumbled as he shuffled across the floor and out the door.

Now there were only two left, and the man who hadn't spoken lit a cigarette and took a long, slow drag. A sinister look crossed his face as his cold, blue eyes followed the little man's path outside and lingered a moment on the open doorway. "What a loser," he said, his cigarette locked between his lips. "Runt." He glanced back at his cards. "Ahh, we don't need him. We got a good game goin'." He studied his cards again. "Tell you what. I'll see you and raise ya another five." Expressionless, he took a stack of coins and carefully placed them in the center of the table. He leaned back in his chair and scowled at the man across from him. The native kept his eyes on his cards. "Well, Joe, what's it gonna be?" the cruel-looking man finally asked.

The native glanced up, rubbed his two-day stubble thoughtfully, and looked back at his cards. Slowly he laid them face down on the table. "Too rich for me, Jarvis."

"I never seen so many cowards in one place before," Jarvis growled. "If you want to play cards with me, you'd better come prepared next time."

Joe glared at his opponent, then purposely relaxed and leaned back in his chair. He stretched and yawned. "Been a long night." The sound of a cock crowing came from somewhere down the street. "Hear that? Even the chickens are up. It's time for me to sleep."

"I should have known. You got no backbone for playin' a real game of cards," Jarvis jeered.

"I am not so simpleminded that I will stay here and let you keep takin' my money. Heard your partner was a real fool, though." Joe leaned his elbows on the table. "What happened to him anyway? No one's seen him since you got into town."

"Ahh, the birdbrain took sick and died on me a couple months back. Just as well—he was nothin' but extra baggage anyway. Stupid as a stump."

Casually Joe relit his cigar. He puffed on it until it glowed red, then took the thick stogie between his thumb and forefinger and studied it a moment as he asked, "What do you plan to do? This is no country to be in without a partner."

"I ain't got time to think about no partner now," Jarvis growled through clenched teeth. "I've got business to settle. I'm lookin' for a man named Enid James."

"What did he do?"

"Let's just say he got in a big hurry when he shouldn't have." Jarvis took a long drag on his cigarette, lifted his chin, and slowly blew the smoke into the air. "He captained a small cutter. Left me and Frank on a beach with nothin' but a bunch of Injuns for company. He's a runty, prissy-looking fella with jet black hair. You seen him?"

Joe thought a moment. "Might have. Seen a man like that a while back, but not since the ice broke up."

Jarvis slammed his fist on the table and cursed. "I should have known! Nothin' goes my way," he griped. He leaned on the table, his anger building. "Until that runt returns, I guess I'll concentrate on finding that no-good trapper."

Joe remained cool, meeting Jarvis's stare. "Who is he?"

"He should have known better than to leave me out there in that icy wilderness," Jarvis continued, unaware of Joe's question.

"Who?" Joe persisted.

"Ah, you don't know him. Just another drifter looking for a fast buck. Last time I saw him, he had an Injun squaw and a kid with him. They were stayin' in a shack down Cook Inlet. I doubt they're still there. He was doin' some trappin' and probably only passin' through. Those kind don't stay in one place long. But he's somewhere here in Alaska, and one day I'll get my hands on him. Some day he'll pay." He raked his money off the table. Half smiling, he snickered as he stuffed the coins into a leather pouch. "Not a bad night's work."

Joe kept his eyes on him. He took his cigar out of his mouth and rolled it between his fingers. "Man could have big trouble out here without a partner. Everyone needs someone to watch his back."

Jarvis eyed the big man suspiciously. "What kind of Injun are you, anyway?"

"My mother is Tlingit, but my father was Russian."

"That explains your looks. Didn't think you were a hundred percent—too good lookin' for that," he said with a laugh. "You talk pretty good for an Injun."

"I lived near a white settlement."

"You from down south?"

"Sitka."

"I figured. Your size is a dead giveaway. Most of the natives up north are so short they look like dang midgets. Sometimes it's hard to tell the men from the women." A crooked grin creased his face, and he added, "As long as they got those baggy, sealskin clothes on, that is." He laughed.

Joe glowered at Jarvis.

Abruptly Jarvis stopped chuckling and leaned back in his chair, throwing his right leg over the left. He met Joe's stare. "What did you have in mind?"

"If a man is going to make it here, he needs a partner. Frank is dead, and you need someone who knows the country. You're pretty good at cards." He paused. "Maybe we could help each other."

"I don't know. I've never been much taken with the idea of associatin' with Injuns."

"Forget it then. I do not need you," Joe cut in. "I will find someone else. Someone who's interested in prospecting."

Jarvis sat straighter in his chair and leaned forward a little. "You know of a place worth minin'?"

"Maybe," Joe answered as he straightened his legs out in front of him and folded his arms across his chest. "Thought you weren't interested in an 'Injun' partner."

"I might be convinced to change my mind," Jarvis answered warily. "Where's this gold at?"

Joe didn't answer right away. He ground his cigar out on the edge of the table and dropped the remaining butt in his shirt pocket. "I do not tell just anyone."

"Okay, cut the bull. I'm interested," Jarvis finally admitted. "Now, can you show me where to find this gold?"

"I will think about it," Joe said with a tight grin. "I will let you know. Now it's time to sleep." Abruptly he pushed himself away from the table and lumbered out of the saloon, leaving Jarvis alone in the gloomy tavern.

Jarvis took the last drag on his cigarette, tossed it to the floor, and crushed it under his heel. "Ahh, I don't need no filthy heathen helpin' me," he grumbled as he slid his chair back. "I don't need anybody's help. All I got to do is keep my ears open. There's always some fool shootin' off his mouth."

But even as he tried to convince himself he could do it on his own, he knew it wouldn't be easy. He didn't know his way around the land. He needed that Indian, and Jarvis hated needing anybody.

With the storm three days behind them, Anna relaxed a little and settled back into her daily pattern. She hoped she'd never have to face another storm at sea. She'd begun to grow weary of the routine on board the cutter and looked forward to setting her feet on solid ground again.

When the cry of "Sitka! Sitka Bay!" came, her heart began to pound erratically. They had finally arrived! Her anticipation was tempered by a sudden sense of panic. What did this new world have in store for her? She wished she could magically see into the future, but she knew the only thing to do was begin her new life.

Activity on board the ship ceased as the crew and passengers crowded to the railing and peered toward the shoreline.

Anna shaded her eyes against the glare of the sun and scanned the coast. "There it is!" she cried as the seaport came into sight.

"Where?" Iya asked, reaching on her tiptoes to peer over the railing.

"There," Anna answered, pointing toward the shore.

"I see! I see!" Iya cheered, grasping the railing in her hands and jumping up and down.

The bay sat tucked between forested hills and steep, snow-capped mountains. It looked peaceful and hospitable, with ships waiting inside its quiet waters. No doubt, after exchanging goods with Sitka's merchants, the crews had gone ashore to enjoy the sights and entertainment the city had to offer.

Long buildings reached over the water, supported by wooden pilings, while smaller structures dotted the shoreline. Beyond this, rows of houses and small business establishments lined the city's narrow dirt streets. Although they were already into the summer months, smoke rose from many of the town's chimneys, attesting to the cool, damp weather common to this area of Alaska.

Anna could see people bustling about town, completely unaware of the new arrivals in their bay. She watched them, hoping to glean some understanding of this new world from its residents. Soon she would plunge into the unknown, into an unfamiliar life that held hopes for a better tomorrow but no promises. She squinted, trying to make out what kind of clothing the people wore. They seemed oddly dressed, but they were still too far away, and she was unable to get a good look.

Erik joined Anna at the railing. "So, what do you think?"

"It is beautiful," she hesitated, "and strange." Pointing toward the dock, she asked, "What are those long houses?"

"The biggest building over there is a sawmill, and the one on the end is the shipyard."

"Oh," Anna said blankly. A moment later, she asked, "What is a shipyard and sawmill?"

"The shipyard is where they work on boats. You know, sprucing them up and repairing them."

Anna nodded and asked, "The sawmill?"

"They cut trees down in the forest and haul them to the mill. Some are sawed up to be used for houses and businesses or even ships. Others are bound together with cables and floated to other mills down the coast."

A large structure on a hill overlooking the town caught Anna's attention. "What is that building?" she asked as she pointed to it.

"Oh, that's known as Baranov's Castle. It was built by a man named Baranov who came from Russia. That's where he and his aides lived while he ruled Sitka. I think it holds government offices now."

"Sitka is big," Iya interjected.

"It's a large town for Alaska," Erik agreed. "But there are cities down south that make this look like a village."

"Like San Fran . . . cis . . . co?" the little girl asked, stumbling over the name.

"That's right. San Francisco is one of the biggest."

"Can we go there sometime?"

"I don't see why not. After we get set up and make a little money, we'll take a trip down."

"Is this our new home?"

Erik looked at the small city and said, "No, we'll only be stopping here for a short while. After I stake out our claim, we'll move farther north on the mainland. And I have to say, I'll be just as glad not to live here. Ever since the U.S. took over, the town's gone downhill and the Indians haven't been too cooperative."

"What does co . . . oper . . . ative mean?" Iya asked, having trouble with the big word.

"What I mean is, the Indians are mad about some of the changes. Sometimes they give folks a hard time."

The travelers remained at the rail while Captain Bradley skillfully maneuvered the ship into the harbor, ordered the sails shortened, and prepared to lower the boats for transporting passengers and supplies.

"We better get our gear packed," Erik said as he lifted Iya onto his shoulders. "It's time to go ashore."

"We go now?" Anna asked a little timidly.

"Sure. No time like the present," he answered as he galloped toward the companionway with Iya on his back. "I'll get my stuff together then give you a hand." He dropped Iya to the floor and hurried down the stairway. Anna followed more slowly, but Erik waited at the base of the stairs to escort her to her cabin.

Wishing she could feel more excitement and less apprehension, Anna surveyed her small cabin. It had served them well for the past several weeks, and she would miss it. She sighed, opened the small cupboard, and began packing their few belongings. When she finished, she stopped to take one more look about, then, trying to keep her voice light, said, "It is time we go," and stepped into the hallway, closing the door behind her.

Erik met her in the corridor. "I didn't expect you to be ready so soon," he said with a grin.

"Not much to do," Anna answered shortly, shifting Luba onto her hip and moving toward the stairway. She kept her eyes averted, not wanting him to see her anxiety.

Once on deck, Anna strapped Luba into her sling and allowed Erik to help her into a small, wooden boat that hung from a hoist and rocked perilously over the water. As Erik lifted Iya into the swaying craft, Anna settled herself on a seat in the center of the dory. She pulled her sister safely alongside her. The little girl fidgeted, unable to contain her excitement. When Erik took the seat across from them, she nearly leaped into his lap, giggling as he planted her securely beside him.

"Don't budge. You'll have to sit still. It's dangerous to be jumping around," Erik said sternly, but he smiled to soften the reprimand.

Iya cranked her head about, trying to take in all the activity.

Before lowering the boat, Captain Bradley strode up to the side of the craft. Looking at Anna, he removed his hat and said warmly, "Ma'am, it's been a pleasure having you on board. I hope it wasn't too uncomfortable for you. Again, I apologize for my men. Good luck to you and your family."

Anna smiled and, nodding her head in respect, answered, "You have been very kind. Thank you."

The captain bowed slightly at the waist, then called, "Lower away!"

The boat shifted away from the ship and slowly descended, swinging slightly. When it slapped against the waves, a sailor quickly severed their link with the clipper and pulled hard on the oars, moving rapidly away from the small ship.

Anna sat very straight in her seat as they sloshed through the small chop. More than once she found herself tugging on her tunic laces, and try as she might, she couldn't keep her hands still. Her heart beat hard against her chest, and she tried to calm herself by taking slow, deep breaths. Luba remained quiet. Anna almost wished the child would fuss so she would have something to do.

Erik reached over and patted Anna's hand. "It's going to be all right."

Anna swallowed hard and nodded, managing a small smile before turning her attention back to the harbor.

The trip ashore passed quickly, and all too soon, they came alongside a small platform with a steep stairway that led up to the pier. The crewman jumped out of the skiff, took a long lead of rope, and tied the craft to the platform. Erik stepped out and lifted Iya onto the landing. Anna stood with her legs braced, balancing as the boat washed from side to side, and gazed at the long stairway.

"Give me your hand," Erik said.

Anna glanced at him, took his hand, and stepped out of the small vessel. For a moment, their eyes met. Neither of them said a word, but they both knew this was the beginning. Anna took a deep breath and started up the steps. Each stride took her farther from the familiar and closer to the unknown. A desire to retreat washed over her. The small cabin back on board the ship seemed safe and secure. She fought the impulse to turn and head back down the steps. She stopped a moment and glanced back at Erik. He looked so hopeful, so unencumbered as he smiled up at her. Anna felt stronger and smiled back. With renewed determination she moved on. She would not let him down.

Iya had already negotiated the steep stairway and called for Anna and Erik to hurry. After they had assembled on the pier, the little girl bounded down the wharf, seemingly intent on starting her new life immediately. However, as she approached a group of men huddled near the end of the dock, she slowed her steps. They watched her approach, looking fierce and unfriendly. One man took a long drag on a cigarette. He stared menacingly at Iya, while slowly exhaling and blowing smoke in her direction. Iya stopped and backed up slowly. When she had put an additional ten feet between herself and the strangers, she turned and ran down the dock toward her family.

"Those men look bad," she whispered as she grabbed hold of Erik's hand.

Erik held the little girl's hand tightly in his, circled his arm protectively about Anna's shoulders, and straightened his back as they walked past the leering men. He looked straight at them. Intolerance hung in the air, but no one said anything, although each man knew what the other thought.

Once on shore, Iya asked, "Why are those men mean?"

"Oh, don't let them bother you. They're just ignorant," Erik explained, trying to shrug off the incident. He stopped and looked about. "I know there's a boardinghouse in town. I'm just not sure where. Let's take a look down this way. Maybe we can find a minister while we're at it," he added with a smile and hugged Anna.

The four of them headed down the muddy street. Anna stayed close to Erik and, although a little frightened by the unusual sights and sounds around her, found herself intrigued. She squared back her shoulders and lifted her chin slightly, determined no one would know how unsure she felt.

Horses and carts moved past them, and from inside one of the saloons, the raucous sounds of the drunken locals reached to the street.

Anna peered through a store window and studied the unusual articles inside. There was so much she didn't know. Excitement began to burn in her chest as she contemplated all that she would learn.

All of a sudden someone collided with her, interrupting her inspection of the shop. She turned and found herself staring into the chest of a very tall Indian. He wore the clothing of a white man, but his hair hung long and loose about his shoulders, and he wore a ring of ivory or bone through his nose. He stared at her but didn't say a word.

Frightened, Anna sucked in her breath and backed away. Erik quickly came to her side. "No harm done," he said to the big man. The Indian only glared at Erik. Without saying a word, he finally moved on.

Erik glanced at Anna, and his face broke into a broad smile as he chuckled.

"What is funny?" Anna asked indignantly.

"If only you could see your face."

"What is wrong with my face?"

"Well, you looked so surprised."

"I never saw an Indian like him before. He . . ." she searched for the right word. "He is very big."

"That was a Tlingit. They're more like the Indians we have down in the states. There's not much likeness between them and the Aleuts. They look pretty fierce. And from what I've been told, they have a reputation for strength and short tempers. You don't need to worry, though. The whites and natives used to battle, but these days they get along pretty well. From what I've seen, the Indians have become part of the town."

"That is good," Anna answered and fell into step beside Erik as they renewed their search for lodging.

A few minutes later, Erik stopped. "I still don't see anything that looks like a boardinghouse." He peered inside the door of a peaceful looking tavern. "This place seems pretty quiet. You and the girls stay out here. I'll go in and find out what I can."

Anna wanted to go with him, but she nodded her head and leaned against the side of the building and waited while Erik disappeared through the doorway.

Chapter 4

$\mathcal{E}$rik blinked, trying to adapt to the darkness inside the saloon. The only light came from two smoky oil lanterns, one on each wall, and a small window that faced the street. As his eyes slowly adjusted to the gloom, Erik glanced about, seeking a friendly face. The tavern was almost empty. *Too early for the evening rush,* he figured as his eyes fell upon two men at the bar. One was tall and lanky, with an air of inertia, the other was just the opposite—a short, squat fellow who looked restless and hungry. His right cheek bulged from a wad of tobacco he'd tucked inside. Both men sported heavy beards and wore their hair long and loose about their necks. *Sourdoughs,* Erik thought, for clearly both men had been living in the north for a long while. *Usually a worthy sort. They should be able to help me.*

A third man appeared from a back room. He was clean shaven and wore what had once been a white apron tightly cinched about his waist. A damp, soiled cloth hung from his hand.

Must be the bartender, Erik decided. He didn't detect any malice from the three, although they seemed wary as they scrutinized him. Erik watched them closely as he made his way across the littered floor of the saloon. "Nice day," he remarked as he stepped up to the bar and rested his arm on the counter.

The tallest of the three nodded in greeting. "A whole sight better'n what we went through a few days ago. That was one of the worst williwaws I've seen come through these parts. Nearly blew us off the map."

"I'll tell you, it was no picnic at sea either," Erik responded and relaxed a little. "For a while I wondered if my last resting place might be at the bottom of the Pacific." He smiled and extended his hand. "Name's Erik Engstrom. Just got into town and hoped someone here could tell me where I might find a boardinghouse."

The barman began mopping the counter with the filthy rag, and Erik wondered what could be accomplished by sopping the bar with the foul cloth. Without stopping to even look at him, the bartender said, "There's one just down the street. A woman named Cora Browning runs it. She's almost always got a room. Good cook too," he added as he flipped the cloth across the end of the bar and looked at Erik. "You plan to be in town long?"

"No, I've got business up north, but my friends will be staying on for a while."

"Friends? I don't see no friends. Where you keepin' em?" he asked, with an edge to his voice.

"They're waitin' for me," Erik answered, a sense of alarm settling in his belly.

"Well, why didn't they come in with ya?" the stubby man asked. "They don't think they're too good for this here bar do they?" He swept his arm through the air as if presenting a grand ballroom. All three men chuckled.

"It's a woman and two children," Erik explained. "They're not friends exactly." The moment the words came from his mouth, he wished he could take them back. *Now why did I tell them that?* he chided himself.

"Well, what are they?" the shorter man taunted.

The three men glanced at each other knowingly and turned to watch Erik as they waited for an answer.

I don't know what set these fellas off, but I better do something or the next thing I know they'll be tossing me out, Erik thought. "They're just my family is all."

The bartender dunked the washcloth in a tub of dirty water and wrung it out. "Family, huh? Well, just a minute ago you said they was your friends. Which one is it?"

"Family," Erik answered shortly. "Well, I guess we'll head on up to the boardinghouse."

The bartender added, "This ain't such a good place for families these days."

"Is that right?"

Without missing a swipe with his cloth, he went on. "Never

thought I'd say this, but since the Russians got booted out, things been goin' downhill. Almost wish things had stayed the way they was." He stopped and looked at Erik. "Don't get me wrong. I'm as loyal to my country as the next guy, but the Americans just ain't doin' much to keep the peace. Most o' the troops pulled out and left us without no protection."

Erik breathed a quiet sigh of relief as the tension relaxed and the men's attention turned toward the town's troubles.

"No government left at all as far as I'm concerned," the lanky man added as he finished off his drink.

The other two nodded in agreement.

"Without no government the Injuns been gettin' pretty uppity. A man can never tell just what might happen. These days my only sleeping companion is my rifle, and," he reached behind the bar and pulled out an old, rusted shotgun, "I'd like to see one of them heathens try and get at me while I'm workin'." He turned his attention to Erik. "Or anybody else, for that matter," he added.

The stocky man turned the conversation back to Erik's family. "You say your family was outside?"

"I didn't say," Erik answered evasively, knowing it would be just as well if these three didn't know about Anna and the children.

Instead of letting it pass, they persisted. "Well, just where are they?" the bartender challenged.

Erik wished he'd found some other place to ask directions. He glanced at the door.

Before he could move, the squat man tramped toward the entrance. He stepped outside and glanced about, noticing something just out of their sight. With a grin, he shuffled back inside and spit a wad of tobacco toward a spittoon next to the bar. He missed, and the sodden, brown mash lay on the wooden floor. "All I seen is an Injun with two Injun brats. Them your family?"

"Yes. Well, not exactly," Erik said, knowing these men meant trouble and wishing there were an easy way out of this. But as he thought of all he and Anna had shared, how she had stood by him, he felt ashamed. There was no easy way out. Either he stood up for what he believed and the people he believed in or he didn't. He slowly eased his eyes over the three men, then let them rest on the offensive runt and said, "She's not my wife yet, but I plan to marry her just as soon as I can find a minister."

The bartender rounded the bar and strode up to Erik. "I just don't understand you Injun lovers. You got no sense. Ya don't have to marry them kind. They're happy enough to keep your bed warm without no license. Only fools wed up with Injuns." The man's voice rose in pitch with each word. "Pretty soon you'll be sproutin' half-breeds all over the countryside."

The tall man cut in. "There ain't no place for you here. Get you and your *family*," he spit the word out as if it were bitter on his tongue, "down the road. We don't need no more Injun lovers."

"Wouldn't close my eyes at night. That squaw will slice your throat just as soon as look at ya," the short man added with a grin, exposing tobacco-stained teeth.

Suddenly Anna came through the door and stood just inside the gloomy room. At first she didn't say anything. Finally she found Erik's face.

The three Sitka residents were taken off guard by her intrusion and momentarily stopped their taunting as they glared at the small Indian woman. The air felt heavy and menacing, as if a thunderstorm were imminent.

Anna let the door close behind her, and in a soft voice ended the silence. "Erik, I hear much talking. Are you all right?"

Next Iya stepped inside and, doing her best to balance Luba on her hip and keep a tight grip on the door, blinked in the dim light. Sunlight slid across the floor, revealing the filth left from the night before.

"Anna, Iya, you wait outside," Erik cautioned, his voice tight and controlled.

"Let the little lady come in," the bartender jeered. "We'll be more than happy to show her a 'real' Sitka welcome."

Erik wanted to pummel the man—all of them—but he held his rage in check. Although he stood ready to fight, a small voice stopped him. *What about the girls?* He glanced at Anna, Iya, and Luba. He'd misjudged the men in the beginning, and while he didn't think they'd actually harm Anna and the girls, he couldn't be certain. He was clearly outnumbered, and though the outcome of an all-out brawl could only be guessed at, he was certainly at a disadvantage.

He stood motionless a moment, fighting with himself. He wanted to hammer them, but reason finally won out and he unclenched his hands and forced himself to relax. Still staring at his challengers, he slipped his arm about Anna's shoulders, took Iya by the hand and, without another word, escorted them out of the room. Malicious hoots and hollers followed them into the street. Erik no longer felt angry, only sorry Anna had been the target of the men's prejudice.

"Guess they don't take to mixed marriages," he said lightheartedly, trying to brighten the mood.

Anna glared back over her shoulder. "They want to hurt you because of me? Maybe it is wrong I come," she said as her anger dissolved into guilt.

"It will never be wrong for us to be together," Erik reassured her. "Don't worry about the likes of them. They're just a bunch of ruffians." He tucked his hands into his suspenders and, putting on an arrogant air, added, "By the way, I did manage to get what I went in for. Those fellows told me about a place to stay just down the street." He smiled. "We'll find it and check in. After that, all we have to do is locate a minister. Hope there's one in town."

They followed the muddy street another block until they came to what looked like a boardinghouse. A sign hanging alongside the front door proclaimed, "Cora's—Rooms for Rent." The two-story building seemed to be the only painted structure in town. Its clean, white exterior looked inviting. A white fence bordered a small yard with a path that lead to the front steps. Wildflowers sprouted from every corner of the yard and climbed up the front of the building, their sweet fragrance hanging heavy in the air.

Anna breathed their perfume in deeply. "It smells good here."

"It sure does," Erik said as he stepped lightly up the broad stairway that lead to a large, shaded porch.

A short, plump woman in her thirties with dark hair pulled back into a bun and a friendly smile, greeted him. "Well, now, I don't remember seeing the likes of you before. Would you be in need of a room?" she asked cheerfully while she dusted flour from her hands. "Ah, what a mess. Sorry. Just finished with my baking. It gets so stiflin' hot in that kitchen I just gotta step out and get me a breath of cool air."

"Are you the Cora on the sign?"

"That I am."

"Do you have any rooms for rent?"

The woman raised one eyebrow as she glanced at Anna and the girls and asked, "Rooms? Well now, I do have *a* room. I'm full up just now and only got one left."

Erik glanced at Anna and blushed slightly before looking back at the woman. "You sure there's nothing else?"

"Sorry. That's all I've got."

Erik only hesitated a moment. "We'll take it then."

"Good. That'll be a dollar a day, which includes meals and baths."

"Sounds more than fair to me," Erik answered.

"Well then, follow me," the stout woman said as she shuffled through a squeaky front door. She edged her way around a small counter and opened a register. "I'll need you to sign here, please," she said and offered Erik a pen.

Self-consciously Erik dipped the pen into the inkwell and scribbled his and Anna's names down. His face burned as he thought, *I'll have to explain this.*

He turned the register back to Cora, but before he could say anything, the neighborly proprietor said, "Erik Engstrom and Anna Dunnak?" She looked a bit surprised, then with a cluck of her tongue, said, "Well, it's none of my business. Follow me. I'll show you to your room."

Erik decided an explanation could wait, and the four weary travelers followed Cora up the stairs.

"My name's Cora Browning. But you can just call me Cora," the woman explained as she opened a door at the end of the hallway. "There's only one bed, but I can bring a mat up for the little ones," she said and smiled warmly at Iya and Luba.

"Thank you," Erik said as he took the key.

"Supper's at six o'clock sharp," Cora called over her shoulder as she headed down the hallway. "If there's anything you need, just holler."

"As a matter of fact, I was wondering if there's a minister in town?"

Cora stopped and turned to face Erik. "We've got us a real nice reverend, but he's out of town just now. He makes a point of visitin' the natives regular and won't be back for a couple days." She thought a moment. "You don't happen to be Russian Orthodox?"

Erik shook his head.

"Well in that case, it's just the reverend then."

"Oh," Erik said unable to hide his disappointment.

"Is it real important?"

"No, not exactly," Erik stated solemnly. "Thanks anyway," he said and started to close the door.

"Is there something you needed right away?" Cora asked, concern in her voice.

Erik glanced at Anna and cleared his throat. "To be truthful, Anna and I wanted to be married as soon as possible."

Unable to conceal her surprise, Cora's face brightened and she tucked a wisp of loose hair back into place. "Considering you'll be sharin' a room, it wouldn't be proper any other way." Kindly she continued, "But I'm sure the reverend will be happy to marry you when he gets back."

"He's the only minister?" Erik asked.

"There's the Orthodox Church, but the priest won't marry you if you're not Orthodox. I'm sorry." Cora paused. "Looks like you have a mighty fine family too."

"Oh, these children aren't mine," Erik explained. "Iya here," he patted the little girl's head, "is Anna's sister, and Luba's father died about a year ago." He glanced down at Anna and the girls and said softly, "But I love them like they're my own."

"I'm sure sorry. Wish there was somethin' I could do. But I'm sure if it's the Lord's will, he'll work somethin' out."

Erik sighed. "I have to agree with you on that. He's never abandoned us yet, and I don't expect him to start now."

"It's good to know you're a godly man, Mr. . . . ."

"Engstrom. Erik Engstrom."

"That's right. I'm just so bad about rememberin' names. Well, Mr. Engstrom, I'm glad to have you. And you too, Anna," she said with a smile. "It's gettin' late. I best get to makin' supper if I'm to have it done by six. And you could probably do with some rest. See you at dinner," Cora said as she marched down the hall with her skirt swishing about her.

Anna turned to look at their room as Erik closed the door. It was simply furnished, with a four-poster bed on the far wall. A lovely quilted spread lay across the foot of it. Freshly ironed white curtains framed the window, and a small desk sat in front of it. A washstand and mirror stood on the opposite wall, and just inside the door a plain, wooden wardrobe waited to be filled. It was a fine room— clean and neat—and Anna liked it. She peeked out the window, which overlooked Sitka's main street. "I like to watch from here," she said, unable to take her eyes from the activity below. "So much I do not know. If I watch I will learn."

Iya plopped down on the bed. "Soft!" she exclaimed and patted the cushion. "You try, Erik."

Erik sat next to the little girl. "It is soft. You and Anna can share this tonight. I'll sleep on the floor."

Anna frowned. *Still we sleep apart,* she thought, but she didn't complain. Instead, she asked, "When will we marry?"

Erik's brow creased in thought. "That I don't know. Looks like things aren't working out quite the way I had planned." To himself he added, *There must be an answer.* Abruptly he stood up and headed for the door. "I've got an idea. I'll be back as soon as I can. Why don't you rest while I'm gone."

"Where are you going?" Anna asked.

"I'll fill you in when I get back," he said, and he kissed her on the cheek. "Just try to be patient. I've got a hunch, but I'm not sure it will work out." He stepped out the door and Anna stared after him as he disappeared down the stairway.

"Why did Erik go?" Iya asked.

"I do not know," Anna shrugged. She strolled over to the mirror, fluffed out her hair, and studied the knotted mess disdainfully. After rummaging through her bag, she found her hair brush and pulled it through her long brown hair until it shone, then she braided it into a thick plait. "That is better," she said with satisfaction.

"Do mine." Iya insisted.

"It is good if you ask," Anna said as she sat on the bed. "I like to help when someone asks, not orders."

Iya planted herself in front of Anna. "I am sorry," she said as she reached out and touched Anna's fine hair, then her own. She looked puzzled and asked, "Why is your hair soft and mine stiff?"

"I do not know. Maybe it is because my father was Russian."

Anna ran the brush through the little girl's straight, black mop.

"I wish mine was like yours," Iya complained, jumping off the bed and staring at Anna woefully.

Anna thought for a moment. "Erik says God made us, even our hair." She pulled Iya back to her and twisted her hair into two braids.

Iya frowned as she mulled over what Anna had said.

"We do not always understand things," Anna explained. "It is all right to wonder." She gave Iya a quick squeeze. "Now it is time to rest," she said as she pushed herself off the bed and pulled the covers down. "You sleep."

Iya didn't argue. Instead she yawned as she climbed beneath the thick blankets and snuggled down into the soft mattress.

Luba seemed content for the moment, so Anna hung their few pieces of clothing in the wardrobe. *A nap would feel good,* she thought as Luba began to fuss, demanding to eat. Irritated, Anna looked longingly at the bed before picking up the whimpering infant and sitting in the chair at the desk. She took a moment and studied her demanding daughter. Unexpectedly, Luba flashed her a vibrant, trusting smile, and immediately Anna's irritation melted away. She chuckled softly and cuddled the baby close before placing her to her breast. She closed her eyes and leaned back in the chair. Even with all there was to watch below, she found it hard to remain awake.

Finally Luba's hunger was satisfied. Anna changed her and crawled into bed beside Iya, tucking the infant in close to her. *I never feel such a soft bed,* she thought as she drifted off to sleep.

Anna stirred, suddenly aware of another's presence. She struggled to free herself from sleep. Someone was in their room and was moving about quietly, as if trying not to alert her to his presence! Frightened and not wanting the intruder to know he had been detected, Anna fought to keep her breathing even as she peeked through half-closed lids. She let out a sigh of relief when she spotted Erik fumbling with an unusual-looking bedroll.

"Oh, Erik, it is you," she murmured.

"Who did you think it was?"

"I did not know. I was sleeping." She pushed herself up on one elbow and, stifling a yawn, asked, "What are you doing?"

"Oh, this is the pad Cora promised us. I'm sorry I woke you."

"Did I sleep a long time?"

"I've only been gone about an hour, but I've got good news," Erik announced as he dropped down on the bed next to her.

Anna sat up, but sleep still clung to her. She tried to concentrate. "News? What news?"

"I told you I had a hunch. I thought I'd heard somewhere that the captain of a sea-going vessel could marry folks if there was no preacher at hand. So I asked Captain Bradley about it, and he told me I was right and he'd be happy to marry us! I don't know why I didn't think of it sooner."

Anna smiled and threw her arms around Erik's neck. "That is good!" she exclaimed, then sat back and looked into his glowing face. "When? When will we marry?"

"Is tomorrow soon enough?" Erik asked as he squeezed her hand.

"No," Anna answered with a smile. "But I will wait." She planted a quick kiss on his cheek.

At dinner, Erik announced their plans. The table was filled with other boarders, but most were more interested in their meal than wedding plans for a couple they didn't know. Their responses were little more than grunts, all except that of a heavyset man who sat at the end of the table and glared at Erik and Anna, making certain they understood how he felt about such a marriage.

Cora, on the other hand, nearly bounced off her chair. "Why, what a wonderful idea, Mr. Engstrom! Of course the captain can marry you! I've heard of that before." She turned her attention to Anna and smiled warmly. "I'm very happy for the both of you. It's clear you two love each other."

Anna blushed and smiled shyly, while Iya announced in a shrill voice, "I am happy Anna and Erik getting married. We will be a family."

"That's right," Cora agreed. Abruptly she swapped her smile for a frown and knitted her eyebrows together. Quietly she studied Anna. "Honey, do you have anything else to wear, other than what you got on?"

"I have more tunics like this," Anna answered as she looked down at her clothing.

"Why, you'll just have to come up with something else if you're to be married tomorrow. I don't mean to be rude, but what you've got on is fine for the trail, but not for a weddin'."

"Wear something else?" Anna asked quietly, uncertain why Cora was so concerned about her garments.

"It just won't do for you to be married in an animal skin," she said matter-of-factly.

Anna looked at Erik and asked, "This is not good?"

Erik thought a moment before speaking. "Anna, you know you're great at tanning hides and your sewing is real good, but Mrs. Browning does have a point. I don't mind your tunic; it's part of who you are, and I want you to wear it whenever you wish, but here the women wear dresses. And for a wedding they would wear a special one."

"Dresses?" Anna asked innocently.

"Yes, like what Cora's wearing. You'd look beautiful in a new dress," he added with a warm smile.

Anna blushed at the compliment.

"Mrs. Browning . . ."

"Oh, just call me Cora," she corrected.

"Cora, could you help Anna find a dress?"

"There's nothin' I could think of that would give me more pleasure."

"Can I have a dress?" Iya asked.

"I think that's a good idea. In fact, I think you both should have at least two," Erik declared. "And some new clothes for Luba too." He downed the remainder of his coffee and scooted away from the table. "That was a fine meal, ma'am."

"Thank you, Mr. Engstrom."

"Erik, please. If I'm to call you Cora, then you'll have to call me Erik."

"Well, Erik it is then," Cora said with a friendly smile. "The sitting room has a shelf of books, and there's some other reading material in the stand against the wall. You're welcome to any of it while you're here."

"Sounds good to me. It's been a while since I've had anything new to read," Erik said as he sauntered toward the parlor and scanned the bookshelf. He ran his hand along the books, and when he found one that looked interesting, he pulled it from the shelf and dropped into an overstuffed chair near the fire. Iya lay on the floor in front of the hearth and poured over the pictures in a magazine. Occasionally she asked Erik to explain something she didn't understand. Anna watched them for a few minutes. It made her feel good to see how much they cared for one another. They'd taken to each other right off, and it seemed they would be forever linked in a special bond of friendship. *It will be like this when we have a home,* she thought.

Cora began clearing away the dirty dishes, pulling Anna out of her reverie. She strapped Luba to her back and joined her hostess.

"Oh, Anna, you don't have to do that," Cora protested.

"I like to help."

"Well, I can use the company, and heaven knows there's more than enough dishes to keep us busy for a while," Cora consented as she balanced a stack of plates and headed for the kitchen. She pushed the swinging door open with her hip and disappeared inside. Anna followed with a load of her own. Cora settled her stack into a pan of steaming water already waiting in the sink, then returned to the dining room to retrieve the remaining utensils and plates. After the table was cleared and washed, Cora handed Anna a towel. She plunged her hands into the hot, soapy water and said, "You dry while I wash."

At first, the two women worked side by side in amiable silence. Anna liked Cora, and the thought of knowing this kind woman better warmed her.

"I can see you and Erik are good folks, Anna," Cora finally said. "I want you to know that no matter what you hear around town, you always have a place here."

"What would we hear?"

"Oh, you know there are folks around who don't take much to mixing of races. And when you and Erik get married, they're likely to get upset."

"I know," Anna answered sadly. "Sometimes I think it is better if we were not together."

"Oh, don't go thinkin' that way, now," Cora scolded kindly. She paused for a minute before continuing. "It is true you'll have a harder road than most, but if you love each other, you'll find a way around the rough places. When I look at you two, I can't imagine God bein' anything but pleased."

Anna's face brightened. "You think so?"

"I sure do."

"I know God. Erik tells me about him. He reads many things from his Bible. Someday I want to read words from God."

Cora washed the last dish, quickly wiped down the counter, and draped her towel across a wooden rack. "You know, I think anything can happen if God's hand is in it. He's mighty powerful, and I believe if you want to learn to read, he'll find a way to make it happen. Don't you worry; everything will turn out just fine." She smiled and gave Anna a quick hug. "Well, I've got some mendin' to do, and I better get at it if I plan to get any sleep. Goodnight, dear. I'll see you at breakfast."

"Goodnight," Anna said as she watched Cora disappear through the door. Alone in the kitchen, she wandered about the large room, examining some of its wonderful gadgets and tools. She picked up the heavy skillet on the stove and marveled at how smooth it felt; it wasn't beaten up like Erik's. The warmth from the stove felt good, and she peeked inside the oven door. *What a wonderful thing,* she thought. *One day maybe I will have one.* Most of the items she had never seen before, and she couldn't imagine what Cora did with them. She hoped Cora would teach her. She warmed herself at the large wood stove a little while longer, knowing she should go up to bed but not wanting to leave the warm, friendly room.

Just then Erik peeked around the door. "Pretty nice, huh? Someday you'll have one like this."

Anna looked at Erik and wondered how it could ever be. She didn't doubt his ability to provide. He had proven he could do almost anything, but it was hard to believe she would ever live in such surroundings.

"I'm going to take Iya up to bed now," he said, and he pointed to Luba, who slept soundly in her pack, "Looks like she was ready a while ago."

Anna smiled and said, "I am ready too."

"Well, after you then," Erik said and held the door for her. As the four of them made their way to their room, the floors creaked and groaned pleasantly. Most of the other tenants had already retired to their quarters, and the large, two-story house felt empty.

When they reached their room, Erik lifted Iya onto the soft mattress and pulled the covers up over her, then went to the table and lit a candle.

"Why do you light the candle? It is not dark."

"Even though the sun only sets for a little while, it still looks dreary at this time of night. I just thought the candle would make it cheerier."

Anna looked about. "You are right," she said as she unstrapped Luba and settled her next to Iya.

Erik stood at the window and gazed out over the town. It was quieter now, although occasional sounds of music and laughter still floated down the empty street. Anna joined him, shyly linking her arm in his.

Two besotted citizens appeared at the end of the street. They sang as they strolled along, leaning against each other for stability. In their drunken stupor, they found their discordant song amusing and laughed raucously, momentarily happy with the world.

"They won't be laughing come morning," Erik commented.

"Sitka is not like my village," Anna whispered.

"Yeah, it's different. That's for sure. You won't have to stay here too long, though. Once I find us a claim, we'll all move north."

"We are not going with you when you look for a claim?" Anna asked, pulling away from him.

"I thought you knew I would be going alone."

Anna could only stare at him in shock. The thought of being separated seemed unendurable.

Erik placed his hands on her shoulders and looked into her eyes. "Anna, it won't be for long. I just can't take you. It's too dangerous. It'll only be for a few weeks at the most. I promise." He put his arm about her waist and pulled her close. "We'll have a good life together, Anna. But this separation can't be helped."

Anna gathered her tattered emotions and snuggled against him. "As soon as we are together, I know it will be good."

For several minutes they stood silently gazing out on the empty street. Anna wondered what Erik thought as he peered out. Did he understand how much it hurt her to have him leave? *No,* she told herself. *He would not go if he knew.* She struggled to control her tears. How many days before she would have to say good-bye? She couldn't bring herself to ask.

Finally Erik yawned and stretched. "Well, we better get to sleep. Tomorrow's a big day." He kissed her gently on the cheek. "This time tomorrow we'll be husband and wife."

Anna kissed him back, only on the lips and more boldly. "I wish we did not have to wait for tomorrow," she whispered as she turned away and climbed into bed beside Iya.

Chapter 5

*A*nna rolled to her side and tried to clear the sleep from her head. She glanced about the room. Erik's bedding had already been taken up and he was gone. She sighed and turned onto her back. For a time, she stared at the ceiling. Luba rarely allowed her to sleep in, and it felt good to have nothing to do. She relished the quiet and comfort. She closed her eyes and burrowed beneath her covers. *Mm, this bed feels good. I do not remember sleeping so deep,* Anna thought.

Suddenly her mind reeled as the events of the coming day flooded her thoughts. Today she would become Anna Engstrom! Her heart beat hard and fast in her chest, and she came wide awake as the realization that Anna Dunnak would cease to exist hit her. Not just her name, but the native girl who had once stood on an empty beach and mourned her family would soon hold little resemblance to the new Anna Engstrom. A year with Erik had already transformed her, and gradually the young girl Erik had rescued off that beach would fade. It seemed so long ago, and like yesterday. She remembered the devastated girl who had believed the gods had snatched away all her happiness. The thought of forever committing to this new world and leaving behind the old seized her, and for a moment she felt threatened and trapped. *No!* she told herself. *It is not a cage, but a new home.*

Gradually Anna relaxed and smiled as she considered what it would mean to be Erik's wife. She knew he would be a good husband. She only hoped she wouldn't be a disappointment to him. Her spirit quieted as she envisioned what her new house would be like and how she would share it with Erik and the children. She promised herself she would never forsake Erik but always stand by him. She would embrace her new life and put the old behind.

"What are you thinking?" Iya asked, forcing Anna's thoughts back to the present.

"Nothing," Anna answered nonchalantly. She wished Iya had given her a few more minutes to herself. She needed time to think over the past, to remember, to spend a little longer with those she had lost.

"You and Erik are getting married?"

"Uh huh."

Iya bounced out of bed. "It is time to get up and get ready."

The smell of coffee, mingled with the aroma of frying bacon and fresh bread, came from the kitchen. Anna's mouth watered. "Something smells good," she said as she pushed herself out of bed. She stopped in front of the window and glanced down on the street. Already people were out, beginning a new day. The sun immersed the little town in a warm glow. Anna lifted her arms over her head and stretched. She wished she could just sit and soak in the sunshine, but today there was no time. She crossed to the dressing table and briskly combed the night's snarls from her hair. After splashing her face with water, she pulled on a clean tunic and settled in the chair to nurse Luba.

Iya had already hurried through her morning tasks and stood at the door, fidgeting with the handle while she waited. "Luba hurry!" the youngster demanded.

"Iya, Luba must eat!" Anna snapped, unable to hide her irritation. The moment the words were out of her mouth, she wished she could have taken them back, or at least have said them more gently. Iya was only feeling the excitement of the day and, as any child would, wished for it to begin. This time, more kindly, she said, "You go. I will be there soon."

Iya needed no urging and said a quick good-bye as she sped off down the hallway.

Her hunger satisfied, Luba smiled at Anna. Anna smiled back and kissed her pudgy cheek, then lay the infant on the bed to change her, all the while chatting pleasantly about nothing at all. The little girl wiggled and cooed at her mother. "Luba, what do you think of this wedding?" Anna asked as she tickled the baby's stomach and pulled off her soiled clothing. Luba only giggled and grabbed for Anna's hands.

For a moment, she could see Kinauquak's face in his daughter's. The young hunter filled her thoughts, and the all too familiar ache settled in her chest. How would he feel about this marriage? As she mulled it over, she knew he would be repelled and unwilling to trust his child to a white man. Doubts momentarily clouded Anna's joy. Was she doing the right thing? She felt uneasy. Kinauquak would not allow this marriage. *But he does not know Erik,* she told herself. *He does not know that Erik is not like other outsiders.* As much as she tried to convince herself that he would understand, she could not. *Kinauquak is not here,* she finally decided. *I am doing what is right. Kinauquak is not here,* she repeated and forced him from her mind.

She hefted Luba onto her hip and headed for the kitchen. When she entered the dining room, most of the other residents were already gathered about the table, quickly devouring Cora's fine meal. Platters of eggs, griddle cakes, and bacon sat in the center. Anna had never seen such a breakfast before. Several patrons stopped and stared at her. The heavyset man from the night before was there, and he stopped shoveling just long enough to glare at her. Intimidated, Anna looked away and found Erik's steady, blue eyes on her. They held no malice, only love and pride. The room and its strangers faded as she met his gaze. Erik grinned and his eyes reflected his smile. Anna felt stronger and smiled back.

Iya scooted the chair next to her away from the table and said, "Anna, sit here."

Glad to have a seat and hoping the others would lose interest in the new arrival, Anna quickly slid in next to Iya.

"Well, good morning to you!" Cora said cheerfully as she entered the dining room, carrying a large tray of fresh pancakes. She glanced around the table. "Well, I don't suppose none of you ever saw a native before," she scolded her residents. "You'd be a whole lot wiser to pay attention to your food than starin' at a newcomer." Embarrassed, the others turned back to their meal, although Anna did catch a furtive glance or two.

"Did you have a good sleep, Anna?" Cora asked kindly.

Anna nodded. "It seems I sleep too long. I am sorry." She glanced at Erik. He still watched her. Energy passed between the two, and Anna wished she could reach out and touch him. *That would upset these people,* she thought, and stifled a smile.

"Oh, no reason to apologize," Cora went on. "There's plenty of breakfast left just yet. Here, why don't you try a couple of these," she said and slid two flapjacks onto Anna's plate. "Looks like you've got a lap full," she added as Anna struggled to keep an overenthusiastic Luba balanced on her lap. "I've got just the thing," she said as she disappeared inside the kitchen. A moment later Cora reappeared with an odd-looking chair on long legs and scooted it in next to Anna. "This will be just perfect for that little dear."

Anna had never seen anything like it and didn't have a clue what the purpose of the strange contraption could be. She waited quietly to see what Cora intended to do.

"Here, let me show you how it works," Cora said as she took Luba from Anna's arms and gently placed the wiggling infant in the chair. After cinching a strap about the child's waist, she swung a tray that was hinged to the sides of the stool over Luba's head and settled it in front of the child. With a satisfied grin, she asked, "What do you think?"

Anna shook her head and smiled. "This is a place of many surprises." She grasped Luba's flailing hands and asked, "Luba like? Now you have your own chair."

Cora placed a scrambled egg on the tray. "Here, this will give her something to do." Using her hands like clubs, Luba smashed the egg, squeezing some of it between her fingers and managing to get a small portion in her mouth. Still, the infant smiled with satisfaction as she tasted the new food.

"Luba likes eggs!" Iya exclaimed.

"She sure does," Erik agreed as he reached across the table for the coffee pot. "Would you like a cup?" he asked Anna.

"Yes," Anna answered, as she turned her attention to Erik. He looked rested and happy.

He filled Anna's cup with the hardy black brew. "It's pretty strong. Cora says, 'If a fella intends to go out and work in the cold, wet weather around here, he needs something strong to keep him going 'til lunch.' This'll do it, I guarantee," he added with a grin.

Anna took a sip of the coffee, and fought to hide a grimace as the bitter liquid touched her tongue. Erik had told the truth, the coffee tasted too strong.

"Here, try some sugar," Erik suggested. "Makes it a little more agreeable."

Anna scooped out a teaspoon of the brown sugar, dropped it into her cup, and tried again. It did help. "Better," she said and took another sip. She glanced down at the pancakes on her plate. She didn't feel the least bit hungry. The butterflies in her stomach had chased away her appetite.

"Good food!" Iya said as she speared a bite of egg.

"It looks good," Anna said tactfully, "but my stomach is not hungry."

"It's just nerves, honey," Cora explained. "Everyone gets a case of the jitters on their wedding day. You just eat up and you'll feel better."

Anna tried to smile. She glanced down at the food on her plate doubtfully, and her stomach churned at the thought of eating any-thing. But she didn't want to hurt Cora's feelings, so she took a small bite, chewed, then swallowed past the lump in her throat. She managed to say, "This is very good." And she meant it too. The eggs tasted delicate and mild. Very different from the ones she had gathered from the cliffs at her beach home. If only her nerves would settle down, she could enjoy the meal, but with her stomach lurch-ing, she feared she would be unable to keep it down. "What kind of egg?" she asked as she thought, *Please stay put*.

"Why, those are chicken eggs," Cora answered cheerfully. "You've never tasted them before?

"No," Anna answered. "They are good."

"Thank you. I must say, I'm known for my cookin' and admit to bein' a bit proud of it too."

"I have to agree with Anna," Erik added. "Excellent meal, Cora."

He pushed away from the table. "I better get over to the captain and make sure of our plans. I won't be gone long."

"Can I go?" Iya asked.

"No, not this time."

Iya pouted.

"Hey, no time for that. You've got to get ready to go to the store."

The little girl brightened a little. "We will be ready when you come back."

Erik donned his hat and headed for the door. He glanced at Anna and smiled. "Bye," he said and stepped outside.

Anna managed to finish most of her breakfast and a cup of coffee. Surprisingly, her stomach did settle a bit by the time she finished. Cora had already cleared most of table. Anna placed a cup and saucer, along with some leftover tableware, on her plate and headed for the kitchen.

"No, not this time, young lady," Cora stopped her. "You've got more important things to take care of. Besides, I'm nearly finished here and don't need the help. You take the little ones and get yourselves ready to go into town. I'll finish up here."

At first Anna didn't move. It didn't seem right to leave Cora with the mess. In the end, Anna had no choice as Cora shooed her up the stairs.

As she tidied up their room, Iya followed her about chattering on and on about a horse and carriage she had seen, then the man who had delivered ice, and how cold the ice had felt, and how she wondered what it would be like to ride a horse and how she was determined to learn one day . . .

Tired of the prattle, Anna sat on the bed and pulled Iya to her. "That is enough talking. Time we comb your hair," she said as she brushed out and braided the little girl's thick hair. After that she changed Luba, then glanced in the mirror before heading downstairs. What she saw startled her. She looked fresh and childlike; the tired shadows had disappeared. Her golden eyes shimmered, and a small smile played about her lips. Even when she tried she couldn't erase it. Pushing an imaginary hair back into place, she followed an overeager Iya out the door.

When she returned to the dining room, everyone had gone. The table had been cleared and was draped with a delicate tablecloth; a bouquet of flowers rested in the center. Anna could hear Cora humming from inside the kitchen. A flood of contentment rushed over her as she took in the scene. This was all so new and different, but still, it felt good.

Anna glanced in the parlor. Erik wasn't there. Instead, two men she had seen at breakfast were relaxing. One sat in an overstuffed chair, smoking a pipe, his nose buried in a book. The other paced back and forth in front of the hearth like a caged animal. The man was clearly agitated, and Anna wondered why he remained indoors. She considered suggesting he take a walk, but thought better of it. He didn't look like the type to accept advice, especially not from a native woman.

Cora bustled out of the kitchen. "You ready to go?" she asked as she rolled down her sleeves and wiped flour from her skirt.

"Yes," Anna answered, her stomach tightening with apprehension and anticipation. She'd never been shopping before and wondered just what it would be like.

"Erik should be back any time," Cora said as she scanned the parlor. "This will make a fine place for a weddin'." She turned and looked at Anna. "I told Erik I thought it would be a good idea if you two were married right here. I hope you don't mind."

Anna thought a moment before answering. "I like this home. It is a good place to marry," she said with a warm smile.

Cora grinned. "Well, it's settled then."

Erik breezed in through the front door. "Everything's all set." He stopped to catch his breath. "The captain will be here at two o'clock this afternoon."

Cora looked at the clock on the mantle, quickly tucked some loose hairs back in place, and said, "We best be movin', then. There's not much time to get the shoppin' done." With that, she hurried out the door and down the steps. Iya scampered after her. Erik took Luba and cradled her in one arm while he guided Anna protectively with the other.

"There's a fine shop just a couple blocks from here," Cora called over her shoulder. "I'm certain we can find things for all of you." She stopped and eyed Erik critically. "You could do with some new clothes yourself, Erik."

Erik looked down at his worn garb and grinned. "I could at that. In all the commotion, I nearly forgot the state of my own wardrobe." He looked at Anna. "It seems we're all shopping today."

With a look of satisfaction, Cora resumed her mission and bustled down the street. A few minutes later, they stopped in front of a shop with a large placard over the door that read "Sam's Mercantile." "Here we are," Cora announced as she scrutinized an assortment of items displayed behind a large window. Items ranging from rifles and wooden barrels to a lovely powder blue cotton dress with a matching wide-brimmed hat enticed passersby.

"Isn't that elegant," Cora said, admiring the dress. She stepped inside with Anna, Erik, and the girls close behind. "Good morning Sam." She greeted an elderly man behind the counter.

"Mornin' Cora," he answered as he snapped the lid closed on a large candy jar. "Just can't stay away from the stuff," he quipped as he popped a piece of hard candy into his mouth and patted his rounded belly. He glanced behind Cora at the children and asked teasingly, "I don't suppose the little ones would like a piece?"

"Why, I don't know that they've ever had candy."

"Yes. At the trading post," Iya said. "I like it," she added with a grin.

"Well, then I'm sure one piece wouldn't hurt." Sam took two long sticks of peppermint candy from another jar, stepped from behind the counter, and held one out for Iya.

The little girl glanced at Anna, and when approval was given, she gladly accepted the man's gift. Immediately she stuck it in her mouth, and her eyes lit up at the sweet taste.

"Can the little one have this?" Sam asked.

"Sure," Erik said and shifted Luba into his other arm. "But I better hold it for her, or she'll make a mighty mess."

Sam smiled at the baby, handed the stick of candy to Erik, then turned back to Cora. "Now, what can I do for you today?" he asked as he pulled a suspender back into place.

"Sam, these are some new friends of mine. This is Erik, Luba, Anna, and Iya," she said as she pointed to each one. "They're all in need of some new clothes. First I figured we'd start with the young 'uns. That should be easiest." She raised Iya's hand and patted it. "After that, the gentleman here is looking for something more fittin' for a weddin', and the young lady needs a couple of dresses. One fine enough for a bride," she added with a sparkle in her eye.

Anna's attention was captured by the rows of cans on the shelf behind the shopkeeper. Pictures of the contents were on the labels, and Anna hoped she'd have the chance to try them one day. Boxes of fruits and vegetables lined the wall next to the counter. Most she'd never seen before. She bent and picked up a large, round red piece of fruit and sniffed it. It smelled sweet.

"Would you like one of those?" Erik asked, his eyes filled with merriment.

"What is it?"

"It's an apple. You'll like it; they're real good. Set it on the counter, and we'll pay for it with the rest of the stuff."

Anna moved toward the counter, but a shelf containing fine needles and thread distracted her. She had never seen such delicate sewing tools. She picked up a spool of bright red thread. Even when the berries were at their ripest, she'd never been able to produce such a bright color.

"Anna, when we have time, I'll help you pick out some of these and teach you how to embroider," Cora said quietly from behind her.

"They are so beautiful."

"That they are, but right now we have other things to take care of. We'll make another trip back here when we have more time."

"I think I've got everything you need," Sam said, drawing his customers back to their original objective. He eyed Luba and Iya. "I have just the thing for you youngsters," he said with a smile and crossed to some shelving along the back wall. "We carry some fine things for little ones, and we even have a couple of dresses I think would fit the young lady," he added with a wink at Iya.

Iya grinned back but kept quiet.

Cora found two tiny dresses—one made of cotton, the other wool. "What do you think?" she asked Anna as she held them out for her inspection.

Anna touched the strange material and rolled it between her fingers. "This will keep Luba warm?"

"Well, of course the cotton is somethin' she would only wear during the summer, and some woolen stockings would do the trick with this one for the winter. Plus she has her warm tunics for the coldest weather," Cora explained.

Anna examined the garments carefully, checking the stitching inside. "These are very pretty." She turned to Erik. "Are these all right?"

"They're real nice, Anna. I think Luba will be pretty as a picture in them."

"We will take them," Anna decided.

"Good, now let's see what we can do for this little girl," Cora said as she patted Iya on the head and began searching through the scant selection of dresses in her size.

Iya quickly made her choice. Holding up a bright red serge dress, she said, "I like this. All right?"

Anna examined the brightly colored dress and smiled at Iya, then looked to Cora and Erik. After they both nodded their approval, she said, "You can have it."

Cora held the dress up against Iya's body. "It looks like a near perfect fit." She turned to the proprietor. "If it isn't, Sam, we'll be able to bring it back and get another?"

"Absolutely, Cora. You know I'm a fair man."

"Iya, you'll need one more. What do you think of this?" Cora asked as she held up a pale green dress with a wide bow at the back.

"Pretty!" Iya cried and hugged the frock to her.

"Cora, I think that's real fine, but do you think it will be practical once we're on our own place?" Erik asked.

"Erik, every girl needs at least one special dress," Cora reprimanded him.

Erik looked at Anna and shrugged his shoulders as if he'd been outdone. Looking down at Iya's beaming face, he said, "I s'pose you're right. We'll buy it."

Iya embraced Erik about the legs. "Thank you. It is the most beautiful I ever saw!"

Cora turned to Anna. "Now dear, it's your turn. Do you see anything you like?"

"Everything is beautiful. I do not know which one."

Cora went to the window. "How about this one?" she asked as she took the powder blue dress from its place in the display.

"That is too nice," Anna said as she glanced at Erik to see what he thought of it.

"In that, I think you'd be the prettiest girl in all Alaska," Erik said, unable to hide his admiration.

Cora held it up to Anna. "Hmm, it might be a bit long. You're not very tall you know, dear. I think you'd better try it on."

"Try it on?"

"Sure. There's a room in the back of the store where you can change." She stepped behind the counter and rounded a corner. "Come on, this way," Cora urged. A little confused, Anna followed. Cora pulled back a curtain draped across a small cubicle. "Just try it on, and we'll see if it's right for you."

Anna stared at her blankly.

"Go on, dear. We'll wait."

Anna examined the dress more closely with all its laces and bows, then stared at Cora. She didn't have the first notion how the gown went on. "I do not know how. It is not like a tunic."

"Oh, of course. I'm sorry, Anna. Here, let me help you," Cora said cheerfully as she ushered Anna behind the drapery.

A few minutes later, they emerged. Anna looked a bit awkward and very uncomfortable. She tugged at the sides and stood stiffly, afraid to breathe for fear the buttons would pop. "I cannot breathe. It is too tight," she complained.

Cora eyed her dubiously and double-checked the fit. "It's perfect. You're just so used to your roomy tunic that anything clinging about your waist feels snug. What do you think Erik?"

Erik's eyes glowed with approval as he assessed the dress, and even more so the wearer.

"Erik," Cora said sharply, "what do you think?" When Erik still failed to answer, she looked at him more closely and grinned. "Put your eyes back in your head, young man. I believe you've already answered my question."

"Anna, you're beautiful," Erik whispered.

"Anna, you should see!" Iya joined in. "You look pretty!"

"It does not feel right," Anna tried to explain as she pulled at the bodice.

"It's just right," Cora interrupted. "Don't worry, you'll get used to it. Now, we'll need at least one more dress and some underthings." She took a yellow checked gingham and held it up for Anna to see. "What do you think?"

Anna nodded. "I like it."

Cora held the dress against her. "Looks like it'll fit perfectly. We'll take this, too, Sam," she said and lay the garment on the counter. With a wink she added, "Erik, why don't you have a look around while we get the other things the ladies will need."

"Uh, yeah, sure," Erik answered and began rummaging through some shirts.

"Sam, maybe you could give him a hand?"

"You bet, Cora."

When they had finished and Erik had made his purchases, Cora ushered them outside, acting like a mother hen. "We better hurry. It's getting late and we've still got a lot to do."

They hustled back to the boardinghouse and, once inside, Cora headed straight for the kitchen. "I better get lunch on before the hungry crowd shows up and finds nothin' to eat. Anna, why don't you and the girls go up and get some rest before lunch," she called over her shoulder as she hustled through the doorway.

"I cannot rest," Anna said, following her into the kitchen. She was much too nervous and knew sleep would be elusive. "Erik, will you take the girls outside? I will help Cora."

"All right, ladies, you heard Anna," Erik said. He took Iya under one arm and Luba beneath the other and galloped across the room and out the front door with both girls giggling.

Anna sliced bread for sandwiches while Cora cut chunks of roasted venison and cheese for her hungry boarders.

Hesitantly Anna asked, "Cora, why did you not marry?"

Cora stopped midslice and stared out the window a moment before answering. "Oh, I was married once. It's been a long time ago. Married a fella name of Patrick. He was a wild one. Like so many of the fellows who come to these parts, he never seemed able to light anywhere—always headin' off for one more adventure. He was a good man, though." She went back to her slicing. "Anyway, one day while I was waitin' for him to return, he washed up on the beach." She tried to blink away her tears, but they fell anyway and she wiped at them with the back of her hand. "They say he must have fallen into the river and washed downstream. Nobody really knows for sure."

"I am sorry, Cora," Anna said quietly.

"Well, that's how I ended up here. I needed to find a way to make a livin', so I started up this place. It's been good for me. At first, it gave me somethin' to do, but it's been a good livin', and I like it real well." She paused. "I like people, and God knows this is a people business. I've been without Patrick now a good long while, and it's gettin' easier." She set her knife aside and rested her hands on the counter. "You know, sometimes I can almost feel his presence. That's durin' the hard times." Matter-of-factly, she continued, "Anyway, I knew what I was in for when I married him, and he died the way he would have wanted. Out in the wild." Her eyes wandered to the hills surrounding the city, and she added softly, "But sometimes I miss him, real bad. I catch myself longin' for him, and then it feels like the pain will never lift."

As Anna watched the grief on Cora's face, she felt close to this new friend and knew Cora understood what it meant to lose somebody you love. "I loved Kinauquak," she began. "A big wave took him. It killed all my people."

"Oh, Anna, I'm so sorry."

Anna felt the tears well up in her eyes. She needed to talk and knew Cora would listen. She blinked, ignoring the salty droplets that spilled down her cheeks. "At first, I think I would die. It hurt to live. But Iya needed me. I knew I must not die." She stopped as she remembered the first time Erik had approached them. She smiled. "Then Erik came. He made me want to live. Now I am happy." She looked into Cora's eyes. "Maybe there is a man who will make you happy?"

"Well, if there is, I ain't found him yet," Cora said lightheartedly as she returned to slicing the cheese.

Voices came from the other room as the boarders began to assemble in the dining room.

"We better get this on the table before they start hollerin'," Cora said with a wink as she took the platter of meat and cheese and headed for the door.

Chapter 6

$\mathcal{L}$ unch seemed interminably long. Anna's queasiness had returned, and she pushed her food from one side of her plate to the other but couldn't bring herself to eat. The other guests seemed unaware of her trepidation and excitement and lingered over their meal. *I wish they would hurry,* she thought in frustration. She glanced at Erik. He hadn't touched anything on his plate either. Anna grinned, knowing he was as nervous as she. He looked up and caught her watching him. Anna blushed and returned to rotating her potatoes around her plate. The senseless chatter at the table dimmed into a monotonous droning as Anna forced herself to remain seated. *When would they finish?* she wondered as a sudden flush and dizziness washed over her. She grabbed hold of the edge of the table for balance and, although she tried to hide her discomfort, Cora's keen eye detected her distress.

"Anna, honey, you okay?" Cora asked with concern.

Anna managed to nod her head. "It is just that the room spins for a moment. I am all right now."

"Well, I say it's time to put an end to this meal," Cora said as she stood up. "We got us a weddin' in a little while, and it's time to get this mess cleared away," she announced.

The other guests stopped visiting and looked at Cora in surprise.

With everyone's attention focused on her, she continued, "So, I'm askin' you politely, now, to hurry up." With that, she began to clear away the dishes. Halfway through the kitchen door, she stopped and looked back. "Oh, by the way, you're all invited. We'll be meetin' right here in the parlor at two o'clock."

Anna piled Iya and Luba's leftover meat and vegetables onto her plate, wrinkling her nose at the pungent aroma. Her stomach churned, and she held the food at arm's length as she headed for the kitchen.

Cora took the stack of dishes from her. "Anna, you've got more important things to think about right now. You go on upstairs. I'll be up in a minute to draw a bath for you and the young 'uns. When you're all cleaned up, I'll help you dress."

Knowing it would be useless to argue with this kind but indomitable woman, Anna bobbed her head in compliance. Erik held Luba on his lap, and as Anna bent to scoop up the infant, her hand touched his. He grasped it and held her there a moment. Anna's heart fluttered as she stared into his warm blue eyes. He said nothing, but Anna could see his love and assurance.

She smiled at him and stammered, "I . . . I will go upstairs." She took the baby and headed for the stairway.

"See you at the wedding," she heard him say quietly as she left.

It wasn't long before a knock came at the door. But before Anna could answer, Cora burst into the room. "I've already got the water in the tub," she said cheerfully. "There are a few things still to take care of, but I'll be back to help you." She stepped out into the hall, then peeked around the edge of the doorway. "You better hurry, now; there isn't much time," she said with a wink.

Anna gathered up the girls and headed for the bathing room where she quickly washed them, and once she had them towel dried, climbed into the tepid water herself. "Iya, you watch Luba," she instructed as she rested her head on the edge of the large tub and closed her eyes, willing her mind to rest. She could feel the tension leave her body. She'd never bathed in such a grand tub, and although the water had cooled, it felt good as it washed over her body. She wished she could soak a long while, but, true to her word, Cora returned and rapped on the door, interrupting Anna's leisure.

Cora peeked inside. "That's enough soakin'. It's time for you to be gettin' ready."

"I will be there," Anna answered as she stepped out and wrapped a rough towel around her.

"I will carry Luba," Iya said as she hugged the infant to her and, still stark naked, followed Anna down the hall to their room.

Cora stood at the door. "Well, I'll be," she said in mock horror as her three guests scurried inside. "Why, you're naked as a jaybird," she exclaimed as she hefted Luba onto the bed and began to dress her.

"What is a jaybird?" Iya asked, leaning her elbow on the edge of the mattress and watching Cora care for Luba.

"Oh, I'm not talkin' about a real bird, it's just a sayin' that means you don't have a stitch of clothing on," Cora answered her good-naturedly. She handed Anna a pair of bloomers and a corset and asked, "Anna, do you need help with these?"

Anna studied the garments. "I know this one," she said as she held up the bloomers. "But not this," she added, letting the corset dangle from her hand.

"Well, why don't you get the pants on, and I'll help you with the other," she said as she turned to Iya and began to dress her. The little girl squirmed and giggled as Cora pulled her dress over her head and tied the sash tight in back.

"Hold still, now," Cora scolded.

Iya looked hurt at Cora's sharp tone. She pouted and crossed her arms defiantly across her chest.

"Oh, look at you," Cora said cheerfully. "Now, I didn't mean no harm."

Iya smiled and looked down at her pale green gown and smoothed the delicate material under her hands. She strolled very ladylike to the mirror and stared at her reflection. "Oh, Cora, it is beautiful!" Giggling, she threw her arms wide and whirled about, laughing at the way her skirt billowed away from her legs.

"Why, if you aren't a sight," Cora said. "I've never seen a prettier girl in all my life."

Iya smiled back and asked, "Will you comb my hair?"

Cora quickly ran the brush through Iya's hair until it was free of snarls, then pulled it up onto her head in a delicate bun. "Perfect," she said as she inspected her work. "You're all set. Now it's time I helped your sister."

Cora turned to Anna, and as her eyes fell upon the half-naked native woman, she clucked her tongue and said, "You are a pretty young thing. I don't believe I ever looked that good, even when I was young." With a playful grin, she added, "Erik doesn't know yet just how lucky he is."

Anna blushed and held up the puzzling corset.

Cora took the garment and quickly slipped it around Anna's torso, laced the ties in back, and cinched them up tight. "You have such a tiny figure. I won't need to pull these real tight. Really, you don't need one of these things," she hesitated. "It's just this bodice; I'm afraid it wouldn't be proper for you to go without it."

Anna stood rigidly still as Cora pulled the laces together and tied them. She sucked in her breath, feeling like she couldn't breathe and wishing she'd never consented to wearing the dress. Just as she was about to protest, Cora crossed to the clothes closet.

"That's done," Cora said as she took Anna's dress from the wardrobe, "now it's time for your dress." She examined the frock for a minute. "My, this is lovely." She bustled back to Anna. "Up with your arms," she instructed. She slipped the gown over Anna's head and pulled it down over her bodice and hips. "All right, then, turn around. I'll button it up for you." She began the tedious job of fastening the multitude of tiny buttons on the back of the dress. "I never did understand why they have to put so many of these darn things on." After fastening the last button, she deftly tied the bow at the back and turned Anna about to see how it fit. She eyed her critically a moment. "It's perfect."

Anna wanted to look in the mirror, but instead Cora steered her to the chair by the window and pushed her into it. Anna thought of protesting, but the warm July sun felt good against her skin, and as Cora ran the brush through her hair she lost her desire to object.

"You can see how you look when we're all finished and not before," Cora teased. "You have lovely hair," she said as she expertly twisted it into a French braid and tied it with a soft blue ribbon that matched Anna's dress.

"There, it's done," she said with satisfaction as she turned to look at Anna. She stepped back. "My, you are a beauty." Cora motioned for her to stand up, then took Anna by the shoulders and turned her about so she faced the mirror.

Silently Anna gazed at her reflection. She barely recognized the woman who stared back at her. The soft blue of her gown deepened the richness of her honey-colored skin and dark brown hair. Her hazel eyes blazed gold. *I do look pretty!* she thought.

"Erik is gonna bust his shirt buttons when he sees you," Cora gushed.

With a rush of emotion, Anna whirled about and hugged Cora. "Thank you, Cora, thank you."

Iya giggled. "Do this," she said as she twirled around. Anna laughed and imitated her younger sister. They stopped and Anna drew Iya back to the mirror. They grew more serious as they stood side-by-side looking at their images.

Quietly Iya said, "We look pretty."

Anna wrapped her arm about Iya's shoulders and gave her a little squeeze. "Yes, Iya, we do, and we are ready for a wedding."

The sound of a closing door and voices of greeting came from downstairs. Anna looked at Cora as her apprehension returned. "What do I do now?" she asked, unable to hide her panic.

"It's very simple, Anna. When you hear the music, you come downstairs. Make sure you stay put until then. It's bad luck for the groom to see the bride before the wedding."

"Music? Is it like a song?" Anna asked, confused.

"Oh, yes, it just wouldn't be a proper wedding without music. And since God has seen fit to bless me with a piano, I'll play the 'Wedding March.'" She seemed lost in thought for a moment. "You know, it's the only piano here abouts, 'cept for the saloon and the church, of course. Anyway, when you hear the music, you walk slowly down the stairs and into the parlor. You and Erik will stand just in front of the captain while he performs the ceremony."

"What then?"

"All you have to do is repeat what the skipper says. He'll let you know when. Don't look so worried. Everything'll be fine."

Anna nodded, but she still felt bewildered and frightened. Why had Erik insisted on their being married? Oh, how she wished she'd put her foot down and insisted on the old way, living together and loving each other as her people had done for generations.

"Well, I better see if the captain is here," Cora announced, cutting into Anna's turmoil. "After all, we can't start without him." She paused and looked at Anna. "Oh, honey, you look like you've seen a ghost. You're almost as white as me. You gonna be all right?"

Anna did her best to smile. "Yes."

"You're sure, now?"

Anna nodded.

"Good, then, I'll see you downstairs," she said and swept out the door.

With Cora gone, the room seemed empty. Even with the children, Anna felt alone. She wandered to the window and gazed down on the street and tried to focus on the people passing by, but her thoughts kept drifting back to Erik and the captain who waited for her in the parlor. She felt ill. *How did all this happen?* she asked herself. She wrapped her arms about her waist, crossed the room, and stared into the mirror. A strand of hair had fallen down on her forehead and she pushed it back into place with a trembling hand. What was taking so long? It seemed like forever since Cora had disappeared.

"Can I take Mary?" Iya asked, breaking the silence and startling Anna.

Anna had nearly forgotten about the children. She glanced at Iya as the little girl cuddled her doll close to her. "Yes," she answered gently.

"Can we go now?"

"No. Cora says not to go down until we hear the music," Anna answered and sat on the edge of the bed, careful not to wrinkle her dress. A soft breeze blew through the window, and she closed her eyes as it bathed her face.

Iya plopped down beside Anna. "Are you happy?"

"Yes," Anna answered hesitantly.

"Then why do you look sad?"

Anna sighed deeply and looked at Iya. "I am not sad," she paused, "only scared a little."

Iya studied her older sister a moment longer. "You are not afraid of Erik?" she asked, her voice tight.

"No. I will never be afraid of Erik. I . . ." She struggled to find the right word. "I feel lost. Everything is new. I do not know . . ."

"It will be all right. Erik will take care of us," Iya said and cuddled close to Anna.

Anna gave the little girl a hug. "You are right. I will try not to worry," she said and smiled to reassure Iya.

Luba began to fuss and Anna cradled her, thankful for the distraction. But as she crooned to the baby, the infant's whimpering grew louder, and she refused to be comforted. Anna looked down at her gown. The buttons were at the back, and she knew it would be impossible to feed Luba until after the ceremony. "Luba, you cannot be hungry," Anna told the infant in frustration. "You ate only a little time ago." She rocked the little girl and paced the floor. "You cannot eat now," she cajoled, but the child's complaining continued.

Desperate, Anna stopped pacing and turned to Iya. "Cora says I cannot go down. Maybe you can take Luba to her? She will feed her something. I will wait here."

With a broad smile, Iya took the baby and said confidently, "I will take care of Luba," as she tucked Mary between her and the baby.

"Hold her tight," Anna cautioned as Iya stepped into the hallway and headed for the stairs.

Anna watched them go. Leaving the door ajar, she returned to the bed and sat down to wait. She glanced at the window. The breeze had stopped and the curtains hung lifeless. After what seemed like hours, the tinkling sounds of the piano drifted up the stairway, down the hall, and into Anna's room.

Anna felt hysteria well up within her. The time had come. As if jolted out of a trance, she stood up and headed for the door. As she pulled it closed behind her, she stopped a moment and tried to slow her breathing. She remembered Cora's instructions and, taking a deep breath, she forced herself to put one foot in front of the other, thankful for the slipper-style shoes Cora had insisted she buy. She remembered the others she had tried on at the mercantile. They had felt like splints of iron laced around her foot—instruments of pure torture. She'd never have managed to make it to the parlor in them.

Cora is very wise, Anna thought as she continued down the poorly lit hallway.

At the crest of the staircase she stopped and studied the steps. They seemed steeper and longer than she remembered. Her legs felt weak and Anna feared they might not hold her. She stood, gripping the banister.

Memories of Kinauquak, her people, and their village flooded her mind. *Is this right?* she asked herself, trying to swallow her panic. The room swayed, and for a moment she feared she might faint. She tightened her hold on the railing and tried to clear her mind. Then Erik strode to the bottom of the stairs. As he looked up at her with love and admiration, Kinauquak and her past quickly faded from her mind. Her pounding heart slowed, and the whirling sensation stopped as she met his steady gaze. Fear retreated and she knew this was right. Slowly she descended the staircase, never taking her eyes from his. She trembled at his intense stare and all else ceased to exist.

Someone coughed, breaking the spell, and Anna glanced about. She saw many faces she recognized. Most of the men and women who had shared meals with her at Cora's table were there. The captain stood in front of the hearth with Sam from the general store. Iya fidgeted at the front of the room, still burdened by Luba, who was doing her best to wiggle free of Iya's embrace. She'd been forced to lay her doll on the floor beside her. Cora sat at the piano, beaming over her shoulder at Anna as she played the "Wedding March." The captain smiled kindly as Anna met Erik at the base of the stairs.

Anna felt a little overwhelmed. She'd never been the center of attention before. Among her people, only the elders and shamans ever found themselves in a position of importance. Others were rarely singled out. She smiled shyly beneath the guests' scrutiny. A smattering of smiles greeted her. Admiration showed on some faces, while others simply watched, openly curious, as if watching a sideshow. Anna searched the faces, but didn't find the heavyset man who had been so cold and unfriendly. The room looked cozy and bright. Cora had opened the curtains wide, and the sun bathed the parlor in a swath of warm light.

Erik took her arm, and the sudden contact sent shivers through her. She smiled at him as she fell into step beside the tall Norwegian. He smelled of soap and had managed to tame his unruly blond hair. Anna thought she'd never seen him look more handsome. She wondered what his thoughts were as they stepped into their future.

They stopped one pace in front of the captain, and Anna noticed the kind man had dressed in his finest attire. He stood erect with his heels solidly locked together and cradled a Bible in his hands. He looked very distinguished. As Cora slipped away from her piano and came to stand alongside her, Anna wondered if her friend had noticed this fine-looking man who stood in her parlor. But Cora seemed unaware of the captain as, eyes brimming with tears, she handed Anna a small bouquet of flowers.

The room fell silent. Captain Bradley cleared his throat and glanced about before allowing his attention to rest upon Anna and Erik. He began, "Dearly beloved, we are gathered here today, in the sight of God and these witnesses, to unite this man and woman in holy matrimony . . ."

As Anna looked up into Erik's face, the captain's voice faded. All she knew were Erik's deep blue eyes. They drew her into him, and she felt as if she had become part of the man, as if they were one person. Passion welled up within her, and her fear retreated; this is where she belonged. Nothing else mattered.

Anna felt a poke in her ribs, and she looked over to find Cora nudging her. "Anna, answer the man," she whispered.

Embarrassed, Anna realized she hadn't heard anything that had been said. She stared blankly at the skipper, hoping he would give her some clue as to what she was supposed to say.

The captain smiled kindly and repeated, "Anna, do you take this man to be your lawfully wedded husband?"

Anna looked at Erik and softly replied, "Yes."

Captain Bradley turned to Erik. "And do you, Erik Engstrom, take Anna Dunnak to be your lawfully wedded wife?"

Erik turned and faced Anna. He took her hands in his and, with a look that took Anna's breath away, answered, "I do." Gently he slipped a plain gold band on her finger.

Anna's chest ached with emotion. She'd never loved so deeply. She had never thought it possible. Captain Bradley continued, but Anna's wash of emotions drowned out what he had to say until he placed his hands on her and Erik's shoulders. He looked at both of them in a fatherly way and said, "I now pronounce you man and wife." With a smile he finished with, "You may kiss the bride."

Erik turned a pale pink and hesitated a moment before looking at his bride. Tenderly he wrapped his arms about her small shoulders and pressed his lips to hers.

Cora snuffled into a handkerchief, and in a flutter returned to the piano where she proceeded to play her slightly off-key rendition of the "Wedding March." The crowd of people spontaneously broke out in applause as Erik and Anna turned to smile at them. Some deliberately kept their hands at their sides, unwilling to celebrate the marriage between these two very different people, but Anna didn't care. She felt too happy.

It was done! They were husband and wife! Erik embraced Anna again, this time with no sign of his earlier embarrassment. Iya pushed between the two newlyweds, trying to hug them both while hanging on to Luba. Erik took the baby from Iya and bent to hug her.

"You are like father now," she whispered.

Erik couldn't respond other than to squeeze her tighter. Blinking back his tears, he stood and shook the hands of the well-wishers flocking about them.

Cora stopped playing and nearly bounced across the room to Anna. She wrapped the small native woman in her arms and hugged her against her ample bosom, holding her close for a moment before letting her loose. Then she held Anna at arm's length and, her eyes brimming with tears, said, "This is just the beginning, Anna. May God be with you both." She wiped the salty droplets from her cheeks and laughed as she gave Anna one more squeeze.

Smiling, she turned to her guests. "Well now, I've made some sweets to celebrate this union, and I've even got a bottle of wine

I've been savin' for a special occasion. I figure this is as special as I've seen in some time," she added as she ushered everyone into the dining room where a grand cake decorated the table.

"Cora, it is beautiful!" Anna exclaimed as her eyes settled on the centerpiece. She'd never seen anything like it. It stood a full three layers, with silky, white frosting laced over it, and in the center a heart covered with red ribbon rested in a bed of wildflowers. As she leaned close to examine the flowers, their soft fragrance greeted her.

Erik circled his arm protectively around Anna's tiny waist. Anna leaned against him. It felt good to be loved, to belong to someone. She glanced up at him and found his eyes on her. Her heart leapt wildly. She felt Erik's arm tighten a little, and as she lay her hand gently over his, she thanked God for his gifts.

"Can we have cake now?" Iya cried, interrupting Anna's thoughts. The little girl leaned on the table, eyeing the elegant dessert and clearly tempted to dip her finger in the frosting.

"Tradition says the bride and groom are supposed to cut the first two pieces," Cora said as she handed a large knife to Erik. Clumsily, the big man sawed off a large chunk. He held it a minute, uncertain just what to do.

"Well, don't just stand there. You've got to give her a bite of it," Cora urged.

Erik put the cake up to Anna's lips. She took a small bite. It tasted deliciously sweet. As Anna smiled at her new husband she decided she would have Cora teach her how to bake this cake.

"It's your turn now," Cora said to Anna.

Erik handed his bride the knife. "I know you know how to use one of these," he quipped.

Anna smiled demurely as she sliced into the cake. She knew he was referring to the time she had tried to teach him the native way of filleting fish, and he had failed miserably. Without a word, she held the sweet up for him to sample. Instead of tasting the dessert, Erik kissed her fingertips. Anna sucked in her breath; the gentle contact sent a rush of emotions through her. Erik grinned and finally took a bite of cake. He turned to their guests and said, teasingly,

"Very good." Anna could feel her face turn crimson as laughter broke out in the crowd.

Cora brought in the wine, ceremoniously uncorked it, and poured a small amount into two goblets, which she handed to Erik and Anna. She divided the remaining wine into several glasses and handed them to the other guests.

Pouring the last bit into her own glass, she said, "Well, it seems we had just enough." Cora raised her glass in the air, and an unexpected shadow crossed her face. Her eyes filled with tears. "I was savin' this wine for me and Patrick's first anniversary. It's some we brought with us when we came here from California. I figured since I couldn't partake of it with him, it would serve well for these two. A toast from me and Patrick," Cora said as she wiped at her tears. "I'm proud to share this with my new friends. I wish you a long and happy life," she continued as she tipped her glass toward Anna and Erik, touching the edge of her goblet to theirs, then sampling the contents.

Erik and Anna did the same. Anna had never tasted wine before, but she had been warned of the dangers it held. It smelled a little tangy and tasted unusual. She decided she didn't like it, but not wanting to hurt Cora's feelings, she emptied her cup.

Cora set her glass down and returned to the piano. She played "Oh Susannah," and soon everyone was caught up in the celebration. The floor of the parlor filled with swirling skirts as the men swept their partners around the room. Cora went on to play one lively tune after another well into the evening.

Erik taught Anna some dance steps and, before long, Anna found herself being twirled about the room on the arm of her new husband. The laughter and merrymaking reminded her of the lively celebrations she had experienced in her village when they heralded a successful hunt or the birth of a son and always when two were joined as mates. Although the music and dances were different, the joy felt the same. Music always seemed to bring a sense of freedom, pushing aside the worries of the world.

The gaiety finally began to fade, and, after a light dinner, people slowly filtered out, seeming reluctant to end their good time.

"Mighty fine party, Cora," Sam said as he shrugged into his coat. "And as much as I hate to go, it's time I got myself home."

Erik shook Sam's hand. "I'd like to thank you for standing up with me today. Since I don't know anyone in town, you did me a great favor."

"Glad to do it," Sam said and patted Erik on the shoulder. "Good luck to you."

Captain Bradley was the next to leave. "I don't s'pose I'll be seeing much of you two. I'll be heading out in a few days. I wish you both luck, and hope you find your gold, Erik."

"Thank you, captain," Anna said. "We could not marry without you."

The friendly sailor tipped his hat good-bye and disappeared out the door. Finally the last guest had gone, and the only ones left in the parlor were Anna, Erik, the children, and Cora. Iya had curled up on a chair with Luba and her doll, Mary. They looked as if they might fall asleep at any moment.

Cora yawned and stretched. "Well, it's time I got myself to bed. Tomorrow is another busy day. You know, I think I'll worry about the dishes in the morning. I'm just too worn out." Then, as if she had forgotten, she added, "Oh, by the way, I moved the extra bedding into my room. I figured the girls could sleep with me. It would be nice if you two had a little time to yourselves," she said playfully.

Anna could feel the blood rush to her face, and when she peered up at Erik he, too, had turned a bright red. Anna looked dubiously at Luba. "Cora, are you sure?"

"Of course I'm sure. We'll be just fine."

"It is all right," Iya interjected. "Cora is nice, and I will help take care of Luba."

Anna crouched in front of Iya. "You do not mind?"

Iya hugged Anna about the neck. "No. Cora says I can help make breakfast," she added enthusiastically.

Anna kissed Iya's cheek and gave Luba a hug. "All right, you sleep good. We will see you in the morning."

Holding Luba in one arm, Cora took Iya's hand and led her into a room off the side of the parlor.

Erik went to the hearth, stirred up the embers, and added more wood. He cleared his throat nervously. "It's still chilly at night. Might as well have a good, warm fire going." He looked at Anna. "Well, it's getting late. I s'pose it's time we went on up to bed." He took Anna's hand, and the two slowly made their way up the creaky stairway.

Once in their room, Anna suddenly felt shy and a little embarrassed. She stood at the window for a long while and watched the empty street. Kinauquak invaded her thoughts once more. She could feel his presence. *No,* she thought, *you are not part of my life now. My people are only with me in mind and spirit. I have a new life—with Erik.* She closed her eyes and tried to dispel the image.

Erik quietly moved up behind her, encircling her in his arms. "What are you thinking about?"

Anna lay her hands over his. They felt rough and worn. She leaned her head against his chest and nuzzled her cheek against his shoulder. "I was thinking of the old ways, of my people. They seem far away, but I care for them."

"Anna, you'll always love your family. That will never change. I wouldn't want you to forget them because they're part of who you are."

Anna didn't say anything for a moment, then very quietly she said, "I am with you now."

Erik tightened his hold. "Anna, I love you," he whispered.

Anna turned about and looked into her husband's eyes. "Erik, I am proud to be your wife. I want only to be with you. And to love you, always."

Erik gently pressed his lips against hers, and as Anna answered his kiss, Kinauquak's presence faded, and Anna knew he would never again be a barrier between her and Erik. Now he could take his place as a part of a past she would always cherish.

Chapter 7

The following morning, the sun reached through Erik and Anna's window and crept across the floor, splashing their room with warmth and color. Anna slowly awakened and squinted through sleepy lids into the bright shaft that blanketed their bed. She blinked at its radiance and sighed as she closed her eyes and nestled against Erik's back. It felt right to curl up next to her husband.

She stifled a yawn, forgetting for the moment that only yesterday she had taken on the name of Anna Engstrom. As the events of the previous day flooded her mind, she opened her eyes and allowed her gaze to rest on her husband's smooth, muscled back. She watched his slow, steady breathing and reached out to caress his skin, startled at how pale he looked beneath her bronzed hand. She'd almost forgotten there were differences between them and found it hard to believe that once a great chasm had separated them—one so deep and wide she'd thought it impossible to span. She closed her eyes and relished his nearness.

Erik let out a deep sigh and slowly rolled onto his back. His eyes still sleepy, he glanced at Anna. He smiled, slipped his arm about her shoulders, and drew her close to him. "Good morning, wife," he said affectionately.

Anna snuggled against him and answered contentedly, "Good morning, husband."

"For a minute I thought I was dreaming when I found you here beside me," Erik said quietly. "I can hardly believe it's true."

"I think it is God's plan that I am your wife."

Erik searched Anna's face. "I know it was him." He stopped and seemed deep in thought. "I never told you, but in the beginning I didn't want to help you and Iya. I just wanted to go on with my life. I'm ashamed to tell you that if not for God's prodding, I would have left the island without you."

"You should not be ashamed. God did not force you to obey, and still you took care of us," Anna said, confident in the goodness of the man who lay beside her.

A light flickered in Erik's eyes, and he smiled. "I guess you're right. Only I know how close I came to leaving you." He stared at the bright blue patch of sky framed by the window, then in a strained voice, continued, "Anna, I want to be a good husband to you and a kind father for the children, but I'm new at this. I know I'm gonna mess up. I'm not going to do it just right . . ."

"I am not worried," Anna interrupted.

"But I am. Sometimes when I look into your eyes, I fear I'll let you and the girls down. You see more good in me than there really is. You're so trusting. Sometimes I wish you were a little more like that girl I met on the beach. Ready to fight and . . ."

"She is still here, within me," Anna reassured him as she intertwined their hands. "But that girl from the beach did not know you. Now she does. Erik, no one does everything right all the time. If we love, that is enough. It will work."

Unexpectedly Erik pulled Anna into a tight embrace and held her as if afraid she might fly away. "I'm so thankful I found you. I'll do my best not to let you down." He stopped and looked into her eyes and grinned. "It's a good thing we have a persistent God."

Just then, a quiet rapping came at the door. Before Anna or Erik could respond, Iya turned the knob and peeked inside. "You awake?" she whispered.

"Yes, Iya," Anna answered, a little irritated. She had wanted more time alone with her husband.

"Can I come in?"

"Of course you can," Erik said cheerfully as he pushed himself into a sitting position, fluffed up his pillow, and rested against it.

Immediately Anna felt guilty about her own selfishness and added, "Good morning, Iya."

The little girl bounded across the floor and leaped onto the bed. Giggling, she landed squarely on Erik's chest.

"Take it easy, there." Erik laughed as he returned the little girl's exuberant hug.

"Did you sleep good?" Iya asked.

"Never better," Erik said and squeezed Anna's hand.

"How did you sleep?" Anna asked.

"Good. Cora has a big bed. Bigger than this, and soft. We already made breakfast. It is time for you to come down now."

Erik sniffed the air. "It sure smells good. What is it?"

"It is a surprise," Iya said with a bright smile.

"I can't wait. We'll be down soon," Erik said.

"No! Now!" Iya demanded. "We made good food." She tugged on Erik's hand.

Erik glanced at Anna and, with a chuckle, said, "It doesn't look like we have a choice, does it?" He pulled Iya to him and tickled her while she squealed with delight. "Okay. We'll get up, but you have to give us time to dress."

"All right," Iya said as she wiggled free of Erik's hold and jumped to the floor. "You will come now," she reminded him. As she opened the door, the sun stretched a long, slender thread of light across the dark hallway, momentarily exposing the dust floating in the air, which quickly disappeared as Iya closed the door. The little girl's steps could be heard as she skipped down the corridor.

Erik yawned and lay back against his pillow. "I feel lazy today."

Imitating Iya, Anna said, "No, you get up now! Breakfast is waiting!"

"Okay," Erik groaned, "but I don't like it. I'd rather lie here with you all day."

"You are the one who promised Iya," Anna teased.

"You're right. It's my fault," Erik replied with feigned guilt.

They both laughed.

When they walked into the dining room, Iya stood proudly beside the table, waiting to serve her two favorite people. Luba sat in her high chair, and it looked like she had managed to get more breakfast on her than in her. She grinned as her mother bent over her and, after searching for a clean patch of skin, planted a kiss on the baby's pudgy cheek. Anna took a seat next to her daughter.

Iya disappeared into the kitchen and a moment later emerged

with a platter of misshapen sourdough pancakes. "I made these myself," she boasted.

"They look good," Anna praised her.

Cora followed with eggs and bacon. "Well, you two look perky," she commented as she set the food in the middle of the table. "You're the last of the lot this morning. Everyone has already eaten and gone their way. Iya here has been a great little helper."

Iya beamed at Cora's praise.

"These look real good, Iya," Erik commented as he speared two flapjacks.

Anna felt ravenous and gratefully accepted Iya's offering of pancakes, along with an egg and several slices of bacon. "Bacon is good," she said as she tore off a bite. "Erik, will we have bacon at our new home?"

"I figured we'd take some with us."

"So, do you two have anything special planned for today?" Cora asked as she settled herself into a chair across the table from Anna.

Erik drizzled syrup over his pancakes. "Actually I've got more to do than there's time for." He took a bite and smiled. "These are fine, Iya. Can't say I've ever tasted better."

Iya grinned and climbed into his lap.

"What do you have to do?" Anna asked petulantly.

He turned to Anna. "I'd like nothing more than to spend the day with you and the girls, but there's still a lot to be done before I can leave. I've got to get a guide lined up. I was told some of the local Auke Indians take folks up north. They're s'posed to know the area real well. And I've still got to get my gear together."

"Today?"

Erik shuffled Iya to his other knee and looked intently at Anna. "I told you, Anna, I've got to get up north as soon as possible."

Anna blinked back her tears. She glanced at Cora, but worry lined the older woman's face and Anna quickly looked down at her hands. Her friend's concern only made it harder to control her own distress. "When will you go?" she asked quietly.

Erik hesitated a moment, then mumbled, "I'm hoping to be on my way by tomorrow morning."

Anna's head shot up and her eyes met Erik's. "We just married and you go?" she asked as her eyes pooled with tears. She pulled at her napkin. "You say you love me."

Erik leaned closer to his bride and took her hands in his. "Anna, please try to understand. I couldn't love you more. I despise having to leave as much as you hate my going. But there's no other choice." He stopped and searched Anna's eyes as if seeking some encouragement from her, but Anna was unable to give it. He looked down at her hands and caressed them. "One good thing is, the sooner I go, the sooner I'll be back. Then we can begin our new life together," he ended with a note of hope.

Anna looked at the wall behind him and fixed her eyes on a lantern sitting on the shelf. Hours before its light had burned brightly, only to be extinguished with the morning. *I am like the lamp,* she thought ruefully. Although she had known this time would come, Anna had pushed it from her thoughts, hoping he would change his mind and allow her to go with him or, at the very least, allow them more time together before he left.

Erik pushed his plate aside. His voice tense, he continued, "Try to understand. I have to go." He stood up as if to leave.

Very quietly, Anna said, "I know you love me. I know. I am just afraid. Afraid you . . . will not come back."

"Of course I'll return. Nothing could keep me away."

"What if something happens? What if you get hurt? Cora's husband . . . "

"Haven't we trusted God all these months?" Erik asked as he pulled Anna to her feet and gently caressed her arms. He searched her face.

Anna nodded ever-so-slightly but couldn't meet his eyes.

"Hasn't he taken good care of us so far?"

Again Anna nodded and wiped at her tears.

"Anna, he won't suddenly forget us. He still cares. And I believe he has a plan for our lives and will see us through."

Anna looked into Erik's steady gaze. "I know you are right. I am sorry for being afraid." She buried her face in his chest and sobbed as Erik hugged her tightly. "I just wish he would not take you away."

"It won't be for long. A few weeks at the most," Erik said as he cradled her against him. Finally he drew back and looked at Anna. With the edge of his shirtsleeve he dabbed at her tears. "Come on now, no more crying."

Anna nodded and managed a small smile.

"I've got to get moving," he said as he took his jacket from its hook and slipped it on.

Her heart sank as he stepped out the door. Tomorrow he would go and maybe never return.

Iya walked around the table and wrapped her arms around Anna's waist. "It will be all right," the little girl comforted her older sister. Silently Anna pulled Iya close to her, and for a few minutes they stood quietly embracing each other.

Anna filled her day helping Cora with the chores. She didn't feel much like talking and quietly went about her work. Later, when Erik returned with a look of jubilation on his face, Anna fumed, unable to understand the ways of this man. *Why is he happy about this?*

"Well, it's all set," Erik said as he pulled off his coat and hung it on the hook beside the door. "Can't believe it worked out so smoothly." He sat down and rested his elbows on the table. "There are two fellows, Aukes, who agreed to guide me north. They speak good English and said they are ready to go anytime I am."

He leaned forward a little, and once again a strange glint lit his eyes, the same look Anna had seen whenever he talked of gold. It made her uneasy.

"They say there's gold on the Schuck, and with a boat, we can be there in a couple of weeks."

Feeling troubled, Anna forced a smile. "That is good. It will not take long. Do you think soon we will have a claim?"

"Yes!" Erik said as he pushed himself away from the table and scooped Anna up in his arms and whirled her around.

His enthusiasm swept over her, and Anna threw her head back and laughed. Finally she said, "Erik! My head spins. Put me down." When he set her back on her feet, she hugged him about the neck and, momentarily forgetting there were others in the room, kissed him. *Everything will turn out right,* she told herself.

As the day wore on, her earlier enthusiasm waned. All she could think about was Erik's impending departure. She wished there were something she could do to stop it, but all too soon the day ended, and after a sleepless night, morning intruded.

Anna looked out the window and instead of bright sunshine, saw dark, sodden clouds resting atop the hills. Although rain hadn't yet begun to fall, the air smelled heavy and damp. The gloom matched Anna's mood. She rolled over and pretended to sleep while Erik quietly dressed and went downstairs.

The moment he closed the door, Anna wished she could call him back—to spend a few more minutes with him. She quickly slipped out of bed and pulled on a tunic. The time had come to say good-bye.

Once more, Cora had taken the children for the night, and Luba already sat in her high chair happily playing with her breakfast, oblivious to the painful good-byes about to take place. Iya sat at the table, leaning on one elbow, with an untouched plate of food in front of her. She kicked her legs back and forth furiously, looking downcast and angry.

Erik walked into the dining room wearing a forced smile. "Well, I'm ready." No one looked up. "Iya, I have to go now," he said as he knelt next to her.

Iya leaned back in her chair and kept her eyes averted.

"I won't be gone long. I promise."

He tried to hug the little girl, but she pushed against him and cried, "I do not want you go. You stay. We are happy here. I do not want to go to the river." She broke into sobs, and this time when Erik reached for her, she clung to him, burying her head in his shoulder.

"I wish there were an easier way," he whispered against the little girl's hair. "There just isn't." He cleared his throat and blinked back his own tears. "One day soon we'll all go north together and live on our own place."

"Why do we not go now? I thought you would change your mind."

"It's too dangerous. I just can't take you until I know more about where I'm going."

"We traveled in the umiak together," Iya argued.

"That was different. We didn't have any choice. It was either that or leave you alone."

"Iya, Erik has to go now," Cora said as she pulled the little girl away from him. She stopped a moment, unable to hide her own concern, and said, "You take care of yourself now, Mr. Engstrom," as she led Iya out of the room.

Next, Erik took Luba out of her high chair and, ignoring the bits of food splattered on her, held the little girl close and gave her a kiss. "You be good for your momma," he instructed, trying to sound cheerful but failing. He gently set the baby back in her chair, but she whined and reached up to him. Erik distracted her with a crust of bread.

Anna hung back, waiting until the last moment. Erik turned to her. She had told herself she would be strong and not make it any worse for Erik, but as he reached for her, she felt her resolve melt away as tears pressed against her eyelids. She waited for Erik to say something.

He took her hands in his and, his voice tight with emotion, said, "Anna, we won't really be apart. I'll be thinking about you every minute. You'll be with me."

Giving in to her emotions, Anna fell into his arms and allowed herself to weep. "I am no better than Iya," she jested, but her attempt at gaiety fell flat as they held each other. Anna could hear the thump of Erik's heart. "Erik, please come back," she finally said. "Let nothing happen to you."

"I'll be careful. I promise."

Anna stood away from him. "I will pray. Do not trust your guides. You do not know what they might do."

"I'll keep an eye on them."

Cora returned and stood just inside the doorway with her arms crossed. Clearly, she had something on her mind. The moment Erik looked at her, she unloaded. "That little girl in there is crying her eyes out. You remember her. She's depending on you. It's a dangerous world out there, Mr. Engstrom, and you've got a family counting on you now."

"Cora, why are you so angry with me?" Erik asked, looking a little bewildered.

"I'm not really," Cora relented. "It's just that I've come to care about these dear ones." She hesitated. "I remember when my husband went out. He promised to return, and I believed him." She stopped short and tucked an imaginary hair back into place. "I'll take good care of your family, Erik," she said more kindly. "No need to worry about them."

"Thanks, Cora. I won't worry as long as they're here with you." He glanced about, as if he might be forgetting something, then hefted his pack onto his back. "Well, I better get movin'." As his eyes met Anna's, she slipped into his arms once more. He held her against his chest for a moment, then gently pushed her away from him and headed out the door.

Anna watched as he ambled down the street. With each step he took, she could feel the loneliness inside swell. She watched until he disappeared from sight, then slowly closed the door. As she did so, she felt as though she were closing off a part of herself. She looked up at Cora and, without a word, dropped into the woman's ample embrace and allowed herself to be mothered. Silently, Iya wiggled between them.

For several minutes Anna took refuge in Cora's arms. Finally, with a deep sigh, she stepped away from her new friend. "Cora, how do we do this?"

Cora reached out and stroked Anna's hair. "You just do, dear. You just do."

Taking a shaky breath, she asked, "How? Erik was with me since my people died. I am alone without him."

"Anna, you're never really alone," Cora reassured her. "God is always here, and I'll help any way I can."

"I do not think he knows this pain."

"Oh, no. That's not true. He knows every kind of pain and trouble. He lived it all."

"How does God know sadness?"

"Well, I suppose he could have been the saddest being who ever lived. He came to earth as a man—Jesus—and lived here for thirty-three years. Why, in the book of Hebrews, God says Jesus experienced all the troubles of mankind. That's why he understands." Cora gently took Anna's chin in her hand. "Anna, God loves you more than you can know. Even more than you love that little baby there." She nodded toward Luba. "He'll always do what's best for you. And I'm sure he'll bring Erik back safe and sound."

"You think so?"

"I sure do," Cora said confidently as she turned to Luba, who was making it clear she'd been confined to her chair far too long. Cora wiped the baby's face clean and lifted her free.

"How about we read for a bit?" she asked as she escorted Anna into the parlor. With the baby cuddled against her, Cora took her Bible from the shelf. Anna settled in a large, overstuffed chair and tucked her feet up under her.

"Erik used to always read," Iya said sadly as she climbed onto Anna's lap.

"Do you have a favorite verse?" Cora asked.

"You pick one," Iya said as she snuggled against Anna.

"Well, how about the book of Proverbs? It always has good, practical things to say." After settling Luba on the floor, she scanned the pages of her Bible. "Here it is," she said. "Proverbs 3, verses 5 and 6: *'Trust in the LORD with all your heart, and lean not on your own understanding; in all your ways acknowledge Him, and He shall direct your paths.'*"

"What does it mean?" Iya asked.

"Well, just what I've been telling Anna. If you trust God to do what's right and don't depend on your own way of thinkin', he'll do what's best every time. Even when life looks real bad, we can trust him to take care of things in his way. We need to remember he knows what he's doin' and will always do what's best."

"I do believe," Anna said and hugged Iya to her.

Chapter 8

*D*ark clouds, heavy with rain, blanketed Sitka. It had been two days since Erik had gone. Unable to shed the heavy mantle of misery that had settled over her, Anna sat at her desk and looked down on the city street. She watched people slog through the mud and cautiously step around puddles. She wished the rain would stop.

Morosely, Anna pulled the shades closed, trying to shut out the cold, damp air that seeped through the window. She stared at the limp curtains. What would she do to fill another day? *I do not feel like doing anything,* she thought and glanced at the girls. They still slept.

With a sigh, she forced herself to her feet, shimmied out of her nightgown, and pulled on her tunic, shivering in the cool morning air. She leaned over Iya and gently brushed a strand of hair off the little girl's face. *She looks more like Mother every day,* Anna thought as she tucked the quilt up under Iya's chin.

She turned back to her vigil at the window. Pulling the curtain aside, she hugged herself and stared out on the wet, dreary world, her thoughts returning to Erik. Was he out in this downpour, or had he found a place to shelter? Was he thinking of her? She scanned the hillsides. *I wonder where he is.* She looked beyond the overcast sky as she whispered a prayer. "Please God, keep Erik safe and bring him back to me." She felt something touch her leg and looked down to find Iya snuggled against her.

The little girl gazed out the window and asked in a small voice, "Anna, are you praying?"

"Yes," Anna answered softly and stroked the little girl's hair.

Luba's cheerful babbling disrupted the quiet.

Iya didn't seem to notice and kept her eyes trained on the hillside as she stated confidently, "Erik will be all right. He will come back soon."

Anna squeezed Iya's shoulder and wished she possessed such assurance. She turned away from the window and crossed to her bed. As cheerfully as possible, she said, "Good morning, Luba," as she lifted the baby into the air and smiled into her sweet face.

Luba chortled and flailed her fists in the air.

Iya patted the infant's leg. "Luba is happy."

"She is," Anna said as she nuzzled the baby's face, "and hungry. I am hungry too. Maybe Cora has breakfast ready?"

Iya headed for the door.

"Dress first, then go," Anna said before the little girl could open it.

"I will change quick," Iya said as she stripped off her night-clothes. She donned her new frock and scurried toward the door.

Anna stopped her. "Do not go yet. First you wash your face and brush your hair."

Iya pouted but did as she was told.

Anna began to change Luba, who giggled and squirmed, trying to make a game of the usual morning routine. But Anna persisted, and Luba finally settled down and babbled contentedly as her mother pulled her dress over her head.

Anna smiled and chatted amiably, telling the infant of their people and the village by the sea where the men used to hunt for the great whale. She told her, too, of one hunter named Kinauquak who loved her very much.

Iya sat on the bed and listened as her sister talked about life as it had once been. When Anna stopped, Iya said somberly, "I do not remember so good."

"People forget, Iya. You have done nothing wrong."

"Do you miss our home?"

Anna didn't answer at first, but pulled Luba to her feet. She glanced out the window. "Sometimes when I think of it, I miss home very much." As her mind wandered to a time and place long past, she continued. "I think of the potlatch when we sing and dance, share fine gifts, and feast on whale meat." She smiled, but as the memories flooded her mind, tears filled her eyes. "I wish I could speak to my family, make baskets with friends, and celebrate good hunting." A surge of emotion choked off her words.

"We have a new life. I do not think of the past."

"We do live a new life, but I will never forget the old." Anna turned to Iya and rested her hand on the little girl's shoulder as she looked straight into her eyes. "We must never forget who we are or where we come from."

Iya seemed to understand and nodded.

Anna smiled, tousled the little girl's hair, and gave her a quick hug. "Now it is time to eat," she said more lightheartedly.

Cora greeted them with a smile as they entered the dining room. "Why, you're up early this morning." After studying Anna more closely, she added, "You look plain worn out."

"I did not sleep good," Anna answered with a heavy sigh.

"I s'pose that's to be expected. It's not every day a woman sends her husband off to parts unknown." Cheerfully she continued, "Well, you two are just in time to help me gather eggs. I figure it's time you met the chickens anyhow."

Puzzled, Anna asked, "Met the chickens?"

"Oh, that's just an expression. You don't actually meet them. You just gather in their eggs."

"How do we get them?" Anna asked, still confused. She hadn't seen any cliffs nearby where they could collect eggs, and this late in the season all the chicks would have long since hatched. She knew of no birds that lay more than once a year. She waited for Cora to explain.

"Why, we'll just go on out to the henhouse," Cora said, unaware of Anna's confusion. "It's just out back."

Anna still didn't understand, but she and the children donned their cloaks anyway and followed Cora to the back of the house. Anna was careful to avoid stepping in any puddles. Iya, on the other hand, skipped along beside her, splashing through every one.

They approached a small wooden shack. Anna hadn't noticed the weather-worn building before. There was nothing impressive about it other than the lively squawks and clucks of proud hens who boasted over their latest accomplishments.

Cora unlatched the door and pulled it open. Anna and Iya hung back, uncertain of what awaited them inside. "Come along you two," Cora said, but when Anna and Iya didn't follow, she stopped and studied her two uncertain companions. A slow smile of understanding spread across her face as she exclaimed, "Why, you've never seen a chicken before have you!"

Anna shrugged her shoulders questioningly and said, "I do not know about chickens."

"Well, I s'pose it's time you did," Cora chuckled. "Come on in. They won't hurt you." She stepped inside and held the door open.

With Luba balanced on her hip, Anna carefully stepped through the doorway. Iya clung to her skirt. As Cora let the door close behind them, Anna felt a moment of panic, suddenly feeling trapped within the gloomy building. The room felt uncomfortably close and warm, and the odor of fowl and damp hay hung thick in the air. As Anna's eyes adjusted to the darkness, she scanned her surroundings. Along one wall, a row of boxes had been secured where a collection of plump, black and brown birds rested contentedly in nests made of hay. With their feathers fluffed up about them, they bristled at the intruders and their small eyes darted about. A large, fierce-looking bird strutted back and forth in front of his hens, clearly unhappy with the interlopers.

Cora opened a small gate leading to the chicken yard and shooed him out. "He can be a bit pesky when he has a mind to. I've been the brunt of more than one of his sour moods," she said scornfully.

"These are chickens?" Iya asked as she crept up to one and studied it closely.

"That they are," Cora answered with a smile, her hands folded across her ample waist. "From May to September the hens lay an egg nearly every day. In fact, some days they lay two. If I don't shut them up at night they never sleep. But come winter, it's another story. I'm lucky to get one a week. I put some aside during the summer to help see us through the long months when they're not layin'. I don't keep many roosters." She peered at the cock she'd booted out. He preened and paraded in front of the shed. "But I have to keep one rooster, or there'll be no chicks. This fella's a bit feisty, but all in all he's a fine one. Keeps these ladies in line and makes sure we have plenty of birds for the stew pot. Won't be usin' him for soup for a while yet."

What Cora did next startled Anna. She reached beneath one of the hens, searched about for a moment, and pulled out two large brown eggs.

Anna could only stare. She'd never seen any bird give up her young so easily.

Cora chuckled as she shuffled the eggs into one hand. "Fine eggs aren't they?"

Anna nodded. "I never saw birds like these. We used to climb cliffs to find eggs, but many times the birds fight us." She stopped and pondered on the strange creatures. "Why do they not fly away?"

"We clip some birds' wings, but most I s'pect just like bein' fed. We throw them a bit of crushed corn every day, and they make short work of any leftovers from the kitchen. In return, they provide us with fresh eggs."

"This is a very good thing. Can I find an egg?"

"Certainly. Most of them don't mind. But you've got to watch that one there with the black and white spots. She's a bit temperamental and might peck at you."

Cautiously Anna reached beneath a golden-brown hen. The bird ruffled her feathers and made a low burr sound in her throat, but she didn't peck. It felt moist and warm beneath her. Anna searched until her fingers closed over a hard, smooth orb. Slowly letting out her breath, she pulled the egg from beneath the hen and discovered she held a perfect, brown egg. Anna stroked it and smiled. "It feels warm and soft," she said as she set it in Cora's basket.

"Can I try?" Iya asked and, before anyone could answer, she reached beneath the nearest hen. A moment later, she pulled her hand out with a small egg clutched tightly between her fingers. Unexpectedly the egg exploded in her hand and splashed yolk down the front of her. Iya squealed. With her arms outstretched, she looked at the gooey mess left in her palm and the splatters on her dress. Her eyes filled with tears, and her chin quivered as she whined, "My egg breaked and ruined my dress."

"Don't worry. It's only one egg, and the dress can be washed," Cora comforted.

Anna wiped at the mess. "Do you think I can have chickens at the claim?"

"I don't see why not. Why, I'll even give you a couple hens and a young rooster to get you started."

Anna smiled. "I would like that," she said and took another egg from beneath one of the hens. "There are many things I like in this new land."

Cora snatched the last egg from beneath the black-and-white speckled hen and steered Iya out the door. "I think it's time we got this one cleaned up and had some breakfast."

Chores kept Anna busy most of the morning. Running a boardinghouse required a great deal of work, and Anna was grateful for the distraction. She dusted and swept, then helped Cora with her baking. After lunch, she put Luba and Iya down for a nap. The day stretched out endlessly before her, and she wondered how she would bear the waiting. Each time she thought of Erik, a deep ache settled in her chest.

It is good to be busy, she told herself as she retrieved one of the pelts she'd started fashioning into a tunic while on board the clipper. She held it up and examined it. It was nearly finished and would be a fine fit for Iya. All Anna needed to do was the final stitching. She draped it over her arm and went to the parlor.

Cora sat in an overstuffed chair close to the fireplace doing some needlework of her own. The fabric she used reminded Anna of the soft, pliable cotton of her new dress. Cora had stretched it across a wooden hoop and now expertly wove a delicate pattern of flowers and lace through it with a fine thread. Anna had never seen this type of sewing, although it reminded her of some of the intricate designs she had woven into her baskets with fine, dyed grasses. She watched Cora closely for several minutes. "What do you call this? It is very pretty."

"It's just embroidery. I'd be happy to teach you."

"I would like that. When I finish this, will you show me?"

"Absolutely," Cora answered and glanced about the room. "It's so quiet. Where are the children?" She stuck the needle down through the fabric.

"They are sleeping. It is good time for sewing."

"What are you working on?" Cora asked as she eyed Anna's pelt with interest.

"First I will make a tunic for Iya, then one for Luba."

"That's sealskin isn't it?"

"Yes. Erik killed it. It is a fine pelt and will make a good, warm tunic."

"It's beautiful and certainly looks like it would keep a body warm. Wouldn't mind having one for myself when the weather turns cold. Could you show me how to do that?"

"Yes, but it takes much time. My mother teached me since I was small." She paused before continuing. "In the village I was a good flesher and tanner of hides." Her eyes suddenly brimmed with tears. Since Erik had gone, she'd felt so alone and, once more, the loss of her family tore at her. She'd found herself dwelling on them and the life she'd left behind. Like an open wound, her grief gnawed at her. "I miss my people," she admitted quietly. "The great wave killed them all, except Iya. It happened long ago, but it still hurts."

"I know," Cora said gently. "Sometimes it seems the pain will never stop. And, in a way, it never really does. It just becomes more tolerable."

Anna wiped at her tears.

"I still miss my Patrick too," Cora went on as she laid her work in her lap and stared at the flames leaping in the hearth. The soft sounds of a ticking clock and crackle of wood settled over the room. Without another word she took up her sewing.

For a time neither woman said anything; both were absorbed in their own thoughts. Then Anna laid her pelt aside and looked at Cora. Quietly she asked, "Cora, do you know God?"

"Yes, I do," Cora answered without hesitation.

"When Patrick left on his trip, did you pray for him?"

"I always prayed for my husband. A day didn't go by that I didn't speak to God about him."

Anna felt confused and a little frightened. "I do not understand. If you know God and he is powerful, why did Patrick die? Why did God not save him?"

Cora didn't answer right away. "I've asked myself that same question a hundred times."

"You do not know the answer?"

"No. And I don't think we're meant to know everything. That's part of walking with the Lord and learning to trust him in all circumstances, even the hard things. I know God loved Patrick. And I know nothing touches God's people that he doesn't allow. I figure if he loves me and always wants what's best for me, then even the hard times are part of a greater plan. Patrick knew the Lord, and I'm sure he's in heaven right now. The apostle Paul said that to die was gain. I believe Patrick's better off. The one's hurtin' are me and his family, but we've managed without him. Still, sometimes when I'm missin' him real bad, I can't help askin' God why. But it's during those times, I always feel his comfort the most. After talkin' things over with him, I feel at peace with it all." Cora returned to her intricate stitching.

Anna worked quietly for a few minutes, but something still troubled her and she couldn't concentrate on her work. She stopped sewing and quietly asked, "Cora, do you think God killed Patrick?"

"Oh no, I don't believe that. It's just that this world is an awful, sinful place and innocent people suffer. In the very beginning, when man chose to disobey God, the whole works fell apart and we ended up living in a land ruled by the devil."

"The devil?"

"Oh, yes, well we don't need to be talkin' about him."

"But I do not understand this devil," Anna prodded.

Cora thought a moment, then lay her stitching aside. "All right," she conceded with a sigh. "He's a bad one. Pure evil. Used to be one of God's angels, but he got so wrapped up in himself and his own beauty and strength, he decided he was more powerful than God. Well, God threw him out of heaven, and he's been doing everything he could ever since to cause trouble. We don't need to fear him, though. God is greater than that old beast, and the Lord lives in us. We just need to remember the devil is on the prowl. But the day will come when he'll get his due. A fiery pit waits for him. When that day comes, we can all shout hallelujah."

"Did he kill Patrick?"

"I don't know. Patrick was a wild one, like I told you. Sometimes we bring on our own troubles. Can't blame Satan for everything. But if it was Satan's dirty work, God used it for good. After Patrick died, I was real lonesome. You know ... grievin'. But my pain only drove me closer to God. There's a verse in the book of Romans that says, *'All things work together for good to those who love God, to those who are the called according to His purpose,'* and I believe it. I've seen it happen just that way, many times."

Anna gazed out the window, then, almost in a whisper, asked, "Do you think Erik will be all right?"

"Anna, I know you're worried about Erik. It's natural for you to fret, but I truly believe he's going to be fine. It seems to me God worked mighty hard to bring you two together, and you've only just started your life. I've a real strong feeling he's got something special in store for you two. Just because my Patrick died young, doesn't mean something will happen to Erik."

"I hope you are right," Anna said, wanting to believe Cora. She picked up her work and pushed the large bone needle through the sealskin.

"Tomorrow is Sunday. I always try to make it to church come Sundays. Would you like to go?"

"Erik talked about church. Father Ermelov used to come and teach at my village, but I did not listen then."

"Well, church is just Christians gatherin' together to worship God. We sing songs and the pastor or one of the leaders teaches from the Bible."

"It is good?"

"Yes."

"If you and Erik both like it, then it must be good. I will go."

Cora smiled as she reached over and patted Anna's hand. "I think you'll enjoy it."

Anna felt better after her conversation with Cora, and the rest of the day passed more quickly. Although many questions still troubled her and there was much she didn't understand about the Christian God, she knew he was real. Despite her loneliness, she felt a peace within her, and it would be enough for now. She knew all her questions couldn't be satisfied immediately, but she hoped she would find answers to some of them in church.

Weary, Anna was glad for her bed at the end of the day. After joining Iya and Luba beneath the warm quilt, she prayed for Erik and, once more, felt an indescribable sense of calm wash over her. Sleep came quickly, and there was no tossing and turning this night.

The following morning, Anna's heavy spirits of the previous day had lifted. She felt more lighthearted and looked forward to attending church. After a hurried breakfast, she and the girls followed Cora down the street.

As Anna cautiously stepped around puddles and avoided the deepest mud, her excitement gave way to uneasiness. Fear settled in the pit of her stomach and tugged at her as she wondered what people would think. What would they say? She had already learned how cruel some could be and knew there would be those who would detest her presence in their house of worship. Even as the thoughts bombarded her, she tried to reassure herself that these people loved the same God as she did and would welcome all believers, no matter what the color of their skin.

Not intimidated by what others might think, Cora seemed in high spirits as she strode the few blocks to church. Her confidence bolstered Anna's.

They stopped outside a small, modest-looking building where a steady stream of people flocked through the front door. Anna could hear singing coming from inside. She stopped on the steps to gather her courage.

Cora took her hand. "There's nothing to be afraid of," she reassured her. "It's just a building like any other, only here we worship God."

Anna studied the church for a moment. It lacked paint like many of the structures in town. The steps were in disrepair, and the curtains hanging at the window looked faded and limp. A large wooden cross hung above the doorway. Painted a bright white, it seemed such a contrast from the rest of the building.

Anna looked at Cora and forced a smile. Taking a deep breath, she allowed the older woman to usher her and the children inside.

The interior of the church looked as humble as its exterior. Plain wooden benches lined up end-to-end were divided by a narrow aisle down the center of the room. Subdued light filtered through two small windows on either side while a large window at the entrance of the chapel welcomed a broad band of sunlight that stretched across the uneven wooden floor. Another wooden cross, identical to the one over the doorway, adorned the front of the church. The room was simple, but spotless, and Anna decided she liked it.

The parishioners sat straight backed with their hymnals propped between their hands, their voices lifted in song. An elderly woman perched on a rickety bench at an antiquated piano moved her hands stiffly over the keys.

As Cora steered Anna and the children down the center aisle, heads turned their way. Anna felt the blood rush to her face. Some smiled, but others stared, openly shocked at her presence. She tried to keep her eyes on Cora's back and off the ogling churchgoers and wished Cora would find a place to sit down. A strong urge to bolt down the street to the relative safety of the boardinghouse rose up within her. She nearly gave in to the impulse.

Finally, Cora found an empty spot on one of the benches and sat. Anna breathed a sigh of relief as she slid in next to her friend. Iya wiggled between the two women, while Luba squirmed restlessly on her mother's lap. Anna had noticed there were no other Indians and wondered why. She leaned close to Cora and whispered, "I do not see any natives."

"Most of them go to the Orthodox Church," Cora whispered back and picked up her hymnal.

Anna tried to relax and listen to the music. She didn't know the hymns. They were very different from the songs she had sung with her people, but they sounded beautiful, just the same, and soon she found herself caught up in the melodies. *One day I will know the words,* she thought with pleasure. But for now, she closed her eyes and allowed the sweet chords with their message of love and rejuvenation to wash over her. She soon forgot her discomfort.

As the last song ended, a kind-looking gentleman stepped up to a wooden podium at the front of the room. Tenderly he laid his Bible on the stand, allowing his hand to rest upon the book as he stood quietly before the congregation. Smiling, he scanned the faces, occasionally nodding at those he knew. When his eyes fell upon Anna, he turned his warm smile upon her, and her sense of not belonging vanished.

"Welcome to the house of the Lord," he said in a deep voice. "I'm happy to see you all here this morning. It seems we have some visitors with us. We're glad you're here." He glanced again at Anna.

Anna liked this gentle minister. He wasn't a big man, but he brought a powerful presence of assurance and peace into the room.

He opened his Bible. "Today, we'll look into the second book of Samuel," he began, and as he read the words came alive.

He spoke of a man named David who had once been a servant of God. Like many men he was tempted by sin, and for a time he allowed evil to rule his life. At one point, he even murdered a man to cover his own wrongdoing. But, as the pastor continued, Anna learned that God never gave up on David, and one day, ashamed and repentant, David turned from his sin and put his life once more into God's hands. David paid a heavy price for his sin—the life of his own son. But with God's help, he went on to do great things for the Lord.

Anna's eyes filled with tears as she envisioned this man prostrate before the Lord with the knowledge of his sin piercing his heart. But even more wondrous was God's enduring love and patience, his willingness to set David back on his feet and welcome him back into close fellowship with himself.

The reverend went on to remind those present that, like David, they too could receive God's mercy. No matter what their past, they could entrust their lives to a heavenly Father who loved them.

Anna clung to every word, feeling as if he were speaking directly to her. She remembered the anger and bitterness that had once controlled her life and how she had hated God. Still he had loved her and drew her to himself. Shame welled up within her, and Anna began to pray she might live a life worthy of his love. She glanced down at the Bible in Cora's hands and a feeling of discontent washed over her. *If only I could read the words,* she thought. . . . *One day, maybe one day.*

The elderly woman returned to the piano, and the small building swelled with song. Anna could feel her spirits lift. With the last note, quiet settled over the congregation, and the pastor led them in a closing prayer. After that, people began filing out.

I love church, Anna thought, and she wished next Sunday would come soon.

Cora linked arms with Anna and nearly dragged her to the back of the church to meet the reverend. Others stood waiting to greet him, so they took their place in line. A cruel-looking man glared at Anna. His mouth slowly turned up in an ominous grin and he spit a wad of soggy tobacco at her feet. She sucked in her breath, feeling as if he'd struck her. She didn't know what to say. Before she could utter a sound, the man turned and shuffled away. *He had no right!* she thought indignantly, but too afraid to confront him, she remained silent.

"Let it go," Cora said quietly. "There's nothin' you can do."

Still angry, Anna stood beside Cora glaring at the floor. As they drew closer to the pastor, she felt a sudden surge of panic. He'd spoken eloquently and seemed kind, but what if he hated her too? How did he feel about an Indian in his church? Her mouth went dry, and her new resolve to trust God faded. She couldn't face another insult. As the line dwindled, Anna convinced herself the pastor was as bigoted as the man who had spit tobacco at her. What would she say? She doubted she'd be able to hold her tongue. In fact, she decided, *I will not allow it! I will tell him what I think.*

"Reverend, I'd like you to meet one of my new borders," Cora said as she propelled Anna forward. "Anna, this is Reverend Nielsen. Reverend, Anna Engstrom."

Anna found herself standing before the minister. With her angry resolve fading, she was uncertain what to say or do, and she merely nodded.

Rev. Nielsen broke into a broad, friendly smile and reached out his hand in greeting. Anna didn't respond. Undaunted by her reserve, he took her hand and gently shook it. "I'm pleased to meet you, Anna. I only got back into town last night and haven't had the pleasure. Although, I must say, I did hear something about you and your husband," he added with a grin.

He seemed so sincere, Anna couldn't help but smile. "I am glad to be here," she said, feeling guilty over her unfair assessment of the man. "I like your speaking."

"Thank you. That's good to hear. I never feel I do God's word justice." He glanced at Luba in Anna's arms then down at Iya. "And who might these two youngsters be?"

Cora answered before Anna had a chance. "Why, this is Iya, Anna's sister," she said, patting the little girl on the head. Iya smiled but stayed close by Anna's side. "And the baby is Anna's daughter, Luba. They're stayin' with me until Anna's husband returns. He's up north scoutin' for a claim. Heard there had been some small finds up that way."

"Well, I wish him luck," Rev. Nielsen said turning back to Anna. "Hope he won't be gone too long. It's always hard being separated from the ones we love." He smiled kindly and, touching his hand to his hat, added, "I hope to see you and the children next week, Mrs. Engstrom."

"We will come again," Anna promised with a smile, her anger long since forgotten.

Loud voices came from out front.

"Well, it looks like I'm needed. Good day," the pastor said as he hurried out the door to take charge of two boys scuffling at the bottom of the steps.

Cora linked arms with Anna again, and the two ambled toward the doorway. "Well, what did you think of it?"

Anna squeezed her friend's hand. "I like it very much. I know Erik will too." They stepped onto the porch and watched as the reverend separated the brawling youngsters and sent them on their way. Anna took a deep breath and scanned the surrounding hills. Almost to herself, she said, "I wonder where he is. If he has found the claim yet."

"I doubt that. He's only been gone a couple of days. Don't expect he's anywheres near that river yet. It's a long way, even by boat."

Anna sighed and, taking Iya's hand in hers, smiled at Cora as she allowed the older woman to escort her down the steps.

"I'm sorry about that fellow back there. But the truth is, Anna, there are those who just don't accept anyone who's different."

"I felt very angry, but I know sometimes there will be trouble. I must not show my feelings. We will come again?"

Cora grinned. "Just what I was hoping you'd say," she said and headed down the street toward the boardinghouse.

Iya skipped ahead while Anna, carrying Luba, followed more slowly. She studied the hillsides and thought about Erik. How long would it be before he came home? *Soon. Please let it be soon.*

Chapter 9

$\mathcal{E}$rik bundled deeper into his coat as he peered through the steady drizzle. He shivered and edged closer to the fire. Although Alaska, with her endless beauty and rare wonders, had claimed him, her unpredictable damp weather still nettled at him. "Can't believe it's the middle of July," he muttered as he glanced at his native guides. They looked at him from beneath their waterproof cloaks but didn't respond. The smaller of the two turned the meat roasting over the fire. Droplets of fat and juice fell from the flesh and sizzled in the flames.

They'd been traveling together three days, and although Erik had made several attempts at casual conversation, they refused to take part. *All they see is an outsider,* he had decided. *They don't understand how Alaska can become home to someone from the outside.* He wished he could explain it to them, but even as he considered telling them, he knew they wouldn't accept what he had to say. Clearly they didn't trust him, and Erik had to admit he wasn't at all sure he trusted them either.

His unfriendly companions seemed constantly on the alert but unwilling to share any insights with Erik. Their behavior unsettled him and, more than once, he found himself glancing over his shoulder. They seemed peculiar, even a little spooky. *If they'd just say something,* Erik thought as he stared into the flames. *I suppose I can't blame them for being reserved,* he reasoned. *It's not like they've been treated with any sense of dignity or justice by most outsiders.*

He wished Anna were with him. It seemed strange to sit beside a fire without her. They'd shared so many nights across the flames from each other. As he thought of her, he could almost imagine that she sat next to him. Her presence had been with him across the miles of ocean. Each day as he moved inland and farther north, his desire to return to Sitka grew stronger. He longed to hold her, but instead he faced another long, lonely night.

He ran his hands through his hair. *This is getting me nowhere,* he thought as he forced Anna from his mind. "Cursed rain," he blustered and wondered if it was raining in Sitka. *I shouldn't have left her,* he reflected, unable to keep his mind from wandering back to his new bride. *She doesn't know anything about living in my world. She'll be lost.* Then he remembered Cora. He'd never met anyone like her. She'd been more than kind; she'd been an immediate friend. *She'll take good care of them,* he reassured himself as he contemplated Cora's open and honest way.

He relaxed a little and looked around. Thick clouds clung to the nearby hills, shrouding the mountain peaks above them. Fog hovered over the beach, giving it a mystical quality, and Erik understood why so many natives believed in ghosts. Soaked with rain, the trees and ferns glistened, their limbs drooping beneath the added weight. Spongy moss covered the sodden earth.

The smaller native nudged Erik's arm. "Here, you take this," he said as he offered a chunk of sizzling meat to Erik.

"Thank you." Erik's stomach rumbled. He'd forgotten his hunger until now. As he bit into it, juice dripped from the skewer and onto his hands. The mild-tasting meat pleased him. "What is this?"

"Mountain goat."

"It's good," Erik said as he took another bite.

The native nodded, but said nothing more.

The rest of the meal was eaten in silence. Erik's companions turned in as soon as they finished. Resting comfortably on beds made of spruce boughs, they quickly fell asleep.

Erik studied them. Unlike the Aleut, they were large boned and tall. The bigger and fiercer of the two wore a bone ring through his nose. It had been honed very thin so it would hang loosely, but Erik thought it looked painful. It gave its wearer a savage look, and he found the ornament a little disconcerting. He'd seen many Aleuts with similar adornments, but instead of wearing the jewelry through their noses, they punctured one lip with a bone or ivory button.

Somehow, the Aleuts' decorations had always seemed less obtrusive.

Erik knew it was just a matter of time before the natives put this practice behind them. Already many had stopped wearing such jewelry. He considered the inevitable changes facing the local Indians and felt a deep sense of loss. It seemed to him that people were too ready to move on to something new before they learned to embrace the present. He thought of his own parents' struggle to adjust after immigrating to America. They never did adjust completely.

He glanced back at his companions. Actually the ring didn't look so bad; it gave the man a sense of character. Erik tossed the last of his coffee onto the ground. *I sure wouldn't want them mad at me,* he thought as he crawled beneath his wool blanket and waterproof slicker. He tucked his hands under his cheek and closed his eyes. Immediately his mind turned to Anna. "Lord, take care of her and the children," he prayed before falling asleep. That night his dreams were filled with images of Anna, a boardinghouse in Sitka, and a cabin left abandoned in the woods somewhere on Cook Inlet.

When Erik awoke the following morning, the people he loved still felt close, and it took him a moment to regain his bearings. He rubbed at his face and looked about. The fire was out and his guides still slept, but the rain had stopped. He pushed himself out of bed and stretched, working out kinks from a night on the ground. After restarting the fire, he put a pot of coffee on and, while it boiled, took out his Bible and sat down to read. Turning to the book of Psalms, chapter 139, he searched the page and found verse one. He read the first five verses carefully, trying to take in their meaning. *O LORD, You have searched me and known me. You know my sitting down and my rising up; You understand my thought afar off. You comprehend my path and my lying down, and are acquainted with all my ways. For there is not a word on my tongue, but behold, O LORD, You know it altogether. You have hedged me behind and before, and laid Your hand upon me.* Erik set his Bible in his lap and reflected on the passage. He felt confidence fill him. As long as he put his life in God's hands, he knew his very steps would be orchestrated by the Creator of the universe. He looked up at the pale morning sky, and his heart swelled with gratitude as the concept settled into his soul. He had no reason to fear. God was in control.

"Thank you, Father," he whispered as he set his Bible aside and studied his surroundings with a fresh eye. Lush forests stretched down to the sea where trees reached over the water as if wishing to explore the oceans. Wide expanses of beach gave way to boulders and deep grasses. Moss covered the earth and crept into the trees where, like plush velvet, it blanketed the limbs and trunks. Heavy tendrils of lichen hung from the branches. The scent of spruce and damp earth mingled with the sweetness of blueberries and salmon-berries.

Erik took a deep breath. It felt good to be alive.

A sharp sting pricked his neck, and instinctively he slapped at the irritant. He looked down at his palm to find the bloodied remains of an Alaskan mosquito. As the sun warmed the earth, hordes of mosquitoes and flies took to the air looking for the nearest warm-blooded animal, but even the presence of these pests couldn't spoil Erik's outlook. It was a beautiful day, and it was the Lord's.

The most hostile of his two guides groaned and rolled to his side. He glanced up at Erik, but said nothing as he pushed himself to his feet and brushed his hair back from his face. In a quick motion, he stepped around the fire and picked up his fishing net. "I will catch fish for breakfast," he said sullenly.

"Before you go, could you loan me some of that salve you use for bugs?" Erik asked hesitantly.

The man grinned knowingly, bent and dug in his pack, then tossed a jar to Erik before striding off toward the beach.

"Thanks," Erik called after him.

He unscrewed the lid and peered at the disgusting-looking con-coction. *Wonder what's in this stuff?* he thought, wrinkling up his nose at its unpleasant odor. After smearing a thin layer of the sticky ointment over the exposed areas of his body, Erik poured himself a cup of coffee.

The other guide rolled onto his back, placed his hands beneath his head, and gazed up at the sky, seemingly unaware of Erik. This fellow seemed less threatening and, although he'd barely spoken to Erik since leaving Sitka, he seemed friendlier than his partner.

"Would you like some coffee?" Erik asked.

The man said nothing, but nodded as he sat up.

Erik poured a cup of the hot brew and handed it to the man. For several minutes, neither said a word. Erik finally broke the silence. "I've been with you several days now, and I don't even know your name."

The man looked at him a moment, as if weighing whether it would be wise to share something as personal as his name with an outsider. Abruptly he answered, "Peter Manook. Your name?"

"Erik Engstrom," Erik answered with a smile as he held out his hand.

Hesitantly, Peter accepted Erik's outstretched hand and shook it.

Erik breathed a sigh of relief. At least he knew one of their names. "Your friend has gone fishing."

"He is good fisherman," Peter said without emotion.

Erik shoved his hands in his pockets. "How far to the river?"

Peter glanced out at the sea and up the coast before answering. "Three, four days, maybe more. When we reach the river, we must leave the boat at the beach and walk."

"How far do we follow the river?"

"From the sea, maybe two days. We will look for black sand. There you will find gold."

Just then, Peter's partner came back into camp with two salmon in his net.

"That didn't take long," Erik commented with admiration.

"The ocean gives many fish in summer," the solemn-looking Indian answered.

"Do you have a name?" Erik asked as cheerfully as he could. The big man glared at him.

"Of course you have a name," he blundered. "I . . . I mean, I was wondering if you could tell me your name. That way I'll know what to call you," he stammered, angry with himself.

The large native kept his black eyes leveled on Erik. In a quiet, decisive way, he said, "My name is Takou." He turned his back on Erik and began filleting the fish.

Probably best to give the man some room, Erik thought. Casually he stood up. "Think I'll scout around a bit before breakfast."

"Do not go far. This is dangerous land," Takou warned, never missing a stroke of his knife. "Take your rifle."

Surprised the man would even bother to caution him, Erik picked up his gun and said, "Thanks. I will."

Since leaving Sitka, Erik had spent all his time with his guides, and the idea of being on his own in this magnificent part of the world appealed to him. Most of what he'd seen so far had been from a boat, and he looked forward to taking a closer look. His feet sank into the spongy ground as he skirted peat bogs and swampy areas. *Probably good moose hunting around these parts,* he thought as he studied the terrain.

He'd only gone a little way when a rotting log resting on a rise caught his attention. It provided a view of the surrounding area and seemed the perfect place to relax and take in the land. Erik climbed the knoll, leaned his rifle on the log, and rested against a limb protruding from the dead tree. The air felt lighter, the odor of rotting plants less pungent. He took a slow, deep breath, and the scent of the sea washed over him. A kingfisher uttered its rattling call as it dove over the marsh and swooped down just above the water's surface, searching for prey.

Erik knew he should return to camp, but the time alone seemed too precious to relinquish. He decided it wouldn't hurt to remain a while longer. As he settled back, a twig cracked behind him, and Erik whirled around to see what lurked in the bushes. A snuffling sound came from trembling shrubs, and Erik tensed as he reached for his rifle and quietly cocked it. Motionless, he held his breath and waited.

A young brown bear lumbered into the clearing, unaware of Erik's presence. Although small for a brown, he was large enough to pose a real threat, and Erik took shallow breaths as he watched the animal. Rid of his heavy winter coat, his light brown fur shimmered in the sun. Erik estimated him to be about three years old. The animal lifted his nose and sniffed at the air. Erik took in a breath and held it, thankful to be sitting downwind of the beast. The bear looked uneasy, sensing Erik's presence. He stood on his hind legs and peered in Erik's direction.

Erik didn't move.

They eyed each other a moment before the animal dropped to his feet and plodded toward the beach.

Erik's pounding heart slowed. *Probably going fishing,* he thought with relief. He smiled as he visualized the magnificent beast swatting at an unsuspecting salmon. Reluctantly he stood up and headed back toward camp.

He could smell the aroma of frying fish as he approached the encampment. *Good thing the wind's coming from the north. If that animal had caught the scent of our breakfast, we might have had uninvited company,* Erik mused.

Peter and Takou glanced up at him as he walked into camp, but instead of greeting him, they returned to their meal. Erik tried not to let their indifference bother him. *It's just their way,* he told himself. His stomach grumbled and his mouth watered as he eyed the fried salmon. He hadn't realized how hungry he was. He took the remaining portion of pink meat and sat down to eat it.

After several bites, he said nonchalantly, "This is very good. Thank you."

Takou nodded.

Erik went on, "Met up with a young bear this morning."

Peter stopped eating and looked at Erik, his interest piqued. Bears were an important sign to the natives. They had immense respect for the great beasts who roamed the land. Many of their totems held emblems of the brown, who represented cunning and strength.

Takou licked his greasy fingers but didn't respond to Erik's statement.

"Spotted him a little way north of here. He was a beauty—well fed by the looks of it."

Peter shot a nervous glance at the nearby underbrush. "He went north?"

"Well, that's the way he was headin' last time I saw him," Erik answered, suppressing a smile.

"There are many bears in this land," Takou cut in. "We do not need to worry. The fishing is good. When their bellies are full, they are content."

"That makes sense. This one didn't seem much interested in me," Erik replied lightheartedly.

"It is time to go," Takou stated as he wiped his hands on his pants and packed up his gear.

Erik quickly stuffed the last of his fish into his mouth, bundled up his bedding, and followed.

Peter doused the fire before taking up the rear, a few steps behind Erik.

The next few days passed agonizingly slow. Each stroke of the oar brought a keen sense of separation as Erik moved farther from his family. Endless hours of rowing began to take their toll. Exhausted and discouraged, Erik wondered if they would ever reach their destination. Maybe the stories of gold were just that—stories.

Erik had nearly forgotten to look for the river when Takou piloted their boat toward a narrow channel and guided them into a rocky cove at the mouth of the Schuck. Erik felt like cheering but held his tongue as they glided into the inviting bay.

"We will leave the boat here," Takou said as he climbed ashore. All three men pulled the skiff into the tall grasses above the waterline and turned it bottom side up.

Takou and Peter hefted their knapsacks onto their backs and headed up river. Erik quickly pulled his on and followed.

The natives kept up an unrelenting pace as they moved inland. Erik had to work hard to keep up, and soon his legs felt like heavy weights. It had been too long since he'd pushed himself so hard.

These two are doing their best to test me, he thought as he struggled for breath, unwilling to give up. For reasons he didn't understand, he wanted the men's respect. So, without complaint, he followed over downed and rotting trees, through spongy bogs and ankle deep ponds, all the while wrestling with clinging berry vines, stinging nettles, and bugs. He couldn't remember being more miserable.

Takou and Peter didn't stop until midday, and then only for a brief respite. Erik's regard for his guides' ability and knowledge grew with each passing hour. They seemed unaffected by the environment, their energy was endless, and they knew where they were heading.

At the end of the second day, they came upon their first miner. Erik felt relieved. Here was proof they had a reason to be there. Where there were miners, one could hope for gold. The man was suspicious, unfriendly, and of little help, but Erik felt better for having stumbled across him. After this encounter, they met several other gold seekers. Most were more than happy to stop their work and expound upon their adventures. Nearly all of them were newcomers and had little to share about the actual diggings, other than that the amount of gold found had been modest. Most were not discouraged, however. They figured it was only a matter of time until their work paid off.

Erik spotted a stocky, redheaded man shoveling mud and sand into a rocker. The man didn't notice Erik and his companions right off, but as they scrambled down the embankment, he turned and planted the tip of his shovel in the loose gravel and watched them approach.

Erik smiled and held out his hand. He noticed the stranger's demeanor relax a little. "Good afternoon to ya," Erik greeted the man. "Name's Erik Engstrom."

The man returned his hardy handshake. "Glad t' meet ye' Erik. Me name's Reid Campbell. What brings ye' oot this way?" he asked with a Scottish brogue.

"Like you, I'm lookin' for gold."

"Figured. Noot much else t' draw a person t' this place. It's noothin' like the strikes made doon in California, boot there's a bit of color here and there. Enough t' keep a man workin'."

Erik looked upriver. "There any claims left?"

"Noot many, but a few yet. Maybe soom good ones too." Reid stroked his beard. "Tell ye' what, why don't ye' stay and have sooper with me and the wife, and I'll tell ye' aboot the Schuck River and her gold."

"Your wife's with you?"

"Oh, yes, wouldna' think of leavin' her behind while I mook aroond in the mud," Reid answered with a grin. "But, it's a lonely life fer a woman. She'd be happy fer someone else's face besides mine at the dinner table."

Erik was about to answer when he remembered his companions. He glanced at them, "Uh . . ."

"Oh, they're welcome t' coom along. Never been troobled by Indians. By what I've seen, they're good people."

"Looks like we've been invited to dinner," Erik said as he turned to Peter and Takou, who nodded their acceptance.

"The day's pretty much played oot, and I'm ready fer a shot of brew, anyway," Reid said as he swept his hat off his head and wiped his brow, then thrust his shovel into the loose rock. "Follow me."

Erik fell into step beside the friendly Scotsman, his mouth watering at the thought of a hot, home-cooked meal. In less than five minutes, they came to a tidy-looking cabin hidden among the trees. Smoke rose from the chimney, and a woman swept the wooden porch that straddled the front of the building. She stopped her work and watched as her husband and the three strangers approached.

Reid bounded onto the porch. "Millie, we've goot company fer supper," he announced as he circled his arm about her small waist and planted a kiss on her cheek.

In mock irritation, Millie pulled herself free of Reid's embrace, smoothed her clean, white apron, and with a smile stretched out her hand in greeting to Erik. "It's nice to have you," she said quietly. Peter and Takou kept their distance. Millie nodded to them. "You're all welcome to share supper with us."

Millie placed three additional places at the table.

Takou and Peter seemed uneasy and, after inhaling the soup and fresh bread offered, left. Erik stayed to swap stories with Reid while Millie kept their cups filled with coffee. She listened without interruption to the men's banter. Erik hadn't realized how much he'd missed the company of a fellow explorer. Like himself, Reid had done a good deal of traveling. And his family, like Erik's, had immigrated. After growing up in North Dakota, Reid had struck out on his own, his need to see the world stronger than his love of home. The two men had much in common.

"Yeah, I was a yoong man like ye' when I got the gold fever," Reid explained. "I headed fer California with big dreams, and I foond one too. That's where I met me Millie." He winked at his pretty wife.

She smiled back demurely. "He was one for big dreams in those days. And don't let him fool you, he may have been real pleased to meet me, but it was the gold that had a real hold on him."

"You were always more important than any gold," Reid maintained. "But I admit to being disappointed when I didna' make it in time fer the big strikes. After missin' oot on the big one, I decided if I ever goot me 'nother chance, I was takin' it. One day I met this fellow who'd been oop this way, and he told me there was gold here. I didna' have much t' lose, so this time I didna' wait, but headed straight here to have a look."

"You said there are still claims to be had?"

"Sure and true. In fact, I'm jest aboot at the end of the line. There're only a few claims bein' doog beyoond here. After thet it's all free and clear fer anyone who's willin' t' work a piece."

"I'm glad to hear that. Figured I'd take a closer look in the morning."

"Have t' tell ye'. There's noot been any heavy lodes found aloong this little river, but she's been puttin' oot gold real regular."

Millie offered to refill their cups. "No more for me," Erik said. He hesitated. "How has it been having your family here?"

"Wee'll, it's joost me and Millie. Never had any wee ones, but we've been happy. Sometimes it's hard on Millie."

"It hasn't been that hard," Millie said. "I'm glad to be here."

"Not many women coom aloong with their men. But me Millie's pretty stroong-minded. Don't let 'er mild manner fool ye'," he said with a grin and patted her on the fanny.

"Reid!" Millie said and shot him an annoyed look.

"She wouldna' stay put while I searched fer our fortune. Have t' admit I'd be real lonesoom without her. Sometimes, though, I worry aboot what she'd be facin' if somethin' were t' happened t' me." He swallowed the last of his coffee.

"God watches over us," Millie said quietly.

"I'm not a religious man meself," Reid said in a conciliatory tone.

Erik couldn't help but notice Millie's pained expression at her husband's offhanded remark. "I believe he does, Millie," he said, glancing up at his hostess. Millie's quiet strength hadn't gone unnoticed, and Erik had wondered if she might be a Christian. *She'll be good for Anna and the children,* he thought as he considered what life would be like for them when they arrived. "I plan to bring my wife and children back with me after I file my claim. Anna will be real happy to know there's another woman about."

"So you've got yerself a wife, too, eh? Did ye' hear thet, Millie? There'll be someone fer ye' t' spend time with."

"It will be wonderful to have someone to talk to," Millie said with a broad smile.

"Well, she's not your typical . . ."

"Who is?" Reid interrupted him. "Any woman willin' t' follow 'er man way oot here has t' be a bit queer, don't you think?"

"So, you think I'm queer do you?" Millie teased.

Reid grinned.

"It's not that exactly." Erik cleared his throat. "She's an Aleut," he blurted out.

Caught off guard, Reid just stared at him for a moment. "Wee'll, thet woon't make any difference," he finally said. "She's a woman isn't she? She and Millie will find somethin' to talk aboot. You know how women are." He chuckled in a friendly way.

Millie gave Reid a reproachful look, then turned a soft smile to Erik. "Your wife's heritage makes no difference to me. I'll be glad for her company."

Erik grinned. "I think she'll like you, Millie." He didn't bother explaining about the children. There would be plenty of time for that. "I better get to my bed. Tomorrow promises to be another long day." He scooted his chair away from the table. "With any luck, I'll find my claim." He stopped at the door. "The dinner was delicious, Millie. Can't remember enjoying a meal more. Hope I'll see you both again soon." With that, he closed the door and headed for camp.

Peter and Takou were already asleep when Erik arrived, and the embers from the evening's fire had grown cold. Erik stretched out on his bedding but couldn't sleep. For a long while he lay on his back, his head cradled in his arms, and gazed up through the trees. He thought of Anna and wondered what she was doing, whether she was all right. The time spent with the Campbells had felt good, but his sense of loneliness seemed even more acute now. He sighed, turned onto his side, and closed his eyes, hoping sleep would cloak his feeling of isolation.

Despite the late night, Erik woke early the following morning. Anxious to get started, he didn't bother with a fire, and a piece of hardtack served as breakfast.

He woke Peter. "I'm scouting ahead. Won't be gone long."

Peter nodded and, with a groan, pulled his bedding over his head.

Erik followed the river as it twisted its way inland, but found nothing of any real interest. He sat on a log to think and survey the waterway. Black sand reached down to the water's edge where the river swept into a tight bend. The water ran shallow and splashed over the rocky bottom. Erik's heart beat hard in his chest. *This might be it!* he thought as he scrambled down the bank, scanning the area for any signs of a claim as he went. When he found none, his confidence grew.

Erik stepped into the water and ran his hand over the rocky bottom, scooping up a handful of gravel and sand.

"Do you see anything?" a deep voice asked from behind him.

Erik whirled around to find Peter standing along the bank.

"You hired me to scout. I will scout," the Indian said as he stepped into the cold river and scooped gravel into his hand. Carefully he sifted through the pebbles, then dropped them back into the water. He took another handful, searching through the dirt and grit. "This is a good place. You will find gold here," he said with confidence.

Erik yanked his pack off his back, dug out a shallow pan, and pitched the knapsack onto the shore. Standing ankle-deep in the water, he brushed away the large gravel and rocks, dipped his pan into the swift stream, and brought it up half-filled with sand and gravel. He gently worked the water around and around the pan, washing away the lighter soils, until all that remained were a few large stones and the heavier flecks of gold. "Look at this! You were right! There's gold here!" Carefully dipping out the gold, he dropped it into a small pouch tied on his belt and dunked his pan back into the muddy water. He repeated the process until only shimmering specks of gold rested on the bottom of his pan. "This is it!" he hooted. "This is the place!"

By this time, Takou had joined Peter. Erik smiled at both men. "Good job fellas. You found it." He reached out and took Peter's hand and shook it heartily, then did the same with Takou. Peter laughed and patted Erik on the back.

Expressionless, Takou said, "Tomorrow we will return to Sitka," then turned and walked up the embankment.

Peter stayed with Erik.

"I ought to be able to make a living here if I get a sluice box set up," Erik told the Indian as he dipped his pan back into the icy water. "There's gold here all right," he said as he washed the rock.

He spent nearly an hour at the river before stopping to mark his claim. He walked off his piece of land and pounded a stick at each corner. After writing up his title rights on a sheet of paper, he nailed it to the front corner stake. "This'll take care of things until I get back to Sitka and file," he said with satisfaction before returning to camp.

Around the fire that evening a mood of celebration hung in the air. Erik shared a meal of fish and sourdough bread with his two guides. He talked of the future and how he would bring his family out and set up a home, while Peter and Takou listened without interruption.

It was late when Takou stood up and put an end to the revelry. "We will leave early. It is time to sleep," he said as he lay down on his bed of spruce boughs and turned his back to Peter and Erik.

"I guess he's right," Erik conceded. "Time to make a night of it." But long after his companions had gone to sleep, Erik lay staring at the evening sky. Only a handful of the brightest stars blinked out of the semidarkness. Now that he'd found what he'd come looking for, the long journey back seemed unendurable. Erik wished he were already in Sitka. He wanted to share his news with Anna, to begin their life together here along the Schuck, to hold her in his arms . . . to love her. As he thought of the future they would share, joy flooded him. "Thank you Lord," he whispered into the night.

The following morning, the three men broke camp early. Erik felt driven, and he abandoned his usual sense of caution as he set a hurried pace. All he could think of was Anna and how he wanted to see her. In his haste he became reckless and nearly tumbled down the bank.

"Careless people pay big price," Takou cautioned.

Erik didn't heed the warning, but instead charged ahead, unwilling to consider the possible consequences of his eagerness.

As he swung around a curve, the soft earth along the bank gave way. Erik grabbed at the underbrush as he slipped toward the turbulent waters below. But the bushes pulled loose in his hand, useless. Erik plummeted into the violent river. The icy Schuck closed over his head, knocking the wind from him. He thrashed at the waters, searching for the surface. Finally breaking free, he sucked in great gulps of air as the strong current swept him downstream.

Limbs and debris along the shore taunted him. A seeming life-hold, they eluded his grasp, becoming instruments of torture as they tore at his flesh. Swiftly the surge washed him toward the sea. The undertow sucked at his feet and dragged him beneath the swirling surface. Tumbling over and over, he lost all sense of direction. His chest burned. He needed oxygen! Suddenly cold air washed over his face and he filled his lungs.

"Dear God! Help me!" he cried.

He searched the bank. Where were Peter and Takou?

The seconds passed, and numbed by the cold, he could no longer feel his arms and legs. He struggled to kick and knew he was facing the last minutes of his life.

Anna, I'm sorry. I didn't mean to leave you alone, he grieved. He could feel his body growing stiffer as the cold gripped him. *Please forgive me.*

The sweet faces of Iya and Luba filled his mind. They would need him. He must live! A familiar verse drifted through his fogged mind. *I can do all things through Christ who strengthens me—Christ who strengthens me—Christ who strengthens me.* He reached beyond his own strength and struggled to endure.

Erik forced his feet to move and wrenched his arms through the water. He spotted Peter and Takou running along the bank ahead of him, and hope swept through him.

Takou waded into the icy river, a rope stretched between himself and Peter. Peter hastily lashed his end around a small poplar while Takou tightly cinched the other end about his waist.

As the river propelled Erik closer to the two men, Takou lunged into the deep water where the current seized him and pulled the line taut. He stretched out his arm and shouted, "Grab my hand!"

Almost to him, Erik tried to move his arms. They felt heavy and stiff. How could he reach out for help? He prayed, seeking the only source of strength powerful enough to meet his need. Forcing his arm free of the water, he reached for Takou's outstretched hand. A sharp pain shot through his shoulder as the Indian grasped his hand and jerked him to a stop. Takou strained as he pulled Erik closer. He grabbed hold of his shirt, wrapped his arm around Erik's waist, and pulled hard.

Peter yanked on the rope while Takou gripped Erik, fighting against the river's current. They edged closer to shore.

Once in the shallows, Erik tried to stand, but his legs felt weak and refused to hold his weight. Both men staggered and fell, sucking at the air while Peter waded in and slung an arm around Erik. Takou pushed himself to his feet and, together, the two natives dragged Erik onto the bank. Soaked and shivering, all three collapsed and lay gasping for breath.

Takou was the first to speak. "You nearly killed yourself," he said with disgust.

Erik could only nod. He knew the big native was right. Shame flooded him. His carelessness had nearly cost him his life, as well as his friends' lives. Struggling for breath, he said, "I'm sorry. I acted like a fool."

In a brotherly way, Peter slapped Erik on the shoulder. "We thought you were gone."

For a while, nothing more was said.

After catching his breath, Erik pushed himself upright, and said quietly, "Thanks for saving my life. You didn't have to."

"We had to." Takou answered matter-of-factly. "It is wrong to watch a man die if you can help." He pushed himself up from the ground and started gathering wood for a fire.

That evening, as the three men huddled around the campfire and shared a meal, they were no longer strangers. Erik described the outside world and its wonders, while Peter and Takou told legends of the bear and wolf handed down for generations by their people.

The relationship between these men had changed forever. Suspicion and fear no longer separated them; friendship blossomed. They would never be the same again.

Chapter 10

*A*nna pressed the heels of her hands against the bread mixture, pushed it flat, then rolled it forward into a smooth sphere. *I have kneaded at least ten minutes,* she thought as she patted the mound of dough and pinched it, testing for its readiness the way Cora had taught her. It didn't feel sticky or lifeless but smooth. Tiny bubbles raised along its surface. *It is ready,* Anna decided. Not yet confident enough to make that decision herself, she asked, "Cora, will you check this?"

Cora slid a pie into the oven, wiped her hands on her apron, and stepped over to Anna. "Well, let's see now," she said as she caressed the dough and examined it closely. "It looks just right to me. You're gettin' better all the time. We'll make a real cook out of you yet," she said cheerfully.

Anna smiled, proud of her accomplishment. She loved the bread Cora baked in the large cast-iron stove that dominated her kitchen and hoped that one day she, too, could provide the tasty treat for her family. Gently she placed the unfinished bread in a bowl, covered it with a cloth, and set it on the top shelf of the stove to rise.

As she looked around for something more to do, Anna's attention wavered and she stopped to gaze out the window. Sighing heavily, her eyes traced the bright path of sunlight as it poured in, bathing the room with warmth. She wished she could saturate herself in it, soak it into her soul, but until Erik returned, she knew there would be no way to warm the cold, hollow sensation she'd carried since his departure. How much longer?

"Looks like you're a long ways from here," Cora said, pulling Anna from her thoughts.

Anna glanced at her, but said nothing.

"You're thinkin' of him, aren't you?"

"Uh huh. I can think of nothing else. It has been weeks since he left. Do you think he will come soon?"

"There's just no way of tellin'. But I'm sure he's fine, honey. He'll be here just as soon as he can."

"I miss him," Anna said quietly.

As Cora embraced Anna, disagreeable chords brayed at them from the parlor.

Cora loosened her hold and smiled as she gently shook her head from side to side.

"Iya likes the piano," Anna said, "but the sound she makes is not good."

"Oh, it's always that way in the beginning. She'll get the hang of it. Little ones don't seem to hear the true tones at first. With a little help, she'll be playing beautifully in no time at all." She patted Anna's back. "I'll spend some time with her this afternoon. Maybe I can teach her a simple song."

"She will like that."

A gleeful chortle came from Luba, who sat amid an assortment of pans and baking utensils she'd scattered about. Clearly she was very pleased with herself.

"Luba, you do beat all," Cora said, propping her hands on her hips.

Anna laughed.

Luba smiled up at the two women and scooted toward her mother. Once she reached Anna's feet, she grinned and lifted her arms, demanding that Anna pick her up. Anna couldn't resist and hefted the little girl off the floor. "Luba, you grow so fast," she said as she held her out at arm's length. "Soon you will walk and run like Iya."

"You know, there's something special between those two," Cora interjected. "I've known a lot of youngsters in my day, but never any who loved each other more than Iya and Luba." She patted Luba's bottom and quickly withdrew her hand. With a wry smile, she said, "Seems this little one's a bit moist. Here, let me take her. It's time for her nap anyway. I'll just give her a change and lay her down."

"Thank you," Anna said as she handed her daughter to Cora. She

---

watched as they left the kitchen. Cora had taken a real liking to both the girls and seemed more like family than a friend. In spite of Erik's absence, life in Sitka had been pleasant, mostly due to Cora's friendship. In a few short weeks, Anna had grown to love the plump woman who had welcomed them into her home.

Cora seemed to revel in sharing her life with Anna. She'd taken her on several outings into town and introduced her to as many modern conveniences as possible, overwhelming Anna with all there was to see and learn. One day, Cora had even convinced a local merchant to demonstrate a hand-cranked washing machine. The contraption frightened Anna; it looked dangerous. But Cora wasn't intimidated by it, and she vowed she would have her own one day. Of all the new things Anna discovered, the one that captivated her most was a beautiful mantle clock sitting in the window of the mercantile. She thought it exquisite, but even more than its beauty, the concept of time kept within a box intrigued her. Cora had one, and Anna enjoyed sitting in the parlor and watching its golden pendulum swing from side to side.

She looked forward to the jaunts into town, although Cora's generosity sometimes went too far. Often Anna returned with clothing and items that she thought were too extravagant, but Cora couldn't be convinced otherwise, and Anna's wardrobe blossomed, as did the girls'.

For the most part, it seemed the residents had grown accustomed to the newcomers. Some greeted her as a neighbor, while others simply ignored her presence. And there were a few who made certain she never forgot natives were a subclass in the human race.

Anna continued to accompany Cora to church, and most of those who attended welcomed her and the children. But she still faced an occasional hostile confrontation. It was often after one of these episodes that even Cora seemed foreign, and Anna would long to return to her own people—to live where the clan trusted and depended upon one another for their very survival. Here people seemed detached, only coming to the aid of another in an emergency. The day-to-day interdependence didn't exist. Anna missed it and thought these new neighbors could learn much from their native friends.

She popped open the oven door and peeked at Cora's baking pie. Warm, apple-scented air rushed up to meet her. Her mouth watered at the tantalizing smell as she closed the door to allow it to finish cooking. When Erik returned she planned to surprise him by presenting him with just such a pie. *I wish he would come home,* she thought. *He is gone too long.* She propped her elbows on the counter, rested her chin in her hands, and gazed out the window. "Please come home soon," she whispered. "God, keep him safe."

"What are you doing?" a small voice asked, interrupting Anna's supplication.

Unaware that Iya had come into the room, Anna jumped a little. "Iya, you startled me."

Iya grinned. "Do you like my music?"

"It is very pretty. Cora says she will teach you more."

"Yes," Iya answered, pumping her head up and down enthusiastically. "It smells good. Are you cooking?"

"Yes, we are."

"Can I help?"

"There is nothing more to do here, but Cora needs vegetables for later. We can pick some."

Iya didn't need any coaxing and ran out the door, slamming it behind her. With a shake of her head and a wry smile, Anna took a bowl from the cupboard and followed. As she stepped outside, the scent of Cora's wildflowers greeted her, and she stopped to pick a rose. She breathed in its sweet fragrance and stroked one of the soft petals warmed by the sun. Everything seemed perfect, and would be, if only Erik were there to share it with her.

Well, it cannot be different, she told herself, tilting her face toward the sunlight. She forced her dreary thoughts to the back of her mind and hurried to the side of the house.

She found Iya already kneeling in the garden loam with her hands wrapped around the top of a stubborn carrot. She wiggled the plant and tugged, but it wouldn't budge.

"Dig away the dirt," Anna instructed.

Iya cupped her hands and began scooping away some of the soil trapping the sweet vegetable, then pulled again. The long, slender root finally came free, and she yelled in delight. "This one is big!" She dusted it off and placed it in Anna's bowl.

After that, Iya scurried down the row, pulling as many carrots as she could until Anna stopped her.

"Iya, I think we have enough. Now we can pick peas."

The little girl wiped the dirt from her hands. "Peas taste good." She plucked a small pod from the vine, popped it open, scooped out the row of small, green orbs, then plopped them into her mouth. Grinning, she chewed contentedly.

"Peas are very good. We can have them for lunch," Anna said as she bent to reach the pods near the ground. It felt good to work beside her sister as she had done at the beach. Anna began to hum a native chant, and Iya joined her.

The pea pods came off easily in her hands. They felt firm and plump with the promise of sweet meats inside. After dropping several into her bowl, Anna stood to stretch her back. She surveyed the small town that reached down to the bay and watched as people hurried about their tasks. She wondered what prodded their hasty steps. In this world, people always seemed in a hurry.

She glanced up at the sun. It no longer felt refreshing but too warm. Small beads of sweat rested on her forehead, and she wiped them away with the back of her hand. She took a long, deep breath, enjoying the scent of warm earth and green plants.

"Good thing the birds did not eat the peas," Iya said. "Cora says she fought them."

Anna nodded and smiled as she remembered Cora's description of her battle to save the young shoots when they pushed up through the soft earth. The pesky birds were constantly seeking out new sprouts, one of their favorite summer appetizers. Anna could see her running at the animals, swinging her broom and threatening them if they dared return, which they always did. In the end, the persistent birds had been no match for Cora. She had outsmarted them by placing a wire dome over each plant until it put down strong roots.

The fruits of her labor were enjoyed by all, except the nasty birds, who went elsewhere to feast.

"Anna, when do you think Erik will come back?" Iya asked quietly.

"Soon."

"Very soon," a deep voice declared from behind them.

Anna whirled about. Erik! It was Erik! At first she couldn't move. Then Erik held out his arms, and without a word, Anna leapt into his embrace. She wrapped her arms about his neck and hugged him tightly. Tears coursed down her cheeks as she laughed and cried at the same time. Erik was back! She forced herself to loosen her hold and look at him. "I felt you would never return."

Erik chuckled, squeezed her hard, and twirled her about. "Nothing could keep me away from you."

Anna clung to him, feeling she would never be able to hold him close enough.

Iya wiggled her way between the two. "Erik, you came back!" she exclaimed as she wrapped her arms about his waist.

With one arm still around Anna, Erik reached down and gathered the little girl up with the other.

Iya giggled and hugged him about the neck. "I miss you."

"I missed you too," Erik said as he squeezed her close.

"Why, Erik Engstrom, it is you!" came a voice from the back of the house. Cora rushed across the garden with her arms flung wide and pulled them into her embrace. "I'm afraid these young ones were missin' you in the worst way." She stepped back and looked at him a moment. "You're a sight for sore eyes, young man, and I must say, you look no worse for wear. Come on in. You must be hungry after so many days on the trail."

"It's good to see you, Cora," Erik said, setting Iya back on her feet and taking her hand. He draped his arm over Anna's shoulder and followed the friendly woman inside.

Cora bustled about the kitchen while Erik and Anna sat at the dining table, their hands clasped tightly together. Anna studied him, trying to etch his features into her mind in case he ever left again. Having him so close seemed like a dream.

Erik squeezed Anna's hands. "I've missed you. Every day my mind was full of you. Sometimes I couldn't think of anything else."

"I thought of you too."

"You and Iya look good. How has it been for you while I was gone?"

"Life is good here. Cora is a fine friend."

"Why, Erik, I feel I know you like a brother," Cora said over her shoulder. "Anna and I had some real good visits while you were away."

"I hated to go, but it was worth it. I found a claim. In fact, I just came from filing. First thing I did when I got into town. It's a great spot, Anna. Shows real promise and it's real pretty too. Just above the diggings, there's a perfect place for a cabin and even room for a garden."

"I like gardens. It is good to grow food." She thought a moment. "Erik, can we have chickens?" Before Erik could answer, she rushed on, "Cora say she will give me some of hers."

Erik broke into a big grin. "Sure we can have chickens. We can have a whole barn full if you want."

Cora filled Erik's cup with freshly brewed coffee.

"Mm, that smells good, Cora. Thanks."

"I'll have some stew warmed up in just a minute. I'm afraid it's leftover from last night, but it's still tasty."

"Sounds great to me. I've been craving some good home cooking."

"When can we go to the claim?" Iya cut in.

"As soon as we get our supplies together. There's plenty of game and more than enough berries and plants, but we'll still need a lot of provisions. The winters aren't as hard down here as they were up on the inlet, but they're hard enough. The heaviest salmon run will be over by the time we get back on the river and settled, but I figure there'll still be enough to see us through. We're about two days travel from the ocean."

Anna was disappointed. She liked living near the sea and would miss it.

"I'm hoping we can make at least one trip down to gather clams and crabs." He looked at Iya and grinned. "Figured we could look for some seaweed too."

Iya wrinkled up her nose.

More seriously he added, "There's a lot to be done, and I don't know for sure if we'll get back down to the beach. We'll just have to wait and see. Cold weather could set in before we get a chance."

"Are there people?" Anna asked.

"I was just going to tell you about that. I did see some other prospectors, and I met a man and his wife who live real close. They'll be our neighbors. Seem like good people. Man's name is Reid, and his wife's name is Millie. I had supper with them one night, and we got to know one another. I think you'll like them. Millie seems real nice, and she's a good cook too."

Anna blushed, remembering some of her previous blunders in the kitchen. "While you were gone, Cora taught me about cooking."

Before Erik could reply, Cora interrupted, "Here you go, Erik." She set a plate of hot stew and biscuits in front of him.

"Thanks, Cora. This looks great," Erik said as he scooped up a spoonful of stew.

Cora sat across the table from him. "So, tell us a little about your trip. Did everything go well?"

Erik stopped eating. "Well, like I said, I found us a good claim. The trip up was wet but beautiful." He stopped and thought a moment and fidgeted in his chair. "I might as well tell you. I did take an unexpected dip in the river."

"Erik!" Anna exclaimed.

"It wasn't that bad," Erik lied. "We were on our way back, and all I could think of was seeing you and telling you about our place. I'm afraid I didn't watch my footing, and the next thing I knew, I was in the river."

Anna's body prickled with fear. "Oh, Erik," she said weakly.

"It's all right. I'm fine. The two guides I hired pulled me out. They're good fellas. I've got to admit, in the beginning, I didn't exactly trust the two of them. I couldn't have been more wrong, though. They're fine men. I've hired them to help us move. We'll need two boats to haul all our supplies, and once we get to the mouth of the river, we'll have to pack in. We're gonna need them."

"You know, I wish more folks understood what kind of people these natives are. Most of them are real kind," Cora interjected. "It's such a shame that the few wicked ones give the rest a bad name. I heard there's some who've been threatening an uprising. I must say, it doesn't give a person a good feelin' with most of the soldiers gone. When the army moved out, they left us with a handful of Federals. Sometimes I think the U.S. would just as soon forget about us Alaskans."

"It's just as well, Cora. As soon as they understand what they've got here, that's all going to change, and the land and people right along with it. It'd suit me fine if they never woke up." He stopped and bit into a biscuit. "Just because things have calmed down the last couple of years, don't believe it's gonna stay like that. I noticed Sitka isn't the boom town it used to be, but I figure it's only a lull before the storm. It won't be long before ships fill the harbor again."

"You make me feel bad. I get to missin' the way things were. The theater in town used to put on a play nearly every week. Sometimes I fear this town will slowly disappear, but I suppose you're right. Change is coming, and we ought to cherish the way things are now."

Erik scraped his plate clean. "Not all change is bad, but I just can't see it helping Alaskans. I've never seen man improve on what God created."

"You're right on that," Cora agreed. "Can I get you something else?"

"No. I'm stuffed. That was great, Cora. Thanks." Erik leaned back in his chair, patted his stomach, and eyed Anna. "I think it's time I took a walk with my wife," he said as he pushed his chair away from the table and took Anna's hand.

Iya jumped up to follow them, but Cora reached out and stopped her. "Not this time, little lady."

Iya pouted, and Anna was about to relent when Cora interrupted, "Iya, why don't we go and check on Luba. I bet she's awake and needin' a change and some company."

Still sulking, Iya replied, "All right," and followed Cora up the stairs.

With their hands clasped together, Anna and Erik strolled down the street. They didn't speak for a long time, as if words would shatter the delight they felt in each other's presence.

Finally, Erik spoke. "I'm glad to be back." He squeezed Anna's hand. "It's good to have you next to me—to hear your voice. I didn't know I could feel such loneliness."

Anna leaned against his shoulder. "I never want you to leave again." She searched for a way to express her feelings. "I felt . . . empty."

"Me too," Erik said, then asked, "Tell me what you did while I was gone."

Anna smiled. "I learned much from Cora. We are good friends. She showed me the town and helped me to meet people. We go to church on Sundays. There," she pointed at the small building that served as the community chapel. "I like it very much. Pastor Nielsen is a good man. He speaks about God. I know you will like him." She stopped and thought a moment. "Will there be a church at the claim?"

"No, there's no town, but we can have our own church at home. We can sing hymns and read from the Bible. There doesn't have to be a lot of people for God to be there."

"That sounds nice," she said, unable to concentrate on the casual chitchat. She gazed up at the hills surrounding Sitka, and as she thought of the lonely days of waiting, her tears came.

"What's wrong, Anna?"

"It is just that when you were gone, I looked at the hills every day and thought of you. I was afraid you were hurt and would not come back." She wiped at her eyes with the back of her hand. "I was scared."

Erik held her close. Anna rested her face against his chest and allowed her weeks of fear and loneliness to spill out in deep sobs.

"Anna, I'm so sorry. I didn't know it would be so hard. I promise I'll never leave you again."

Anna stepped away from the tall man who had changed her life and looked up at him. "Do not promise. We do not know the future." She sniffed and added, "Some things cannot be different. We will do what we must and trust God." She smiled. "I survived."

Erik pulled her back into his embrace.

After a few minutes, Anna glanced up at the sky. "It is late and time to go back. Luba will be hungry."

"I can't wait to see her. Is she walking yet?"

Anna laughed. "You were not gone that long. She is still too little. But soon, maybe."

The next couple of days flew by. While Erik purchased supplies and made arrangements for their delivery, Cora and Anna prepared food for the trip and constructed cages for the chickens Anna planned to take with her.

When they were finished, she showed them to Erik.

"Anna, you never cease to amaze me. I believe there's nothing you can't do if you put your mind to it. These are great. Why, if I were a chicken, I'd be proud to be shipped in these," he teased.

Anna laughed. "You will not make fun when you have a chicken in the pot."

"No, that I won't," Erik agreed.

With all the preparations completed, they had one free day before they were to leave.

"You know," Cora began over breakfast, "I was thinkin' you two ought to take a trip down to the hot springs. This might be the last chance you'll get. It's a grand place, I'll tell you that. And it's not far by boat. You'll be sorry if you miss it."

"Hot springs?" Anna asked.

"You never been to a hot spring? It's a place where the water boils up from underground, all warm and smellin' of minerals. It's a real pleasure to just rest in the soothing waters. I did it once. It was wonderful. You don't know what you're missin'. Besides feelin' real good, it's s'posed to have healin' powers too."

Anna looked at Erik, uncertain.

"I'd be glad to take care of the little ones while you two go," Cora pressed.

"What do you think?" Erik asked.

Anna shrugged. "I do not know. It sounds nice."

Erik leaned back and locked his hands behind his head. "You know, I believe it's a good idea. We've been working pretty hard, and a day resting in a warm spring sounds real fine. Everything's ready to go. Peter and Takou are set and plan to meet us at the pier in the morning. I don't see any reason why we shouldn't."

"Then it's settled," Cora jumped in. "I'll make a picnic lunch for you two, and I'll bet Sam from the store could set you up with a guide."

In less than an hour, Anna and Erik found themselves in a dory, accompanied by a small native man, heading for the hot springs. The guide pulled hard on the oars, and Anna liked the feel of the boat as it coursed through the water. The sound of the waves slapping against the sides and the smell of sea and salt brought pleasant memories. The sea would always feel like home.

As they moved away from Sitka, the town didn't look nearly so large and frightening as it had when Anna first sailed into the bay. But it appeared strong and stable, ready to stand against anything that threatened its existence, and Anna had a sense it would continue for many years.

Soon their escort guided the boat into a small cove. "I will be back in three hours. You be here," he said and pointed at the beach.

"We will," Erik assured him as he helped Anna out of the small craft. They watched the skiff pull away, and soon they were alone.

"It seems this is a popular place," Erik said as he pointed toward rock steps fixed into the hillside. He took Anna's hand. "This way," he said as he headed up the uneven stairway. The smell of the springs told them when they were near.

Anna wrinkled up her nose. "It smells bad, like eggs."

"It's only sulfur. It's harmless; you'll get used to it."

Anna wasn't so sure but followed anyway.

They climbed the steps until they came to a small cottage built around the pool. Steam rose from the warm water and hovered above it, giving the place a mysterious quality. Anna stopped and stared at the wonder. "I never saw this before," she said in a hush, "but the elders say such pools have great power."

"Well, I don't know about any power, but I do know they feel real good. I say we try it," he added with a devilish grin as he knelt down and ran his hand through the water. "It's warm. Feels just like a bath. This is great!" he said as he stripped off his shirt. "Last one in is a sick walrus," he teased as he skimmed off his breeches and leaped into the lagoon.

Anna quickly slipped off her dress, but still hadn't quite conquered the technique of her underthings, so when she had finished, Erik had already settled himself comfortably along the edge of the warm pool. Unashamed, she stood naked before her husband.

Erik's eyes showed his approval as he held out his hand to Anna, and she stepped into the water. She settled herself next to him, and he draped his arm over her shoulders and pulled her close. "This must be a little like heaven," he said as he leaned his head back and rested it on the rock ledge behind him.

"Mm, it feels nice," Anna agreed and swept her arms through the water. She enjoyed the sensation of the warm water as it swirled about her. She leaned against Erik. It felt good to sit beside her husband. All things were as they should be.

Erik turned his young wife's face to his and cradled her chin in his hand as he touched his lips to hers. Anna gently answered his kiss.

"I thank God for you, husband."

Erik wrapped his arms about her, crushing her to him. His voice tight with emotion, he said, "I love you, Anna. You are a gift from God."

Anna pulled away for a moment and caressed his cheek. "He loves us both. I think we are a gift to each other." She kissed him again, only this time with passion. And for a time, the outside world ceased to exist.

Chapter 11

*I*mpatiently Erik leaned against the door frame and waited for Anna to say her good-byes. She glanced at him and knew he was eager to be on his way, but sorrow wrenched at her and she was unable to hurry. There had been too many partings in her short life.

"Here, enjoy," Cora said, handing Anna a basket filled with sandwiches, cake, fresh fruits, and vegetables.

Anna took the basket. "Thank you," she said, unable to meet the woman's eyes. She'd known Cora only a short time, but she seemed like a lifelong friend. Anna's throat constricted and her chest ached as she fought back her tears.

Cora picked Luba up from the floor and kissed her. "Now you be a good girl and don't give your mother any trouble or you'll have to answer to me," she said, trying to sound cheerful as she handed the infant to Anna.

Iya made no attempt to hide her distress. She wrapped her arms tightly around Cora's waist and clung to her. Tears slipped from her eyes and washed down her cheeks. "I do not want to go away from you," she cried.

"Now, now, it's not all that bad," Cora comforted the little girl. "We'll see each other again. It's only good-bye for a short time." She knelt in front of Iya and folded her in her arms. "You know, the Schuck River isn't so far away as all that. I'll be lookin' for you come spring when Erik returns for supplies." She blinked back her own tears.

Iya glanced at Erik. "Will we come in the spring?"

Erik nodded and smiled. "I believe Cora'd have my hide if we didn't."

"That's a certainty," Cora said with a wink. She turned back to

---

Iya. "We'll see each other before you know it." She gave Iya a quick hug and looked at Erik. "Mind you now, bring the whole family."

"They wouldn't let me come without them," Erik assured her with a grin. His smile faded as he turned to Anna. "It's time to go," he said quietly.

Anna crossed to the doorway and handed the baby to Erik. Why did it seem she was always leaving those she loved? She turned and faced Cora. For a moment, the two women looked at each other, their eyes brimming with unshed tears.

"I was not going to cry," Anna said as she wiped at her eyes in frustration. "Cora, you are my good friend," she choked.

"Dang it all!" Cora uttered as she pulled Anna into her embrace. "I'll be missin' you, honey. It's gonna be real empty around here without you and the little ones." She took a deep breath and held Anna away from her. Trying to smile, she continued, "Like I said, I'll be lookin' for you come spring."

Anna nodded and hugged her once more. She took Iya's hand and headed for the door. Anna's eyes met Erik's, and she was surprised to find that his eyes shimmered. She managed a small smile before stepping outside.

Cora extended her hand to Erik.

He took it, then wrapped his other arm around the small, plump woman. "Thanks, Cora, for everything."

"I didn't do nothin' but enjoy your company. You're the ones who gave me something special." She sniffled. "Now, get on out of here. You've got a boat to catch."

Erik bowed slightly, then walked through the door and down the stairs.

Anna looked back at Cora and waved before following Erik down the path. Some of the flowers along the walkway had wilted and no longer stretched up to gather the sun's warmth. Their sweet fragrance had faded. As Anna walked by, she decided she felt like the flowers—parched and damaged.

I should be happy. I am beginning a new life with my husband. Why do I feel so sad? she wondered, unable to comprehend that this additional parting represented a far more devastating and permanent farewell—that of the loss of her people. In a matter of minutes, through one of nature's cruel misfortunes, she'd said enough good-byes for a lifetime.

Please let this be the last time, she prayed. But even as the thought entered her mind, she realized it would be impossible. There would be many partings to come and she knew it.

"Good-bye," Cora called.

Anna swung around and forced a stiff smile.

Cora waved.

"Good-bye," Iya choked.

Erik doffed his hat, then eagerly strode on. Anna turned and followed him, forcing herself to not look back at the boardinghouse she'd called home for so many weeks. The time had come to move ahead.

Two boats waited at the dock. One held their supplies and sat low in the water, while the other bobbed freely on the swells. Peter stood on the landing and waved at Erik, while Takou climbed into the loaded skiff.

"Mornin'," Erik said as he descended the stairway that lead to the boat landing. "I'd like you to meet my family," he said proudly as he pivoted around and took Anna's hand. "This is my wife, Anna, and this is Luba," he continued, hefting the baby into the air. Iya jumped from the bottom step and stood beside Erik. He patted her head. "This young lady is Iya, Anna's sister."

Peter smiled. "It is nice to meet you."

Takou only nodded and tipped his oars into the bay.

Erik rested his arm around Anna's waist and continued, "Anna, I'd like you to meet Peter. And the tall fellow in the boat is Takou," he added with a grin.

Anna nodded and smiled. Peter seemed friendly, but as she met Takou's steady gaze she felt troubled. He looked fierce and un-friendly. But she remembered what Erik had told her about the man and relaxed a little.

Iya grinned at the two natives and asked, "Are you the ones who saved Erik from the river?"

Takou broke into an unexpected grin. "He looked like a drowned otter when we pulled him out."

"Let's get started," Erik interrupted. "Now's not the time to go into all that." He hefted Iya into the empty boat while Peter held the craft close to the pier. Anna and Luba were next. Peter stepped into the supply boat with Takou and pushed them away from the dock.

"We will lead the way," Takou said as he pulled hard on the oars and headed the boat slowly into the bay.

Erik, with Anna and the girls, followed the two natives.

"How long before we get to the river?" Iya asked.

"Several days," Erik answered. "I'm not sure just how long because we've got the supplies this trip. But after we reach the river we'll have another two or three days of walking ahead of us."

"Will we build a house?"

"You bet. There's plenty of good timber, and I figure we can build us a real nice place. But until that's done we'll have to live in a tent."

"Tent?" Iya asked. "What is a tent?"

Erik thought for a moment. "It's kind of like a house only it's made of cloth."

Iya looked confused.

"You remember the men who took you and Anna?"

Iya nodded.

"They slept in a tent."

Iya grinned. "I know now," she announced.

"I do not like to talk about those men," Anna cut in.

Iya frowned, a hurt look on her face. "I did not talk of them, only of a tent."

Sitka quickly disappeared into the mist as the small group headed north and wound their way through the ocean channels toward the mainland. Once again, Anna found herself enchanted by the scenery. They moved past powerful waterfalls that cut through sheer rock faces and washed into the sea, and they saw moss-covered lowlands nestled between large sections of forest. Meadows freckled with wildflowers carpeted the massive feet of snow-capped mountains.

Beside God's awesome creation Anna felt small and insignificant. She wondered how a God of such power could be interested in her. She dipped her hand into the water, leaving a rivulet behind as they coursed through the channel. Even the water captivated her as it changed from a deep blue to aqua, then took on the green of the surrounding forest.

Colonies of sea lions rested on outcroppings of rocks along the shore. As the travelers approached, most waddled across their craggy homes and dove into the sea, but some held their ground, barking defensively at the intruders.

Iya found the animals amusing, and as they approached a group, she leaned forward in the boat and imitated their husky yelping. Even Takou smiled at her antics.

As the sun rose higher into the sky, the light fog burned off, leaving a mist that lingered along the beach. A shrill screech came from overhead, and Anna shaded her eyes to peer into the sky. An eagle soared above them, hunting for a midday meal. He floated on the warm currents, searching the waves with his keen eyes. Then he hesitated, folded his wings against his sides, and hurtled himself toward the water. At the last moment, he pulled up short and stretched his claws out in front of him. With a small splash, he dipped into the sea and, without breaking his momentum, lifted back into the sky clasping a large salmon in his talons.

"Beautiful aren't they?" Erik said.

"Yes," Anna answered, never taking her eyes from the magnificent bird. "They are a good omen. Our people used to tell stories of the eagle." She touched the walrus-tooth necklace at her neck. Memories of the desolate beach where Erik had found it flashed through her mind. There had been no eagle that day. She looked at Erik and repeated, "It is a good omen."

As the day wore on, the sun no longer felt warm and inviting but began beating down mercilessly upon the boats' occupants. Anna longed for a shady place to rest. Her body ached, and she wished they would put ashore where she could stretch her weary muscles then lay upon the cool earth. Luba began to fuss and Anna put her to her breast, but even that did not comfort the infant. Iya grew restless and whiny. Anna suggested a song, but after only a few measures, Iya's voice faded and Anna sang alone.

When the song ended, Erik said, "I like to hear you sing. You have a beautiful voice."

Anna managed a small smile. She didn't feel much like singing.

The wide, flat-bottomed boat made slow progress. Anna missed the umiak. Streamlined, it had cut through the water much faster. This craft seemed to wallow in the waves. Anna wished there were something she could do to hurry them along.

When she felt she couldn't stand one more minute confined in the slow craft, Takou called out, "We will put ashore here," and pointed toward a small stretch of sand. Expertly he nosed his craft toward shore.

Anna sighed with relief and smiled at Luba as Erik followed.

Iya stood up, bracing her feet against the sides of the boat as it rocked. The moment the bottom scraped against the rocks, she leaped into the shallow water and darted up the sandy beach. "Iya, come back here," Erik ordered.

Either Iya didn't hear him or refused to obey, and she disappeared into the tall beach grass.

In a strong, controlled voice, Erik repeated, "Iya, come here."

This time the little girl stepped out of the deep grass and guiltily looked at Erik as she edged toward him.

"Iya, you can't go wandering off," Erik explained, unable to hide his irritation. "Stay close to camp." He glanced up and down the beach. "There are a lot of wild animals in this area. And you might stumble across one in a foul temper."

"I am sorry," Iya said and headed for a clump of seaweed that had washed ashore.

Anna gathered firewood while the men set up camp. After Erik had a good fire going, Anna made fish soup and warmed the biscuits Cora had packed.

"That smells good," Erik said as he sat down next to the fire.

"It is ready."

Peter and Takou sat across the fire from Erik as Anna ladled soup into bowls.

Iya raced into camp and announced, "I like it here. Can we stay?" She took a seat next to Takou and smiled up at the stern-looking man.

"It is a good place," Takou answered.

"We can't stay here. There are no claims," Erik explained.

Iya frowned, but didn't say anything more as she dipped her biscuit into her soup.

"The loaded boats are slowing us down," Erik complained.

"It will take longer with the supplies, but we will make it soon enough," Takou said.

Luba sipped greedily from Anna's bowl.

"She's got quite an appetite," Erik joked.

Anna nodded and handed the little girl a piece of her biscuit.

"I wish there were some way to move faster," Erik commented.

"We all do," Peter said as he held his bowl out to Anna. "This is good. Can I have more?"

Anna refilled Peter's cup, then Takou's and Erik's.

Iya drained hers and yawned. "I am tired," she said as she curled up on her bedding. She fell asleep almost immediately.

Anna put Luba to her breast and the infant suckled greedily, but soon her eyes, too, began to droop.

"Looks like Iya's had a hard day," Erik said as he lay a blanket over the little girl.

Anna looked down at Luba. "It is the same for this one." Gently she wrapped the infant in a blanket and lay her beside Iya. "This is a long day. I think they will sleep good." She stifled a yawn.

"Looks like you ought to join them," Erik teased.

"I think you are right," Anna said as she rolled a blanket out and lay down. She tucked her hands under her head and smiled at Erik. "It is cold without you beside me."

Erik blushed and grinned at Peter and Takou. He emptied his cup. "Well, goodnight. I'll see you in the morning," he said as he joined his wife beneath their cover.

The days blended into a blur of sea and sky as the travelers continued their journey. Each day Anna looked for the river, anxious to see her new home, and when Takou finally announced that they had arrived, she searched the shoreline expectantly.

Iya jumped up and down in the boat and shouted, "We are here! We are here!"

A small beach lay along the base of the river. After navigating into the quiet waters, the men hauled the boats ashore, unloaded them, and dragged them into the deep grasses that lined the beach where they would remain until Takou and Peter returned to Sitka. They would leave one craft for Erik and Anna.

Anna sat on a log with Luba on her lap and waited to see what they would do. Iya raced to the water's edge and waded in. "Iya, do not go far. You do not swim," Anna warned, shivering as the cool wind swept across her bare arms.

Erik glanced at the sky. "It's still early. Do you think we ought to head upriver today?"

"We have a few hours left," Peter answered and glanced at Takou, who would make the final decision.

Takou looked at Anna. "Can you travel?"

Anna felt exhausted and wished she could rest, but unwilling to slow their progress, she nodded yes.

"We will go then," Takou said with authority.

Each man filled a pack with supplies and hefted it onto his back. Iya took a lighter pack while Anna carried Luba on her back. What they couldn't haul, they stashed beneath the boats to return for later.

Takou led the way, with Erik next, then Iya, and Anna with Luba on her back. Peter followed.

The damp earth and numerous ponds along the way were a perfect breeding ground for mosquitoes and black flies. Hordes of the pests descended upon the travelers. Anna swatted at the unrelenting insects, but they were not to be thwarted and seemed to grow in number and aggressiveness as the travelers moved away from the ocean.

Finally Takou stopped. He dropped his pack to the ground and slid down the bank to the river. While the others watched, the big Indian squatted along the river's edge and filled a cup with water. He carried it to the damp bank and added some of the soft earth, which he mixed until it was the consistency of pancake batter. Then he scooped out a handful and spread it on his face and arms. "This will help."

"What happened to your salve?" Erik asked.

"It is gone. This will work."

"We did this in the boat to protect us from the sun," Anna said as she carefully spread mud on Luba's tender skin.

Iya wrinkled up her nose as she slopped the gooey brown mess on her arms. "I do not like it," she complained.

"You will," Peter said matter-of-factly. "The bugs will not bite so much. I have seen it so bad that small animals die."

"I've heard of such stories," Erik said.

Anna looked at Erik and broke into laughter.

"What's so funny?"

Anna tried to stifle her laughter and answered, "I never saw you brown before."

Erik grinned. "Well at least I fit in," he quipped.

The mud worked well, and the travelers continued on in relative comfort.

That evening after supper no one sat by the fire to swap stories. Instead the exhausted travelers took to their beds. Anna's last thoughts were of the land that awaited her upriver and how good it would feel to have a place to dwell, where she and her family could remain always.

Two days later, they came upon Reid tirelessly shoveling gravel into his sluice box. His red hair blew about his face, hiding his eyes, and he jumped when Erik called, "Hello there!"

Reid brushed his hair from his eyes. "Weel, hello t' ye'," he called back.

Erik waved at the friendly redhead and scuttled down the bank with his family close behind.

"Why, it's good t' see ye', lad," the older man declared, slapping Erik on the back. "Me and the missus been woonderin' if we'd be seein' ye' again. She'll be glad t' know yer safe and soond."

"I filed my claim, and now I'm back to work it," Erik answered with a grin.

"Looks like the skeeters have been after ye'," Reid said as he wiped at Erik's muddy face.

"They've been fierce all right. It'll feel good to clean up."

"Would ye' like to have soopper with us?"

Erik glanced at Anna. "Sounds good, but we're kind of anxious to get to our place. Another time maybe?"

"Any time, then." He glanced at Anna and the girls. "I take it this is yer family."

Erik stepped beside Anna and draped his arm across her shoulders. "Yep. This is Anna. Anna, I'd like you to meet Reid Campbell. The man I told you about. He and his wife, Millie, will be our closest neighbors."

"I am glad to meet you," Anna said with a smile.

"This is Iya, Anna's sister, and the baby's name is Luba. She's Anna's daughter," Erik explained.

Reid squatted down in front of Iya. "It's a pleasure t' make yer acquaintance, little lady," he said and reached out his hand.

Iya smiled, took his hand, and shook it hard. "It is nice to make your ac . . . qua . . . ?" She couldn't pronounce the word and finally said, "Good to meet you."

"It's good to see you, Reid, but we've got a home to get to," Erik said as he headed toward his claim.

Anna nodded at Reid and followed.

A few minutes later, Erik stepped into a clearing and stopped. "Well, what do you think?"

Anna stood quietly beside him and clasped his hand. "This is it?"

"This is our claim."

Anna looked over the property. Tall grasses and bushes with delicate flowers covered the earth while poplar and spruce grew side by side, creating a cool canopy overhead. She gazed down at the river. It tumbled over rocks and poured into deep pools where it slowed into quiet coves before descending downstream. She looked back at the parcel of land Erik had said was theirs. The sun reached through the covering of leafy branches and illuminated a small patch of open ground. Dust and pollen floated aimlessly in the shaft of light.

"It is beautiful," Anna finally answered. "I love it."

"Will we stay here?" Iya asked.

Anna glanced down at the little girl, then gazed out at the open ground again. Taking a deep breath, she answered, "We are home."

Jarvis leaned over the railing and retched as the cutter dipped its nose into another wave. Choppy seas and the smell of burning coal had proven too much for his stomach. Shaky and weak, he stood up and glowered at his partner.

"You do not look so good," Joe said, then added with a grin, "You look pale even for a white man."

Gripping the railing, Jarvis retorted, "I've been sailin' a long time and never been sick. This is your fault. What did you give me?"

"I did nothing. Do not blame me for your weak stomach."

Jarvis moaned and slid to the floor as the ship plunged down another deep trough. "It's not my stomach. It's this blasted weather. This is your fault. You're the one who said we ought to go to Sitka."

"You said you wanted gold. To find it we go south." He grinned again. "I could not know the sea would make you sick." More seriously he added, "Can never tell about the weather." He thought a moment. "You know I hear if a person is sick he should lay flat on his bunk and tilt his head back over the edge."

Jarvis shot him a sour look.

"It is supposed to help. Also, I hear if you eat a big meal it will help."

"Eat? How do you expect me to eat?" Jarvis glared at him. "Nothin's gonna help except to get off this stinkin' ship."

"Captain said we are not far from Sitka."

"Anything other than being at the dock is too far. How soon before we can get up to the diggings?"

"Not until spring. Winter will be here soon. There is no time to find a claim and file it," Joe explained as he lit a cigar. Smoke rolled off the stogie and into Jarvis's face.

Jarvis blanched. "Get that thing out of my face," he hollered as he pulled himself to his feet and leaned on the railing. "I'll get you for this," he growled. "Should have trusted my instincts. Never partner up with no Injun."

"You do not need me? Fine. When we get to Sitka I will find another partner, and we will find gold."

Jarvis reeled back toward the deck. "Wait a minute. A deal's a deal. You said you'd take me. I paid for your passage. You can't back out now. You owe me." He glared at the big man. "I knew I couldn't trust you."

Joe scowled at him.

Jarvis swung at the big man, but missed. Weakly, he sprawled across the deck and lay there a minute before slowly pushing himself to his knees. He peered up at Joe.

Joe took another puff on his cigar and stared calmly at Jarvis. "I always keep my word. I will show you where the gold is."

"You bet you'll show me," Jarvis said through gritted teeth.

Joe didn't respond; he merely puffed on his cigar. He took the stogie from his lips, rolled it between his fingers, and studied it. "You talk big, but you are a little man. I choose what I will do." He grinned. "Even that drifter outdid you."

Jarvis pushed himself back to his feet. "That's what you heard, huh? Well the game's not over yet. When I find that sorry excuse for a man, he'll wish he never knew me. I'll get another crack at him. One day it'll be my turn." Almost to himself he added, "Wonder if that half-breed's still with him."

"What?"

"Nothin'. It's not important." Jarvis narrowed his eyes, and a smile crept across his face. "Maybe you might be interested at that." He studied Joe a moment. "He had himself a nice squaw. Real pretty for an Injun." He laughed. "You interested? Maybe if we find them, she'll take a shine to ya."

"I do not need another man's woman."

Jarvis steadied himself and scanned the shoreline. "Sure you don't," he mocked. He took a deep breath. "I think I'm feelin' better," he said smugly. "You'd better watch your back." Just then, the ship dropped into a rather deep trough and quickly swept back up the crest of the wave. Jarvis's bravado disappeared as he made another lunge for the railing.

Joe stood back and watched the despicable man and wished he'd never teamed up with him. *If I had the money, I'd pay him every cent I owe and be rid of him,* he thought. *I am no saint, but this man is evil.* He flicked the butt of his cigar overboard. *After we find the gold, I'll find a way to lose him.* But he knew it would be tough to do so without embittering the vicious man. If he wasn't careful, he'd spend the rest of his life looking over his shoulder, waiting for him to turn up. Jarvis wasn't the sort who'd let a wrong done to him go by. A shudder swept through Joe. The thought of dealing with this repulsive man long-term sickened him. *I'll think of something before spring,* he decided as he turned and headed for his cabin.

Chapter 12

The good weather held, and the Engstroms spent their first night on the claim beneath the stars. With the children already asleep, Anna lay with her arms folded beneath her head, staring at the dark canopy overhead. The long summer days were behind them, and fall's brightest stars winked down at her.

"It is beautiful," Anna whispered to Erik.

"Nothing prettier than an Alaskan night sky. Thousands of stars twinkling from above. It can't be matched. As many miles as I've traveled, I've never seen anything as grand. It almost makes a person wish for winter."

Anna pushed herself up on one elbow and peered at him. "You want winter to come?" she asked incredulously.

Erik chuckled. "Not exactly. I don't like working in the cold and wet. It's miserable. But I have to admit there's something about Alaskan winters—I can't explain it exactly, except that you know you've really experienced one when you've been through a season. It's real and alive. And when the Northern Lights prance across the heavens . . . well, there's just nothing as impressive."

Anna rolled to her side and snuggled against him. "Hmm, I understand. But they used to frighten me. When I was young and the lights danced in the sky, I hid beneath my coverings. Only when I grew older did I see their beauty."

Erik nuzzled her neck. "Tomorrow I'll put the tent up."

Anna gazed into the dying embers of the fire and murmured, "I do not mind sleeping outside."

"When the weather's good neither do I, but around here you can never tell when the rains are going to come. From the looks of things, it stays pretty wet. The sooner we have a shelter the better."

Anna nodded and closed her eyes. It felt good to lay beside Erik, to feel his breath against her neck and the warmth of his body against hers. "This is a good place," she said quietly. "We will build a home and have many children."

Erik didn't respond.

"You do not want children?"

Erik wrapped his arms around her and pulled her closer. "Of course I do—lots of them. Why would you think anything else?"

"We did not talk about it," Anna answered flatly. "You are like a father to Iya and Luba. I do not know if you want others."

"I want all we can have. A whole passel of them running about would be fine by me."

Anna remained quiet a moment then asked hesitantly, "What if we have no more children?"

Erik didn't answer at first.

Fear welled up in Anna. Would Erik be angry with no sons to carry on his name?

Erik hugged Anna. "If we have children or not is up to God."

"Do you think he will give many?"

Erik chuckled and squeezed Anna tighter.

"It is not funny," Anna protested.

"Anna, I'm not making fun. I just think you're worrying about something we have no control over. We have to wait and see what happens. God knows best."

Anna wondered at Erik's unwavering faith. Quietly she asked, "Erik, you always believe, always trust. How is it so?"

Erik thought a moment before answering. "I get scared just like everyone else. Sometimes I'm quaking in my boots. It's just that I've walked with God long enough to know he cares. He's never let me down. He's wise enough to do what's best—always. And because he knows the beginning and the end, he always makes the right choice." Erik rolled to his back. "There have been times I didn't accept his decision. I've argued with him and done things my way." He paused. "The great thing is he loves me anyway. And teaches me even from my mistakes."

"Does God ever stop loving?"

"No—never," Erik answered with conviction.

"I wish I knew more. Some day I will read his book."

"I read it for you and the girls every day . . ."

"I know," Anna cut in. "But I want to read it myself."

Erik yawned and stretched. "Maybe some day," he murmured. "But for now, we better get to sleep. Morning will be here before we know it." He turned toward Anna and hugged her. "Mm, you smell good. Like spring grass." He planted a kiss at the nape of her neck. "I wish we were alone," he said in a husky voice. "First thing tomorrow, I'm putting up that tent."

Anna turned toward him. Cradling his face in her hands, she studied her husband. Blue eyes, the color of the delicate flowers of her home, gazed back at her. She ran her thumb down his cheek and across his lower lip. Love welled up within her, and tears pricked at her eyelids. "I love you," she said, her voice trembling.

"I love you," Erik whispered, then kissed her.

The shrill cry of blue jays and magpies were the first sounds to greet Anna the following morning. She pulled her blanket over her head and tried to shut out their persistent racket.

Iya peeked beneath the cover. "You sleep a long time. Erik already made breakfast. Time for you to get up."

Anna could hear the crackle of the fire and smell the sweet fragrance of burning spruce. She blinked her eyes and peered up at her younger sister. "I am not ready to get up," she argued good-naturedly.

With a smirk Iya stood up, planted her hands on her hips, and said firmly, "Anna, I say it is time you get up."

Anna smiled at Iya and grabbed at the youngster's ankle.

Giggling, Iya jumped out of Anna's reach.

The smell of frying saltpork and biscuits made Anna's stomach churn, and she realized she didn't feel well. She wished she could roll over and return to the peaceful world of sleep, but finally conceded to Iya's insistence and said, "All right, I am getting up."

Iya grinned triumphantly.

Erik squatted next to the fire, holding the frying pan above the flames. He peered at Anna over his shoulder. "Good morning. Breakfast is nearly ready. How about a cup of coffee?" Without waiting for a reply, he set the pan down in the coals and poured her a cup.

Anna pushed herself into a sitting position and folded her legs beneath her.

"Here you go," Erik said as he handed her the coffee. "Give this a try and see if it doesn't wake you up."

Anna brushed her hair out of her eyes and looked around camp. Takou sat across the fire from Erik with a plate of biscuits on his lap. Peter stood along the bank, staring at the river.

Takou finished his food and drained his cup of coffee, then said, "It is time we went to get the supplies."

"I'll go with you," Erik offered.

"No. Peter and I will go. You stay with Anna and the children."

Peter stepped up to the group and hefted Iya onto his shoulders. The little girl squealed in delight. Peter laughed. "I will not miss this one," he teased as he set her back on the ground.

"Yes, you will," Iya insisted.

"You sure you don't want me to go along?" Erik asked.

"No, it is better if you stay," Peter insisted. "Take care of your family."

Takou hefted his pack onto his back. "We will return soon," he said and headed into the woods.

Peter smiled and waved as he followed his friend.

"Once they make up their mind to do something, it doesn't take long for them to act," Erik said as he shoveled two biscuits onto a plate, drenched them in thick gravy, slid a slice of saltpork alongside, then offered the meal to Anna. "Here, I saved some breakfast for you. It's not bad."

Anna looked down at the greasy meal and immediately pushed it away as nausea nearly overwhelmed her. "I do not feel good," she managed to say.

Iya sat Luba on her lap and, as if the infant's dietary habits would make Anna eat, said, "Luba ate some."

Hearing her name, Luba began bouncing up and down and nearly tumbled to the ground.

Iya giggled. "She is happy today."

"Anna, are you all right?" Erik asked with concern.

Anna set her cup aside. "I am fine, just not hungry." She averted her eyes from the food and forced herself to think of something else, hoping her queasiness would pass. She looked at the forest surrounding the clearing. The songs of birds and chirps of squirrels seemed to come from all around. An abrupt gust of wind nudged the animals from their perches. The birds took to the air while squirrels dashed to find more secure branches.

"I'd better get at that tent," Erik said, removing his hat and smoothing his hair down before replacing it. "Wish I could get the cabin up right away, but it'll have to wait a while." He scanned the small open area. "No need to worry, though. These trees will help protect us from the wind. And I'll have the house up long before the cold weather gets here."

Luba began to fuss, and Iya handed the infant to Anna.

"Good morning, little one," Anna said as she settled the baby at her breast.

Iya turned to Erik. "Can I help you look for gold?" she asked.

"I can use all the help I can get," Erik said as he swept Iya into his arms.

She giggled, then stopped and looked at him soberly. "Erik, you are like my father."

"I'm not your father . . ." Erik began.

Iya frowned.

"But I wish I were. Any man would be proud to have a little girl like you."

Iya smiled softly. "After the wave, I had no family but Anna. Then you came. In here," she patted her chest, "you are my father."

Erik blinked back tears and took a deep breath. "I feel the same way. You seem like my own. Even if I'm not your real father, I love you just like I were. We're a family."

Iya grinned and hugged Erik hard about the neck.

Erik returned her embrace. "If you want, you can call me Daddy."

Iya broke into a wide grin.

Erik cleared his throat. "I guess it's time we got to work," he said, and he reluctantly set Iya on the ground and hauled out one of their packs. "Let's get the tent up." He tipped one of the bundles on end and dumped its contents onto the ground. "Ah, here it is," he said as he stretched out a large piece of canvas.

Anna watched as Erik put up their makeshift home. It looked complicated, but Erik seemed to know just what to do. Iya helped by holding lines taut and handing Erik poles when he needed them. In less than an hour, their canvas dwelling stood ready to occupy.

"Well, what do you think?" Erik asked as he pulled back the front flap. "Not bad for an old piece of cloth and a few poles."

Anna walked up to the structure and ran her hand over the coarse material. She peeked inside. "Will this keep out rain?" she asked doubtfully.

"The canvas is made to keep the moisture out. If you cinch the front flap up tight, it'll stay warm and dry. We used these during the war. They'd be our home for months at a time."

"You spoke of a war before. What war?" Anna asked. The thought of Erik battling against another tribe made her uneasy. One day would he be called to fight again?

Erik looked across the river and, for a moment, seemed lost in another time and place. Finally he said solemnly, "There was fighting between the Americans in the north and in the south, and I was a part of it. It's not something I like to think about."

Anna wanted to know more but could see the subject pained Erik, so she kept quiet.

Turning his attention back to the tent, Erik said, "Go on in. Take a look."

Anna smiled and stepped inside. The room smelled musty, and the air felt heavy and warm.

"I know it smells kind of bad, but if you leave the door open a while it will air out," Erik explained.

The wind gusted and the sides billowed. For a moment, Anna thought it might fall.

"I know it doesn't look like much, but it'll stand," Erik explained.

Anna doubted it would remain upright if a big storm blew through, but for now she felt content at having the shelter.

Erik stood up straight and his head pressed against the ceiling. "I don't think these were made for tall men," he said with a smile.

Iya began running around the center of the small room, and Luba laughed at the little girl's antics.

Although this was only a temporary dwelling, a sense of celebration filled the room. This would be their home. Permanent or not, it didn't matter. It represented everything Anna and Erik had hoped for for so long.

"This is good," Anna said as another gust of wind whipped through the door and surged against the sides of the structure. She watched, afraid it would collapse, but when the wind died down, the tent grew quiet and stood just as it had. Anna felt a little more secure. "Maybe it will not fall in a storm."

"It'll hold up all right," Erik said with confidence. "But you won't have to worry about storms. We have plenty of time before the weather turns bad."

"Say neighbors!" came a cry from downriver.

"Sounds like we've got company," Erik said and stepped outside. Anna followed.

Reid greeted Erik with a warm handshake. A delicate-looking woman in her late thirties or early forties stood by his side. Her light yellow hair had been pulled back and caught into a tight knot at the nape of her neck. Small wisps had blown loose and fluttered around her face.

"Anna, you remember Reid. You met him yesterday."

Anna nodded and smiled.

"This is me wife, Millie. Remember I told ye' aboot her?"

Millie bobbed her head politely. "It's real nice to meet you," she said sweetly, her blue eyes crinkling as she smiled. "It's been a long time since I've had the pleasure of another woman's company. Sourdoughs seem to be about all we get around here."

Reid draped his arm over his wife's shoulders and said teasingly, "Yeah, weel, soom of us aren't so bad."

Millie smiled at her husband. "I guess not. I married one," she teased.

"I am happy to meet you," Anna said, warming to the woman immediately.

Iya pulled at Anna's tunic, demanding attention.

"This is Iya, my sister," Anna explained.

"It is nice to meet you, Iya," Millie said with a smile.

Iya grinned. "You smell like Cora."

Millie chuckled. "I hope that's good."

"Yes, Cora smells very good."

Millie looked at Luba, and her eyes warmed as she gazed at the baby in Anna's arms. "And who might this little angel be?"

"This is Luba."

Millie reached out and gently caressed the baby's cheek with the back of her hand. "She's beautiful. You must be very proud of her."

Anna nodded. "Do you have children?"

Millie glanced at Reid. "No, the Lord never blessed us with any," she answered quietly.

Reid cleared his throat, then went on a little too cheerfully, "Weel, enough of this chitchat. We joost coom by t' ask if ye'd share supper with us. Figured with ye' jest gettin' set up and all it might be simpler fer ye'."

"We'd like that," Erik said.

"Good, then we'll plan on seein' ye' two a bit later," Reid said as he tipped his hat then turned toward home. Millie smiled and followed him.

As Anna watched them disappear into the underbrush, she decided she liked her new neighbors. Reid's Scottish brogue sounded warm and rich, and Millie seemed kind. Anna looked forward to seeing her again.

"They seem like real decent folks," Erik said, cutting into Anna's thoughts. "They ought to be fine neighbors."

"Yes," Anna agreed. "I like Millie very much." She paused. "In a way she reminds me of Cora." Tears came to her eyes as she thought of her friend. "I wonder how she is?"

"You miss her, don't you?" Erik asked kindly as he slipped his arm around Anna's shoulders. "One of the hardest things about this wanderer's life is the friends and family we leave behind."

Anna nodded. She knew time would ease the pain of leaving, but she missed the good-natured woman.

"It's time to get to work," Erik stated. "First thing we've got to do, Iya, is build a sluice box. After that I'll need your help hauling gravel and water."

"I have much to do here," Anna said.

"We'll be working down at the river." Erik kissed Anna's cheek. "Come on, Iya." He took the little girl's hand and set off for the stream.

Anna set Luba on a blanket and got to work. First she shook out their bedding. She lay the girls' mats side by side on the north edge of the tent and hers and Erik's opposite theirs, then she spread a fur rug down in the center of the room. *This will feel good on bare feet,* Anna thought as she folded their clothing and stacked it in one corner.

When she had finished, she stood back and surveyed her work. The room was small and a bit crowded, but she decided a table would be useful, so she went in search of a suitable chunk of wood. When she found one, she rolled it inside and stood it on end next to her bed. *This will make a fine table,* she thought as she set a lantern on the makeshift stand.

With the tent in order, she went to work to make their camp more comfortable. First she rolled several small logs close to the fire pit, then she went in search of wood with a level side. She found two pieces and, after hauling them into camp, pushed them together, flat side up. "This will work," she said with satisfaction as she draped a canvas bag over the top, creating a clean, flat surface for dishes and eating utensils. She wiped the sweat from her brow and sat down to rest. A mosquito landed on her forearm and she swatted it. "At least we will not be bothered by you when winter comes," she said with relief as she flicked away the dead insect.

Her nausea had subsided and she realized she felt hungry, so she rummaged through a knapsack until she found a piece of jerky. She sat down and munched on the tough meat, washing it down with a drink of cool water.

Erik and Iya returned midday. They looked dirty and wet, but seemed cheerful about their labors.

"Looks like you've been busy," Erik said happily as he glanced about.

"We are hungry," Iya said as she sat down on one of the stumps Anna had hauled into camp.

Erik peeked inside the tent. "Looks great, Anna—just like home."

"I am glad you like. Did you build the slu . . .?"

"The sluice box?" Erik cut in. "Yep, we've just about got it done. Only a few more boards to hammer in, and we'll have her ready to go. Iya here is a good worker."

Iya beamed with pride. "I like to do carpenter work."

"She's a good one, too, if I do say so myself," Erik said, patting her on the back. "I'm starved. Why don't we head over to Reid's?"

"I am ready," Anna said as she gathered up Luba and followed Erik into the forest.

Millie met them at the door. "Come on in. Supper's nearly ready."

The smell of fresh biscuits greeted Anna as she stepped inside and looked about the tidy cabin. It was small, but warm and inviting. Fascinating pictures of places Anna had never seen decorated the walls, and knickknacks adorned a hodgepodge of shelves. A brightly braided rug rested in front of the hearth and filled the room with color.

Anna relaxed and took a deep breath.

"Would you like to sit down?" Millie asked with a smile as she pulled a chair away from the sturdy wooden table in the kitchen. "I'll bet you're hungry. Setting up a home is a lot of work."

"I am hungry," Iya said, taking a seat at the table.

Anna sat beside Iya and settled Luba on her lap while Erik and Reid remained in the living area, swapping the latest news from up and down the river.

Millie hurried back to the stove, hefted a large pot from the back of the firebox, and set it in the center of the table. She lifted the lid and, with a wooden spoon, swirled the contents. Steam rose into the air and filled the room with the aroma of meat and vegetables.

"Something smells good," Erik said.

"Thet's Millie's stew. Ye've never tasted anythin' like it," Reid boasted.

Millie blushed as she placed a pan of hot biscuits beside the stew. Next she filled the tall glass tumblers at each place with water from an elegant glass pitcher.

"These are the only pieces of glassware I was able to salvage from my mother's things," she said as she set the pitcher on the table. "Most everything else broke on our way out from Nebraska. Mother loved nice things," she added quietly.

"They are pretty," Anna said as she touched the etching on her glass.

Millie smiled at her, then, turning toward the living room, said, "Well, men, supper's on."

Erik took a seat across from Anna.

"Reid, could you say grace?" Millie asked a little hesitantly.

Reid pulled his chair up to the table and looked at his wife, a mixture of shock and irritation on his face. He cleared his throat. "Millie, ye' know I'm noot a prayin' man."

Anna could feel the tension in the air and shifted uneasily in her seat.

Luba whimpered.

"I'd be more than happy to say grace, ma'am. That is, if you don't mind," Erik offered.

Reid gave him a look of gratitude. "Thet would be jest fine with me."

They bowed their heads. Anna noticed Reid give Millie a knowing look before he lowered his.

"Dear Lord," Erik began, "we thank you for bringing us safely to this land and for providing us with good neighbors. And we thank you for this fine food. Amen."

Amen's were whispered around the table. Millie lifted the lid from the pot and began dishing out the thick, savory stew.

"I managed t' get me a yoong moose early this season," Reid said as he eyed the heaping plate in front of him. "Millie can do amazin' things with moose meat. Help yerselves t' a biscuit."

"Don't mind if I do," Erik said. "They look delicious."

Anna didn't remember ever tasting a better meal. Not even Cora's cooking compared. "This is good. You might have Erik here every day. I do not cook so good," she said with a crooked smile.

"If you'd like, I could teach you," Millie offered. "Most of my recipes I got from my mother. Back home she was known for her cooking."

"I would like that."

"You say you shot that moose around here, Reid?" Erik asked.

"Sure did. There is always plenty of game." Reid leaned forward on his elbows. "Early this spring the Indians had been stirrin' oop a bit of trooble, but we were runnin' low on our meat so I told Millie I'd be headin' oot. She wasn't noon too happy aboot it, with the Indians and all, boot a man's got t' feed his family now doesn't he?"

"Reid likes to hunt and would have gone whether we needed it or not," Millie added with a grin.

Reid cast her a look of feigned annoyance. "As I was sayin' before I was so rudely interrupted, I set oot jest before daylight. It was dark as pitch it was—a thick layer of clouds blockin' oot any light from the stars or moon."

He leaned back in his chair and slipped one leg over the other. "Weel, I knew me way aroond so I wasn't worried. Figured if I followed the river I couldna' miss the pond. Thet's where ye'll find the mighty beasts most days. Weel, I was goin' aloong, happy as ye' please when I heard this crackle in the underbroosh. Now, like I said, the Indians had been a bit cranky, soo I felt a little tight. Withoot knowin' it, I stepped back and right oof the edge of the bank. Next thing I know I'm slippin' doon the hill and into thet unforgivin' river."

"I know what that's like," Erik interjected with a grin. "Had the same bad luck on my trip out of here. It's a mighty cold river."

"Weel lad, then ye' know what I'm talkin' aboot. It was still dark as sin, and I didna' know what I might be facin'. I'm not ashamed t' tell ye' I was scared. I thought I was a goner. Mighty hard t' swim when it's pitch dark and ye' got no idea where ye're at. Weel, anyway, I was flailin' aroond, and by pure loock I grabbed hold of a limb stickin' oot over the water. I'll tell ye', I hung onto thet branch." He glanced at Millie. "I figure Millie here moost have been prayin' cause the good Lord was smilin' doon on me, thet's fer sure."

He stopped long enough to take another bite of stew. "Well, I managed t' drag meself oot of thet cold river and while I was restin' on the shore, I heard the same rustlin' sound in the bushes. I was sure somethin' was followin' me. So I hid in the tall grass and waited. By this time, the mornin' light had begoon t' brighten things oop jest a bit, so I figured if I held real still I might get the joomp on whatever was stalkin' me. Weel, pretty soon I can see the bushes just above me start quiverin', and I hear the cracklin' of brush. It looked like somethin' big was coomin' me way. I feared it might be a bear, and when I saw a bit of brown fur, a chill went right oop me spine. I thought fer sure it was a brownie. I try t' stay clear of them. Ye' know, they've been known t' track a man."

Iya's eyes widened with alarm.

"Now, Reid, hurry up and finish your story before your supper gets cold," Millie chided him.

"I'm almost doon," Reid answered with a twinkle in his eye. "I figured I ought t' meet me adverseery straight on, so I stood oop and set me sights on thet bush. All of a sudden an animal breaks through, chargin' straight at me . . ." He let the sentence hang in the air.

"What happen then?" Iya asked.

Reid chuckled. "Well, I'll be darned if it weren't a moose. He startled me soo bad I nearly fell back into the river."

"A moose." Erik blurted out.

"Yep." Reid answered with a grin, dipping his biscuit into his stew and stuffing it into his mouth. "I figured if thet's what I coom huntin' fer, I sure better git him in the bag, so I blasted him. He never knew what hit him."

"Lots of moose around, huh?" Erik asked.

"There sure is, lad. But remember we've goot competition from the Indians, not t' mention the wolves and bears. When you're oot and aboot, you'd best be watchin' ye're back." Reid scooped out the last of his stew. "How's the work goin' on ye're place?"

"The tent's up, and Anna here did a great job of making it real homey. And Iya and I nearly got the sluice box finished. I figured tomorrow I'd start washing some rock."

Reid grinned. "I remember when I first goot here. I did me best t' git right to it."

"I figured the sooner I got started, the sooner we'll be able to make a real home for ourselves," Erik answered as he glanced at Anna.

Anna smiled.

"Would you like your pipe, Reid?" Millie asked.

"Thet I would. How aboot you Erik? You enjoy a smoke?"

"Nope, never took it up."

Millie went to the hearth, took Reid's pipe and tobacco down from the mantle, and returned to the table. After handing them to him, she began to clear the table.

The Scotsman filled the bowl of his pipe, tamped it down, then struck a match and held it over the tobacco while he sucked hard. A moment later, a whisper of smoke rose into the air and the tobacco glowed red. Reid puffed on it and leaned back in his chair. "Nothin' quite like a good smoke," he said as he removed the pipe from between his teeth. "I've had this since I was a yoong man. Me grandfather brought it over froom Scotland with him. Never had another thet smoked as good." Reid leveled a serious look at Erik, "Somethin' ye' need to know, Erik, winter's unpredictable aroond here. It can coom on ye' real sudden. Some years summer seems t' hang on, but there are times thet the wind cooms blastin' doon from the north as early as September or October." He paused and studied his pipe. "If I was ye', I'd be workin' on a cabin first thing."

"I plan to. Just figured I'd take a quick peek at what I've got first."

"Be careful, lad. Sometimes a quick look turns into a lifetime of searchin'. Gold-fever ken git ahold oon ye' before ye' know it and then nothin' else matters. I've seen it more than once." He drew on his pipe. "One time I watched a whole band of men, soom of them with wives and children, forget aboot everything but gold. If noot for the kindness of neighbors, they'd of all died."

"Don't worry about me," Erik reassured Reid. "The gold won't get a hold on me like that."

"Weel, if ye're noot worried, then ye' weel should be."

"Would anyone like a piece of pie?" Millie interrupted.

"I like pie," Iya said without hesitation.

"Well, you can have the first piece, then," Millie said as she carved a large slice out for the little girl. "Anyone else?"

"I wouldn't miss it," Erik said.

"Anna, how about you?"

Anna nodded and gladly accepted a piece, but an uneasiness settled in the pit of her stomach as she considered Reid's words of caution and Erik's seeming lack of concern. She'd feel better if Erik would build the cabin and outbuildings first, but it was his decision when the work would be done. She could only wait.

Chapter 13

*T*akou hefted his pack onto his back and held his hand out to Erik. "It is time for Peter and me to leave," he said soberly.

"I'm sorry to see you go," Erik replied. "You've been a real help to me." He shook Takou's hand, then Peter's. "I will always consider you friends."

"And you are our friend," Peter said with a smile.

Iya held her hand out for Takou. "Good-bye," she said, as grown-up as she could.

Takou's expression softened as he shook the little girl's hand. "Good-bye."

Peter crouched down in front of Iya. He handed her a crow's feather. "You keep this. It will bring you luck," he said.

Iya took the gift and hugged her friend. "It will remind me of you until I see you again," she said and wiped at her tear-filled eyes.

"I'll see you on my next trip south," Erik said jovially.

"Good-bye," Anna said quietly, sorry to see them go. It had taken a while, but she had grown fond of Peter and Takou, and she would always be grateful to them for saving Erik from the river. "I hope we will see you again."

Both men nodded and headed downriver.

The weeks passed and Erik worked hard along the Schuck. Each day he rose early, and often he didn't return to camp until forced to by darkness or fatigue. Sometimes, too weary to eat, he would drop into bed with barely a word to his family.

The claim had proven to be a moderate success and Erik seemed compelled to work it, always hoping for the big strike that lay only a few more shovelfuls away.

Anna's alarm grew as she watched the change in Erik. He had little time for her or the girls, and although the weather seemed to grow colder each day, the tent remained their only shelter against the elements. Frequently the wind whipped under the canvas sides, blowing in cold air and rain, leaving their living space cold and damp.

On the coolest days, Anna and the children huddled together beneath fur blankets, trying to keep warm. Anna quickly learned to avoid contact with the tent walls when it rained. If touched, the canvas leaked, and anything near it ended up soaked.

Erik continued to promise to build their cabin, but each day he headed for the river for gold instead of the forest for timber. Anna began to worry that they would spend the winter in the cold, wet tent. The days had grown shorter, and the leaves had started to turn varying shades of yellow and orange. Some mornings, a thin layer of frost covered the ground.

Anna visited Millie as often as possible. Her home looked bright and cheerful, and a warm fire always greeted her and the children. Millie seemed to enjoy having company, and Anna always felt at home. They shared sewing techniques, and Millie taught Anna some of her mother's recipes. Anna was becoming a good cook.

One morning, after making corn dodgers, Millie and Anna sat at the table to enjoy them.

"Mm, these are good," Anna said as she bit into one of the small biscuits.

"And you made them yourself," Millie praised.

"No, you helped me. But I will make them for Erik now."

"You're getting good at cooking."

"Thank you. I wish Erik would notice. Sometimes he is so tired, he goes to bed without eating."

Millie looked at her hands, then hesitantly asked, "Anna, is something wrong? Between the two of you, I mean."

Anna sighed. She hadn't shared her concerns with Millie, but now that her friend had asked, she knew she needed to talk about her fears. She glanced out the window and took a deep breath. "Erik only digs for gold. I do not see him until it is dark." She paused and studied the corn dodger in her hand. "He is not the same."

"Not the same how?"

Anna looked up at her friend. "He only washes rock. He does not talk to me or the girls. He does not read his Bible." Her eyes filled with tears. "I am afraid."

Millie took Anna's hand. "Oh honey, he hasn't changed, not really. It's just the gold. I've seen it before." She hesitated. "I'll talk to Reid and see if he will say something to him. All right?"

Anna sniffed and nodded. "I just want Erik to be the way he was."

"Don't worry. Everything will work out," Millie reassured her.

But Anna wasn't so certain. The spells of illness in the morning had passed, but she had missed her last two cycles, and she was sure that she carried Erik's child. How would he feel when he learned about the coming baby? He'd grown so distant, and he seemed to only care about gold.

Millie must have spoken to Reid immediately because the following morning he came by.

"Hello there, little one," he said as he swung Iya into his arms.

Iya giggled. "Twirl me!" she demanded.

Reid gave her two swift spins then set her back on her feet.

"Hello," Anna said.

"Nice t' see ye', Anna." He grinned at Luba. "I swear thet baby's growin' like a weed."

Anna smiled. "She is getting big."

"Is Erik aboot? I was hopin' t' have a word with him."

Anna liked his lyrical way of speaking. When she'd asked him about it, he'd explained that his family had come from Scotland when he was just a boy, and although he'd tried to shake his accent, he hadn't succeeded. Anna was glad he'd not been able to overcome it.

"He is at the river," she answered.

"Well, I'll jest go on doon then." He tipped his hat and strode off.

Iya started after him, but Anna called her back. "This time you stay. You can help me bake." As she watched Reid disappear over the bank, she twisted a towel between her hands, fearful of what might follow. She felt certain he'd come to talk with Erik about what she'd shared with Millie. Now she wished she hadn't said anything.

"Iya, would you collect the eggs? We will need them for the bread," Anna said as she gathered up some of the utensils she would use.

Iya grinned and set off in search of the eggs.

Anna looked forward to the day they would have a shed like Cora's and Millie's so they wouldn't have to search for eggs. She stopped to listen when she thought she heard shouting coming from the river. She watched the bank and told herself, *It is just the wind.* But she listened harder. When she heard nothing more, she relaxed a little and went back to her mixing.

A few minutes later, Reid stormed up the bank. "There's no talkin' t' the man," he muttered, shaking his mop of red hair as he headed down the trail toward his place.

Anna's stomach tightened. Something had happened between Erik and Reid, and clearly it wasn't good.

"What is wrong with Reid?" Iya asked.

"I do not know."

"I found two," the little girl said, handing the eggs to Anna.

But Anna barely noticed as she watched Erik march up the bank, glowering angrily. He charged into camp and silently paced back and forth in front of the fire. Anna waited, her apprehension growing with each moment. She'd never seen him so upset. Iya felt his wrath and huddled next to Anna as her eyes followed Erik's pacing.

Abruptly he stopped, shoved his hands into his pockets, and glared at the ground in front of their feet. In a tight, controlled voice he asked, "Why did you feel you had to talk to someone else about us? Why didn't you talk to me? No, instead you had to go to the neighbors and tell them about my stupidity."

"I did not say that," Anna defended herself. "I do try to talk to you."

"Well, it seems they think I'm half-witted. Reid came down here just to let me know how irresponsible I am. That if I really cared about my family, I'd be getting ready for winter." He glared at Anna. "Is that what you think? That I don't care?"

"No," Anna said. She backed up a step. "I never thought that." Her anxiety began to dissipate and anger moved in to replace it. She straightened her shoulders, thrust her chin up a notch, and locked her eyes on his. "I told Millie the truth. I tried to tell you, but you would not listen."

She could see the hurt her words inflicted, but she was too angry to stop. "We live in the tent too long. You promise us that you will build a house, but even when the rain and wind come you do not. Luba has been sick. Her eyes run and she coughs. What will happen when the cold dark days come? We have no meat or fish—no wood for the fire." She wiped at hot, angry tears. "We cannot eat gold. But it is all you think of." She stopped long enough to take a deep breath. "Iya and I, we pick berries, plants, but that is not enough. We do not know hunting."

"I've been working hard, and I haven't forgotten about what needs to be done. I said I'd do it and I will."

"Erik, you are not the same man I marry. Like Reid says, the gold has changed you. It controls you. I do not want it!"

"It is the only way we will ever be able to have a real home and the things we need."

"It is more important than us?"

Erik swept his hat off and slapped it against his leg. "Of course not."

Now vented, Anna's anger began to ebb. She tried to blink back her tears, but they spilled down her cheeks despite her efforts and she wiped them away, annoyed at her weakness. "If we are important, why are you not with us?" she asked, unable to keep her chin from quivering. "You are always at the river."

"It's not that I don't want to spend time with you, but there's a lot of work to be done and I'm tired."

"You do not read your Bible," Anna challenged.

"I know, but that's going to change. When I'm not so tired . . ."

"When will that be?" Anna interrupted.

Erik didn't answer. He folded his arms across his chest as he searched for something to say. "I don't know, but soon," he finally declared.

Anna held his gaze. "When winter comes it will be too late," she said woodenly. She felt empty and didn't want to argue any longer.

The fire needed tending, so she turned her back on Erik and crossed the yard to a small stack of wood she had gathered.

Erik watched as Anna lifted the ax and began chopping firewood into smaller chunks. *I should be doing that,* he thought, but he couldn't bring himself to say or do anything. He couldn't believe what Anna had accused him of. How could things get so bad? How could she believe he wouldn't care for her? He worked hard to make a better life for them. His anger began to build once more as he considered her accusations.

He stormed into the forest, not conscious of where he was heading, only knowing he needed to get away. After trudging downriver for several minutes, he stopped and sat on a log. A man he had seen along the stream before, but hadn't taken time to get to know, worked his claim. Erik watched him. After a while, his emotions calmed and he began to actually observe the man. Unaware of his filthy appearance, he worked diligently, first shoveling rock and hauling water, then shaking and sifting the sandy soil. The man had a single-mindedness about him that made him completely unaware of the world around him. He was so wrapped up in his work that he didn't even notice Erik.

As Erik continued to watch, an uneasiness settled in his belly. Was this man him—working mindless hour after mindless hour, thinking of nothing but gold? Anna had been right. Erik suddenly felt sick at the sight of the man as he realized what he had become. The unthinkable had happened—gold had become his god.

As the immensity of his sin gripped him, grief swept through Erik. *How could I have done this? How could I turn my back on the people and things that matter most? All for gold?* He covered his face with his hands. "Lord, forgive me. I didn't mean for this to happen. I'm sorry, so sorry."

He glanced up at the sky. Billows of dark clouds hung low over the hills. *Snow could be here any time,* Erik thought. *How could I have done this? God, what do I do now?* he pleaded in anguish.

Then he heard it deep within, the quiet voice he had come to know as his Lord's. "Trust me and do what you know is right."

Erik sat there a while longer before forcing himself to his feet.

He needed to talk to Anna and Iya, to let them know how sorry he was and how things would change—immediately. He took one more look at his neighbor and headed back to camp.

Iya saw him first. "Anna," she said quietly.

Anna took Luba in her arms and watched Erik draw near. The anger was gone from his eyes, and Anna cringed as she saw the shame and grief he carried.

Erik smiled weakly at Iya as he approached Anna. He stopped a few feet from her. "Anna, we need to talk."

Anna sat down and quietly waited for him to speak. Luba wiggled out of her arms and grabbed a wooden spoon from among the dishes, then sat down and chewed on it contentedly.

Erik sat on a stump close to Anna. He studied his hands a moment, then cleared his throat. "Anna, I've been a fool," he began.

"Erik, you . . ."

"No, let me finish. You and Reid are both right. I haven't been taking care of what's really important. My desire for gold has ruled me."

He lifted his eyes to Anna's and what she saw filled her with guilt. She hadn't meant to hurt him so. He was a good husband, a good man. She wanted him to know that, but she waited, knowing he needed to speak.

"I wish there was something I could do to erase what's happened the last few weeks, but all I can do is say I'm sorry and begin to do what I should have from the start." He paused. "Please believe that I love you and the girls more than anything on this earth, and if I have to stop mining altogether then I will." His eyes brimmed with tears. "I let you down." He looked up at the sky and let his arms drop to his sides. "And I let God down. I'm so sorry. Please forgive me," he ended abruptly.

Anna stood up and went to Erik. She cradled his head against her chest, smoothing his hair beneath her hand. "Erik, it is all right. We can begin again. You are only a man, not God. We make mistakes. I do not want you to stop your work, only do not live for it." She looked down at him tenderly. "We love you."

Iya stepped up to Erik. "Daddy, I am not mad," she said as she wrapped her arms around his broad shoulders.

Erik looked at Iya and Anna. "I don't deserve you, but I'm thankful God doesn't always give us what we deserve. He knew how much I needed you." He hugged them both. And for a few moments, the three held each other.

"Well, I better get at it," Erik said and stood up. "I've got a lot of work to do before the snow flies."

"Wait," Anna said softly. "I must tell you something."

His face lined with worry, Erik asked, "What? Is something wrong?"

"No," Anna said hesitantly. "I . . . it's just that I am going to have a baby."

Silently Erik stared at Anna as if what she had said made no sense.

Anna swallowed hard and said a little louder, "I carry your child."

"A baby!" Erik whispered, and a grin spread across his face. He gently pulled Anna toward him again. "A baby!"

Anna smiled and nodded.

Erik swept her into his arms. "When?"

"Late spring."

Erik kissed her then repeated softly, "A baby. Our baby."

Anna breathed a sigh of relief. "I did not know if you would be happy when you work so hard."

"Of course I'm happy."

"We are having another baby?" Iya asked.

"Yes, Iya." Anna answered kindly.

"Luba, did you hear? We will have a big family," the little girl announced as she lifted Luba.

"I'd say this calls for a celebration," Erik said. "Why don't we have Reid and Millie over? We'll tell them the news. Besides," he added soberly, "I've got an apology to make."

Anna nodded her approval. "Millie has taught me much. I will make biscuits with fish stew."

"Sounds good to me. I'll go and invite them right away." He headed toward their neighbors, then stopped and returned to Anna. He rested his hands on her shoulders and said, "I love you." Then he turned to Iya. "Come on Iya, you can come with me, but don't tell them the news. We'll do that after supper."

As Anna watched Erik and Iya disappear into the thicket, she marveled at how quickly things could change. Only minutes earlier, she'd felt hopeless and alone. Now her spirits soared like the eagle.

In the days and weeks that followed, Erik made good on his promise. He worked hard and, with Reid's help, quickly constructed a cabin, a smokehouse and cache, and a shed for their chickens. The house was bigger than the one they had shared the previous winter, and it even had two glass windows Erik purchased in Sitka.

With the cabin finished, Anna began moving in their belongings. She stopped and looked at the light filtering into the rooms and felt joy sweep through her. She'd never lived in a home that was so bright. At the beach, the huts made from mud and grass did not have windows, and the shuttered windows in their first cabin only allowed sunlight on the warmest days.

Erik came in, carrying an armload of blankets. "It is very good," Anna told him. "I could not wish for a better house."

Erik grinned and, humming a tune, swung her around in a slow waltz.

Erik worked hard building furniture for their new home. He didn't quit until he had a table and chairs for the kitchen and two beds, one for Anna and himself and another for Iya and Luba.

Soon after the house was finished, Millie came for a visit. "This is for you," she said as she held out a brightly colored quilt.

Anna took the precious gift and studied the intricate stitching. "Millie, it is beautiful! I will put it here," she said as she draped it across the foot of her bed. Anna took real pleasure in preparing coffee for her friend that day and in being able to sit down in her own home and visit with her neighbor. It was something she had dreamed of.

"This is a fine house," Millie said as she sipped her coffee.

Anna surveyed her home. "Yes, it is good and strong. We thank you and Reid for your help."

"I didn't do anything; it was Reid. And he was more than happy to do it."

"Erik said he will make better furniture after he goes to Sitka. He will buy material for stuffing. I am saving feathers for the cushions."

"He's planning to head down to Sitka this late in the season? The weather's already turned bad. The channel will be real treacherous."

"I wish Erik would not go," Anna said sullenly. "But he says he must." Anna shifted her weight and pulled at her dress. "Already my belly grows. Soon I will have no dress to wear," she muttered.

"How are you feeling?"

"Good. No trouble."

Millie glanced out the window, then back at Anna. "I worry about you. You're working too hard."

"I am strong and the baby is strong. You do not need to worry. We are good," Anna reassured her friend. She patted her belly. "But soon I will have to make a bigger tunic," she added with a wry smile. "Erik said when he goes to Sitka he will shoot sea lions and otters for furs." She stopped and gazed longingly in the direction of the ocean, momentarily forgetting her guest.

"What's troubling you, Anna?"

"Nothing. Only I miss the sea, the sounds of gulls and the barking seals, the waves pounding the beach. I used to sit and watch the waves come in and go out again. I never tire of it. I miss the smell." She closed her eyes, trying to capture the sounds and pungent aroma. When she opened them, she looked intently at Millie. "I will not forget. The sea will always be part of me."

"I know what you mean. I still miss the open plains. Sometimes this forest seems too close. I grew up where I could look across an ocean of grass. You could see for miles. I remember feeling so free there."

They were quiet a while as their minds wandered to days long since past.

Millie finally asked, "Anna, what will you do when the baby comes?"

"I will have the baby, no problem."

"But who will help you?"

"I do not need help."

Millie studied her cup. "I've never had a baby of my own." She looked at Anna. "I spent my life on a farm and have had a hand in many births. I seemed to have a way with the animals, so my father called me when it was time for a new calf or lamb to come into the world. Once I even had to give our old hound dog a hand having her pups. Momma and Poppa had gone into town and left me to look after my younger brothers and sisters. Anyway, when old Jewel started having her pups, she didn't know how to take care of them, so I had to do it for her. We didn't lose a single one." She glanced back at her cup. "I know I'm not an expert, but if you want someone here, I'd be honored to help when your time comes."

Anna smiled and took her friend's hand. "I would like that. When I had Luba, I wanted a woman to help, but there was no one, so I did it alone. It was hard." She took a sip of coffee.

"I suppose you're wondering why Reid and I don't have any young ones," Millie said quietly.

"Yes, I have thought about it, but you do not need to tell me."

Millie cradled her empty cup in her hands and studied it. "We always wanted children; it just never happened. When Reid and I were first married, we planned on having a big family." She forced a smile. "We both love children. We couldn't wait to fill our home with exuberant youngsters, but there were never any babies." Millie's eyes sparkled with unshed tears. "At first we cried and pleaded with God. We couldn't understand why the Lord would withhold his blessing. Then we became angry with each other and those around us. It seemed every woman had a baby except me. Sometimes I would look at a new mother and hate her just because she could have a child and I couldn't. It was awful. I ended up hating myself."

"I am sorry," Anna said quietly.

Millie smiled and took a deep breath. "Somewhere along the line, I found God to be enough. I'd still like to have a baby, but it's all right that there's just the two of us. I believe some things just aren't meant to be. And Reid and I became closer when I put my anger aside." She tipped her cup on its edge and studied the contents.

"Sometimes it still hurts, but we've had more than a lot of folks. We truly love each other. I only wish it hadn't hurt Reid's faith. He used to be a believing man, but now he says little about God." She stopped and thought a moment. "I don't suppose we'll ever completely understand why until we're with the Lord, but for now, all I know to do is to trust him." She patted Anna's hand. "Anna, don't look so sad. I'm not unhappy. I couldn't have a better husband, and we have much to be thankful for."

"You are very strong. I wish I could be like you. I know I could not trust like you."

"That's not true. God gives an extra helping of mercy and peace to us when we need it." She drank the last of her coffee. "I used to think it was important to leave our name through our children, but I've discovered an even more important heritage: that of knowing Jesus Christ. And I can do that by sharing what I know with others and living for him."

"When we came to live here, I knew only a little about God. Erik teaches me many things, but I want to know more." Anna smiled. "I think God gave you to me so I can learn."

"Well, I will tell you all I know, and the rest we can discover together."

"I would like to read the Bible."

Millie smiled. "Maybe we can work on that," she said as she got up, leaving her empty cup on the table. "It's time I got home. I still have some baking to do."

Anna waved to Millie and watched until she disappeared down the trail that led to her home. She felt a little sad as she thought of the hardship of her friend's barrenness. "God, please give Reid and Millie a child," she prayed. She caressed her rounded abdomen and was reminded how God had blessed her beyond what she had even known to ask.

Erik had spent several days chopping wood while Anna and Iya stacked it beside the cabin.

"Well, that ought to see us through the winter," Erik said, surveying their work. "Now I can make that trip down to Sitka."

The morning Erik was to leave, Anna wished she could keep him home. She always worried when he was away. "I am glad Reid is going with you."

"Me too. He's made the trip several times, and I'll feel better if I go with someone who knows the route well."

"I thought you would not go until spring?"

"Things change."

"I wish you did not have to go. Snow has already fallen. What about ice in the channel?"

"The inlet stays ice free," Erik said as he wrapped his arms around Anna and pulled her close. "Don't worry, we'll be back before you even notice we're gone."

"Will you give this to Cora?" Anna asked as she handed Erik the tunic she had made for her friend. "Tell her I miss her, and tell her about the baby."

"I will," Erik promised. "Now, if you need anything, Millie's close. She's been living out here longer than you and will know what to do if there's a problem."

"We will be fine," Anna reassured him as she picked up Luba.

"I wish I could go," Iya whined. "I want to see Cora and Takou and Peter."

"Not this trip," Erik said as he knelt and gave her a hug, "but next spring we can all go. I'll tell everyone hello for you."

"Give them a hug too," Iya said, trying not to pout.

"You can count on it," Erik said and kissed the little girl. He wrapped his arms around Anna and Luba. "I'll miss you," he whispered against Anna's hair. He held her tight for a moment then stepped back. "Well, I better get moving. Reid will be wondering what happened to me. Now keep the bolt locked. Do you remember how to use the rifle?"

Anna nodded. "There will be no trouble."

Erik gave her one more quick kiss and was gone.

Anna watched him through the window. "God, please keep him safe," she prayed.

Anna managed to keep herself busy while she waited for Erik's return. She picked the late-season berries and did some sewing, but the hours seemed to drag by. She tried to envision where Erik might be and marked the days on the calendar, hoping he would return ahead of schedule.

Often she sought Millie's company. The afternoons seemed more bearable when she spent them with her friend. Millie taught Anna how to crochet delicate stitches and shared some new recipes with her, while Anna showed Millie how to prepare some of her people's favorite foods and told her stories of the old ways. She showed Millie the native way to sew skins so that moisture couldn't penetrate and promised to teach her the art of tanning and softening hides when Erik returned with new pelts.

One day while Millie and Anna visited over tea, Millie spotted one of Anna's baskets on the shelf. She carefully took it from its perch. "This is lovely," she said as she examined the beautiful work. "Did you make it?"

"Yes. The women in my village made many baskets. The grasses on the bluffs above my home were good for baskets, but I cannot find any here. I would like to make more."

"I hear the Indians in this part of Alaska use the bark from trees to fashion their baskets."

"How would they do that?"

"I think they tear it off in narrow strips and soak the bark until it is pliable. They also use spruce roots. I've seen some of them. They're beautiful." She turned her attention back to Anna's handiwork. "But not as nice as this."

"Maybe I will make one from the bark of a tree," Anna thought aloud.

"It wouldn't hurt to try."

Iya squealed from outdoors and Anna dropped her work. With her heart pounding against her ribs, she ran to the door and yanked it open. What greeted her, however, was not what she had expected. Iya was gathered into Cora's embrace! Unable to believe her friend had actually traveled from Sitka, Anna stood in the doorway and silently stared at her.

"Well, are you gonna stand there all day, or are you gonna give me a hug?" Cora teased.

"Cora!" Anna cried as she found her voice and leaped off the step and into Cora's outstretched arms. The two women hugged each other tightly. "Cora, I cannot believe you are here!"

"In the flesh. It's wonderful to see you," Cora gushed as she stood back and looked at Anna.

"I did not know you would come back with Erik. It is so dangerous at this time of year," Anna said as she cast an exasperated glance at her husband.

"We couldn't talk her out of it," Erik explained as he wrapped Anna in a tight hug. "Mm, it feels good to hold you."

"This woman is a stubborn one," Reid added. "*No* is one word she doesn't understand."

"I wasn't plannin' to come up this way, but when Erik told me about the baby, well, I just couldn't stay in Sitka while you had that child way out here by yourself. My, you look wonderful. It seems pregnancy agrees with you," she added and indiscreetly patted Anna's stomach.

"I am glad you came, but Millie is here to help with the baby," Anna explained as she turned to her new friend. "Millie, this is Cora."

"I'm glad to meet you," Cora said as she reached out and took Millie's hand.

"I've heard so much about you," Millie said with a smile. "It's good to meet you at last."

"I've missed all of you," Cora said as she swept Iya back into her arms.

"You still have the boardinghouse?" Anna asked.

"Of course. A friend of mine is takin' care of it for me while I'm gone. I hope I won't be in the way here," she added as she eyed the small cabin.

"Never," Anna reassured her. "At the village many people live in one house. We liked it very much."

"Well, it's time we were gettin' on home," Reid said, his voice heavy with fatigue. He wrapped his arm protectively around his wife.

"Good-bye," Millie said. "It was nice to meet you, Cora."

Reid tipped his hat to the ladies and headed toward his place downriver.

Anna grinned at Cora. "It is so good to see you. I have a lot to tell you," she said as she ushered Cora inside.

"Now, where is Luba?"

"She is asleep, but will be awake soon," Anna answered as she took a closer look at her friend. "Cora, you look tired. You need to rest."

"I don't ever remember being more exhausted. Erik told me it would be a bit of a hike up the river, but I had no idea. Why, I believe I've lost a few pounds," she added with a smile. "I could do with a drink and a place to sit down."

Anna steered her into the most comfortable chair. "You sit and I will get you a drink," she said as she went into the kitchen. "Cora, you will have to stay until spring." She returned with a glass of water. "It will be nice to have you here," she said as she handed the water to Cora.

"I wouldn't dream of leaving before you have that baby. I'm here to make sure you take good care of yourself."

Anna smiled and sat across from her, still unable to believe her dear friend had come to stay. This time when she brought a child into the world, she would not be alone.

Chapter 14

$\mathcal{E}$ rik and Reid had been successful in their hunt for sea lions, and their first evening home, the two families feasted on the sea's provision.

"This is good," Iya said, ignoring the juice dribbling down her chin.

Anna nodded. It had been a long time since she'd tasted sea lion. "At the beach we ate this often. I have missed it."

Cora looked at her plate disparagingly. "I think I'd rather have a nice piece of beef or venison."

"You'll get used to it, Cora," Erik said as he took another bite. "It's very mild tasting. Now, seal is another story. It's good only if you make sure to scrape away all the fat and then soak it in strong saltwater." He leaned his elbows on the table. "We found plenty of seals and sea lions, but the otter are few. They've been hunted out. We didn't even get a shot at one." He took another bite. "We'll have to make a trip back to the beach and bring up the rest of the hides and meat. I figured I'd lay out a trap line once the cold weather sets in. The pelts we get from that ought to keep you women busy during the short days this winter."

Anna smiled ruefully. "We do not have enough work?"

Erik grinned. "I just wanted to make sure you weren't bored," he teased.

"I will teach Cora how to clean hides," Anna said with a wink.

"I'm not so sure I want to learn," Cora countered.

"I am a good flesher," Iya said proudly. "Anna taught me. It is hard, but you can do it, Cora."

"I've never been one to shirk when it comes to work," Cora said as she pushed her plate aside. "But I must say, cleaning out a nasty hide doesn't much appeal to me."

"Reid and I figured we'd do some fishing while we're down at the coast."

"Can I go?" Iya asked.

Erik glanced at Anna. "Well, I don't see why not."

"When can we leave?"

"I buried the meat, but that's still no guarantee a bear or wolf won't come along and dig it up. I think we'd do best to head back right away. What do you think, Reid?"

"I'm ready when ye' are."

"Well, tomorrow it is, then."

Luba shoved herself up off the floor, balancing on the tips of her toes and her palms. With a grunt, she pushed herself upright and teetered a moment before plopping back to the floor. In frustration, she let out a wail. Anna quickly picked up and soothed the toddler.

"Won't be long before that young 'un will be walkin'," Cora remarked. "Why, she must have doubled her size since I last saw her. Children grow so quickly," she said wistfully.

"I am growing too," Iya boasted, vying for her share of the attention.

Cora eyed the youngster. "Why, you sure have. It looks like you might of grown a foot or more," she exaggerated.

"Is that a lot?"

"That's more than a lot," Erik cut in, with a sideways glance at Cora. "I'd say an inch or so is more like it. But you are definitely sprouting up."

Iya grinned.

"Well, Reid, if we plan on heading back to the beach in the morning, I'd say we'd best get to bed," Erik said, stifling a yawn.

Cora stretched. "I'm afraid I'm worn out too. Where would you like to put me?"

Anna glanced about the room, uncertain just what to do. She hadn't expected company. "You sleep with Iya and I will keep Luba with me."

"That sounds fine," Cora answered good-naturedly as she gave Iya a quick hug. "You don't mind sharing a bed with me do you?"

Iya shook her head no and pulled on Cora's hand. "I will show you."

"It seems I've got a guide to show me the way," Cora said as she followed Iya to their bed. "Goodnight everyone."

Reid rose from the table. "We'll be goin' then. I'll see ye' in the mornin'."

"Thank you for dinner," Millie said as she followed Reid out the door.

Erik kissed the top of Anna's head. "I'm going to bed."

"I will be there soon."

Anna washed up the evening dishes and nursed Luba before climbing into bed beside her husband. Luba gladly snuggled next to her mother and quickly fell asleep.

Anna leaned against Erik. He breathed evenly and deeply. She liked the feel of his body next to hers, warming her. She always felt safe beside him. She closed her eyes and tried to sleep. The soft scent of spruce from their bedding smelled good. *When I replace the boughs with feathers, I will miss the perfume of the forest,* she thought. She opened her eyes to gaze out the window for a moment. Stars flickered through wisps of clouds in the night sky. Anna pulled her covers over her shoulders and snuggled deeper into her bed.

Thoughts of her people flooded her mind, but the painful bite she had come to expect didn't touch her. Instead, she felt a sense of peace as she considered her mother and father, her brothers, and Kinauquak. At first she didn't understand, but as she considered Erik and the girls, Reid, Millie, and Cora, she realized she had a new family now. Like Ruth in the Bible, she'd truly found kinship with these kind people. She was no longer an orphan at the mercy of some unknown god's whims, but a child of the one, true God.

She slept soundly that night without fear of the future.

The next morning, Erik and Reid left for the coast, following Iya who sprinted down the path ahead of them. They were gone only a few days before they returned with a makeshift litter carrying the sea lion meat, hides, and several fish.

"Looks like we've got us enough to last for some time," Cora said as she took some of Erik's load.

"It looks like a lot, but it's not nearly enough. I'll have to do more hunting."

Anna and Cora helped unload the packs. "We have much work to do," Anna said as she lay a large cod out on a smooth stone and began filleting it.

Cora worked beside her and proved handy with a knife. Cora noticed Anna watching her and explained, "Just because I don't like butchering, don't mean I'm not any good at it."

Anna laughed. "You are very good. We will have much meat for smoking. It will taste good on a cold winter night."

Cora glanced about. "Well, I just hope there are no pesky bears or wolves around to steal the fruit of our labors."

"We see them, but they do not come near."

"I hope the smell of this fresh meat doesn't change their mind."

"I do not think we need to worry."

"Hope you're right," Cora said, glancing into the forest.

"When we lived at other cabin, a wolve . . ." Iya started to say, but couldn't remember the word.

"A wolverine," Erik interjected as he strode up to the women. He reached around and planted a kiss at the base of Anna's neck.

Anna smiled up at her husband, then turned back to Cora. "A wolverine did steal our food, but Erik made it into a fine skin."

"Nasty creatures," Cora said with a shudder. "I had a run-in with one myself years ago." Still looking around, she finished, "I hope I never see one of those devils again."

"Don't worry, I'll protect you, Cora," Erik teased as he raised his gun and pretended to hunt for one.

Cora sniffed derisively and turned back to her work.

The days had grown much shorter. Mornings felt crisp and chilly, and the ground became soggy from frequent rains.

Erik added a room to the cabin for Cora, then fashioned a rocking chair for her so she would have a comfortable place to sew.

Anna had gathered enough feathers from butchered chickens and the fowl Erik shot to begin stuffing the bedding. She started with Cora's then did her own. Although she missed the fragrance of spruce, the luxury of feathers far outweighed the absence of aromatic evenings. She never wanted to return to the lumpy mats made of spruce boughs.

When he completed the work at the house, Erik returned to mining. The claim provided a steady supply of gold but no big strikes. Occasionally Anna joined him while he worked. She'd sit and visit while he shoveled rock and washed it through the rocker. Sometimes she helped shovel or cleaned the debris and gold from the screen. When the clouds parted and the sun broke through to dry the sodden days, she and the girls stayed and shared lunch with Erik along the river's edge.

Erik no longer hungered for gold, and Anna's worry that he'd be gripped by its call dissipated. For Erik, it had become nothing more than a way to make an adequate living, and Anna felt relieved as it took its rightful place.

Erik returned to reading from the Bible during the quiet evenings. Cora and Anna kept their needles busy while Erik read, only looking up occasionally when he came to an especially exciting passage or when they had a question.

One evening, Anna stopped her sewing and quietly said, "I want to read."

Erik set the book in his lap and looked at Anna. "Do you know any of the words?"

"No, but you could teach me."

He glanced at Cora. "It's not as easy as all that, but all right. You sit here beside me and follow along while I read."

Anna set her sewing aside and sat on the floor beside him.

Erik began, "Psalm 127:3: *'Behold, children are a heritage from the LORD, the fruit of the womb is a reward.'*"

"What does it mean?" Anna interrupted.

"Well, I believe God is saying that our children are a blessing from him, his reward, so to speak, for us here on earth. And we need to treat them as his gift." He leaned over and patted Anna's protruding belly. "And by the looks of things, he's blessed us abundantly," he added with a grin.

Anna ignored him. "What is this word?" she asked, pointing at the page.

"Behold."

Anna looked at him in frustration. "I hear the words when you speak, but I do not know which ones you are saying."

"Anna, honey, you can't learn to read in a day," Cora said. "And this isn't the proper way to learn. You have to begin with one letter then one word. It takes time."

"I don't know anything about teaching someone to read," Erik defended himself.

Anna sighed, "It is all right. I will listen. Maybe later I will learn reading." She pushed herself up from the floor and sat down in her chair with her arms folded over her stomach. "You will read more?"

Erik turned a guilty look on Cora then returned to the passage. Before long, Anna, Luba, and Iya had all nodded off to sleep.

"Poor dears," Cora said as she lifted Iya up from the floor and carried her to her bed in the corner of the room. She returned to gather up her sewing. "I'm afraid Anna's working too hard and that baby's taking a toll on her. She needs more rest."

Erik hefted Luba onto his shoulder and carried her to bed. She whimpered slightly as he lay her down, but she stuck her thumb in her mouth and quieted as she snuggled close to Iya. "I've been a little worried," Erik whispered. "Anna hasn't seemed herself lately."

"Oh, I'm sure it's nothing to worry about. It's natural for a woman to be a little worn out. I just wish she'd do a little less is all. I'd better get some rest myself. Goodnight," Cora said as she retired to her room.

"Anna, it's time we got to bed," Erik said, gently shaking her.

Anna blinked her eyes and looked up at him. She nodded her head drowsily and smiled as she stretched.

A sudden gust of wind ripped at the roof, and a puff of smoke blew down the chimney.

Erik looked up at the ceiling as the rafters rattled beneath the blast of air. "Sounds like a storm. Maybe winter is finally on the way. We haven't had much snow so far."

"It is due," is all Anna said as she shuffled to her bed.

Winter did arrive. The storm piled snow around the cabin, and when the weather cleared it remained cold and cloudless for several days. A hard, crusty layer formed on top of the heavy white blanket.

Erik made an effort to work on his diggings, but the river froze over and the ground became hard. He decided his time would be better spent working his trap line, so he focused on keeping it in good shape. Trapping was excellent, and he rarely went out that he didn't return with one or more furs.

The weather along the Schuck was sporadic at best. Very cold air would sometimes be followed by warmer days. Rain fell occasionally, melting the snow and ice that had built up around Erik's equipment, allowing him to return to work for short periods of time.

Anna continued to make winter clothing from the furs Erik brought in from the trap line, and even Cora had taken to wearing the warmer, comfortable tunics, although the clothing gave her a more rounded appearance.

"I feel like a doggone bear in this," Cora said one day as she looked down at her overstuffed form.

Anna and Iya chuckled.

"But you are a very friendly bear," Iya jested.

"Well, I would hope so," Cora retorted as she opened the door and peeked outside. The wind whipped into the room. "Looks like another cold one." She glanced at the dwindling stack of wood beside the stove. "We'll be needing more wood before this day is done. Iya, would you give me a hand hauling some in? After we've got that done, we'd best get started on our Christmas baking. You know, it's just around the corner."

"Baking?" Anna asked.

"Well yes, it wouldn't be Christmas without my grandmother's sugar cookies." She studied the room. "We could put a tree over there," she said, pointing at the far corner of the room. "And how do you feel about inviting Reid and Millie over for Christmas dinner?"

"I would like that," Anna answered and smiled knowingly. She'd not forgotten Christmas. For weeks now she'd been working on presents for everyone and looked forward to watching their expressions as they discovered their gifts. She'd designed a birch-bark basket for Millie. It wasn't as exquisite as the baskets she'd woven at the beach, but she was certain Millie would like it. Erik had long admired the knife Anna had carried since leaving her home at the beach, and she decided it would make a fine gift. It had been crafted by a man from her village, who had carefully balanced its weight and honed the blade to a fine edge. She'd designed a leather sheath he could strap to his belt to carry it in.

Without complaint, Cora had been sleeping on an ugly, scratchy pillow. Anna had taken a piece of fine linen Erik had brought back from Sitka and made it into a pillow cover, then stitched an intricate pattern of wildflowers along one edge.

Iya would discover a new dress and a warm pair of mukluks for her growing feet. And Anna even managed to sew a small quilt for Luba. The toughest gift idea had been Reid, but when Erik mentioned that he'd brought some special tobacco back from Sitka, Anna felt certain Reid would appreciate it.

This Christmas she would be prepared, and Anna found herself counting the days, excited about spending the holiday with her friends and family.

"So, do you suppose Erik's got anything special planned for this Christmas?" Cora asked, interrupting Anna's thoughts.

"I do not know," Anna answered with a shrug. "But I do not think he will forget," she added with a smile.

Just then Erik swung the door open, his arms piled with wood, and tramped inside. "It's turning cold," he said as he dumped the wood in a pile next to the hearth, then pulled off his coat and hat and hung them on a hook just inside the doorway. "Got two more mink and a rabbit this morning. At this rate, we ought to have a good supply of furs come spring."

"Christmas is very soon," Anna commented casually. "Cora says we should invite Reid and Millie."

"Sounds like a good idea to me. Couldn't imagine Christmas without them." With a twinkle in his eye, he continued. "Let's see now, how many days is it?" He looked at the calendar tacked on the wall and counted off the days. "Only ten days!" he said, feigning surprise. "I wonder if we'll have a visit from Saint Nicholas this year?"

"Saint Nicholas?" Iya asked, her eyes bright with curiosity and excitement.

"He's the jolly little man who brings presents for little girls," Erik explained.

Iya grinned. "Will he come here?"

"Well, if you're real good, I bet he'll stop by," Erik answered with a grin, then picked her up and set her on his shoulders with a groan. "You're getting so big, soon I won't be able to lift you."

Iya giggled. "I am not that big."

"You sure are," Erik teased.

The spirit of gaiety rousing her, Luba squealed with delight and pulled herself up by her mother's skirt. Anna lifted her into her arms. "Luba will walk soon. She grows so fast."

"The older she gets, the more she looks like you," Erik said with unmistakable admiration.

"She does look a lot like Anna," Cora said. "But her eyes are more brown than hazel, don't you think? And I don't believe she's going to have her mother's wavy brown hair. It looks like it'll be straight and black like Iya's." She cinched her hood tightly about her face. "Come on, Iya, why don't we gather up some more wood? Then we can get to that baking," she added with a wink.

The time passed quickly, and the day before Christmas Erik disappeared into the forest with Iya tagging along behind. He returned just before dark and pounded on the door. When Anna opened it, she was surprised to find him dragging a small hemlock behind him.

"I figured we ought to have us a Christmas tree," he explained as he dragged the tree inside, "This looked most like the ones we used to have at home. So here it is," he said as he propped it up against the wall.

Puzzled, Anna asked, "Why bring it inside?"

"It's an old custom. On Christmas Eve we cut the finest tree we can find and bring it indoors and decorate it. On Christmas Day we all place our gifts beneath it."

"It's a beautiful tree," Cora gushed. "And I think it would look best in this corner." She walked across the room and stood, with her hands planted on her hips, in the spot she suggested.

"Looks like as good a place as any," Erik said as he tipped the little tree on its side and nailed a few pieces of wood to its trunk to make it stand upright, then set it in the corner Cora had chosen.

Everyone stood back to admire the hemlock, enjoying its rich scent. Cora shuffled out of the room, and a few minutes later reappeared with a small bag.

"I brought some decorations with me just for the season," she explained as she pulled out a string of brightly colored beads. She set the bag aside and admired the ornaments. For a moment, she seemed to be in another place. Looking up at Erik and Anna, she said, "Patrick and I strung these on our first tree." Carefully she arranged them on the branches. "These go on first, then everything else." She stood back and admired the shiny red droplets.

Iya reached into the bag and drew out a handful of handcrafted ornaments. "These are pretty."

"Iya, be careful," Anna admonished as she took the decorations from the little girl. "You must hold them gently."

"That's all right," Cora said. "I've been dragging them around with me for years. Don't suppose they'll break easily." She took a handcarved, wooden angel. "See, each has a string on it. You just tie it around a branch like this," she explained as she hung the angel from an upper limb.

"Can I do one?" Iya asked.

"Certainly," Cora said. "Why don't you do that while I pop some corn?"

Iya and Anna finished hanging the ornaments, and when the corn had popped, Cora showed them how to string it. After they had laced the plump white trimming on the tree's branches, Erik brought out a finely carved wooden cross and placed it on the top.

"I made this," is all he said.

Everyone stood back to admire their creative handiwork.

Erik rested his arm around Anna's waist and pulled her close to him. "It feels like home," he said quietly.

"It is pretty," Iya declared. "Can we keep it?"

"Only a few days. Soon it will wilt and turn brown, and if Luba has anything to say about it, she'll have it down before tomorrow," Erik said as he bent and scooped Luba up, stopping her headlong drive toward the nearest branches. The infant squealed in annoyance at the disruption.

"I think some Christmas carols would be in order," Cora said brightly.

"Christmas carols?" Anna asked.

"Carols are songs we sing at Christmastime," Cora explained. "You just listen and you'll get the hang of it. Why don't we begin with 'Silent Night?'" She began in a strong alto voice. Erik joined her, and soon Anna picked up the words and added her voice to theirs. For the next hour, Anna, Erik, Cora, and Iya sang one song after another. The joy of Christmas filled the room as they sang of their Savior's birth and remembered the miracle that had taken place so many years before on a dark night in Bethlehem.

Later, when Anna lay in bed snuggled next to Erik, she thought over the evening. "He is so good to us," she whispered into the darkness.

"Who?"

"God. He has given us so much."

"He has at that," Erik agreed and rested his hand on Anna's abdomen. The baby moved beneath his palm. "I'll never get used to it. To know there's a life inside you. It's a miracle. God's gift."

Anna turned to face her husband. "It is our miracle. Yours, mine, and God's," she said softly.

Erik pulled her close. "Life seems almost too good. Sometimes I'm afraid I'm going to wake up, and it'll all be just a dream. Other times I fear something awful will happen," he said, his voice growing tight.

Unable to think of anything that would put his mind at ease, Anna just rested her head against his chest. After a while, Erik's breathing became deep and regular, and she knew he slept.

The next morning Anna awoke to the mingled aroma of biscuits and coffee. She rolled to her side and looked across to the kitchen.

Cora stood at the counter slicing chunks of moose meat into steaks. Anna closed her eyes and relished the indulgence of a few extra minutes of sleep. Suddenly she remembered—*It is Christmas!* She opened her eyes and peered around the partial wall that gave them privacy from the rest of the house and glanced at the tree. No gifts. *That will change,* she thought with a smile. She looked toward the kitchen. Iya was meticulously setting places at the table.

Anna pushed herself up on one elbow and looked for Erik, but he had already gone. As Anna climbed out of bed, she left her sleepiness behind. It was Christmas!

"Why didn't Saint Nicholas come?" Anna overheard Iya ask. "I have been good," she whined.

"He will come," Cora said. "Don't worry about that."

"The table is done," Iya said as she skipped across the room to the tree and knelt next to it to lift the branches to see if she'd missed any packages.

"Iya, you'll just have to be patient," Cora said. She looked up to find Anna watching Iya. "Why, good mornin', Anna," she said cheerfully.

"Good morning. Where is Erik?"

"Oh, he said he had a few things to take care of," Cora answered with a playful grin. "Said he'd be back shortly."

The sound of someone knocking snow and mud off his boots came from outside. Erik pushed open the door. "Another cold morning," he said as he stripped off his gloves.

"Why don't you sit down and I'll get you a cup of coffee?" Cora said. "That'll take the chill out of you."

Erik hung up his coat and hat and took his place at the table. "Looks like someone did a mighty fine job of setting the table," he said with a smile.

"I did it," Iya boasted as she climbed into his lap.

Anna sat across from Erik and cradled Luba on her knees, allowing the infant to nurse. She looked down at the baby in her arms. "Soon there will be another to feed."

"You'll have to wean Luba soon," Cora advised. "Or she'll raise a real fuss when she's booted off the teat by another. She's not one to take something like that easily."

Anna sighed. "I know. Soon."

"Well, maybe we can tempt her with some of these," Cora said as she placed a platter of hot biscuits on the table.

Anna allowed Luba to nurse a few minutes longer then offered her a biscuit. Grinning, Luba shoved a large piece in her mouth and chewed contentedly.

"She's a good eater, that's for sure," Erik commented.

Iya gulped down her meal, then sat with a look of expectancy on her face while swinging her legs back and forth.

"Iya, you best find something to do," Cora said. "It's gonna be a while before any celebratin' begins. Anna and I have a whole meal to fix before Reid and Millie come by." She thought a minute. "Why don't you take Luba outdoors for a spell?"

Anna swallowed the last of her coffee. "It is very cold."

"A little cold won't hurt them as long as they bundle up," Cora asserted.

"I will keep Luba warm," Iya pleaded.

Dubiously Anna peered out the window and finally said, "Only for a little while."

Iya quickly donned warm clothing while Cora dressed Luba.

"I'll keep an eye on them," Erik said as he pulled on his coat and lifted Luba into his arms. "They can give me a hand with some of the chores," he added as he and the girls went outside.

Anna and Cora got to work. After clearing away the morning dishes, Cora placed a moose roast in the Dutch oven and set it in the coals of the fire. "I'm afraid I'm a little weary of moose. A turkey sounds so good. When I was a little girl, we always had turkey for Christmas dinner. It's just never seemed right havin' anything else." Her eyes misted. "You know, holidays are always such a mixture of joy and sorrow. Joy at what's comin' up and sorrow for all the good times and people from days past." Cora wiped at her eyes. "Well, at least I've got some sweet potatoes for my sweet-potato pie," she added with a smile.

"When you smell the roast and taste the bread and pies, you will not think of turkey," Anna assured her as she began kneading the sweet-roll dough. Both women worked quietly. When Anna thought she had worked it long enough, she asked, "Is this right?"

Cora poked the dough and when it sprang back, said, "Seems ready, but a little milk would make a world of difference. I wish we had a cow. Wouldn't that be something to have a cow out here?"

Erik managed to keep the girls busy most of the morning, and when they came in, their cheeks glowed red from the cold.

"Is it time to eat now?" Iya asked.

"No, but you can have a snack," Anna said as she set tea and bread on the table. "When you finish, you can rest."

Iya frowned. "I do not feel sleepy," she complained.

"Now, that's enough of that," Cora corrected. "We have a big day, and you *will* rest."

Iya relented and sat down to eat her bread and drink her tea, then she lay down for a nap.

Reid and Millie arrived just as Cora was removing the roast from the pot. "Merry Christmas. You're just in time," Cora said cheerfully, her face red and damp from the heat of the fire.

Rubbing the sleep from her eyes, Iya wandered to the front door to greet their guests, but before she made it, she noticed the tree. "Presents! There are presents!" she exclaimed.

"I believe Saint Nicholas visited us while you slept," Erik teased.

Iya knelt next to the tree and studied the many packages beneath it.

Millie hung her coat on a hook and handed Anna a jar filled with a peculiar-looking substance. "I brought some sauerkraut. It's my mother's recipe. In our home, Christmas dinner wasn't complete without it."

"Thank you, Millie," Anna replied as she took the jar and set it on the table.

Millie reached into a deep pocket of her coat and took out a small packet wrapped in cloth and tied with string. "And I thought you might like a little butter with your bread," she said with a smile.

"Butter! Where on earth did you get butter?" Cora asked.

"It's a sourdough's secret," Reid said with a hint of mischief.

Everyone waited for him to explain, but the redheaded Scotsman kept quiet.

"Well, you know you're dying to tell us," Erik finally prompted.

Reid grinned. "Well, this sourdough told me aboot a surefire way ye' kin have butter any oold time ye' want. What ye' do is take a set of caribou horns and choop them into pieces. Then ye' put them into a pot and boil them fer two nights and a day. After thet ye' set them aside a while and let them cool. When thet's doon, there'll be an inch or two of white butter restin' on top of the water."

"I don't believe it," Erik said.

"No, it's true all right. I've heard of it," Cora cut in. "But I've got to admit, I never had the guts to try it." She eyed the butter in Millie's hand dubiously.

"It really is good," Millie said. "I doubted Reid when he told me about it, but I figured there was nothing to lose, so I made some. It really tastes quite good."

"Well, I guess we'll find out," Cora said lightheartedly as she took the butter, emptied it into a bowl, and placed it in the center of the table. "Thank you, Millie."

Finally the meal was ready. Everyone sat around the table, and Erik gave the blessing. Anna had been right. Cora didn't miss the turkey she'd been so fond of while growing up but became involved in the good food and friends of this Christmas. They ate until they could eat no more. The consensus was that the meal had been delicious—even the butter.

After they had eaten, the women cleared away the dishes and washed them. Only then did they turn to the tree.

Iya scooted away from the table and sat beside it, eagerly eyeing the packages.

Erik joined her. "Well, do you think we ought to open them?"

Iya nodded heartily.

As everyone gathered about the tree, Cora said with a wink for Iya, "Seeing as there's someone here who doesn't seem able to wait, I suppose I can start." She reached beneath the tree and pulled out a small box tied up with a red gingham bow. She handed the package to Iya.

Her eyes sparkling, Iya turned the package over in her hands, then pulled the tie loose. The cloth fell away and Iya yanked off the lid. She gasped as she gently lifted out a delicate horse figurine. She turned it over and over in her hands, running her fingers over its intricate lines.

"I know you like horses and thought you might like to be reminded of them now and again," Cora said quietly.

"It is beautiful," Iya said, unable to take her eyes off the wonderful gift. "Thank you, Cora," she finally managed as she hugged the woman.

After that, gifts were quickly exchanged. Everyone exclaimed over the beauty or usefulness of each item received. Finally, only one gift remained. Erik handed it to Iya.

The little girl tore through the wrapping, and as a beautiful porcelain doll emerged, she seemed to stop breathing as she stared.

"When I was in Sitka, I decided it was time you had a real doll," Erik explained.

"She is beautiful!" Iya exclaimed. "But Mary is a good doll. You did not have to buy another."

"Well, now Mary has a friend," Cora interjected.

Iya smiled and hugged the doll to her, then ran to get Mary. When she sat down with both dolls side by side she said, "I will need to name this new one." She thought, and her eyes landed on Millie. "She has hair like Millie and blue eyes. I will name her Millie."

"Weel, thet's what I call a real coompliment," Reid said with a grin.

Everything turned quiet. Erik looked at Anna. "Oh, I forgot one thing," he said with a glint of mischief in his eye. "I'll be right back. Reid, could you give me a hand?"

"I'd be more then happy t'," Reid said with a conspiratorial air.

The two men disappeared outside, and Anna looked around the room at her friends. She could tell by the look on their faces they knew the secret. A moment later, clumping and thudding sounds came from the porch, then the door swung open. Erik propped it with his foot and stuck his head inside. "I wanted to wrap this for you, but there just wasn't any way," he puffed as he and Reid gave one more heave and lifted a sturdy little cookstove into the room. Anna covered her mouth to suppress a gasp. She'd never imagined owning something so wonderful. It wasn't nearly as large nor as elegant as the one at Cora's boardinghouse, but to Anna it couldn't have been finer.

"Well, what do you think?" Erik finally asked.

"It is wonderful! I do not believe I have such a fine thing."

"See, here. There's a compartment for baking bread," Erik explained as he pulled open a latch on the side of the stove, exposing a small cubicle.

Anna crossed the few steps between them and hugged Erik.

"I take it that means you like it," Erik teased.

Anna nodded and hugged him again before turning to the stove and running her hand over its smooth surface. "Now I will cook even better."

That evening they sang more Christmas carols, and Erik read the story of Christ's birth.

Anna's mind returned to the previous Christmas when she'd heard the story of Christ for the first time. So much had happened since then. It seemed like a lifetime ago. Anna remembered her reaction to the news of the babe—the Savior of the world—a living sacrifice for all mankind. She had rebelled openly and had been unwilling to listen to anything Erik had to say. She smiled as she remembered how he'd prayed for her, unintimidated by her defiance. She was thankful for his diligence.

When Millie and Reid had gone and the others were in bed, Anna lay beside Erik as she pondered the power of God. He had given her even more than she had known to ask. She didn't understand it all yet, and doubted she ever would, but one thing she knew, she could trust him. He held the world in the palm of his hand, yet had chosen to show favor on someone as unworthy and insignificant as her.

The baby within her moved, and Anna placed her hand on her abdomen. This child had been designed by the hands of the Creator of the universe. In his mercy and love, he had chosen to be involved in her life. Anna's eyes filled with tears. "Thank you," she whispered.

Chapter 15

$\mathcal{T}$he months passed, and the cold of winter melted into spring. Rain fell relentlessly, saturating the land. Anna often stood at the window and watched the steady downpour, feeling nearly as wretched as the plants and trees that drooped beneath the weight of the deluge. She longed for the sun's warmth to dry the earth. Most days Anna, Cora, and the children remained indoors. Visits to Millie's were rare. Cora's company became invaluable to Anna. Her positive disposition helped to lift the spirits of those around her, and she never seemed to lack for stimulating subjects of conversation.

Anna's lessons in embroidery and fine stitching continued, and Erik and the girls became the recipients of her loving labors. She also taught Cora native basketry and tanning methods, and as the weeks passed, new baskets adorned their shelves.

Although Cora had little education, she understood Anna's desire to read and attempted to teach her. In the beginning all went well. Anna quickly learned the letters of the alphabet and their sounds, but as they progressed to combinations of letters and word pronunciations, Cora found herself unable to teach what she didn't understand. After several frustrating attempts, both realized that Anna would have to wait until a more capable teacher could be found.

"I'm so sorry, Anna," Cora apologized one afternoon. "I wish I could teach you, but my own reading is poor at best."

Fighting disappointment, Anna answered, "That is all right. Maybe some day there will be someone who can teach me."

Cora patted her hand. "Why don't we plant some of the seeds I brought with me? If we start them indoors, they'll be sprouted and growing by time the weather warms. Then we can transplant them into the garden."

Anna smiled, eager to move onto something she did well. She

liked working in the soil and making things grow. She and Cora quickly set to work. First they built planter boxes out of used lumber and shipping crates, then they filled them half-full with mud from the river bank. After allowing the soil to dry for two days, they loosened it with their hands and pushed seeds into the dirt. They set the boxes in the light of the windows and each day checked for signs of growth, excited about the promise of new life.

Iya checked the boxes every day. One afternoon, she studied the soil closely, her nose nearly touching the soft earth. She let out a squeal of delight. "There is a plant! There is a plant!"

Everyone gathered around, and sure enough, a tiny green shoot had broken the surface of the river dirt. Iya jumped up and down and clapped her hands, and she began checking the other boxes. Anna smiled at Cora. It didn't matter that the plant had sprouted indoors—it still represented the first sign of the warmer weather to come.

While they marveled at the little plant, a rapping came at the door.

"I do not know who would come out in such bad weather," Anna said as she went to answer it.

A wiry little man, sporting a full winter's growth of beard, stood on the porch. "Good day, ma'am," he said as he tipped his hat and grinned, showing tobacco-stained teeth. "My name is Hubert Bitner."

Anna studied him a moment. He was filthy and rain-drenched but didn't look threatening. He wasn't the first miner to visit the Engstrom's. It seemed word had spread that a family lived along the river, and some of the lonely men in need of a touch of home found their way to Erik and Anna's doorstep.

Anna glanced behind the man to make certain he was alone. Since Jarvis's intrusion on Cook Inlet, she couldn't help but feel a little suspicious. Cora, however, always insisted on welcoming the unexpected visitors in, feeling that comforting the lonely was part of what God had called her to do. Although rough around the edges, most of the men came from solid families.

"Hello to you," Cora said from behind Anna. "Come on in."

Anna opened the door a little wider, and the man slipped inside.

"You sit right down, and I'll get you some coffee to warm your bones," Cora said.

Dripping rainwater on the floor, the man hobbled to the table, his eyes shifting warily beneath heavy brows as he scanned the cabin.

Iya left her dolls on the floor and stood beside the table studying the stranger closely.

"You go and play now," Cora said and shooed Iya away from the table.

Anna felt uneasy, but she sliced off a piece of cornbread for the man.

Cora set a cup of steaming coffee in front of him and sat down. She leaned on her forearms and asked, "You have a claim around these parts?"

"Down thet way," Hubert answered, pointing downriver.

"Been here long?"

He scrubbed at his beard. "Well, near as I can tell, 'bout two years. Like everybody else, I figured I'd strike it rich." He snickered. "Truth is, I ain't pulled 'nough gold out of this land t' buy me a good plug of tobacca. I hoped t' buy my own place, but seems thet ain't never gonna happin'. These days one season jest blends into 'nother."

"You could move on. Do something else," Cora suggested.

He pushed his tobacco farther into his cheek. "Ah don't feel much like it." He leaned forward and stared hard at Cora, his eyes red and watering from age and the cold. "Truth is, minin's kind of settled in my bones. Don't know what I'd do if I weren't scratchin' in th' dirt." He loudly slurped his coffee.

Anna didn't like the man and wished Erik had stayed home instead of insisting on working in the rain. She set the piece of cornbread in front of the visitor.

"Thank ya' ma'am," Hubert said as he pushed his tobacco aside with his tongue and took a bite of the bread.

Anna tried not to gag as she watched him eat; the tobacco juice dribbled from one side of his mouth, while crumbs of cornbread dropped from the other. He swallowed, and Anna wondered how he managed to not down his tobacco at the same time.

Then the wiry man closed his eyes; a look of pure pleasure crossed his face. "Mm, good, real good. I can't 'member th' last time I had anything so tasty." He leveled his gaze on Cora. "Your man down diggin' in the dirt?"

Cora chuckled. "The only man here is married to Anna," she said, nodding at her friend.

Hubert turned a surprised look on Anna, then glanced at Luba and Iya playing on the floor.

"He havin' any luck?"

Anna could feel herself growing angry, but she forced herself to smile. "He finds enough," she answered curtly.

"He better watch his back. A feller came through couple a weeks ago. Said he'd been down ta Sitka. Says they're havin' Injun trouble and figgered they might just come up this way."

Anna swallowed her anger. "We have no trouble with Indians," she said, wishing the man would leave.

Hubert eyed her sharply and grinned. "Well, you cain't never tell," he went on. "This feller told me them natives been murderin' women and children." He waited for a response, his face twitching in anticipation.

Anna forced herself to remain calm.

Cora moved uncomfortably in her chair. "Well, we've never had any trouble with the natives around here, and I don't figure there's anything to worry about," she said a little sharply.

Hubert wasn't put off. He turned his attention back to Anna. "I can see," he said as his eyes rested on Anna's rounded belly, "you're 'bout ready t' pop 'nother papoose. If I was you, I'd skedaddle out of here. Yer wouldn't want nothin' to happen to these young 'uns. Ya know what Injuns do t' babies, even Injun babies . . ." he said, allowing the sentence to hang in the air.

Anna clenched her jaws and forced her hands to remain at her side. How dare he sit at her table and speak that way? She glanced at a wide-eyed Iya who hadn't missed a word.

He's scaring Iya, she thought indignantly. She wanted to throw him out. Raising her chin a notch, she leveled a look of disgust at him. "I do not think Indians will make trouble here." She kept her eyes on his.

Finally, the vile little man shifted his gaze to the floor. He wiped his mouth with the back of his dirty hand and pushed himself away from the table. "Well, don't say nobody didn't warn ya," he said defensively as he tottered to the door. He pulled it open. "I thank ya fer yer hospitality," he said with a nod and closed the door behind him.

Anna shuddered and forced herself not to latch it.

"He's really somethin'," Cora said. "Gives me the shivers." She tucked her hair back into place. "But we never know when we might be helpin' someone God sent us," she added, as if defending herself for allowing the miner inside in the first place.

Anna didn't say anything. She only hoped she never saw the man again.

In the weeks that followed, Anna kept a close watch on the forest, unable to push the miner's dreadful words from her mind. She knew he was probably talking nonsense, but his warning weighed upon her and she kept Iya close to home.

As the days passed and the weather grew warmer, life abounded along the Schuck, as it did within Anna. She grew large and began to feel as clumsy as a sea lion out of water. She longed for the birth, and when the baby settled lower in her pelvis, she knew she hadn't long to wait.

One morning as Anna helped Cora clear the table, Cora stopped and studied her. "Looks to me like that baby could come just about any time."

Anna looked reproachfully down at her belly. "Sooner would be best." She smiled. "I think it will be soon."

Iya placed her hand on Anna's stomach. She waited a moment, and Anna's abdomen rolled beneath it. Iya's eyes lit up. In a hushed voice she said, "He is awake. Do you think he will come today?"

Anna shrugged her shoulders. "I do not know. Maybe. I will tell you when it is time."

"Millie made me promise to send for her if anything happens," Cora said as she slipped a dish into a bucket of warm, sudsy water.

Anna shuffled to the window and looked at the green clearing about their house. The sun warmed the trees and wildflowers. "I think a walk would be good," she said as she glanced at the cloudless sky. "There is no rain today."

"Oh, I don't know," Cora cautioned. "If you're ready to start laborin', I'm not sure that's such a good idea."

Anna laughed. "The baby will not fall out. We will eat lunch with Erik. It is good to walk. I like to watch the river when it is full and wild in the spring."

"Okay, but I'm not lettin' you go by yourself."

"I will carry Luba," Iya offered.

Anna smiled at Iya and nodded her permission.

After the dishes were done and the cabin tidied, Anna took a chunk of leftover moose roast and sliced it into thick slabs. She placed them in a basket with several pieces of bread.

Cora added sliced johnnycake. "It looks like we've got everything," she said as she slipped a drinking mug in beside the food and tucked the basket under her arm.

When Erik saw them, he stopped his work to watch as they carefully made their way down the bank. He wiped the sweat from his brow with a kerchief and sat on a large rock along the water's edge. "Good to see you," he called out. "I could use a break. My stomach's been grumbling for a good hour."

"We brought meat and bread," Anna said as Erik helped her settle on the rock beside him.

"Sounds good."

Cora pulled out two pieces of bread, slapped a slice of meat between them, and handed the sandwich to Erik. "Eat hardy. A workin' man's got to keep up his strength."

Cora offered Anna one. Anna looked at the sandwich doubtfully. "I am not hungry."

"I am," Iya said and took the meat and bread from Cora.

Cora eyed Anna warily. "You feelin' all right?"

Anna smiled and looked out over the river. "I am fine."

Cora gave Anna a questioning look, then hefted Luba out of her pack and handed the little girl a piece of bread. Luba crushed it between her fingers and shoved a hunk into her mouth. "Don't be such a hog," Cora reprimanded the girl playfully. "You try to eat too much and you'll choke."

Anna felt an ache in her lower back. She rubbed at her back and changed position, trying to ease the discomfort.

Erik looked at her with concern. "Are you sure you're all right?"

"I am fine. The baby is too big."

"Anna said the baby may come soon," Iya announced.

"By the looks of things, I'd say she's right," Erik said with a grin.

Although she felt uncomfortable, Anna remained perched on her rock. The sound of the turbulent water renewed her, and the sun against her skin warmed her. She looked at the top of a nearby hemlock and spotted two eagles soaring high above it. Silently she watched them as they glided across the sky.

"They say eagles mate for life," Erik commented.

Anna watched as the pair flew above the trees and out of sight. "They are beautiful," she said softly and turned her attention to the forest around them. It seemed life had bloomed overnight. Birds fed their young. The ducks and geese had returned to the quiet pools along the edge of the river, where they ferociously defended their nests. She remembered seeing a family of otters playing along the shallows only a few days before. She tipped her head back and allowed the sun to warm her face. She sat for a while with her eyes closed, then looked back at the river and thought how good it would feel to dangle her feet in the cool stream. She slipped off her shoes, and just as she was about to dip her feet in the cold water Erik asked, "What're you doing?"

"I want to feel the river," she answered and plunged her feet into the swift stream. Immediately the cold penetrated her skin and shot up her legs. With a gasp, she quickly withdrew her feet from the frigid water.

Erik laughed. "Just because that sun feels warm doesn't mean the river is. It'll stay ice cold long into summer."

Sheepishly Anna said, "It feels so warm, I forgot." She leaned back and yawned. "The sun makes me sleepy."

"I'd better get back to work," Erik said as he pushed himself to his feet. He took Anna's hand and helped her up. "I think a nap might do you some good."

Anna nodded.

Erik kissed her. "I'll see you later," he said and headed back to his shaker.

Anna returned to the house with Cora and the girls. All she could think of was bed. "I do not know why I am so tired," she told Cora.

"Well, don't worry about the why, just get yourself into bed and rest," Cora said matter-of-factly.

Anna nodded and shuffled across the floor. The pressure against her pelvis sent slivers of pain down the tops of her legs. *It will feel good to lay down,* she thought as she sat on her mattress and swung her feet onto the bed. She rested her head on her pillow and almost immediately fell asleep.

Some time later, she struggled awake. In the quiet she heard the steady ticking of the clock. Anna forced her eyes open and looked around her. Cora slept in her chair with her chin resting on her chest and a book in her lap. Iya and Luba lay cuddled close together on their bed. Anna wondered how long she'd been asleep. The sun no longer slanted through the windows and the house felt chilled.

I should get up, she thought as she rolled to her back and stared at the rough hewn beams angled across the ceiling. Relishing the quiet, she lay a while and closed her eyes, trying to return to the world of sleep.

A deep ache settled across her back and slowly wrapped itself around her abdomen. Anna tried to ignore the pain, but it increased and nudged her fully awake. She'd felt this before. She smiled. A new life would soon join them.

Anna couldn't remain in bed. She got up quietly and walked to the window to gaze out on the clearing. Sunlight still brightened the spring flowers that had pushed their way through the moss. Velvet petals in shades of yellow, blue, and red basked in the last rays of the day.

There is no better time to be born, Anna thought as she rested her hands on her stomach.

"You're up," Cora murmured. "What time is it?"

Anna looked at the clock, but it was in the shadows and she couldn't read it. "It is time to begin supper."

Cora blinked her eyes and glanced at the window. "Looks like it's long past that. I don't know what happened to me. One minute I was reading and the next . . ." She shrugged her shoulders.

"I will start dinner," Anna said, but another contraction stopped her.

Cora yawned again. "I feel so lazy. Why, I don't believe the eggs were even collected today."

Iya wandered into the center of the room and leaned against Cora's legs. "I will get the eggs," she said drowsily and wandered toward the door. Still not completely awake, she stood in front of it for a moment, staring at the boards as if not recognizing them, then she pulled it open and stepped outside. A moment later, her cries carried into the cabin. Her face streaked with tears, Iya reappeared, holding up her index finger. "The chicken would not give me her egg. She fluffed up her feathers and bit me," Iya whined.

"Well, I'll be," Cora said with a smile.

Iya stared at Cora in shock. Clearly this was not what she had expected to hear.

"I bet one of those hens is settin'. Why, in a few weeks, she'll present us with a batch of new chicks." She looked at Iya. "She wasn't mad at you, hon. She's just protectin' her young 'uns."

Iya's frown transformed into a smile. "We will have more baby chickens?"

"That's right. Until those eggs hatch, we need to leave that hen to herself."

A strong contraction surprised Anna, nearly doubling her over. A moan slipped from her lips.

Cora looked at Anna and hurried to her side. "Are you all right?"

Anna tried to smile and took a slow, deep breath. "Yes." She took another breath. "I was not going to say anything until after supper, but the baby seems in a bigger hurry." The contraction eased and Anna straightened and smiled.

"It's time?"

Anna nodded.

"Well, you better sit down," Cora instructed, steering Anna toward the nearest chair.

"I am fine," Anna tried to reassure her.

"Well fine or not, you're taking it easy."

Anna looked at her, incredulous. She knew what to do. Cora did not. Irritably she snapped, "I know how to have a baby."

Taken back, Cora stared at Anna a moment. She seemed to be fighting with herself and finally said, "You're right. I'm sorry. I do have a habit of taking over. You do what you think is best."

Immediately Anna felt bad for losing her temper. "Maybe I will sit down," she said and allowed Cora to guide her to a chair. She smiled up at her friend. "Thank you. I am sorry. I am glad you are here. When the baby comes, I will need you."

Cora relaxed. "Do you want me to get Erik?"

"No, he will come for supper soon. There is time enough."

Cora tied an apron around her waist. "Well, we best get to it. He's gonna be mighty hungry when he comes in," she said and began slicing carrots and potatoes into a skillet.

Iya set the places on the table while Luba began to cry. Anna stood up to get the baby, but another contraction stopped her. She sat back down. "Iya, would you take care of Luba?" she asked weakly.

Iya looked at the baby dolefully. "Luba always cries," she complained.

"Iya, all babies cry. Luba does not cry too much," Anna said kindly.

Iya stomped across the room, picked the baby up from the floor, and carried her to the nearest chair, where she plopped down and tried to soothe the infant.

Cora watched Anna with concern. "I wish Erik would get home," she fretted.

Anna tried to smile, hoping her unruffled appearance would calm Cora, but another contraction hit, this one stronger than the last. Anna did her best to disguise her discomfort. When it passed, she said, "Luba took a long time to be born, but I think this one will be here much faster."

Erik knocked the mud off his boots and opened the door.

"Mm, something sure smells good," he said as he hung his coat up. He crossed the room and bent down to kiss Anna. "You look a little flushed. You feeling all right?"

"Anna is having the baby," Iya declared.

"Iya," Anna shushed her sister.

"You're having the baby?" Erik asked, his nonchalance of a moment before gone.

Anna smiled and nodded.

"How soon? Are the pains close together? Are you hurtin'?" Erik's words tumbled from his mouth.

Cora laughed. "And I thought I was a greenhorn. Calm down, Erik. It's not her first, you know. Babies come in their own time. You can't rush them."

As another pain cut through her, Anna gripped the edge of her chair. She tried to relax and when the pain finally passed said, "I do not think this one will take long."

"You haven't been laborin' very long," Cora said, unable to hide her concern.

"Like you said, the baby will come in its own time," Anna answered with a grin.

"Well, I think someone better get Millie. She made me promise to send for her as soon as your labor started."

"I will get her," Iya volunteered.

Cora eyed the youngster dubiously. "I don't think you ought to be wanderin' around the woods by yourself."

"I'll go with her," Erik offered. "I won't worry with you here." He shrugged into his coat.

Iya set Luba on the floor, pulled on her boots and cloak, and stepped outside.

"I'll be back as quick as I can," Erik said as he pulled the door closed.

Cora scooped Luba off the floor. "Have you been abandoned,

little one?" she crooned, then suddenly held her out at arm's length. "My, it feels like you need a change."

After replacing Luba's soiled clothing, she set the little girl back on the floor and handed her a hard crust of bread to chew on. "I'll get your room ready," she said as she bustled toward the back of the cabin.

Anna pushed herself out of her chair.

Cora stopped. "And what do you think you're doing?"

"I will make some tea."

"I'll get it. You sit down."

Anna knew it would do no good to argue, so she sank back into the chair.

A few minutes later, Cora handed her a cup of hot tea. "Now, you just sip on that and relax," she said and headed for Anna's room.

Anna took a drink of the steaming brew. It had a strong bite to it, and she thought it appropriate under the circumstances. As it washed down her throat, she thought how good and warm it felt, so unlike the painful cramps that swept through her body.

Another pain crept across her back and reached around her abdomen, gripping her like a vise. She closed her eyes and tried to focus on something pleasant. Her mind filled with images of the beach. Oh, how she missed the sea. With one hand she gripped the edge of the chair, breathing slowly until the pain subsided.

"I've got everything ready," Cora announced. "Just like you showed me. Do you think you'd like to lie down?"

Anna nodded and handed her the unfinished cup of tea, then awkwardly pushed herself up and out of the chair. Cora wrapped her arm around Anna's waist for support and guided her toward the back of the cabin.

After only a few steps, another sharp spasm pierced Anna, and she had to stop. "Ahh," she moaned and gripped her abdomen.

"Oh, dear, I'm sorry it hurts so," Cora soothed, brushing Anna's hair back from her face.

Anna waited for the contraction to subside. "It is all right, Cora. It is good to have pain. That is the way. When I had Luba, it was much harder. I had no one to help." She smiled at her friend and squeezed her hand, then leaned on Cora and shuffled the rest of the way to her bed.

Just as Anna got herself settled, Erik returned with Millie and Reid. Reid remained in the living area, but Millie peeked in around the partition.

"Is it all right if I come in?"

Cora nodded.

"How are you?" she asked as she sat on the bed beside Anna.

Anna smiled. "It seems this baby is in a hurry."

"Is there anything I can do?"

"It is good you are here. I will tell you what to do when it is time."

Millie looked surprised.

Cora gave her a sharp look and took Anna's hand. "We'll do whatever you ask, honey."

Another pain began to build, and Anna rolled to her side, struggling to keep the agony from overpowering her.

The next two hours crept by. Barred from Anna's side, Erik sat at the table with Reid, where the two men talked of hunting and gold. Occasionally Erik pushed himself away from the table and walked to the window or the hearth. A deep moan came from the closed off bedroom. "I want to be with her, but she insists it's bad luck. Some foolish belief of her people. Men aren't allowed."

"It's joost as weel. A birthin' is noo place fer a man," Reid said.

"I don't know if I can stand this waiting anymore."

Just then, Cora peeked out. "Millie," she said, her tone sharp, "We need you."

Millie nearly tipped her cup over as she jumped from the table. She looked at Reid. "I'm scared," she whispered. "Just because I've helped deliver calves and puppies doesn't mean I know anything about delivering babies."

Reid took her hand and kissed it. "Ye'll do wonderful," he reassured her.

Millie managed a tremulous smile and bustled to the back of the cabin.

She stepped into the poorly lit room and hesitantly made her way to Anna's side. In the throes of another contraction, Anna seemed unaware of her. Millie took Anna's hand and held it tight while Cora held a cool cloth to the young mother's face.

The pain finally relented and Anna sat up.

"What are you doing?" Millie gasped.

"I must push," Anna explained.

Cora and Millie looked at each other.

"When the next pain comes, I need you to help me sit and keep my legs bent." She felt the edge of another contraction beginning. "It is coming," she gasped. She grabbed a small, smooth branch and bit down on it. Gripping her knees, she fixed her eyes on the wall in front of her, and as the pain built, strained to expel the infant.

As the spasm relented, Anna leaned against Millie. Cora wiped the perspiration from her face and neck with a cool cloth. "That feels good," Anna said and closed her eyes, enjoying the cool sensation against her skin . . . then she felt a new contraction begin to build.

"Ahh," she cried out as an explosion of pain gripped her. She bore down and labored to push the child into the world. It seemed the agony would never end . . . and then it was finished. Together, Anna and Cora reached down and lifted the child. Cora quickly cleared the mucous from his mouth.

Suddenly liberated from her pain, Anna relaxed and gazed at her son. Tears mingled with the sweat on her cheeks as she took the baby into her arms. "A son," she whispered as he began to wail.

"Oh, my, will you listen to that set of lungs," Cora said, barely able to speak, so overpowered by her emotions.

"He's a strong one," Millie agreed. With tears streaming down her cheeks, she cut the cord that attached the child to his mother.

Cora wrapped the afterbirth in the delivery cloth and set it discreetly in the corner of the room.

Millie helped Anna settle back in the bed. She wiped away her tears with the back of her hand and smiled broadly at Anna and her baby. "I've never seen anything so wonderful in all my life," she said. "He's a beautiful baby. Thank you for letting me be here."

Anna looked up at her dear friend. "I needed you." She gazed back at her son. Already he gripped her finger as he suckled at her breast.

"Can a father come in?" Anna heard from the door.

"Come. Come," Cora said, ushering Erik into the room. "Well, you've got yourself a son, Mr. Engstrom," Cora said, wiping away fresh tears.

Erik sat on the edge of the bed and stared at the baby in Anna's arms. For a long time he didn't say anything. "He's beautiful," he finally whispered.

"He looks like his father," Anna said quietly.

"He looks like both of us."

Anna searched Erik's face. "This baby is part of two worlds." She paused. "What will we call him?"

Erik cupped the baby's head in his hand. "I've been thinkin' on that. I'd like to name him after my father. What do you think?"

"You are from your father. It is good."

"Evan then," Erik said, his eyes brimming with tears. "Poppa would be proud of his grandson."

"It is a good name," Anna said, then looked at Cora. "Is it not right that in this land people have three names?"

Cora nodded.

Quietly Anna said firmly, "I would like his name also to be Patrick."

Cora's eyes brimmed with tears. "My Patrick would be honored."

Iya pushed her way through the circle of people.

"Meet Evan Patrick," Erik said holding the baby up so Iya could see him.

Iya stroked the soft, fuzzy hair on his head. "He is pretty, but he does not look like me. He looks like you."

Erik grinned and held his son up in front of him. "Welcome to the world, Evan Patrick Engstrom."

Chapter 16

*J*arvis chewed on the end of his cigarette as he stared out the window. He had been quiet all morning, contemplating some scheme, and now he stood glaring out at the street, his jaw twitching as he thought. Joe knew something was up and waited to hear what Jarvis had to say.

Still gazing out the window, Jarvis ended his silence. "I think it's time to head up north. Winter's long past, and there's nothin' to keep us here. Time we did some of that prospectin' you said we'd do." He turned to Joe, a wicked glaze in his eyes.

Joe had seen that look before and knew it meant trouble. "Why do you want to do that? There isn't enough gold to worry about up there."

"There's a lot of things a man could prospect for. There's more than one kind of treasure in this world," Jarvis answered with an ugly grin.

Joe stared back at his partner and wondered why he'd stayed with him. But it was too late now. Jarvis couldn't be reasoned with. Even if he left, Joe knew the man would track him down and one of them would end up dead.

"You don't care about gold," Joe accused. "It's that Engstrom fella you're thinking about. The one who left you and Frank and made you look like a fool."

"I ain't no fool," Jarvis thundered. "That weasel deserves whatever he gets, and I figure I ought to be the one who gives it to him." He stopped, turned his back to Joe, and looked out on the dirty street again. "Heard he's up north somewhere. Got himself a claim." He took a drag on his cigarette and slowly turned and stared at Joe. His eyes remained untouched as a slow grin spread across his face. "Never know, if we head up that way we just might happen upon him. Give him a hand with his claim, and his squaw. Heard he married that Injun. The man's stupider than I thought. Marryin' an Injun," he spat. "Never did understand why a white man would do that." His eyes turned colder. "If I remember right, she wasn't too bad lookin'. Wouldn't mind getting next to her myself." He laughed. "Take his claim and his wife. How would that be?"

"Forget it. There is nothing there for us—only trouble. The reports coming back are not good—no gold, and that man will not let you take his wife or his land."

"I wasn't gonna ask him," Jarvis asserted. "The element of surprise can work wonders."

Joe leaned back in his chair, trying to look relaxed. Life had been easy here in Sitka, and he had no wish to go traipsing off to some unknown river just so Jarvis could vindicate his hurt pride. Greed was the only thing that might hold him here.

"Seems to me," Joe began slowly, formulating his thoughts as he went, "we done pretty well here. A game of cards here and there has seen us through. Drifters let loose of their money real easy. I don't see any reason to move on. There's plenty of shiners to be had right here."

"Ahh, we ain't made enough to buy a chamber pot," Jarvis argued.

Joe pushed himself to his feet. "If you'd stop drinking up so much of it, we would have plenty."

"I don't drink that much," Jarvis defended himself. "If we made any real money, there'd be enough to drink ourselves to bed every night and still have somethin' left over."

"Real money? Is that what you want? I got real money," Joe shouted as he jumped to his feet and pulled open the closet. "I've been keeping this hidden so you wouldn't get at it," he said as he pulled a pouch from a small alcove in the back of the closet. He dumped the contents onto the bed. A wad of bills and several gold pieces fell into a pile.

"You've been holding out on me, you scum," Jarvis growled.

"I did not try to cheat you. I only kept you from spending all our money on booze and whores."

Jarvis wasn't listening as he lunged at the big man.

Joe grabbed his partner by the collar and shoved him against the wall. "Do not make me break your neck," he threatened through clenched teeth.

Jarvis glared back at him, then seeing the uselessness of struggling with a man twice his size, relaxed. "All right, all right. Let me go."

Joe loosened his grip and stepped back.

Jarvis slumped into the nearest chair and scowled at his partner. He picked up his cigarette and sucked on it, but it had gone out. He tossed it into a tin tray and sat glowering at Joe. "Okay, tell me your plan."

Joe leaned against the wall and crossed his arms casually. "We've been doing pretty good with cards, but you drink too much and throw money away on whores."

Jarvis grinned. "Gotta admit they got some fine fancy women around here."

"Yeah, well how fine are they when we've got no money left?"

"They're always fine. We'll just get some more money."

"And then what? In the end, you got nothing. I plan to have my own place someday, and nobody, including you, is going to stop me."

Jarvis lit another cigarette and took a long drag off it while he eyed Joe warily. "It seems to me, it was you who said you knew where we could get our hands on some gold. What happened to that plan, huh?"

"Can't depend on gold. It comes and goes. We are too late for California gold, and up north there's not enough to sweat about. You can make more right here in the saloons. Only a foolish man would leave a sure thing to hunt for a maybe."

Jarvis flicked his ashes and watched them fall to the floor. "So, what's your plan?"

Joe grinned. "We stay put. As long as people keep moving through, we work the saloons like we have been. When we got enough money stashed, we can split what we have and go our own ways."

Jarvis leveled his sharp blue eyes on the big native. "Who's in charge of the dough?"

Joe met Jarvis's hard stare. "I do not get drunk and sleep with whores. I will keep the money."

"How do I know I can I trust you?"

"You do not have a choice," Joe answered evenly.

Jarvis's face turned red with rage and he clenched his fists. Joe waited, ready to fight if he had to.

Slowly Jarvis seemed to relax. His gaze returned to the window. "What about Engstrom?"

"Forget about him."

Jarvis dropped his cigarette to the floor and ground it out under his heel. "Okay. We'll stay, but if you do anything that makes me think you're trying to cheat me . . ." Jarvis let the threat hang in the air.

Joe smiled and nodded his head, purposely casual. He knew Jarvis would carry through if given a chance, but he never intended to give him the opportunity.

"I'll keep my eyes open for that drifter," Jarvis continued. "Sooner or later he'll come through this way. Then we'll square up. I'll get my chance."

Disgust welled up in Joe. He'd be glad to be rid of this man, but for now they had a good thing going. He'd stay with him only long enough to make the money he needed, then he'd be gone. The sooner the better. Eventually Jarvis's rage would mean trouble, real trouble. In his gut, Joe knew he should leave, but he couldn't—not when there was so much money to be made.

Along the Schuck, the flowers bloomed in the warm sun. Evan thrived, and with each passing day he looked more like his father. His hazel eyes and honey-colored skin were all that set him apart. He rarely cried and nearly always had a smile for anyone who would pay attention to him.

Luba thought Evan was another doll and, more than once, the little boy had to be rescued from his sister's affectionate play.

One afternoon, Cora bounced the baby on her lap. "Evan is

growing so fast. I can hardly believe he's nearly two months old already."

Anna nodded and smiled at her son. "It seems the days go by faster and faster."

Cora cleared her throat and seemed a little uneasy. "You know, it's time I got back to my boardinghouse."

Anna looked at her blankly. Although she'd known the time would come for Cora to leave, she had hoped it wouldn't be so soon. She didn't want things to change. Life seemed perfect. "Cora, I wish you would stay."

Cora looked down at the baby, and her eyes glistened with tears. "I wish I could, but I've got a business to run. It can't go on without me indefinitely. Besides, Captain Bradley said he'd be by this summer. If I'm not there, I don't know what he'll think."

Anna smiled as she remembered the man who had captained their ship and then performed her wedding ceremony. "Captain Bradley?"

Cora blushed. "Oh, I know what you're thinkin'. We're not keeping company, but you never know."

Anna smiled. "I think he is a good man."

"That he is." Cora kissed the baby. "Anna, I'm real proud of you. You've become a fine wife and mother. You're more than able to take care of your family. You don't need me."

"There is still much I do not know."

Cora shook her head. "You know everything you need to." She lifted Evan up and nuzzled his cheek before hugging him. "You're growin' so fast, young man," she said, then glanced at Anna, unable to hide her grief. "You know we won't be apart forever. Erik comes down to Sitka real regular, and I expect to see you and the children."

"We will come," Anna promised.

Two days later, Cora was ready to leave.

Reid and Millie came by with a gift of blueberry tarts and a quilt Millie had made. "We'll miss you," Millie said as she hugged Cora. "You take care of yourself now."

"That I will do," Cora said good-naturedly.

Iya clung to Cora's legs. "Please stay," she begged.

Cora stooped down in front of Iya and kissed her tear-stained cheeks. "We'll see each other soon. Next time Erik comes to Sitka, you can come and visit me. We'll have a wonderful time."

Iya nodded and wiped her nose with the back of her hand.

Anna's eyes stung as she tried not to cry. It was time to say good-bye. Her chest ached as she looked at her friend. The house would seem so empty without her.

Cora held her at arm's length. "I'm gonna miss you, Anna. You're like my own daughter."

Tears leaked from Anna's eyes as she embraced Cora. "It seems I am always saying good-bye," Anna stammered. "I will never get used to it. I do not know what I will do without you, Cora."

"You'll be just fine," Cora said and stepped back. As matter-of-factly as she could manage, she said, "It's time to go. We've got a long ways ahead of us, and the sooner we get started the better. I will see you next time Erik comes south."

Anna nodded.

Cora gave her a quick kiss on the cheek and headed downriver.

Erik gave Anna a hug. "I'll see you in a few weeks."

Through tear-filled eyes, Anna watched them disappear. "Please, God, watch over them," she prayed, wiping away her tears. "And do not let it be too long until I see Cora again."

Clutching Anna's tunic, Iya leaned against her. "I do not want Cora to go," she said and wiped at her runny nose.

"We do not always get what we want," Anna said as she stroked Iya's hair. "God's ways are not our ways."

"I think he made a mistake."

Anna smiled. "He does not make mistakes. Sometimes we just do not understand." Trying to cheer Iya, she added, "Erik said he will bring gifts when he returns."

"Presents?" Iya asked, momentarily distracted.

"Uh huh."

But soon Iya's frown returned. "I want to see Peter and Takou."

"We will see them again," Anna promised.

Scowling, Iya tramped to the river bank and sat on a log, where she stayed for a long while staring at the river.

"Now, Erik, I don't want any arguing. You're stayin' here and you won't be payin' me a cent. You and Anna had me in your home for months."

"Yes, but you were a guest."

"And so are you here."

"But this is your business," Erik argued.

"I won't hear any more," Cora said as she pressed his money back into his palm. "Now, I've got work to do."

She glanced around at the dust and dirt. "A lot of work," she added with a sigh. "But first I better get supper started. Before I know it, I'll have hungry guests around the table and no food." She hustled off to the kitchen.

"I've got some business to take care of," Erik called after her. "I'll be back in time for supper."

Cora peeked around the door. "Six o'clock. Don't be late."

"Never late for your cookin', Cora," Erik said with a grin, then donned his jacket and headed for the door.

He headed straight for Peter's. Several months had passed since he'd said good-bye to his native friends, and he looked forward to sharing the latest news and swapping stories. Peter lived on the outskirts of Sitka, and it didn't take long for Erik to reach his home.

Doesn't look like things have changed, he thought as he approached Peter's tiny, run-down cabin. Two small windows peered out from between old, worn planks. The house had never been painted, and each passing season had bleached the wood a shade lighter. A plume of smoke drifted out of the tin stovepipe in the roof, and Erik felt heartened to know his friend was home. As he stepped onto the porch, the old wood creaked beneath his feet. He knocked on the door.

Almost immediately the door flew open. Peter stood there a moment in stunned surprise. Finding his voice, he said, "Erik!" and slapped his friend on the back, then hustled him inside. "It is good to see you. What are you doing here?"

"Had to come down for supplies."

"Have a seat," Peter offered, pulling one of two chairs away from the table.

Erik sat down and glanced around the cabin. The small, one-room house looked neat and clean, and except for a bear skin hanging on one wall, a lumpy bed in the corner, and the table and two chairs, it was empty.

"Would you like a cup of coffee?" Peter asked.

"Sounds good. Thanks."

Peter poured them each a cup and sat across from Erik.

"Is Takou still living around here?" Erik asked.

"Yes."

"I hope to see him while I'm in town."

"I will take you to him. He lives close." Peter took a drink of coffee and looked into his cup as if contemplating something important. Worry creased his face.

"Is something wrong?"

Peter looked up. "Maybe," he said with a shrug. "There is a man in town who looks for you. He said if anyone sees you they should tell him."

"What's this fella's name?"

Peter thought a moment. "I think he is called Jarvis. He is a bad man, I am sure."

"Yeah, I know him. And you're right, he is a very bad man." Erik set his cup back on the table. Rage seethed just below the surface. *I've had about enough of you, Jarvis,* he thought. "It seems the time has come to have a talk with Jarvis," he said with determination as he stood up.

"No. He will kill you."

"Is that what he says?"

"Yes. He has been saying lies about you and that he will kill you if he ever sees you again."

Erik smiled thoughtfully. "Seems he's gotten real bitter since our first meeting."

"What happened then?"

"He and another man kidnapped Anna and Iya when we were

living up on Cook Inlet. When I left him out there in the snow, I hoped I'd never have to look at him again."

"You do not have to."

"I'm not gonna hide from this guy, Peter. And if I don't confront him I'll have to watch my back, always wondering when he's going to come at me. It's better to get it out in the open and taken care of. Where can I find him?"

Peter didn't answer.

"If you won't tell me, someone else will."

Hesitantly Peter said, "He's usually at the saloon down by the pier." He paused. "We will take Takou and go together."

"No. This doesn't concern you and Takou. Jarvis is my problem. I'll handle it," Erik said as he opened the door. "Tell Takou I'll see him later." Before Peter could argue with him further, Erik pulled the door closed and headed toward town. He strode down the street and headed straight for the pier. "I can't believe that guy's still around," he muttered. "I didn't do anything to him he didn't deserve. What's he think? He knocks me over the head, takes my family and furs, and I'm just s'posed to leave him to it? How dare he hunt me!" Increasing his pace a little, he continued his tirade, "Well, this time, Jarvis, you bit off more than you can chew."

By the time Erik reached the saloon, he was angrier than he could remember. Recklessly he pushed the door open and marched into the center of the room. As his eyes adjusted to the murky interior, he looked about. "Jarvis. I'm looking for a man named Jarvis," he demanded.

There was a long silence, followed by a slow, deep chuckle. "Well, if it ain't Mr. Engstrom," said a voice from a dark corner.

Erik whirled around to face the speaker. He could only make out the outline of a man sitting at a corner table. The man took a long drag on a cigarette and the smoke swirled about him.

"I heard you were looking for me, Jarvis," Erik challenged.

"Yeah, I've been lookin'," Jarvis sneered as he pushed his chair away from the table and stepped into the light to face Erik. "We've got business," he continued, his cold, blue eyes boring a hole through Erik's head.

A chill crept up Erik's spine and he suppressed a shudder.

Joe pushed himself away from the table and stood beside Jarvis.

Erik glanced at the giant of a man and asked, "This your new partner?"

Jarvis didn't answer.

"You always need someone to help you take care of your filthy business, don't you?"

Jarvis bristled. "Who this is is none of your business. When you left us to die, Frank didn't have a chance. It won't happen again."

"You two made your choice," Erik countered.

"You left us with no choices," Jarvis said through clenched teeth.

Erik's anger grew. "You came into my house and took my family."

Jarvis glanced around the room and relaxed his shoulders. "A man's got to take his opportunities where he can find them. And you were a perfect opportunity," he jeered. "Too bad you didn't stay where we left you. What a sight—you sprawled out in the snow, laying in your own blood. You'd have been better off dead than married to a squaw." His hand moved closer to his gun.

"I would not touch that," a deep voice said from the front of the bar. Takou stepped up beside Erik, then Peter.

A look of disbelief crossed Jarvis's face as he let his hand slowly return to his side. With loathing, he looked from Takou and Peter to Erik. "Now you're not only married to an Injun, but you've got them doin' your fighting for you too," he taunted.

Erik smiled. "It's good to have friends. 'Course you wouldn't know anything about that," he added sarcastically. His grin disappeared. "I've had enough of you, Jarvis. Now, I'm a God-fearing man, but I can only be pushed so far. I'm warning you, stay away from me and my family, or I'll forget about restraint and come lookin' for you. I don't like killing, but if you push me, I don't figure I've got any other choice."

Jarvis silently stared at him.

"Did you hear me?"

Jarvis glared. Finally he said, "Yeah, I heard you. I've got better things to do than worry about some whining outsider and his Injun bride."

Erik held his eyes a moment longer, his anger seething just below the surface. He wanted to pummel this man, to leave him bleeding on the floor, the way he had been left in the snow, but instead he turned and walked out of the saloon. Takou and Peter followed.

Erik took several paces before stopping. He worked hard to compose his emotions, then patted Takou and Peter on the back and said, "Thanks, friends." He eyed Peter ruefully. "Thought I told you to stay put."

Peter grinned. "You do not always know what is best."

"Good thing Peter came and got me," Takou said.

Erik smiled. "Yeah, I guess you're right. I could use the help. I don't think we'll need to worry about him from now on. He knows when he's outmatched."

Laughing, the three men wrapped their arms about each others' shoulders and headed toward Cora's and the promise of a hot meal.

Chapter 17

$\mathcal{T}$wo days after his encounter with Jarvis, Erik left Sitka and headed back to Anna and the children. The Schuck had become his home, and he longed to return.

His first evening home, Erik shared what he had seen in Sitka and his visit with Peter and Takou. Anna and Iya listened to every word, anxious to hear about the distant city and their friends. Purposely, Erik failed to mention his meeting with Jarvis, hoping there would be no reason for Anna to ever know of their confrontation.

The years passed, and Erik continued to work his claim in good weather and his trap line during the winter months. He managed to make a meager living, and the Engstroms were content.

Two years after Evan's birth, Anna presented Erik with another son. They named him Joseph Erik Engstrom. He was a perfect blend of both parents. More short tempered and demanding than Evan, Joseph made his presence known right from the start. Erik often teased Anna that Joseph was his mother's son. He had dark hair and eyes, telling of his native heritage, but promised to grow tall and broad-shouldered like his father.

The family made regular trips to Sitka for supplies and to visit friends. Occasionally Erik saw Jarvis on the streets, but the evil man didn't seem to relish another encounter and, except for a sneer thrown Erik's way, ignored his rival.

The children loved their trips south. Cora was one of their favorite people, and, while staying at her home, they raced up and down the stairs of the boardinghouse and down the long hallway. They often convinced Cora to make visits to the general store and chased each other down the street while Cora followed. Once inside the mercantile, they studied the glass jars filled with candy and waited for Cora, who always purchased treats for them.

Visits with Peter and Takou were a must, and the two natives seemed to relish sharing their heritage with the youngsters. Iya's friendship with Peter grew, while Takou made sure to take Evan and Joseph hunting and fishing, teaching them the native ways. Both boys proved to be naturally skilled, and Takou often said he believed they must be part Tlingit.

During their visits, Anna pitched in and helped Cora just as she had when she'd lived at the boardinghouse. The two friends managed to make time for shopping and long chats over coffee, and Anna relished Sunday visits to church. If there were one thing she missed along the river, it was church.

One Sunday after services, while she and Erik walked back to Cora's, she said, "Maybe we will live near a church one day."

"Maybe."

"Do you think we will ever leave the river?"

"Can never tell," Erik said cautiously. "The gold won't hold out forever."

Anna didn't want to think of the possibility and quickly pushed it from her mind. She loved her visits to Sitka, but soon longed for home, even though farewells were always painful. Anna never ceased trying to convince Cora to join them on the river.

"You know I belong here in Sitka," Cora answered.

"No, it is that Captain Bradley you wait to see," Anna teased one day.

Cora smiled knowingly and didn't argue with Anna.

Along the Schuck, Anna's friendship with Millie deepened. The two women spent hours swapping recipes, sharing sewing tips, and piecing quilts together. Anna loved to hear stories of Millie's growing-up years in Nebraska and her family's trek across the prairies and deserts to Sacramento. Likewise, Millie always listened with interest as Anna described what her life had been like on the beach. Both women believed their heritage was something of value, something they needed to share with friends and family.

After Joseph's birth, Erik added another room to their cabin. Small as it was, their three-room home became known as the finest place along the Schuck. Passersby often stopped to visit and always commented on their house, often wondering aloud why someone would build such a fine place on a temporary mining site.

Each time the temporary status of their home came up, Anna felt an old uneasiness settle over her. She couldn't imagine leaving and refused to consider the possibility. This was home.

Aside from the occasional reminders of their temporary residency, life seemed perfect, and Anna felt certain nothing could disrupt her joy. But nothing remains the same, and the years 1879 and 1880 would bring great changes to the Engstroms' lives.

Since taking over the territory of Alaska in 1867, the Americans had done little to govern the land, and rumors of Tlingit uprisings began to drift up from the southern coast. Over the years, there had been small skirmishes, but now it seemed the natives were determined to make their presence felt throughout southern Alaska. Reports of brutality and terror inflicted upon miners and their families, and even in homes in Sitka, flourished. At first Erik didn't take the reports seriously, thinking them nothing more than the overblown tales of paranoid whites. Then one evening, after putting the children to bed, they heard a frantic knocking at the door. Erik sprang from his chair and flung the door wide.

Reid stood on the porch, clearly shaken and out of breath.

Immediately thinking something had happened to Millie, Anna quickly pushed herself out of her chair and joined Erik. "What is it?" she asked, unable to disguise her alarm. "Is Millie all right?"

"Yes, she's fine," Reid said as he glanced over his shoulder into the gathering dusk, "but I left her home aloon, and I've got t' git back. I only coom by t' tell ye' there's been a real bad uprisin' by the Tlingits. Guess they've goon plain loco. They've been killin' whites and burnin' homes all aloong the coast."

"Slow down," Erik said calmly. "Where did you hear this?"

"A yoong man just up from Sitka. He says he saw it. And things doon't look good. With no troops left t' help folks, they're in a real bad way doon there. Guess the local government's sent fer help . . ."

His voice faded and he shrugged his shoulders. "I doon't know what'll be left by time anyone gets there t' help."

"Come on in and . . ."

"No, I left Millie aloon. I'd be lockin' me doors and windas until things calm doon." He paused. "If they do."

"I don't think we have much to worry about," Erik tried to reassure his friend. "We've never had any trouble with the local Indians, and I don't see why we should now."

"Weel, I'm noot one t' judge unfairly, ye' know, but with human nature the way 'tis—ye' git one riled oop and the next thing ye' know, the whole lot of 'em are oop in arms." He paused. "I can't say thet I blame them exactly. This was their land before all of us coom bargin' in. If only folks would joost let the natives be."

"Change will come no matter what," Erik said thoughtfully. "There's nothing any of us can do to stop it."

Reid tipped his hat to Anna. "I've goot t' go."

"Say hello to Millie," Anna said.

"I'll do thet," Reid answered and was gone.

Anna pulled her cloak tighter about her shoulders and shivered involuntarily as she watched their friend disappear into the night.

"Is something wrong?" came a small voice from the back of the cabin.

Anna turned to find Iya and the other children huddled together, their eyes wide with fear. She crossed the room, picked up Joseph, and smiled at him. "Everything is fine. Some Indians down by Sitka are causing trouble, but not around here."

"What about Cora and Peter and Takou?" Iya asked.

Their friends had been Anna's first concern, but she put on an air of confidence and answered, "I am sure everyone is fine. Now, you get back to your beds." She handed Joseph to Iya and watched as the children reluctantly returned to their rooms.

Reid's words came back to haunt her—"They've been killin' whites and burnin' buildins'." What about Cora? Was she really all right? Were Peter and Takou fighting against the whites? Panic welled up in Anna as she returned to her chair. Scenes of torture and murder filled her mind, and try as she might, she couldn't dispel them. She looked at Erik, hoping to find comfort. "What will happen to Cora?" she asked quietly.

"Anna, this whole thing has probably been blown way out of proportion. I'm sure she's fine. And it wouldn't please her to know that you were worrying." He stopped and let his eyes wander to the darkened window. "Besides, she's got more spunk than the both of us put together. I'd fear for any Indian who tries to bother her," he added with a grin.

Ignoring Erik's attempt at humor, Anna said, "But she has never faced this kind of trouble."

"That may be true. I don't know. The last time we were there, things were on edge and I tried to convince her to come back with us, but she refused. She said she understood the natives, and if trouble flared up, she wanted to be there to help. Anna, she wasn't afraid, and I don't think we should be either." Erik paused. "She's not alone, you know. God's with her."

Anna knew Erik spoke the truth. Over the years, she'd watched Cora's unwavering faith and knew she was a strong woman. *I wish I knew what was happening,* she thought as she glanced at her children's rooms and fought her own fears. *If they come here, will they hurt my children?* She looked at Erik. "What if the Indians attack here?"

Erik drew Anna out of her chair, wrapped his arms around her, and held her close. "You worry too much. There's no reason to believe they'll bother us."

"I have seen them—watching from the forest."

"Yes, watching. Never hurting."

Anna stepped away from Erik and, with her hands pressed against his chest, said quietly, "When the trouble is over, what then? I am a native, and the children . . ." She couldn't finish.

"There's always been tension between the whites and the Indians. That isn't going to change, but I don't believe people who have known you for years are suddenly going to mistrust you and the children because of this."

"I hope you are right."

Later, as Anna curled up next to Erik, sleep eluded her. The night seemed endless as frightening possibilities played through her mind. Erik's sleep was also restless. She watched the window, waiting for the first morning light to penetrate the darkness.

In the days that followed, Anna and Erik spoke little of the uprising, but both knew it occupied much of their thoughts. The air felt heavy with tension, and Anna kept the children close to home, alert to any threat. Erik continued to work the claim but kept his rifle at his side.

Once Anna caught a glimpse of a group of natives as they skirted their clearing. They stopped for a moment to peer at the house, then quickly disappeared into the forest. Anna hurried indoors with the children and secured the door, where she waited for Erik's return, her heart pounding as she listened for any unusual sound. When her fear subsided, she chided herself for her irrational alarm.

When the days stretched into weeks and the uprising in Sitka still hadn't touched those along the Schuck, people up and down the river began to relax. Word finally came that a ship called the *Man-of-War* had steamed into Sitka waters and aimed its big guns on the natives' stronghold, threatening to beat the rebels into the ground. Realizing the futility of fighting against such power, the Tlingits surrendered. American troops moved in and quickly extinguished small outbreaks of discontent.

All along the river, stories of what had happened in Sitka spread—many of them creating frightening pictures. Anna wondered how their friends had fared and became preoccupied with their well-being.

One evening over dinner Erik cautiously suggested, "I was wondering," he began, "I mean, I was thinking I might go on down and check on Cora."

Anna's interest was immediately piqued. She set her fork aside and waited to hear what he had to say.

"We're in need of supplies anyway," he continued.

"I think it is a good idea. I will go with you."

"No. I'll go alone. We still don't know what's going on down there."

"I am going," Anna repeated stubbornly. "Millie will watch the children."

Erik stared back at her, his face painted with frustration. He sighed. "All right. You can come along."

Anna smiled and went back to her meal.

Two days later, Erik and Anna kissed the children good-bye and set out for Sitka. Although they had made the trip many times over the years, it always seemed new. Anna never tired of the wildlife or the contrast between the aqua blue of the sea and the sheer gray cliffs. During the early spring, chunks of iridescent blue ice floated on the water. If not for their mission, Anna would have enjoyed this trip, but uneasiness and concern for her friends tugged at her, and her sense of urgency destroyed any enjoyment she might have found in the beauty around her.

As they rowed into Sitka Bay, things looked fairly routine. Ships were tied up at the docks and anchored in the bay, although there were fewer than usual. When they came closer, Anna could see that activity along the docks seemed subdued, as did the town. As they walked the streets they saw some burned out buildings and several others with broken windows. Few people roamed the walkways, except for uniformed men who seemed to be keeping watch. Anna felt their eyes boring into her and wished she weren't a native.

"I do not like it here any longer. It is not the same," she whispered to Erik.

"No, it's not. Try not to let them bother you. They're paid not to trust people. Eventually all this will blow over, and you won't even be noticed." He paused and pushed his hat a little farther back on his head. "You have to remember, they were just at war with the Indians. Things don't change overnight."

Anna stopped and looked squarely at Erik. "We were here first," she blurted out. "Your people pushed their way into our lives. It is not wrong for the Indians to want the old ways."

Stunned, Erik didn't answer immediately, then calmly he said, "Anna, I didn't say that what has happened didn't have a reason, but murder is wrong. I know it's been rough on your people. I'm sorry, but there's nothing I can do to change that."

Anna glared at Erik, anger surging through her. They had never argued about the right and wrong of their two peoples, but that didn't change the fact that she was native and he was . . . not.

She turned away and tried to gather her thoughts. She wished she could find some justification for what the Indians had done, but Erik was right, there was no valid reason to kill. She looked back at Erik and her anger faded. "What the Tlingits did was wrong, but the outsiders are wrong too. We do not know that they killed people," she ended feebly.

"Well, that's what I heard. If we can find Peter and Takou, I'll be able to find out for sure. But first things first. Let's go find Cora."

As Anna and Erik approached the boardinghouse, they were stunned to find it no longer looked neat and tidy. Tall, spindly weeds had taken over the yard, replacing the profusion of flowers that usually grew there.

Cautiously, Erik walked up the steps. Anna followed, her mouth dry. Something was wrong. Erik rang the bell and waited. When no one answered, he rang it again.

Anna looked at Erik. "Where is she?"

His face creased with worry, Erik opened his mouth to answer when the door creaked open. A small, timid-looking woman peered at them from the dark interior. "What can I do for you?" she asked suspiciously.

"We are friends of Cora's. Is she here?" Erik asked.

The woman looked Erik up and down, then studied Anna. "What do you want with her?"

"We just want to see her. She is our friend," Anna explained, trying to control the alarm rising within her.

The woman studied Anna a moment longer. "She's been sick nearly three weeks now, but follow me," she said as she pulled the door open. "Maybe seeing friends will perk her up."

Anna and Erik quickly stepped inside.

The woman closed the door and, with mincing steps, escorted them into the parlor.

There were no guests lounging in the chairs, no fire in the hearth, or smells of baking bread or simmering soup. Instead, the boardinghouse looked dark and smelled musty. The shades were drawn tight to keep out the sunlight. The house felt like a tomb.

The little woman pushed open the door to Cora's room. "Mrs. Browning, you've got visitors." When there was no answer, she repeated, "Mrs. Browning?"

Anna's stomach tightened as she followed the strange little woman into Cora's bedroom. Like the rest of the house, it was shrouded in darkness and smelled musty and dirty. Anna peered through the dim light to where Cora rested on a stack of pillows. She looked small and frail. Anna took a tentative step toward the bed.

Cora's mouth turned up in a small smile. "Anna. It's good to see you," she croaked.

Anna tried to keep her tears in check as she looked down at her friend. Her plump, ruddy cheeks were sunken and pale. Dark circles framed her dull-looking eyes. Anna sat on the edge of the bed and took Cora's dry hand in hers. "Cora, I did not know you were sick."

"How could you?"

Anna pressed the back of Cora's hand to her cheek. "Oh Cora, I wish we would have come sooner."

"It's all right," Cora said tenderly.

"What happened?" Erik asked.

"During the trouble, some of the native children were separated from their parents." She stopped to catch her breath. "Several of them became ill, but we couldn't get a doctor to help. I did the best I could, but two of the little ones died." She stopped and motioned for Anna to help her with the glass of water on the stand. Anna held it up to her friend's lips. Cora took a sip and lay back on her pillows.

"Thank you," she said weakly. "It never occurred to me that I might catch what they had."

"Has the doctor seen you?"

"Yes. But he doesn't know what to think of it. Whatever it is, it just seems to keep hangin' on. It's in God's hands. I don't have the energy to worry about it."

"We will pray for you," Anna said quietly.

Erik walked around to the other side of the bed and sat down. As Anna began to pray, he took Cora's hand in his.

"Heavenly Father, we know Cora is one of your special people and that you love her. She is so sick." Anna had to stop and fight back her tears. "She needs you now. You are a powerful God, and we know there is nothing you cannot do. Please touch Cora—heal her body." Anna faltered. "We do not wish to say good-bye to our dear friend." Anna paused. "Yet your will, not ours. Amen." Anna looked into Erik's eyes, then Cora's. Tears ran in streaks down her cheeks as Cora smiled and squeezed her hand.

"Please don't be afraid, dear. There is a wonderful verse you must hear. Erik, could you read Philippians 1:21?" Cora asked. "The Bible is on the bed table."

Gravely Erik took the Bible and looked up the verse. "'For to me, to live is Christ, and to die is gain,'" he read.

Cora added, "Remember when we were talkin' about Patrick's dyin'. . . and I told you how the apostle Paul faced death? That he wasn't afraid?"

Anna nodded, unable to answer.

"Well, you see . . . it's like this," she wheezed. "I feel just like Paul. If I live, that is good, then I can go on servin' my Lord, but if I die, it's even better, because I will be in his kingdom." She stopped to catch her breath. "Do you see? No matter the outcome, we can rejoice. God has a plan." She smiled. "Now, stop that cryin'. Where are those children of yours?"

"We left them with Millie."

A look of disappointment momentarily crossed Cora's face. "Well, you give them a big hug for me."

"Why don't you do it yourself next time you come to visit," Erik said with a smile.

Cora nodded.

"Anna, I'm gonna' see if I can find Peter and Takou," Erik said as he rose from the bed.

"Erik, be careful," Cora warned him. "Things are better, but they're not as they should be. Most of the natives have been keeping to themselves and out of the town." She swallowed and took a couple of slow breaths. "From what I hear, some of them are still pretty angry. Most folks are keeping pretty much to town."

"I'll be careful," Erik reassured her. He bent to kiss Anna before leaving the room.

Anna remained by Cora's side until her friend fell asleep, then she quietly crept away and went in search of the woman who had let them in. She found her in the kitchen slicing onions into a pot of boiling water.

"I'd like to thank you for taking care of Cora," Anna said as the door swung closed behind her.

"I don't mind. She's a good woman."

Anna nodded in agreement. "My name is Anna."

"Name's Jane," the woman said, wiping her hands on her apron and holding her hand out in greeting. "It's nice to meet you."

Anna looked around the kitchen. It looked dreary. Hesitantly she asked, "Why is the house is so dark?"

Jane shrugged her shoulders. "Seemed no reason to open the shades. And the darkness suited my mood, I guess."

"Well, if you do not mind, I will open them. I think Cora would like that."

"It's fine by me."

Anna went to the parlor and pulled back the heavy curtains. She blinked as sunlight flooded the room, illuminating the layer of dust that had settled over the furnishings. Anna ran her hand across the top of the lamp stand and studied the grime that came away on her fingers. She dusted her hands off and went to the kitchen for an apron.

Anna spent the remainder of the day cleaning house. When Cora was awake, she made sure to spend time with her and managed to spoon a little broth between her parched lips.

When Erik returned, the main rooms sparkled, and a pot of stew simmered on the stove. "This feels more like home," he said as he walked in and settled himself in a chair. His face was lined with concern.

"Did you find Peter and Takou?" Anna asked.

Erik looked glum. "I talked to Takou. He said he hasn't seen Peter for weeks now. He's afraid something's happened to him."

"Oh no! Not Peter!" Anna exclaimed. "What will we tell Iya?"

"Nothing. Hopefully he'll turn up."

"Are the stories we heard true?"

"Many of them, but most of the natives weren't involved. Only a handful did any real damage. Still, they'll all pay the price," Erik added morosely. "Some have lost their homes, and they're all afraid to come into town for supplies. Conditions are pretty bad."

Anna sat on the arm of his chair and took his hand in hers. "Life is not always as we want it," she said quietly.

Erik sighed deeply. "That's for sure. How's Cora?"

"No better. Erik, she seems so sick. Do you think she will die?"

Erik wrapped his arm around Anna's waist. "I don't know. All we can do is pray."

A loud wheeze followed by a burst of coughing came from Cora's room. Erik and Anna hurried to her side. Erik bent over her listless form and helped prop her head up on the pillow. "Here, Cora, why don't you try a sip of water?"

Cora managed to swallow a bit. "Thank you," she whispered in a hoarse voice.

"Cora, what can we do?" Anna asked, frightened.

Cora ignored Anna's question and allowed her gaze to wander to the ceiling. "You know, it will be nice in heaven. I'll be able to see my Patrick again. I've been missin' him so. The Bible says there is a time to be born and a time to die. I'm not afraid of dying. Soon I'll be reborn into a life without pain or suffering. There'll be no death."

"No. Please, Cora, try," Anna protested.

Cora finally seemed to notice Anna. She looked into her young friend's eyes. "I will try," she whispered as she closed her eyes.

All through the night, Anna sat next to Cora's bed and prayed. She couldn't bear the thought of her leaving this earth. "Please God, save Cora," was Anna's continuous prayer. In the small hours of the morning, she couldn't keep her eyes open and fell into a restless sleep.

"Well, you couldn't even stay up with me," Cora teased.

Anna sat up and stared into the lucid eyes of her friend. "Cora? Are you all right?"

"Well, I've felt better, but not recently. I think I'm gonna make it, though," she said with a smile.

Anna broke into a big grin, reached across the bed, and hugged her friend. "I am so glad. I prayed so hard."

"It seems your plans and God's are real similar. You know, I even feel a little hungry. Do you think you could find something for me to eat?"

Anna nodded and hurried to the kitchen.

Anna and Erik remained at Cora's until she completely recovered. There was still no word of Peter, but they couldn't delay their departure longer—they needed to get back to the children.

The day before they were to leave, Anna discovered Jane feeding a small native child at the back door.

"Jane, who is that?" she asked.

The small, frail woman looked over her shoulder guiltily. "Just one of the mites who was orphaned during the uprising."

Anna looked into the sorrowful, suspicious face of a little girl. "What is your name?" she asked.

The girl said nothing.

"She never talks," Jane explained.

"Does she have anyone?"

"Not so far as I know. Just figured I'd keep on feedin' her until someone took her in."

"Does Cora know?"

"No. I didn't say nothin' with her bein' so sick. I know she wouldn't mind, though."

As Anna stared at the little girl, an idea began to form. "I'll be right back," she said and sprinted out of the room.

She found Cora and Erik in the parlor. "Cora, did you know Jane has been caring for a little orphan girl?"

"No, but I'm not surprised. There are many children without families now. Poor things."

Anna turned to Erik. "Erik, I was thinking," she paused. "Millie and Reid can't have children. Maybe they would like this little girl?"

Erik glanced at Cora then looked back at Anna. "Oh, I don't know, Anna. We can't say what they'll do."

"Well, we could take her with us and see."

"What happens if they don't want her?"

"I would want her."

"I'm not surprised," Erik said with a grin. He thought a moment. "You sure she has no family?"

"Jane says not, and she hears most of what goes on in town. She ought to know."

"Reid and Millie would make fine parents," he said half to himself. A wry smile crept across his face. "I'll check in town to see if she has any family, and if not, I suppose it would be all right."

"Oh, thank you, Erik," Anna gushed as she threw her arms around her husband's neck. She looked up at the ceiling. "Thank you, Father. I've been praying for Millie so long now. I know she will be so happy."

Chapter 18

$\mathcal{T}$he little girl never spoke during the journey home. She watched Erik and Anna with a mixture of fear and need but was never able to reach out to either of them.

Their last evening on the trail, Erik and Anna climbed beneath their blankets for the night. Anna whispered, "Millie will be good for her."

Erik studied the sleeping child. "She has a lot of love to give, and this one's going to need an abundance it seems."

Anna smiled as she thought of introducing the child to Reid and Millie. "They have wanted a child for so long," she said as she snuggled closer to Erik.

"Yeah." Erik responded doubtfully. "I hope we're doing the right thing."

"I know it is right. She is a gift from God to Reid and Millie," Anna reassured him.

Late the following day, Erik, Anna, and their little charge approached Reid and Millie's home. Tired and anxious, Anna was glad to see the smoke rising from their chimney. Erik walked up to the door while Anna waited on the steps with the little girl.

But before Erik could knock, Iya rushed outside and caught him in an exuberant embrace. The next thing Anna knew, all the children were crowded around demanding their attention.

Millie emerged with the bright glow of the cookstove on her cheeks. "Welcome home. It's good to see you," she said as she hugged Anna. She glanced down at the native girl who was trying to disappear behind Anna. "And who do we have here?" she asked kindly.

Before Anna could answer, Reid filled the doorway. "Well, I thought I heard soom commotion oot here," he said jovially. "Did ye' have a good trip?" he asked as he patted Erik's shoulder.

"Real fine," Erik answered.

"How were things doon in Sitka?"

"It seems the government has everything under control, but it's just not the same."

"I'm sorry t' hear thet."

"It'll all iron out in the end, I expect."

Anna stepped onto the porch, leading the little girl by the hand. Now that the moment had arrived, butterflies stirred in her stomach and her mouth felt dry. What if she'd been mistaken? What if Reid and Millie were unwilling to care for this child? She swallowed past the lump in her throat and hesitantly said, "Millie, Reid, we brought a friend with us." She nudged the girl forward. "We do not know her name. She won't talk. Her parents were killed in the uprising, and she has no one." Anna paused and waited for their reaction. Millie's eyes softened, but Reid's expression was guarded. Anna continued. "She needs parents . . ." She cleared her throat. "We thought that maybe you . . ."

Before she could finish, Millie moved a step closer to the child and knelt in front of her. She placed her hands on the youngster's shoulders and looked into her mournful eyes. "I've been waiting for you," she said, her eyes brimming with tears. She looked at Reid. "God has answered our prayers."

Reid's expression was still cautious, but as he looked into Millie's joy-filled face and then into the sad eyes of the little girl, his look softened. "Weel, I guess we've goot us a yoong 'un," he said in a husky voice.

"What should we call you?" Millie asked.

The little girl blinked her dark brown eyes, and a tear slipped from one corner. She looked hard at Millie and said quietly, "My name, Nina."

Anna looked at Erik with brimming eyes.

"Nina. That's a lovely name," Millie said as she took the little girl's hand and led her inside. She stopped and turned around. "Anna, Erik, would you like to come in for some tea?"

"No, I think we better be getting home," Erik said.

"After you have had time with Nina we will visit," Anna added and herded her children off the porch.

Winter seemed long and wet that year; spring hung back nearly until summer. When it did arrive, Anna and the children wandered the fields picking wildflowers and enjoying the land's rebirth. Millie and Nina often joined them. It was comforting to see Nina smile and laugh with the other children. Anna wondered at the difference love could make.

As the weather warmed, Anna took to standing along the riverbank and watching the water sweep past as it surged toward the sea. She tried to imagine how it widened and slowed when it flowed into the vast ocean. She wished she could float the swift currents all the way to the great Pacific. *I miss the sea,* she thought, then sighed and looked about. She had a good life along the Schuck. There was no reason for discontent.

One day, near summer's end, Erik sat beside Anna during one of her afternoon interludes at the river's edge. He tugged at a long slender blade of grass, breaking it off at the ground, then leaned back on his elbows and chewed on it. "Pretty spot isn't it?"

"Mm. It is beautiful here."

Erik sat up and took a deep breath. "Anna, the gold has played out," he blurted.

"It is gone?"

"Not all of it, but there's not much left. Not enough to take care of us."

Anna's throat tightened. She knew what Erik had to say and didn't want to hear it.

Erik lay his hand over Anna's. "We'll have to leave."

"But winter is almost here. How can we go?"

"We'll wait 'til spring. We've got enough to see us through until then." He paused and studied the river. "I heard of another strike up north. Thought it might be a good place for us to start over."

As Anna considered leaving their home and friends, tears pressed against the back of her eyelids. "I do not want to go," she said quietly.

"I wish we didn't have to, but there's no choice."

"Where is this place you speak of?"

"It was only a mining camp a few months ago, but already it's grown into a small town called Harrisburg. There might even be a church or a school. I don't know how fast claims are going, but if we head out in early spring, there might be a few left."

Anna looked at her husband. "If you think it is a good place, then we will go."

Winter passed quickly, and all too soon Anna and Erik were packed and ready to leave. Reid and Millie stood with Nina between them, waiting to say their good-byes.

Anna and Erik walked through the house one last time. Anna gripped Erik's hand tightly as memories flooded her—evenings spent reading around the hearth, visits with Reid and Millie, Luba's first steps, the birth of the boys. Anna felt as if a spear had pierced her chest, and her vision blurred with tears. "There is too much of us here," she lamented and leaned against Erik's arm.

Erik wrapped it around her and held her close. They stood quietly for a moment, then turned and walked out, closing the door behind them.

Millie kissed each of the children, then wrapped her arms around Anna. The two women clung to each other.

"Millie, you have been a good friend," Anna said through her tears. "I wish you were coming with us."

"You never know, we just might see you in Harrisburg one of these days. The gold on our place won't hold out forever." She blinked back her tears. "You take care of those young ones, now."

"I will. And you take care of yours," she said with a tremulous smile as she gathered her children about her.

"Well, we better get t' it," Reid said cheerfully, hefting a pack onto his back and kissing Millie. With a glance at Erik, he headed up the trail.

Erik grasped Millie's hand in a firm grip. "You've been a good neighbor and friend. I'll miss you," he said before turning and following Reid.

Iya stood in front of Nina. "I wish we didn't have to go. Take care of my flowers for me."

Nina forced a smile and nodded.

Anna glanced at Millie and waved. The boys sprinted on ahead while Luba and Iya walked beside Anna. *I wish there was another way,* Anna thought as she wiped her tears away.

Sitka seemed bursting at the seams with would-be prospectors heading north. Erik and Anna went straight to Cora's, hoping to find peace from the deluge within the walls of her home.

"Why, it's good to see you," Cora greeted them.

Anna always enjoyed her visits with Cora, but this time she was unable to smile as she thought of telling her about their plan to move north.

"Something's troubling you," Cora prodded.

"We're moving to Harrisburg," Erik explained.

"Along with the rest of them," Cora said, nodding toward the town.

"The gold played out on our place. We don't have a choice."

"Always the gold. Well, I guess I can't blame you. But the town isn't called Harrisburg anymore, they renamed it Rockwell."

"Do you think there'll be any trouble getting supplies here?"

"Maybe, but I heard they've got a pretty fine town already. You can probably get all you need there."

Erik nodded. "I'll see about booking us passage on a steamer then."

"You go on ahead. I'll get Anna and the children settled. We're pretty full up, but there's always room for you."

"Thanks, Cora," Erik said as he headed for the door.

Later that evening, with the children tucked into bed, Erik and Anna stood looking at the streets of Sitka. Erik stood behind Anna and cradled her in his arms. "Seems like only yesterday doesn't it?"

Anna nodded and leaned against him. "I wish things didn't have to change."

"Me too," Erik said with a sigh.

Only a week later Cora ushered them to the pier. "You were lucky to get a cabin. There's a lot of folks waiting."

"It looks like God's hand to me," Erik said. "They got a cancellation just as I was buying tickets."

Anna was disappointed at how quickly Erik had managed to get them booked. She had hoped to spend more time with Cora. "Cora, do you think you will come to Rockwell to visit?"

"Well, I don't see why not. You know Captain Bradley offered to take me on his ship any time I like." She smiled knowingly. "I believe I'll take him up on the offer."

Anna hugged Cora and quickly boarded, not wanting to drag out the good-byes. Once on board, she leaned against the railing and looked back toward the pier. She found Cora's face in the sea of people and waved. Cora smiled and waved back.

The gangplank was pulled in, and the ropes securing the steamer were released as the ship's horn blew. Slowly they eased away from the dock. Anna picked up Joseph and grabbed hold of the railing. Frantically she searched the faces below, looking for Cora. There she was. The corners of her mouth drooped, but when she saw Anna looking at her, she forced a smile and waved once again with big, broad sweeps of her arm. Anna took Joseph's arm and waved back.

"I don't want to go," Iya said.

Anna wrapped her other arm around Iya's shoulders. Her stomach lurched as the ship's horn blasted once more. The dock grew smaller, and soon Anna was unable to make out the faces of the well-wishers. As Sitka disappeared into the fog, a growing sense of dread pulled at her, and she wished she could stop their departure, but there was nothing that could be done except to move forward and see what awaited them.

Five days later, they steamed into the small town of Rockwell. It had been built along the beach and stretched into the surrounding hills. The town looked like it had been built in a hurry. Shabby shops and businesses lined the streets, and stumps still stood as reminders of the forest that had recently stood there.

A stampede of optimistic miners and their families clogged the narrow roads. Children played while men haggled with shopkeepers over inflated prices of mining equipment and supplies.

Erik stopped outside a mercantile. "Looks like sheer thievery is going on here," he said with disgust as he looked at some of the advertised prices. "Six bits for twenty pounds of sugar! We should have stocked up in Sitka," he added before disappearing inside.

Anna gathered the children close to her and leaned against the side of the building to wait. As she watched the throng of people, she wondered if they had made a mistake in coming to Rockwell. *At least Erik could trap on the river,* she thought.

"I'm hungry," Evan whined.

"Me too," added Luba.

"Do not worry about your stomachs now. We will eat soon enough," Anna reprimanded them. Her own stomach gnawed at her, but until they set up camp, food would have to wait.

After what seemed like hours, Erik emerged from the small shop. He smiled as he held up five sticks of hard candy. "I wonder if anyone here would like something sweet?" he teased.

"I do, I do," the children all chimed at once.

Erik handed one stick to each, then turning to Anna, he bowed ever so slightly and, holding out the last piece, said, "For you, dear lady."

Anna chuckled and took the gift. "Thank you," she said and took a lick. It tasted delicious. She broke off a piece and handed it to Erik.

Erik stuck it in his mouth with a grin and said, "Let's get moving." He led the way down the street. "Fellow inside says there are still some claims to be had up on Gold Creek. Nothing to brag about, but a little color." He unfolded a map and examined it. "By the looks of things, it's not so far."

"Joseph, you are getting too heavy," Anna said with a sigh as she set the little boy on his feet and took his hand. "Iya, you watch Luba and Evan." She hitched up her skirts and followed Erik down the street, taking two steps for each one of his. Joseph jerked free of his mother and ran ahead until Erik scooped him into his arms.

"We'll need a wagon and a couple of horses to haul our supplies," Erik said as he ducked into a livery.

Anna followed. She'd never been inside a stable before. It smelled of animals and hay, and as her eyes adjusted, Anna could see several stalls, some with horses peering out.

A whiskered, heavyset man stepped up to Erik. "What can I do for you?"

"Well, I need a wagon and a couple of good horses."

"Where you heading?"

"Gold Creek."

"Wagon's not gonna do you no good up that way."

"Why not?"

Casually, the man leaned on his pitch fork. "No decent roads. Just a trail that follows the creek through a deep gorge. You'd do better to hire a couple of men to pack in your supplies."

"Where do I find someone?"

"There's a handful of natives who do nothin' but pack for folks. I'll send a boy up to find a couple for you." The man stopped to snuffle into a dirty handkerchief then, tucking it into his back pocket, put his fingers to his lips and whistled.

A moment later, a tall, gangly young man strolled around the corner of the building. "Yeah?" he asked.

"This man needs a couple of packers. Why don't you see about findin' him some."

"Sure," the boy said and turned back the way he had come.

"Well, in that case, I guess one horse would do me fine," Erik said as he ambled down the row of stalls and studied the animals. He stopped in front of the last stable. "Can I have a look at this one?"

The man took a lead rope down from the wall, strolled over to the stall, and led out the stocky black gelding. "This is a fine animal. Strong. He'll make a good pack horse."

"How much you want for him?"

The man scratched at his whiskers. "Well, he's a good 'un. I'd probably have to ask fifty dollars for him."

"How about twenty-five?"

"I'll throw in the saddle and tack, and you got him for forty."

Erik thought a minute. "Thirty-five."

The man glanced out the door and back at the horse before conceding. "All right. You have a deal."

Erik paid the man, then saddled the animal and turned to Iya. "Well, Iya, you always wanted to own a horse. I figure you ought to be the first to ride him."

Iya's face beamed with excitement as she slipped her foot into the stirrup and pulled herself aboard. With a big smile, she looked down on her family. "It is nice to be tall," she said as she shifted her weight in the saddle.

Erik led her outside just as the young man returned with two native men.

"These fellas said they'd help you," the boy said.

"How much you charge?" Erik asked.

"Two bits each," the smaller of the two answered.

"Sounds fair to me. My supplies are back at the mercantile. I need them hauled up Gold Creek."

The packers nodded and headed for the store.

As the Engstroms and the two natives made their way upstream, they passed dozens of men working claims along the waterway. Anna had never seen so many miners in one place before. She felt stifled and even more certain they had made a grave error in coming to Rockwell.

The trail was rough and steep in some areas. It didn't take long before the children began to lag, and Anna wished they could stop and rest. After a while, Erik stopped. He studied the land for claim markers and, finding none, waded into the water and examined the sand. Tiny flecks of gold winked at him from the rock. He stood up and with a grin and said, "This is it. Our new home."

Anna sighed and looked about. The country looked similar to their home on the Schuck, except here they were hemmed in on both sides by the walls of a canyon and as far up or down the stream as she could see, men worked sluice boxes. *How will we learn to live among so many?* she wondered. Aloud she said, "I will fix supper," and began searching through their supplies. "Iya, would you take the children and gather wood for a fire?"

The children dispersed in search of firewood, while Anna prepared their cooking utensils and Erik began setting up camp.

After eating, Anna's mood lifted a little. Sitting beside Erik on a log overlooking the creek, she took another look at their new home. Her eyes roamed across the river to the mountain peaks that rose up all around them. Dense forests clung to their slopes and thinned just below the summit where they were replaced by scrub and rock. She looked across the water and followed it as it wound its way seaward.

"It's not what you expected, is it?" Erik asked quietly.

Anna leaned against his shoulder. "I did not know what to expect," she answered softly. "It is beautiful. I only wish there were not so many people."

"It'll take some getting used to, that's for sure." He glanced at the clearing where they had shared their dinner. "I'll build us a place right there in that open area."

Anna smiled. "I am not worried about a house. We are together, that is what matters, and God is here just as he was on the Schuck."

Erik hugged her. "I love you."

Anna rested her cheek against his chest. She liked the feel of his wool shirt and the smell of dust and sweat. She turned and gazed down the river. As dusk gathered, the men were no longer so distinct, and she could almost imagine that they weren't there. She sighed deeply.

Their new home wasn't as large as the one they had shared on the Schuck, but Anna didn't mind. She fashioned simple cotton curtains for the windows, made coverlets for their chairs, and decorated her shelves with her knickknacks. Soon it felt like home.

Slowly they met their neighbors. Most were not unfriendly, but they weren't the type to embrace newcomers, either. Some of the miners had brought their families, but for the most part, the area remained a bachelors' haven. The few women who had traveled north with their husbands seemed distant and a little suspicious of

Anna. She wished Millie still lived nearby. Life seemed lonely without her friend.

One evening after supper, Erik sat reading his Bible. He lay the book in his lap and looked up at Anna. "I heard there's a woman downriver who teaches school. Wondered if she might take on Iya and Luba."

Anna's hopes soared. For so long, she had wanted her children to attend school. "Do you know what place it is?"

"I was told it's about a mile down from us, right across from the big bend."

Then and there, Anna decided she would visit this teacher. Iya and Luba were old enough, and she intended for them to go.

The next day, Anna dressed the children in their best, put on her finest dress, swept her dark brown hair on top of her head as she had seen the white women do, and set off downriver.

Anna had no trouble finding the woman's home. Just beyond the big bend stood a tidy cabin with flowers growing in a neat row in front and a wooden rocker sitting on the porch. Clearly this wasn't a bachelor's cabin. *This has to be it,* Anna thought as she stepped onto the porch.

She could see crisply starched curtains at the windows, and apprehension welled up within her. Everything seemed a little too perfect. She fought the desire to turn around and head for home and, instead, took a deep breath, clasped Joseph's hand tightly in hers, and rapped on the door.

Almost immediately a tall, reed-thin woman opened it. For a moment she stared at Anna from pale blue eyes.

Anna's mouth went dry.

"Can I help you?" the woman asked, and her expression softened a little.

Anna swallowed hard. "I heard you teach?"

The woman looked back at her blankly as if she didn't understand the question.

"Do you teach children?" Anna repeated.

"Yes, I do."

Anna glanced down at the woman's feet, which had been stuffed into pointy black shoes, then looked back into her cool, blue eyes. "Would you teach my children?"

Luba, Evan, and Joseph hid behind Anna's skirts, while Iya hung back on the porch step. The woman glanced at them and asked, "All of them?"

"No, only Iya and Luba," Anna answered as she pulled Luba forward and nodded toward Iya. "They want to learn to read."

"How old are you, Iya?" the teacher asked.

"I am almost twelve," Iya answered proudly, pulling herself up to her full four-foot, eight-inch height.

"And, Luba, how old are you?"

Luba held up six fingers.

The woman managed a tight smile. "Has the older one ever been in school?"

"No."

The teacher looked them over once more. "Well, they'll do just fine."

"You will teach them?" Anna asked, unable to keep the delight out of her voice.

"I suppose I can handle two more."

"Thank you. Thank you," Anna burst out, taking the woman's hand and shaking it hard.

An unexpected smile broke out on the teacher's face.

"It has been my dream that my children would learn to read and write."

"I am glad to do it. What is your name?"

"Anna Engstrom. My husband and I live upriver."

I'm glad to meet you, Anna. My name is Emily Connelly." She tucked a strand of thin, blond hair back into place and glanced inside. "I've got to get back to my students. Why don't you bring the girls tomorrow? They will each need a slate and slate pencil. We start right at nine o'clock, and I don't tolerate tardiness. Make sure to pack them a lunch. We always work through the afternoon."

"Tomorrow," Anna repeated as she backed away, feeling her welcome had ended. "They will be here."

Mrs. Connelly closed the door.

Anna stood on the porch a moment longer. "Thank you," she said again before turning for home. As she headed up the path, she thought back over the brief encounter. *She seems a peculiar person. But if she will teach my children, it does not matter.*

Iya lagged behind, her face drawn into a frown.

Anna stopped and waited as Iya strolled toward her, keeping her eyes on the ground. When she caught up to her, Anna asked, "Iya, is something wrong?"

Iya looked across the creek, allowing her eyes to wander over the hills. "I am not sure I want to go to school."

"Not go to school?"

"Maybe I am not smart. What if I cannot learn?"

"Of course you are smart. Didn't you learn to make fine baskets when you were still a little girl?"

Iya nodded, unconvinced.

"And didn't you help build a cabin and make fine skins?"

"But that is not the same as learning from books."

"Smart is smart," Anna said with assurance, ending the discussion.

That evening over dinner, Anna told Erik about her visit to Mrs. Connelly's.

Erik sipped his soup thoughtfully.

"What are you thinking?" Anna asked impatiently.

Erik leaned back in his chair and looked squarely at Anna. "Why is it so important that the children go to school?" he asked evenly.

Anna stared at him, unable to believe his response.

"I'm just wondering about your reasons," Erik prodded.

"You do not want Iya and Luba to learn to read?"

"Yes, I do. I think it's a good idea. I just want to know why it is so important to you."

Anna pondered Erik's question a moment. She had never thought about why. It was just so. Finally, she answered, "They need to know about the world and they cannot without reading."

"Is that all?"

Anna pushed her food around her plate. Quietly she admitted, "People respect someone who can read."

"So it's respect you're looking for."

"That is not all," Anna answered indignantly. "Life will be better if they can read . . . and people will respect them. Is that wrong?"

"It's not wrong to want those things, but you need to remember people are more than what they know—it's who they are that counts."

"You are right, but some do not see beyond how we look. To some we are nothing."

Erik leaned forward and took Anna's hands in his. "That isn't going to change just because they can read. Nothing we do will change how some feel. We need only care how God sees us. He sees to the heart." Erik paused. "I want all the children to go to school. I think it's important, but even more important is that we remember, with or without schooling or anything else, we're significant. Gaining more knowledge won't make us any better, but what we do with that knowledge can make a difference. We have to stop worrying how the world sees us."

Anna knew he was right, but sometimes it was so hard to live what you knew to be true.

Before Iya and Luba left for school, Erik gathered the family together. "I think we ought to pray before the girls leave," he said as he took Luba's hand.

They formed a circle, clasped hands, and bowed their heads.

"Heavenly Father, this is a special day, one we've hoped and prayed for. We thank you for your blessing. We know it won't be easy, that there will be hardships, but we ask you to watch over these girls and help them be a light to those around them. Remind Luba and Iya that they are never alone, that you walk every step with them. Calm our hearts and help us to trust in your guidance and your will. Thank you, Father. Amen."

Amens were whispered around the room.

"Here are your lunches," Anna said as she handed a small tin to Iya and kissed her cheek.

"Thank you," Iya said and crossed to the door. "Good-bye, Daddy."

Luba wrapped her arms around Anna's waist. "Bye, Momma," she said, her voice tinged with fear.

Anna tried to hide her tears as she looked down into the round, sweet face of her daughter. *What would Kinauquak think to see his daughter going off to school?* she wondered.

Erik scooped the little girl up and kissed her squarely on the cheek.

"Daddy, let me down," she protested with a giggle.

Erik set her on her feet. "You have a great day," he said with a smile.

As Erik and Anna watched the girls head downriver, Anna said, "I wish Iya was not so stubborn. I do not like to see them go alone today."

"They're not alone," Erik reminded her. "And she's old enough. We have to let go a little."

Luba dawdled along; the flowers seemed to beckon to her. She stopped every few steps to pluck one of the bright blossoms that bloomed along the trail.

"Luba, hurry up," Iya scolded. "We do not want to be late our first day."

"I will give these to the teacher," Luba announced as she skipped up to Iya.

Iya barely glanced at the little girl's treasures, her mind full of what lay before them. She forged ahead and tried to quiet the butterflies in her stomach.

When they came to Mrs. Connelly's, Iya stopped several paces from the house. She studied it as she struggled to find the courage to go inside, then she gripped Luba's hand tightly, stepped up to the door, and knocked.

Mrs. Connelly answered and peered down at Iya with a tight-lipped expression. "You girls are late," she said sharply. Then she spotted Luba and the flowers she held up, and her expression softened. "But better late than never," she added more kindly. "We'll not count it against you this time, but after this please make sure to be on time."

"I am sorry," Iya apologized.

"These are for you," Luba said shyly, holding out her flowers.

"They are lovely. Thank you," Mrs. Connelly said as she took the bouquet and opened the door for the girls.

Iya pushed Luba into the room ahead of her.

The house looked bigger inside than it did from the outside. It was clean, but sparsely furnished. Several children with slates on their laps sat on the floor, peering at the newcomers.

"Please have a seat over there," Mrs. Connelly said, waving toward the far side of the room.

Clutching her slate to her chest, Iya gripped Luba's hand and towed her to the far wall where they sat down. Iya glanced at the other children and felt the blood rush to her face as eight pairs of eyes studied her and Luba.

"Children, meet Iya and Luba. They will be joining us," Mrs. Connelly explained. She cleared her throat. "Now, if I could have your attention up here."

The students turned and looked at the board at the front of the room, all, that is, except for one big boy. He stared at Iya. Iya tried not to look at him, but when he stuck his tongue out at her, she couldn't help but stare back at him, wide-eyed and angry.

"Jason!" Mrs. Connelly snapped.

Immediately the boy turned around and stared at the board.

During the midmorning break, Mrs. Connelly stopped Iya on her way outside. "I know it will be a bit difficult to catch up, but with hard work, I believe you can do it. Please let me know if there's anything you need help with."

Iya smiled and decided Mrs. Connelly wasn't so bad after all. "Thank you. I will try very hard," she assured the teacher before following the other children to the yard.

Luba waited for Iya on the porch. Meekly, she stood against the front wall and watched the children playing tag. Iya joined her, feeling very much out of place. She'd never played with any children other than her brothers and sister and Nina.

The boy who'd stuck his tongue out at her tugged on another boy's arm, and the two purposely sauntered up to the edge of the porch. "Well, Ethan, it looks like we got ourselves a couple of Injuns," he sneered. "What do you think of that?"

"Not much," Ethan said as he stepped up onto the porch and stood directly in front of Luba.

The little girl cringed.

He rapped his knuckles on the top of her head. "You s'pose there's any brains in here?" he snickered.

"Nah, I heard Injuns ain't got no brains."

Iya stepped between Ethan and Luba, glaring at the skinny, redheaded boy.

A short, stocky girl with thick brown hair hanging in her face joined Iya. "You leave them alone, Jason. They didn't do nothin' to you."

"Stay out of this," Jason threatened.

"I'll tell your Ma."

Jason stepped back, still glaring at the girls.

"Come on," the daring girl said to Iya. "Let's get out of here." She jumped off the porch and strode around to the side of the house. "You can't let them bother you. They ain't worth it. Mrs. Connelly is Jason's Ma. If he gives you any trouble, jest tell her, and she'll give him a real lickin'. My name's Elspeth. What's yours?"

Iya smiled. She liked the spunky, friendly girl. "It is nice to meet you, Elspeth. My name is Iya, and this is Luba."

"Them's real funny names."

"I guess," Iya said with a shrug.

"Where you from?"

"We just moved up from the Schuck River, but once I lived on an island."

"Did you live with Indians?"

Elspeth's curiosity held no meanness in it, so Iya didn't feel offended by her questions. "Yes. We lived in a village."

"That sounds exciting. I never been in a real village before."

Emily Connelly called the children back to class.

Once inside, Elspeth made room beside her and motioned for Iya and Luba to sit next to her.

Iya gladly took the offered seat and thought of how she would tell Anna about her new friend. Thoughts of the troublesome boys faded as Iya considered all of the wonderful days ahead.

Chapter 19

*A*nna poked her needle through the soft cotton material in her hand while Iya and Luba sat at the table working on their schoolwork. Anna stopped and watched the girls. It felt good to know they would learn to read and write. She set her sewing aside, pushed herself up from her chair, and strolled across the room to the table. With her hands clasped behind her back, she stood beside Iya and watched as the youngster struggled to duplicate the letters in her speller onto her slate. *It is like magic,* Anna thought as she pulled a chair out and sat beside Iya. She studied the strange symbols and tried to remember what Cora had taught her. She recognized some of the letters, but the words were unfamiliar. She sighed deeply. *I wish I could read.*

Both girls looked at her. "Is something wrong?" Iya asked.

"No," Anna answered hesitantly, then blurted out, "I just wish I could read too."

"You can."

"I cannot."

"Yes, you can. You will learn like me."

"Who will teach me?"

"You can work with us."

Anna looked back at the words on Iya's slate. "You think I can?"

"Yes. It is hard, but we will work together."

Was it really possible? Did she dare hope? "I do want to," Anna said quietly, then with more confidence, added, "I will try." She pulled her chair in closer. "But we will not tell Erik."

"Why not?" Luba asked.

"When I know more, I will surprise him," Anna answered with a smile. She looked at Luba. "You must keep the secret."

The little girl grinned and nodded her head.

"I will not tell," Iya assured Anna.

After that, Anna hurried Erik out of the house in the morning and rushed through her morning chores so she could begin working on the lesson Iya had given her from the previous day. Gradually the letters and their sounds began to make sense, and Anna found that putting words together could be fun. She gained confidence as she learned.

Iya and Luba both did well in school. They devoured every piece of information given them, as if afraid they would lose the opportunity, and it wasn't long before they were both reading simple tales from the readers supplied by Mrs. Connelly. Often in the evening, they proudly read stories for the family. Their progress thrilled Anna, and she hoped it wouldn't be long before she, too, would be able to read to the family as they all sat around the hearth.

It was a time of joy for the girls. Learning was exciting, and Iya's friendship with Elspeth grew. They often explored the countryside together and sometimes helped their fathers at the river. Occasionally Elspeth shared dinner with the Engstroms, and afterward she and Iya poured over their studies together.

If not for Jason and Ethan's continued taunting, life would have been perfect. Iya had not told Anna about the boys' cruelty, and she made Luba promise not to tell. "It will only upset Anna," she had explained. "I will take care of you," she promised Luba, who agreed not to speak of it.

But being the daily target of the two nasty boys became a burden. Iya tried to ignore their abuse and managed to take their verbal blows pretty much in stride, but one day, when they decided to make Luba the butt of their nasty jibes, she lost her temper. She strode up to Jason and, before she realized what she was about to do, balled her hand into a fist and swung her arm as hard as she could. She hit him squarely across the cheek and knocked him to the ground.

Before Iya could revel in her victory, however, Mrs. Connelly appeared behind her and grabbed her by her collar. "Iya! What kind of behavior is this for a young lady?" she demanded, sticking her face close to Iya's. "This will not be tolerated! You march straight home and tell your father what you have done."

An explanation rose in Iya's throat, but she couldn't defend herself against Mrs. Connelly's unfair attack. She dropped her head and said, "Yes, ma'am." With a quick glare at Jason, who wore a look of triumph, she ran down the trail toward home before anyone could see her shameful flood of tears.

When she'd cried herself out, she slowed and stopped to skip rocks across the top of a pool. At first she threw them hard and angrily, but finally more gently, taking pleasure in how far the stones would skim across the water's surface. Knowing she would have to face Anna sooner or later, she tossed her last rock and headed toward home, feeling empty and bruised but less agitated. She shuffled into the yard, sat down on the porch, and tried to decide what she would say. She propped her face in her hands and gazed out at the forest.

It didn't take long before Joseph announced, "Iya's home. Momma, Iya's home."

Anna came to the door. "Iya, why aren't you in school?" She sat down next to her sister. "Is something wrong? Are you sick?"

Iya sighed. "No. I am not sick."

"There is something wrong," Anna prodded. "Tell me."

Iya looked up at her sister, her eyes brimming with tears. "Mrs. Connelly sent me home."

"Why would she do that?"

Iya took a deep breath. "I hit Jason."

"You what?"

"I hit him. He was being mean to Luba and I hit him," she said in a rush.

"What was he doing?"

"He was calling her names." Iya hesitated. "He and Ethan call me and Luba names because we are Indians."

"They call you names?" Anna asked as she wrapped her arm around Iya's shoulder and pulled her close, willing her building anger to the back of her mind. "What kind of things do they say?"

"They call us dirty Injuns and say we are too stupid to learn to read and do 'rithmetic." She swallowed hard. "Sometimes they hit us."

"Mrs. Connelly allows this?" Anna asked, trying to control her growing rage.

"She does not know."

"How could she not know?"

"They are only mean when she is not around." Iya sighed. "And Jason is Mrs. Connelly's son."

"Is there anything else you have not told me?"

Iya swung her feet back and forth, but didn't answer.

"Well?" Anna persisted.

"Sometimes Iya and I speak our people's language, like you taught us, and some of the others asked us to teach them. When Mrs. Connelly found out, she got real mad and said we cannot speak it anymore."

Anna's rage threatened to explode. She clenched her fists and forced herself to remain still. *How could she? Why do people act like this? Will it never end?* she fumed. *Well, they are not going to get away with it,* she decided and pushed herself to her feet. "Iya, why didn't you tell me before?"

"I did not want you to worry."

Anna paced in front of the house, then stopped. Trying to control her voice, she said, "You must always tell me when you have trouble. I will talk with your teacher." Determined, she stepped inside and a moment later reappeared with a wrap thrown over her shoulders. "Iya, you watch the children. I will be back soon." With that, she swept down the steps and charged up the trail.

Tears stung Anna's eyes, and a heavy pain pressed against her chest as she hurried toward Mrs. Connelly's. *It is so unfair! Why do people have to hurt innocent children?*

Over the years, Anna had shouldered the burden of others' prejudice and hatred. She'd never once retaliated, but no longer. "God, we have done nothing to deserve this," she raved as she walked. "I will tell them what I think!" As she trudged on, she began to hear another voice—a voice of reason and calm. Grudgingly she let go of her rage and replaced her angry thoughts and words with prayers for wisdom and peace.

"Father, help me to focus on you and not my own anger. I know this rage will only bring more pain. Do not let my anger speak, but your justice."

When she finally stepped into the clearing in front of Mrs. Connelly's tidy home, she was thinking more rationally. She stopped to gather her thoughts and wished she had talked to Erik before rushing into a confrontation.

She considered leaving, but Elspeth saw her. "Oh, Mrs. Engstrom, I'm real sorry about Iya," the young girl said as she stepped up to Anna. "She didn't do nothin' wrong. It's that mean old Jason."

Anna forced a smile. "Iya is fine," she reassured Elspeth. "I'd just like to talk to Mrs. Connelly." Anna took a deep breath, stepped up to the door, and knocked.

A broad-shouldered young man with a sullen expression answered.

"Jason, who is it?" called Mrs. Connelly from the back of the house.

"I dunno," he replied, staring at Anna.

Anna felt her resolve wither under the boy's unfriendly scrutiny. But unwilling to allow him to get the best of her, she swallowed past the lump in her throat and as sternly as she could, said, "I would like to speak to your mother."

Without taking his eyes off her, the young man silently swung the door open.

"Oh, Mrs. Engstrom," Emily Connelly twittered as she hurried to greet Anna. "Where are your manners, Jason?" she chided her son. "Please come in. Jason, you go on out and play with the other children."

The adolescent plodded to the door. As he opened it, he threw an angry look at Anna, then pulled the door closed behind him with a loud thud.

Unaware of her son's rudeness, Mrs. Connelly crossed to the table and said, "Please have a seat."

Feeling awkward, Anna followed her and sat down.

The two women sat across from each other, neither seeming to know what to say next.

Anna glanced at the frail, kind-looking woman and wondered

how she could have thought of her as an enemy. *Anger changes reality. I must never see things through anger but put it aside,* she decided and silently sought wisdom and guidance from God. She folded her hands in her lap and leveled a steady gaze on the delicate woman. "Iya came home and told me what happened," Anna began.

Emily Connelly said nothing but waited for Anna to continue.

A steady thumping sound came from the porch, and Anna guessed that Jason was kicking the steps. She glanced at the window, half expecting to see his sullen face watching them. Her heart pounded hard then slowed when she found the window empty of anything but the stiffly starched curtains fluttering in the breeze.

She took a deep breath and started again. "Iya said there are boys who call her and Luba names and sometimes hit them."

Mrs. Connelly's mouth tightened into a pinched line, and her cheeks bloomed with anger. "Who? Did she say who is doing this?"

"Two boys," Anna answered as she rested her hands on the table and stared at them a moment. "One is called Ethan . . ."

"Oh, yes. A rascal, that one. I'll make sure to speak to his mother."

Quietly Anna continued, "Another boy, also." She looked directly into the teacher's eyes. "Jason."

The woman blanched. "Jason? My Jason?" she asked, her hand fluttering to her throat. Before Anna could answer, Emily Connelly stood up and went to the door. "Jason! Come in here at once," she commanded.

A moment later, the young man inched inside the door, looking like he wished he were invisible. He knew his mother's wrath was about to come down on him.

"Mrs. Engstrom tells me you and Ethan have been mistreating her girls."

Jason glanced at Anna then back at his mother, but didn't answer.

"Well, is it true?"

Mrs. Connelly clutched the back of her chair so tightly her knuckles turned white.

"Ah, we didn't do nothin'," Jason finally said. "They're just a couple of babies."

"What would you call nothing?" she persisted.

Jason's face turned red with rage and he glared at Anna.

Anna fought not to cringe under his stare and forced herself to meet his gaze. He turned back to his mother. "We just called them a couple of Injuns," he said, then added petulantly, "That's what they are, ain't they?"

Now his mother's look turned cold. "What else?" she pressed him through clenched teeth.

Anna almost felt sorry for the boy. The teacher's frail appearance masked a very strong woman.

"We told them they better stay home," Jason answered belligerently. "That school was no place for Injuns, and that they ought to stay with their own kind." He looked at the floor.

"And did you hit them?"

"Yeah. But they asked for it."

"No one asks to be hit, Jason." Mrs. Connelly took the boy by the ear and led him off toward the back of the cabin. "I'll deal with you later. For now you'll stay in your room," she said scornfully as she let loose of his ear.

Throwing a look of contempt at Anna, the young man trudged into a back room.

Emily didn't look at Anna, but walked to the window and stared at the wild grasses that grew at the edge of the clearing. Her hand trembled a little as she smoothed an imaginary wrinkle from her neckline.

"I'm very sorry, Mrs. Engstrom," she finally said and turned to face Anna. "I didn't know. It won't happen again, I assure you."

"Thank you," Anna answered quietly. She considered leaving the other issue for another day; clearly Mrs. Connelly was already shaken. But as she glanced at Luba playing in the yard, she knew she must deal with it. "There is something else," Anna said hesitantly. "Iya said you will not let her speak our language."

Emily's tired blue eyes flamed at Anna's comment. "That is true."

"Why?"

Emily cleared her throat and folded her arms across her chest. "You no longer live with your kind, Mrs. Engstrom. I believe if natives intend to live among the whites, they should live like us. You need to put your heathen pasts behind you," she said sternly. "And I don't want the other children exposed to such things."

Anna could feel her anger begin to flare. Her first impulse was to retaliate, but something stopped her, and she looked beyond Mrs. Connelly's cool exterior to the fear hidden deep within the woman. Instead of giving a verbal thrashing, Anna took a deep breath. "I agree we live here now and need to learn new ways. I have learned much since I left my home, but my past is a part of who I am. I cannot change my blood, and I do not wish for my children to forget who they are."

Emily sat down and primly folded her hands on the table in front of her.

Anna noticed they bore calluses from hard work, but her nails were neatly manicured.

"Mrs. Engstrom," Emily said sweetly, "I understand how you must feel about your heritage . . ."

"No. You cannot."

Emily's jaw twitched irritably, and she let out an exasperated sigh. "I don't know *exactly* how you feel, but I can imagine it, after all, we're all transplants here." She gave Anna a hard look. "The children in my school will speak English. I can make no exceptions," she said firmly.

Anna looked at the woman, hating the tears that threatened her. She wanted to lash out and tell her how hard it was to live where people always looked down on you, treating you as if you had no right to walk the same ground; to tell her what it was like to try to make a life for your children, only to have the world you live in snatch away even your smallest hopes and dreams. But she couldn't say any of these things. Mrs. Connelly wouldn't understand— couldn't understand.

"Here at school they will speak English," Anna said woodenly.

"Good. I'm glad we have that settled," Mrs. Connelly said with a stiff smile as she stood up, putting an end to their meeting.

Anna walked to the door. "The girls will be here tomorrow," she said as she stepped outside and closed the door behind her.

Luba joined her. "Momma, is everything all right?"

"Yes," Anna answered shortly, wanting to run into the woods and lose herself in the wilds—to weep—to allow all her pain to wash away. "You stay here. Iya will come and get you at the end of the day," she said evenly as she bent and kissed the little girl on the cheek. With her shoulders thrown back and her body rigid, Anna headed home.

Erik met her at the door, his face lined with concern. "Iya told me what happened. I was just about to come and get you."

"I spoke to Mrs. Connelly," Anna managed to say, still close to tears.

"What happened?"

"She will punish her son," Anna answered as she hung her wrap on the hook inside the door, then unable to stop the flow of anger and hurt, she turned to Erik, her eyes brimming. "Why are people so mean? Sometimes I hate whites!"

"Whoa there! I'm white, remember?" Erik said with a grin.

"It is not funny," Anna said coldly.

Erik got up from his chair and wrapped his arms around his tiny wife. "I know it's not. I was just trying to lighten the mood, that's all."

Anna burrowed into this chest. "I know, but sometimes I get so angry. I try not to, but it's still there."

"Anna, some folks just don't know any better. I know that's not an excuse, but it's just the way things are. We can't let ourselves fall into the same trap—hating just because of color. Not all whites are cruel or insensitive." He tipped her chin up so she had to look into his eyes. "God created each of us unique. He doesn't draw a line and say, 'On this side all dark skinned people stand and on that side all whites.' He doesn't point to one group and say, 'All of you are good, and all of you are bad.'"

Anna smiled.

"We all bleed red blood; we all hurt; we all feel joy. It's what's on the inside that counts."

Anna moved away from him. "I know you are right, but it is not easy living in a world that does not see through God's eyes."

"Anna, the world will never see through God's eyes," Erik said softly. "I understand your anger. You even have a right to it, but in the end all it will do is hurt you and the girls."

Anna turned back to her husband and wrapped her arms about his waist. "I will try not to let them anger me," she said and closed her eyes as she rested against Erik's chest. She always felt safe within his arms. "You are so good for me," she whispered.

Erik tightened his embrace.

In the weeks that followed, Mrs. Connelly kept a close eye on the children. The boys' taunting stopped, and the girls continued to learn in a more congenial atmosphere.

Anna promised herself she would love those around her no matter what, and each day she asked God to help her see the world through his eyes. Life did not change much, but Anna found a new peace and confidence as she saw people with a fresh perspective. It wasn't easy, but she knew her example was what the children would learn, and she hoped they would grow up knowing how to love, not hate. She continued to teach them of the old ways, while at the same time helping them to accept the new.

Anna and Erik hadn't been in Rockwell long before the local miners took a vote and renamed the town Juneau. Their new home grew rapidly with the influx of miners and their families. Small businesses flourished, and mining companies sprang up as men of wealth dug deep into the earth to expose great pockets of gold buried beneath the land. Holdings on the small placer claims were soon taken up, and disappointed new arrivals, who had come in search of wealth, sometimes struck out in anger by trying to force their way onto another's claim. Fights broke out with the loser sometimes paying with his life. Erik began carrying his rifle with him and, although challenged once or twice, never had to use it. He had a thief in his sights one day, but couldn't pull the trigger over the theft of his horse.

He managed to make a steady profit on his claim, and slowly the Engstrom home took on a different look. It grew in size, and the latest gadgets filled their shelves. Anna's favorite was a new mantle clock. Each time she looked at it, she thought of Cora and longed for the day she would see her friend again.

Saloons and show-houses blossomed along the main street, sharing space with houses of worship. Anna's prayer of one day living near a church had been fulfilled, and the Engstroms became regular attendees.

One afternoon, on their way home from worship, Erik took the boys and went to price some equipment needed for the claim while Anna and the girls headed for the mercantile. A man shoved past Anna, nearly knocking her off her feet.

"Watch where you're goin'," he growled.

"I am sorry . . ." Anna began as she looked into familiar, iceblue eyes. Her heart pounded in her chest, and she felt Iya move closer to her. She found herself speechless as she looked into the face of Jarvis Moyer.

"I know you," Jarvis muttered as he studied them. Then a menacing sneer slid across his face, and he broke into a grin. "You two," he spat. He turned and called over his shoulder, "Hey, Joe, I want you to meet Engstrom's squaw and his brats."

Anna watched a big native join Jarvis. He studied them, but his eyes didn't hold the same ruthlessness as his partner's. Unwilling to drop her gaze, Anna stared back at the man.

Joe turned away abruptly. "Let's get out of here," he said and headed down the street.

"We're not finished yet," Jarvis threatened. "I'll see you two around," he said as he turned and followed his friend.

Anna let out her breath, realizing she'd been holding it.

"What is he doing here?" Iya demanded.

"We better get what we came for and go," Anna said, not bothering to answer Iya's question. She took Luba's hand and headed for the mercantile on shaking legs. *Erik will be angry if he finds out Jarvis threatened us,* Anna thought. *He cannot know,* she decided. "Iya, Luba, do not tell Erik about Jarvis."

"Why?" Luba asked.

"He is a bad man and it will upset Daddy."

"Can I tell him we saw him?"

"No. Do not say anything."

As it turned out, a few days later over dinner, Erik brought up the subject of Jarvis. "Saw an old friend in town today," he said wryly.

"Who?" Iya asked.

"Jarvis Moyer. I don't want you to have anything to do with him. He's a dangerous man."

"We saw him," Anna said quietly.

"Did he bother you?"

Anna shot a warning glance at Iya. "No. We only saw him."

"I wish he would leave," Iya added and leaned forward on her elbows.

"So do I," Erik agreed. "But I doubt he'll go until the money dries up and that could be a long while."

The weather turned cold, and as Christmas approached, Anna could barely contain her excitement. This year she had a special gift to present to Erik, and as she thought of his delight when he discovered she could read, she smiled. She'd been working hard, snatching bits of time with Iya when Erik was away, learning to read the Christmas account in the Bible.

One afternoon, after spending time studying, she closed the Bible and held it to her chest. *I can read it!* she thought and envisioned the joy on her family's face when she shared the story with them on Christmas.

Two days before Christmas, a knock came at the door. Iya raced to answer it and as she pulled it open, a blast of icy wind blew in. Anna pulled her shawl tighter around her shoulders. "Iya, who is it?"

Iya giggled and said, "Come and see."

Feeling impatient with silly games, Anna pushed herself out of her chair and repeated her question, "Iya, who is here?"

A gust of wind pushed the door open wide. There standing on the porch stood Reid, Millie, and Nina. Anna sucked in her breath. "Millie!" she cried. "Reid!"

Immediately Anna was in Millie's arms. For several moments the two women held each other tight until Anna forced herself to take a step back. With her hands still on Millie's arms and tears in her eyes, she said, "It has been too long. I have missed you."

"Doon't I get a welcoom?" Reid teased.

"Oh, Reid," Anna said taking his hand and squeezing it. "It is good to see you. Erik will be so happy. He is down at the stream."

Anna bent and patted Nina on the head. "And Nina you have grown so much."

Nina grinned. "Where is Luba?"

"With her father."

Millie's eyes sparkled with delight. "We figured it was time to move on. The claim's pretty much played out, and to tell you the truth, the river became too lonely without you. I just couldn't stand it. So here we are," she said flinging her arms wide.

"Oh, Millie! I am so glad! Come in out of the cold and have a seat. I will make some coffee. You must stay and have supper."

"Absolutely. In fact, we doon't have mooch of anyplace t' go. If you doon't mind us campin' on yer place until we c'n find one of our own, we'd sure appreciate it." Reid said.

"Camp? In this weather? We can make room for friends."

"Yer sure we're noot puttin' you oot?"

"There are never too many people in a house if they're good friends," Anna reassured Reid.

"Weel, thank ye'. Where'd ye' say Erik was?"

"At the creek. Iya will show you."

"I think I'll be goin' on doon, then."

Iya pulled on her heavy coat and ushered Reid and Nina out the door.

"Millie, I can't believe you're here. I have missed you so much. Many times I've thought of the visits we used to have." Anna patted her friends hand. "Will you stay in Juneau?"

"We don't have anyplace else to go, so I suppose so." A shadow of concern crossed her face. "Is there work?"

"The claims are all taken, but some of the mines are hiring men. Reid could work for one of them."

Millie sighed. "It will be so good to have our own place set up here."

"It will happen," Anna assured her. "It is a wonderful gift to have you here for Christmas," she added with a smile.

"Where are the little ones?"

"They went with their daddy. They have become Erik's shadow."

That evening seemed like old times. Reid and Erik swapped stories over dinner while Millie shared the news from Sitka with Anna and the children played.

"While we were in Sitka, we stopped to see Cora," Millie said.

"How is she?"

"Good. Very good. She told me Captain Bradley came to see her. She tried to explain away his visit by saying he had business in Sitka, but as far as I can see, that man has his sights on our Cora. After all, he didn't have to stop and visit."

"Now, Millie, ye' doon't know thet," Reid corrected his wife.

"Well, a person doesn't have to know. You can see it when Cora talks about him."

"Wouldn't it be wonderful if Cora married again?" Anna said. "I like Captain Bradley. He is a good man."

Millie nodded.

Reid threw a look at Millie and Anna and changed the subject. "Are there any claims left t' be had?" he asked Erik.

"They've long since been taken. Only way to get one these days is to steal it or inherit one. Neither option seems to fit you."

"Yeah, I think I'll pass oon the theft, and I doon't know anyone willin' t' give me theirs. What aboot jobs? Is there any fer a man willin' t' work?"

"The real gold is deep underground, but a man needs a lot of money to dig for it. Some of the big money men from California have opened mines. It's dirty, dangerous work, but you shouldn't have any trouble finding someone who needs you. That is if you're willing to do it."

"Work is work. I doon't mind dirt or danger."

Millie gave her husband a sidelong glance, then looked at Erik. "How dangerous is it?"

"If a man's careful, he should probably be all right, but accidents happen. You just don't know."

"Weel, I figure the good Lord's got me life in his hands, and I doon't need t' fear." He patted Millie's hand. "But I won't be doin' anything foolish," he reassured her.

Later that night, after the house was quiet and all had gone to bed, Erik lay next to Anna with his arms folded beneath his head. "It's almost like old times. I didn't realize how much I missed Reid until today. It feels good to have him here."

"Mm, I know," Anna agreed. "It will be nice to have a friend."

"I guess we've both been kind of lonely," he said as he pulled Anna close to him.

With three additional people sharing the Engstrom home, the cabin seemed crowded, but no one really minded. Besides, Christmas was only a day away, and there was much to do. Having friends to share the holiday only made it better.

With much fanfare, Christmas arrived. There were gifts to open and special treats to feast upon and a trip to church through the blistering cold. It was wonderful. That evening Christmas candles cast shadows on the walls as the two families gathered together around the hearth. After tea had been distributed, Erik went to the shelf and took down his Bible.

He settled back in his chair and turned to the book of Luke. All the children watched expectantly. Quietly he began to read about the angel's visit to Mary, telling her of God's Son who would be born to her. Everyone listened intently, quietly sipping tea. Anna never tired of the story, and each year she was reminded of her first Christmas with Erik when he had read the story and how Iya had embraced God's gift and she had rejected it.

Just as Erik began to read of Christ's birth, Anna quietly interrupted. "Erik, wait," she said as she stood up and crossed to him. "Please, may I read?" she asked as she gently lifted the Bible out of his hands.

Erik looked at her with a puzzled expression.

Anna returned to her chair and continued where Erik had left off. *"'And it came to pass in those days that a decree went out from Caesar Augustus that all the world should be registered . . .'"*

With only a few stumbles, Anna read of the miraculous birth of their Savior, the worship of the wise men, and the final flight into Egypt. Gently she closed the Bible. No one spoke.

Erik's eyes glistened with tears. "Why didn't you tell me?"

"I wanted to surprise you. And this seemed the right time—the day of his Son's birth. It is the most wonderful thing to read God's words."

Erik pushed himself out of his chair and swept Anna into his arms.

Anna clung to him. "You were the first to read this to me. Today it is my gift to you."

Erik hugged her tighter and whispered, "I'm so proud of you."

"With God, I can do all things," Anna quoted and smiled up into her husband's proud face. "I will read another," she announced as she opened the Bible. She read the first verse she came to. *"'For everyone to whom much is given, from him much will be required; and to whom much has been committed, of him they will ask the more.'"*

Anna's eyes met Erik's. *Will much be required of us?* she wondered as she closed the Bible and set it back on its resting place upon the shelf.

Chapter 20

Spring thrust aside the cold of winter, and flowers pushed through the soft earth and stretched toward the sun. Buds emerged on the trees and new grasses sprouted. Anna and the children spent hours exploring the nearby fields and forests. After a morning's exploration, they rested on open spaces where the sun could warm them, then returned home with armloads of the early spring wildflowers. Their sweet fragrance filled the house.

Anna made sure not to let the children wander far from home. The forests held many dangers and stretched into great expanses of wilderness waiting to swallow up careless travelers. She didn't fear the woodlands or its creatures but rather felt a great respect for its grandness. Within its cool shadows, she found contentment and peace. She loved to sit quietly and watch moose browse the bottoms of ponds and patiently stand in the tall grasses while their calves nursed.

Blending into the busy society of Juneau had been difficult for Anna. She avoided trips into town whenever possible, preferring the company of the forest over crowds of people. One day, however, finding herself short of staples, she was forced to make the trip. The children, on the other hand, relished such excursions and skipped ahead of Anna, stopping occasionally to wait for her to catch up. When they arrived in town, the children scurried down the street to the mercantile where they waited for Anna.

"I wish I had your energy," Anna said with a sigh as she stepped onto the porch, then went inside with her children trailing behind. Mr. Stevens, the proprietor, was helping a customer, so Anna waited quietly. The children scattered, fascinated by the wide variety of interesting items on the store shelves. Anna smiled as she remembered her first visit to a general store. It had been a wonderful time of discovery. Everything had been new and interesting, and she'd felt like a child as she'd inspected one gadget after another.

A loud crash yanked Anna out of her reverie. She whirled around, searching for the one responsible for the racket and, to her horror, found her son Joseph sprawled out on the floor with the pickle barrel tipped over and pickles scattered all about him. Juice crept across the wooden floor boards and ran between the cracks.

Sheepishly Joseph looked up at the adults staring at him.

"Joseph!" Anna exclaimed. "What have you done?"

"He was trying to get a pickle when he pulled it over," Luba explained.

"I'm sorry, Momma," Joseph said in a high-pitched voice.

Anna marched across the floor and helped the embarrassed youngster up. "Joseph Engstrom! You know not to touch anything," she scolded.

Mr. Stevens chuckled behind her. "Don't be too hard on the boy. I can remember a time when my own desire for a pickle got me into hot water." He hefted the barrel up from the floor, then eyed Joseph. "This is a mighty tall barrel for such a little fella."

"I will pay for the damage," Anna said.

"Not necessary. I'm expecting another shipment any day. The barrel was nearly empty anyhow."

"You are very kind, Mr. Stevens. Thank you." Anna said softly before turning a frown on Joseph.

The stout woman Mr. Stevens had been helping cleared her throat.

"Oh, Mrs. Mullins, I'm sorry. I'll take the rest of your order now," Mr. Stevens said as he scuttled behind the counter to finish helping her.

"Iya, you take the children outside and wait for me until I am finished," Anna said as she gave Joseph's shoulder a gentle squeeze. "And watch this one," she added with a smile as she smoothed her skirt and returned to the counter.

Mrs. Mullins peered down at Anna through a pair of wire-rimmed spectacles perched on the bridge of her nose. She sniffed and turned a steely gaze on the store owner.

"You serve natives?" she bristled.

The proprietor leveled an even look at the woman. "We serve whoever comes through that door."

"But Indians?" Mrs. Mullins asked as she leaned over the counter, cupped her hand next to her mouth, and whispered just loud enough so Anna could hear, "I don't want to buy merchandise that some Indian might have touched. A person never knows what they might catch."

Anna felt rage well up within her and glared at the woman. She forced herself to remain silent.

Mr. Stevens's face reddened and he crossed his arms. "You don't have to buy from us," he said coldly. "If you have a mind to, you can go elsewhere."

"Well, I never," the woman sputtered as she gathered her parcels against her ample bosom, lifted her nose in the air, and flounced out of the store.

The owner smiled apologetically at Anna. "What can I do for you, Anna?"

Now that the dreadful woman had gone, Anna felt her anger diminish and hurt well up in its place. Tears stung her eyes, and she swallowed hard as she tried to control her emotions. Why were people like that?

"Thank you, Mr. Stevens," she managed to say. "I need a pound of sugar and ten pounds of flour."

"I've got it right here," the friendly man said as he stepped from behind the counter, lifted the lid off a large bin, and began scooping flour into a burlap bag. He set it on the counter then did the same with the sugar. "That'll be one dollar," he said as he returned to the cash register.

Anna handed him the coins and with a sad smile left the store.

"What happened?" Iya asked. "That woman looked real mad when she came out."

"Nothing happened," Anna answered shortly and strode down the street.

Overall, life in Juneau had been good, but the continued cruelty of some still had the power to wound Anna. She just couldn't get used to it and found with each additional rude remark or hateful look she became more angry. Within her warred a battle against her own bitterness. It would be so easy to allow the anger to rule her life, but she knew it wasn't God's way. Many times she sought him, knowing only that he held the power to love all people. As long as she was willing, he provided the ability to forgive. Still, Anna found she had to seek his help more and more often.

She prayed quietly as she walked. *God, give me peace. Help me to see that woman as you see her.* She turned toward Millie's. Anna knew she needed to talk to Millie. Chewing on her lip, she picked up her pace as she thought of her longtime friend. Many times she had helped Anna through turbulent waters. *Father, thank you for Millie,* Anna prayed as she hurried on.

Reid had found work at a local mill and built a log home on the outskirts of town. Anna knew the way well. She and the children had visited many times.

"Are we going to Millie's?" Evan asked.

Anna nodded and immediately the children broke into a trot. They loved visiting Millie and knew she always had goodies waiting for them.

When Anna arrived, the children were already sitting on the porch, munching cookies. Millie smiled. "It's good to see you, Anna. Please come in." She took a closer look at her friend. "There's something wrong, isn't there."

Anna shrugged her shoulders. "Not really."

"Oh? I've seen that look before. I know you well enough to know when something's bothering you." She grinned. "Why don't I make us a cup of tea, and we can have a nice chat," she said as she draped her arm over Anna's shoulders and ushered her friend inside.

Anna set her packages on the table and slumped into a chair.

Millie measured tea into a strip of cheesecloth, pulled it together at the top and tied it, then placed the pouch into a kettle of hot water. While it steeped, she set a platter of cookies in the center of the table. "I just made these this morning. They're quite good, even if I do say so myself."

Anna smiled and took one, but she didn't taste it. "Thank you,

Millie," she said and took a long, deep breath. "Your house always smells of baking."

"Well, it seems I do a lot of it. You know Reid's got to have his sweets."

"You love it," Anna teased.

"I must admit; I do enjoy cooking." She glanced out at the porch where the children chatted. "Especially since Nina came to live with us. She's such a good little girl." Millie's eyes filled with tears. She quickly blinked them away, squeezed the excess water from the tea bag, then filled two cups with the fragrant brew. She set a mug in front of Anna, then took hers and sat across the table from her friend.

Anna nestled back into her chair with her mug cupped between her hands. She felt better already. Sunlight streamed through the front window, warming the room and brightening Millie's tufted rugs and assorted knickknacks. An old woodstove stood in the center of the room, smelling of spruce and hemlock. The house felt cozy and friendly.

"I always feel at home here," Anna said.

Millie smiled warmly.

Halfheartedly Anna nibbled on her cookie. It tasted sweet and flaked into crumbs in her mouth.

"Now, tell me what's got you so down in the mouth?"

Anna looked at her hands. "I do not want to complain."

"Sharing isn't complaining. After all, God told us we are to share one another's burdens. That way the load doesn't feel so heavy." She smiled and sipped her tea.

"It is nothing, really, just a woman at the mercantile."

Millie waited quietly.

"I needed some flour and sugar. While I was waiting, Joseph spilled the barrel of pickles and . . ."

"I'd like to have seen that," Millie interrupted with a chuckle.

Anna frowned. "There was a woman who did not think it was funny. She became very angry and did not want Mr. Stevens to sell to us."

A hard line replaced Millie's smile.

"She told Mr. Stevens that if he let Indians shop in his store she would not buy from him."

Millie patted Anna's hand. "And what did Mr. Stevens do?"

"He told her she could go to another store."

"Well there you see, he doesn't care that you're an Indian."

Tears welled up in Anna's eyes, and she ran her finger along the wood grain of the table. "Millie, when will the hating stop? Why is it wrong to be an Indian?"

"It's not wrong. It's just that some people's thinking is depraved. God made you just the way he wanted."

Tears escaped the corners of Anna's eyes.

Millie stood up and knelt next to her friend. She wrapped her arms around the small woman. "Anna, most people don't give a hoot what color you are. And those who do, well you can't let them bother you. What's most important is that God made you, and he is pleased with his creation. In fact, he says we are made in his likeness."

Anna leaned her head against Millie's shoulder. "I knew I needed to see you. You always know what to say to make me feel better."

Millie gave her a hug. "I'm glad you came."

"Millie, do you think it will always be like this? Or will people learn to love each other?"

"Change is always slow. I don't think we'll see the end of this in our lifetime, but maybe some day. You have to remember there has been a lot of hurt on both sides."

"Sometimes I feel I cannot listen to one more cruel word."

Millie studied her cup then looked up at her friend. "Anna, God will see you through. He understands. After all, he suffered the greatest rejection of all—that of his own people." She sipped her tea. "There are only a handful of mean folks. Those of us who know you, love you. Just try to remember that."

Anna managed a small smile and nodded, then dipped her cookie into her tea and took a bite. "This is very good."

That evening, Anna told Erik what had happened in town. At first, Erik's anger at the injustice boiled to the surface; it was quickly mingled with irritation at Anna's reaction. "You've got to stop letting people upset you," he said sternly.

"What can I do?"

"Just ignore them. If you let people know you're hurt, it only gives them more reason to bother you."

"You do not understand what it's like, Erik. I try not to show what I feel, but sometimes it is impossible." Her chin quivered as she continued, "To have people degrade you . . ." She couldn't finish.

"What makes you think I don't understand? I've been living with you for many years now. I've seen what happens," Erik almost shouted.

"If you understand, then why do you yell?" Before Erik could reply, Anna went on, "What will there be for the children? What more will they face? It is not fair. Sometimes I think it would have been better if you had left Iya and me on the beach." She kept her eyes averted, unable to meet his stare.

"Leave you!" Erik spouted. "I can't believe you'd say that."

"Well, I did," Anna answered haughtily and lifted her eyes to his in a challenge. For a moment, they stared at each other, then in one swift movement, Anna threw a cloak over her shoulders, flung open the door, and ran outside. *He does not understand,* she lamented as she ran into the forest. "Oh, Father, why doesn't he understand?" She wept as she raced on, flailing through the thick underbrush.

Winded, she finally stopped and leaned against a tree for support. She rested her face against its cool surface and cried, releasing years of hurt. "It is too hard," she sobbed. "I cannot do it anymore. God, you have to make it stop."

Feeling empty, Anna sank to the ground and tucked her knees up close to her chest. Gradually her pounding heart steadied and her breathing slowed. She inhaled and looked up through the trees. A full moon was just beginning to reach above the horizon. A cloud threaded itself across its face, momentarily blocking the brightness. Anna stared at the golden sphere and remembered a time when such an apparition would have frightened her. She knew now it was not an evil omen but part of God's creation.

Anna's mind returned to her quarrel with Erik. She could not remember ever having such a serious fight. She rested her cheek on her knees, and the reality of how wrong she had been began to sink in. She knew Erik tried, that he did his best to understand. *How could I have been so mean to him? He has felt my pain and stood by me through it all.* A picture of Erik defending her against a sailor on the first ship they sailed on came to mind. *Why am I so stubborn?* she asked herself. As long as she could remember she'd always been so. The elders of her tribe had had such a time with her. She smiled as memories from her childhood flooded her mind. Her stubbornness had put her under their authority more than once, but they'd always forgiven her and set her back on course. Erik had been like that—gently guiding and encouraging.

He looked so hurt and startled when she'd run from the cabin. "I must go back and tell him I am sorry," she said aloud as she pushed herself to her feet.

She looked about, trying to get her bearings, but nothing looked familiar in the shadowy light of the moon. Goose bumps rose on her arms and her heart pounded a little faster as she realized she didn't know the way back. She'd been in such an emotional state when she'd run into the woods that she hadn't bothered to pay attention to where she was going. She forced down her rising panic and attempted to think. But no matter how hard she tried to recall her steps, she couldn't. *How could I be so foolish?* she asked herself.

She looked at the moon. "Dear God, please show me the way," she prayed. "Give me wisdom." Taking a deep breath, she took one more look about and headed in the direction she felt was right.

The moon slipped behind a blanket of clouds, and the forest was thrown into darkness. Anna stumbled over a protruding tree root and fell. Her hands sank into soggy moss, and the smell of damp earth and rotting plants assaulted her. She pushed herself to her knees and sat back, fighting tears of frustration. The night sounds that had always seemed so comforting from the protection of her home frightened her now. The cry of an owl sent shivers up her spine, and the croak of frogs sounded disturbing and unreal. She felt like a child and longed for the comfort of her mother's arms. It had been so long since she'd known her mother's tenderness.

"I am afraid," she whispered into the still night air. She knew she might never be found in the endless forest. *People will wonder what happened to me,* she thought. "God, I need your help."

Light and shadows mingled as the moon reappeared from behind the clouds. As Anna pushed herself back to her feet, a rustling came from the nearby bushes. She held perfectly still and listened, afraid to even breathe. Something moved stealthily into the forest. When Anna could no longer hear it, she breathed a sigh of relief and moved on.

Several minutes later, she stopped to rest on a downed log. She shivered and brushed her hair back from her face. *How do I know if I'm going the right way?* she wondered. Her throat felt parched, and she longed for a cool drink of water. Closing her eyes, she thought of how good her warm bed would feel and once more chided herself for her foolish outburst.

A light breeze tousled her hair, and Anna thought she detected a hint of salt on the air. She sniffed. *Yes! It did smell like the sea!* Hope sprang within her. If she found the beach, home awaited her.

Barely able to contain her excitement, she headed in the direction of the salty aroma. She had to force herself to be cautious and not run. Soon, she could hear the pounding of surf, and the wind began to whip her hair about her face. She knew she was close. Finally she broke free of the forest, and an open expanse of beach greeted her. She raced onto the sand and looked about. The moon no longer hid behind clouds or trees but shone so brightly her shadow stretched across the sand. A familiar silhouette of a jagged rock protruded from the waves.

"Thank you, Father," she called before setting off toward Juneau and then inland, toward home.

Late into the night the cabin emerged from the landscape. Bathed in moonlight, Anna thought it had never looked so good. As she stepped onto the porch, she whispered, "Thank you, Lord." She opened the door and stepped inside. What she found stunned her. The cabin, lit by a single small lamp, felt cold. No fire burned in the stove, and Erik sat at the table with his head in his hands, a whiskey bottle and glass beside him. He peered up at Anna as she closed the door.

His face looked old and lined with grief and remorse. Guilt washed over Anna. She had caused this. "Erik," she said as she crossed to the table, "I am sorry. I did not mean what I said. You have been the blessing of my life. I thank God for you every day. Please forgive me."

"No. I'm the one. I didn't listen. I wasn't fair to you and the girls. It hurts so much to watch the people I love get wounded time and time again. I just didn't want to hear any more. I'm sorry." He stood up and pulled Anna into his arms. "Please forgive me."

Anna buried her face in his chest, then looked up into his eyes and caressed his cheek. "There is nothing to forgive. I am only grateful for you."

Erik kissed her gently. "I love you."

Anna wrapped her arms around him and rested against his broad chest. She felt safe and wished she could remain in his embrace always.

A chill passed through her and she shivered.

"You're cold. Here, let me get you something hot to drink," Erik said as he released her and went to the stove. He started a fire and put a pot of coffee on to boil, then disappeared into their room. A moment later he returned with a quilt. "Put this around you," he said kindly as he draped the blanket over her shoulders.

Anna took the covering gratefully, but as her eyes fell upon the bottle and glass on the table, she couldn't help but ask, "Why the drink?"

Looking a little sheepish, Erik took the bottle and corked it. "Reid left it. I felt so bad, I guess I thought it might help. It didn't," he added.

"Erik, over the years, you and I have watched many natives be destroyed by liquor," Anna said, her voice grief laden.

Erik sat down heavily at the table. "I know. I've never really been one to drink much; it just seemed the thing to do." He looked at his hands. "After you left, I got to thinking about my own past and how much it hurt when people teased me about my accent and my parents' 'foreign quirks.' I realized how bad it's been for you. And I wasn't helping. Of all people, I should understand. When I was a boy, the kids teased me unmercifully. They made fun of the way my parents dressed and talked. I used to pretend they weren't my folks. But of course everyone knew. It was tough, but I worked hard to fit in; I even managed to overcome my accent. But now I know who I am. I'm the son of immigrants, and Norway is where I'm from and that will never change." He looked at Anna. "I know what it feels like to have someone judge you based on your parentage."

Anna cringed. *He still does not understand,* she thought. "Erik, why did you not tell me this before?"

"It was something I tried to forget. I didn't want to think about it."

Anna bit her lip. "Erik, you can hide who you are. I never can."

"I know it's not exactly the same thing, but I remember how much it hurt."

Anna smiled. "It is good that we share this thing. God knew we needed each other when he sent you to Iya and me." She sighed and picked up the bottle of liquor. "Tomorrow I will take this to Reid," she said as she set the bottle on the counter.

"I almost went over there tonight."

"Why?"

"I figured that's where you were."

Anna considered letting him believe she had been there, but immediately dismissed the idea, knowing honesty is what God wanted. Quietly she said, "I did not go to Millie's."

"Then where have you been?"

Anna hesitated. "In the woods."

"Anna! You know better."

Anna poured two cups of coffee. She handed one to Erik and sipped hers. "I know it was foolish, but I let my anger control me. Before I knew it, I was lost."

The color drained from Erik's face. "Anna, do you know what could have happened?"

Anna nodded. "I made it to the beach and found my way home from there," she explained quietly.

"If I had known . . ." Erik began.

"You did not," Anna answered matter-of-factly. "But God did. And even though I was foolish, he took care of me." She smiled softly. "He always cares for me." She took another sip of coffee and set her cup on the counter. "I feel so tired. It is time for bed."

Erik draped his arm around Anna's waist and pulled her close. "I will try to be more understanding. I promise. I thank God for you, Anna," he said as they walked to their room.

Anna leaned against him. "And I, you," she said softly.

Chapter 21

*A*nna slapped at a mosquito, then resumed fanning herself with a folded newspaper. Nothing seemed to ward off the persistent pests. She leaned back in the deep grass along the bank and gazed up at the sky. Billowy white clouds rested against a blue backdrop. *If not for the bugs this would be a perfect day,* she thought as she turned her attention back to Erik who worked along the river. Her heart fluttered as she studied the tall, blond man. She never tired of watching him.

With a sigh, she pushed herself to her feet. "I have things to do," she told herself. She'd invited Reid and Millie for Sunday dinner and still had baking to finish.

She scanned the riverbank. Her three youngest children had ventured so far upstream she couldn't see them. *The older they become the farther they wander,* she thought sadly. Iya worked alongside Erik. Of all the children, Iya spent the most time with Erik. From the beginning, they had shared a special bond.

For a moment, Anna considered what her life had once been. She hadn't thought about it for a long time. It seemed so long ago. Life in Juneau had been good, although their claim produced only modest quantities of gold. Still, Anna felt content. She had a fine home and a wonderful family. *I have no complaints,* she thought as she slapped at another mosquito. "Except these bugs!"

She went inside and started a fire in the stove, then set out the ingredients she needed to bake a berry pie. When she went to get the lard, she found the container nearly empty. "This is not going to be enough," she said with a sigh. "Now I will have to go to town." She glanced out the window. "Well, it is a beautiful day," she conceded and took a jar from the top shelf. She poured out its contents and counted out enough change for her purchase, then replaced the money and put the jar back on the shelf.

Before leaving, she stopped at the top of the embankment and called to Erik. "I am going into town."

Erik nodded and waved.

Anna waved back, not minding so much that she had to make the trip. It would be nice to walk along the river's edge on such a nice day. She strolled down the path, enjoying the fresh air and sunshine. Fireweed bloomed all along the hillsides, and Anna decided that on the way back she would pick a bunch of the bright pink flowers.

Once in town, she headed straight for the mercantile. After buying the lard she needed, she rushed out of the store, determined to make it home early. She'd taken far too long coming into town. With the handle of the lard container slung over her arm, she hurried down the street while tucking her money into a leather pouch. She was so engrossed in what she was doing, she didn't see the man who blocked her way and ran straight into him.

"I am sorry . . . " she began, then stopped abruptly when she looked into the man's face. A mixture of fear and anger wedged itself beneath her ribs, and she sucked in her breath. Staring into the cold, hard eyes of Jarvis Moyer, she tried to maintain her composure.

His mouth turned up in a sinister grin. "Well, if it isn't little Anna. It's been a while."

Anna stared at him, then without a word tried to push past.

"Whoa there. I didn't say you could go."

"No one tells me what I can do," Anna retorted, lifting her chin defiantly and trying to step around him.

Jarvis grabbed her arm. "I'm not finished talkin' to you."

"I will scream if you do not let go," Anna threatened.

He smiled. "Go ahead. Try it. I don't think the yell of one little Injun lady'll bring much attention."

"I have many friends," Anna said as she glanced around, looking for a familiar face. Finding none, she yanked her arm free.

A tall Indian stepped up beside Jarvis. "Let's get moving," he said nervously.

"I'll go when I'm good 'n ready. If you're in such a dad-blame hurry, go ahead without me."

Anna watched the big native, curious at his reaction.

"We have better things to do than mess with this woman. Let's go."

As Jarvis looked up at his partner, his grip loosened, and Anna saw her chance to escape. She quickly slipped past him and headed down the street toward home.

"I'll see you around," Jarvis called after her and laughed.

As Anna hurried away, she didn't look back. Her heart pounded and her mouth felt dry, and she couldn't seem to draw enough oxygen into her lungs. Only after putting a lot of space between herself and town did she finally stop. She leaned against a tall fir to catch her breath and watched the path to make sure Jarvis hadn't followed. When she saw no sign of him, she relaxed a little and headed home at a hurried pace.

She was uncertain whether she should tell Erik about her encounter or not, but later that afternoon decided it would be best. Erik sat at the table working on his rifle while Joseph sat beside his father and watched. Anna joined them. "Would you like some coffee?"

"No thanks."

Anna hesitated, then said quietly, "I had to go in to town for some lard this afternoon."

"Looks like you put it to good use," Erik said, eyeing the pies on the counter.

"While I was there I met someone."

Erik looked keenly at Anna. "Who?"

Trying to calm herself, Anna clasped her hands in her lap.

"Momma, when can I go to school?" Joseph asked, taking advantage of the lull in the conversation.

"Not until next year, Joseph."

"Why?" he whined.

"You won't be old enough until then," Anna answered, thankful for the diversion.

"You were about to tell me about someone you met in town?" Erik prodded.

"Oh, yes." She cleared her throat. "I, uh, ran into Jarvis Moyer."

"Jarvis? What's he still doing in town?" Erik bristled. "I haven't seen him for a while and thought he'd moved on. I guess that's too much to hope for. Did he bother you?"

Anna glanced down at her plate. "No," she lied. "He only said hello."

"I can just imagine his greeting," Erik scoffed as he pushed himself away from the table. "I've got some work to do," he said and stormed out the door.

When Erik returned later that evening, they said nothing more about Jarvis. Anna knew Erik would be watching for the man and felt uneasy. His temper sometimes got the better of him and she worried, knowing how intensely he disliked the evil drifter.

The following day, Anna's meeting with Jarvis was forgotten as Reid and Millie came for lunch after church. The weather remained fair, so they picnicked at the stream. Erik and Reid took the children wading while Anna and Millie watched.

"Do you remember playing in the river when you were young?" Millie asked dreamily.

"Yes, I always loved the water, but at the beach it was very cold. When the summer sun came and warmed the land, I would sometimes swim out into the surf." Anna smiled. "My brothers would yell at me from the shore, threatening to tell, but they never did."

"My parents used to take us to a quiet spot on the creek by my home where the water washed into a deep pool. While my father fished upstream, my sister, Eleanor, and I would jump into the deepest spot and try to touch the bottom. Then we would join Momma in the warm grass and rest in the sun while she told us stories of her own childhood." She smiled softly at the memory.

"If we both like swimming, why are we sitting here?" Anna asked, feeling a sudden surge of youthful enthusiasm.

A look of mischief crossed Millie's face. "Why, I don't know." She jumped to her feet. "The last one in is a gallinipper," she called over her shoulder as she scrambled down the bank.

Anna laughed and followed her. Squealing as the cold water hit them, both women plunged into the icy pool.

Anna found bottom and stood up. "Ohh, that is cold," she said, shivering as she brushed her hair back from her face.

"Yes, but it feels wonderful!" Millie gushed.

"Weel, I'll be," Reid said, clearly amused.

Millie eyed her husband playfully and splashed him with water. Reid immediately reciprocated, and soon all the adults as well as the children participated in the play.

Still laughing, Anna waded to the edge of the creek and sat down. "I cannot remember having so much fun. We should do this more."

"I still can't believe ye' did that," Reid told Millie. "I guess I always knew ye' were a real spitfire," he teased and hugged her.

Millie smiled.

A scream came from the stream. Instantly alert, Anna stood up and looked for the trouble. "It's Iya! The current's got her!" she cried, a knot forming in her stomach as she watched her sister struggle to stay afloat.

Erik flung himself into the creek. She hadn't gone far and he reached her quickly, grabbed hold of her shirt, and easily pulled her into the shallows. Shivering with fear, Iya clung to him. Erik steadied her and helped her walk to shore.

"Oh, Iya, you scared me!" Millie said.

"Me too," Iya answered, wrapping her arms about herself and trembling.

"It's high time ye' learned to swim, yoong lady," Reid reprimanded.

"Someone has to teach me."

"I guess that's my responsibility," Erik said. "This summer's nearly gone, but I promise next year I'll teach the whole lot of you."

The days passed quickly and quietly, and as autumn approached, Anna spent many hours working in the garden. One morning, she stopped her work and leaned on her hoe as she studied the rows of healthy plants. "This year we will have enough to see us until next summer," she told Erik. She patted Evan's shoulder. "It is because of the children that we have such a fine garden. I will miss their help when they go back to school."

"We will need another slate for Evan," Iya said. "And we need more slate pencils. May I go into town and get them?"

Anna thought a moment. "I do not like you to go alone, Iya. There are many people we do not know, and Jarvis is there."

"I don't like him hanging around. He's always looking for trouble," Erik added.

"He does not frighten me anymore. He is hateful, but I do not think he will hurt me."

"I wouldn't be so sure of that."

"Can I go?" Iya pleaded.

Anna felt uneasy. She looked at Erik. "She is growing up. What do you think?"

"She's nearly thirteen. I s'pose it's time to give her a little more freedom," Erik admitted.

Anna thought a minute. "All right, Iya, you may go, but you must not speak to strangers, and if you see that Jarvis Moyer, stay away from him."

Iya smiled and raced toward the house. "I will get the money jar," she called over her shoulder. A moment later she reappeared with the treasured crock that held their savings.

Erik frowned. "We ought to open an account at the bank. We're accumulating enough cash these days that I worry about leaving it in the house."

"Here," Iya said thrusting the container into Anna's hands.

Anna counted out just enough coins for the needed items. "This should be all you need," she said, and she placed the money in Iya's hand. "Do not lose it."

"I will be careful," Iya assured her.

"All right, then," Anna said, still uncertain she was doing the right thing.

"I won't be gone long," Iya promised as she headed down the trail.

"Why can't I go?" Luba and Joseph both whined in unison.

"Today Iya will go alone," is all Anna said as she watched the young girl disappear around the bend.

Iya enjoyed the sensation of freedom. There was no one to tell her what to do or how to do it. She felt very grown up. Each time she met a neighbor, she greeted him or her in her most mature voice and made sure to be very polite.

When she came upon old Mr. Vanguard, she stopped and said, "Good morning, Mr. Vanguard. How are you today?"

"Oh, fair to middlin' young lady. How about yourself?"

Iya liked Mr. Vanguard. He had bright blue eyes that sparkled when he talked, and his long white beard reminded her of the pictures she'd seen of Santa Claus, although he wasn't at all rounded, but very thin and a little bent. A tattered cap crowned his shoulder-length silver hair, and he always wore a smile. Whenever he had goodies, he shared them with the children along the river.

"Where's the rest of your family today?" the old man asked.

Iya squared her shoulders and answered, "They are at home."

"They know you're off by yourself?"

"Yes. I am old enough to go into town on my own," she stated proudly.

The old gentleman eyed her closely. He grinned and said, "Why now that you mention it, seems you are at that. Just the same, you watch out for strangers and don't dawdle."

"I won't," Iya promised and hurried down the trail. Swinging her arms, she took long strides, enjoying the sensation of the breeze against her face and the strength in her legs. A squirrel scampered across the trail and hurried up a tree. Iya stopped to watch the creature scoot across an overhanging branch where it stopped and looked down at her, its nose twitching and its tail bristling nervously.

Iya grinned. *I wonder what it's like to be a squirrel.* "Good morning Mr. Squirrel," she said, then glanced at the sky and realized noon was quickly approaching. *I better hurry, or Anna will skin me alive,* she thought and moved on.

Iya loved the town with its busyness. She watched the flood of homesteaders and prospectors bustling through the dusty streets. Iya was so enthralled with watching people that she quickly lost track of time and was barely aware that she had arrived at the mercantile.

"You going to stand out here all day?" Mr. Stevens asked as he swept a pile of dirt off the front step.

Iya blushed as she turned to look at him. "I was just watching all the folks," she explained as she followed him indoors.

"Some pretty interesting characters in town these days, I have to admit," Mr. Stevens said with a smile. "What can I do for you today?"

"I need one slate and three slate pencils."

"I think I can manage that." He searched his shelf. "Ah, here they are." He took the items from the cupboard and laid them on the counter. "Will you be needing anything else?"

"No, that's all today," Iya said, feeling very grown-up as she placed her money on the counter.

Mr. Stevens sorted through the coins and, when he finished, handed two coppers back to Iya. "You've just enough left to buy yourself a couple pieces of hard candy," he said with a twinkle in his eyes.

Iya thought a moment. *What will Anna say if I spend the money on sweets? She doesn't have to know,* she reasoned and slid the coins across to Mr. Stevens. "I would like one peppermint stick and some gumdrops please."

Mr. Stevens smiled, pulled a stick of peppermint from one jar and a handful of gumdrops from another, and dropped them into a bag.

"Thank you," Iya said as she took the candy and school supplies and left the store. She was in no hurry to return home, so she strolled along the street with her packages carefully tucked under her arm. She found a shaded spot and sat down. Digging into her bag, she counted out the pieces of candy and decided she would share them with her family. *Anna won't be mad if I share,* she thought as she stuck the peppermint stick in her mouth and settled back to watch the passersby. The street seemed emptier now, and Iya figured everyone must have gone in for lunch. Her own stomach grumbled.

She stifled a giggle as a woman with eight children walked by. Round and plump, the woman reminded her of a fat hen with her brood of chicks flocking about her. With a stern look, she glanced at Iya, then gathered her children closer and moved down the street.

Iya leaned against the building and relished the feeling of maturity. *One day I will have my own children,* she thought. A group of tough-looking boys migrated up the street, and Iya's stomach fluttered. Would they harass her? As they came closer, she could see some of the boys were part native and, thankfully, barely gave her a glance as they walked by. She breathed a sigh of relief and remembered Anna's warning not to dawdle.

Gathering up her packages, she set off for home. As she passed a tavern doorway, she heard shouting coming from inside. She knew better than to stop but couldn't resist and decided a peek wouldn't hurt. She swung open the door and glanced inside. The room looked dark after the bright afternoon sunlight. Iya peered into the gloom, and as her eyes adjusted, she saw five men standing around a table. They looked angry as they glared at each other. With her heart pounding, she waited to see what would happen. Then she recognized one of the men and stifled a cry. It was Jarvis Moyer! *I should go,* she told herself, but didn't move. Instead she eased inside to watch.

"You were cheatin' and you know it," a bearded man sputtered at Jarvis.

"Prove it," Jarvis taunted.

"I don't have to. Everyone knows you're a cheat."

Jarvis lunged at the man, grabbed him by the collar, and pulled him to within inches of his face. "I'm a what?" he asked through clenched teeth.

"You're a cheat," the bearded man repeated, meeting Jarvis's stare.

Joe thrust his arm between the two men. "Hey, that's enough. Jarvis, let's get out of here."

Jarvis scowled at Joe and tightened his grip on the man. With a deadly glare, he suddenly flung him free.

The man lost his footing and fell to the floor.

Jarvis smirked as he grabbed his hat off the table and headed for the door.

Iya tried to squeeze into the shadows, but she wasn't quick enough. Jarvis stopped and stared at the little girl pressed against the wall. At first he didn't seem to know her, but then a glimmer of recognition crossed his face and a cruel smile played on his lips. "Well if it ain't the little Injun girl. Pretty grown up now ain't ya?" he added with a gleam in his eye.

Iya's fear became anger, and she thrust her shoulders back as she tipped her face up to her enemy and glared at him. "I am not afraid of you."

"Oh, is that so?" Jarvis sneered as he bent down, his face only inches from hers.

Iya could smell liquor on his breath. The odor sickened her.

"We don't have time for this," Joe said. "Come on, let's go."

"Shut up!" Jarvis shouted. "I'll do what I like. I'm tired of you tellin' me what to do all the time."

Iya tried to escape, but Jarvis grabbed her by the sleeve. "Where do you think you're going? I didn't say you could leave."

Instinctively Iya kicked, hitting Jarvis in the shin. As he grabbed at his leg, she slipped out the door and ran down the street. She could hear Jarvis cursing, then the sound of his boots beating the ground behind her, but she didn't dare stop to look. *If only my legs were longer,* she thought, willing them to move faster. She knew he could easily outrun her. Fear gripped Iya and her heart raced as she pushed herself to move faster. *If he catches me . . .* she couldn't finish the thought. She scanned the streets, looking for anyone who might help, but they were empty. *Where can I go?* she asked herself, as she tried to fill her lungs with needed oxygen. Her chest burned and her legs felt like lead. The pier was almost always busy. She turned toward the bay.

Jarvis's labored breathing was close behind her. *He is getting close! God help me!* Iya's mind screamed. She raced onto the dock, but the boats were out with the tides and the fishermen with them. She ran until the pier ended and then she stopped. There was no one who could help. She stared down into the murky waters of the bay and considered jumping, but she couldn't swim. She was trapped. Iya turned and faced her pursuer.

"I've got you now, you little brat," Jarvis said as he stopped and struggled to catch his breath. He swaggered confidently toward her. "Thought you could outrun me, huh?" He bent in a half-crouch with his arms extended slightly from his sides as he approached.

Iya's heart pounded and she felt like she might be sick. *Maybe I can get around him,* she thought and took a step sideways.

Jarvis moved with her and blocked her way. "You're not getting away this time," he threatened as he closed the distance. He lunged at her and grabbed her arm, pinning it behind her back.

Iya struggled to pull free, but a pain shot through her shoulder and down her arm. She stifled a cry.

He gripped her around the waist, and Iya turned and pummeled his chest with her fists. "Let me go!"

"Not on your life. You ain't gonna give me any more grief," Jarvis growled.

Iya felt smothered by fear, but kicked at him again.

"That's enough of that," he said as he held her out at arm's length and struck her across the face. The blow knocked her to the edge of the pier. Like a cat ready to pounce, Jarvis came toward her. Iya tried to scramble away, but her foot slipped and she knew she was going to fall. She tried to grab for the wood pilings, and a scream wrenched itself from her throat as she plunged into the bay.

The icy water washed over her, and she tasted salt as she struggled toward the surface. Choking, she flailed at the water and tried to stay afloat, but again and again the water closed over her head. "Help me!" she cried in a strangled voice as she looked into the dead eyes of Jarvis Moyer. For a moment, he stood on the pier and watched, then turned and walked away.

Chapter 22

*A*nna set her sewing aside and went to the window. With a growing sense of alarm, she looked across the clearing and up the trail that led to town. *Iya should be back. Where is she?*

She watched as Luba, Evan, and Joseph played a game of tag. Momentarily distracted, she smiled as Evan chased after Luba and easily caught her. *He is growing so quickly,* she thought as the boy swung away and sprinted out of his sister's reach, avoiding being retagged. He'd grown out of his childhood chubbiness and promised to be tall like his father.

Anna sighed and glanced back at the trail, her stomach churning with apprehension. *She is probably just dallying,* Anna told herself as she returned to her sewing. But no matter how hard she tried to push aside her growing sense of foreboding, it tugged at her. She stabbed the needle down through the material of Iya's new church dress and told herself, *She is fine.*

The door flew open, and Anna put on her sternest look, ready to give Iya a tongue-lashing for her tardiness. She looked up, but it was only Luba. Disappointed, Anna forced a smile as Luba closed the door.

"Momma, is something wrong?"

"No," Anna answered pensively. "Is Iya back?"

"I have not seen her. We are waiting. It's a lot more fun when Iya is here."

Anna sighed and lay her sewing in her lap. *Where are you, Iya?* she inquired silently. Then she asked Luba, "Is your daddy still down at the river?"

Luba nodded, her cheerful expression replaced by a look of trepidation.

As Anna thought of all the possible reasons for Iya's tardiness, her fear grew. Unable to remain still, she crossed to the window and paced back and forth, occasionally stopping to look up the trail. Her breathing became rapid, and she fought tears of anxiety.

"I cannot wait here any longer," she finally said, grabbing a jacket from the hook by the door and heading for the river and Erik. She stopped a moment and studied the pathway, hoping Iya would appear, but when she didn't, fresh tears filled her eyes and a choking fear swept through her. She ran down the bank and across the rocks to Erik.

Erik stood up and wiped his brow as he watched Anna, concern creasing his face. "Anna, what is it? What's wrong?"

"Iya has not returned."

Erik glanced at the sky. The sun would be setting soon. "It's late. She should have been back long ago. Why didn't you tell me?" he asked, his voice sharp and worried.

"I kept telling myself she had only lost track of time," Anna explained as she glanced nervously toward the bank, still hoping Iya would appear wearing a sheepish grin for being so late.

Erik tossed his shovel aside. "That's probably all it is, but I'll go see if I can find her. Maybe she's at Millie's."

Hope leaped in Anna. *Millie's! Yes, that is it. She went to Millie's.*

Erik planted a quick kiss on Anna's cheek. "I won't be long. I'll probably meet her on the trail," he said hopefully as he headed up the bank.

"Erik, please hurry. If anything happens to her . . ."

Erik stopped and looked at Anna. "I'm sure it's nothing," he tried to reassure her.

Anna wished she could go but knew her children needed her. She trudged up the embankment. Luba and the boys were waiting. They sensed that something was wrong.

"Where is Iya?" Joseph asked.

Anna forced a smile. "Iya is just a little late coming back from town. Daddy went to get her." Feeling a need to gather her children close, Anna said, "Please come inside."

"I want to play," Evan complained. "Why do we have to stay inside just because Iya is late?"

"I know." Anna steered the little boy toward the house, and she searched for a reason. "I . . . I will need your help to fix supper."

The six-year-old looked at his mother accusingly. "Something is wrong. Why hasn't Iya come home?"

Anna swallowed and tried to hide her concern as she walked up the front steps. "Everything is fine. Iya will be here soon." She ushered the children indoors then went into the kitchen and pulled a bag of potatoes from a lower cupboard. "Evan, you and Joseph can wash these. Luba, would you slice some carrots? I think soup will be good. Just what Erik and Iya will need when they get home."

Once more, she crossed to the window and stared out. She longed to see Erik and Iya walk into the clearing hand-in-hand, but all that greeted her were the tree boughs bending in the breeze and a shower of autumn leaves carelessly pitching about in the wind.

She turned back and checked the rising bread dough she'd left earlier. She'd nearly forgotten it. "This looks almost right," she said as lightheartedly as she could while she started a fire in the stove.

When another hour passed and Erik and Iya had still not returned, Anna couldn't bear the waiting any longer. She set the children's meal on the table and pulled on a coat. "Luba, I am going to town. You are in charge."

Luba stood straighter. "I am more than seven now," she said proudly. "I will take care of everything. We will stay right here until you get back," she promised, eyeing her brothers sternly.

Anna bent and gave them each a quick kiss before stepping into the chilly evening air. She barely noticed the cool, brisk wind as she hurried toward town. The sun lay low in the sky, its warmth lost. Long shadows stretched across the path. Anna's stomach churned. She knew something was terribly wrong. It was far too late. Iya should have been back hours ago. And where was Erik?

She broke into a trot. *Heavenly Father, please protect them. Please don't let anything happen to Iya,* she prayed as she ran. She breathed a sigh of relief when Juneau came into sight. Everything seemed fine. But she felt shocked at the world's normalcy while she carried so much turmoil and anguish within.

She searched the streets. Erik and Iya seemed to have disappeared from the face of the earth. *Where are they?* she asked herself.

Erik strode down the street, his heart pounding hard in his chest. Iya hadn't been at Millie's, and he'd looked everywhere else. Where could she be? Mr. Stevens said she'd been in the store earlier. He said she'd purchased a slate, pencils, and some candy. After that he hadn't seen her.

At least I know she made it this far, Erik reasoned. *But what could have happened to her?* "Dear God, show me where she is," he prayed as he hurried down the street.

A few minutes later, he spotted Jarvis's partner, Joe. Taking long strides, he confronted the man. "You seen my little girl?"

Unable to meet Erik's eyes, Joe nervously looked down the street.

Erik's heart pounded harder. This man knew something. "You know where she is," he accused. "Where? Tell me."

"I don't know," the big man lied.

Erik studied him. "You're lying." He moved a step closer. "What happened to her?"

"I had nothing to do with it. It was Jarvis."

"You had nothing to do with what?" Erik demanded, panicked by the man's words. "What are you talking about? If you've, hurt her..." Erik threatened, his rage and fear taking control. He grabbed the man by the front of his shirt. "Tell me!" he shouted.

"I don't know, really. She and Jarvis got into a scuffle. Jarvis took off after her. I haven't seen either one since."

Erik loosened his grip. "Where did they go?"

Joe pointed down the street. "Toward the harbor, I think."

Erik shoved Joe out of his way and sprinted toward the pier, scanning the streets as he went. *Dear God! Help me!* He prayed as he ran. Anything could have happened to her if Jarvis was involved. His mouth felt dry and his heart beat wildly. *Why did I let her go alone?* he mourned. *All this is my fault.*

As he approached the docks, he slowed his pace. He searched the quay, but saw no sign of Iya or Jarvis. "God, where are they?" he asked hopelessly, panic engulfing him. He could find nothing.

Fearfully he scanned the water, searching the waves that broke against the pier and swept ashore. He breathed a sigh of relief when all he saw were empty waves and gulls. *At least she's not in the water,* he thought as he ran down to the beach to search the shore.

He walked the waterfront, but found nothing. As his eyes moved back and forth over the pilings, searching, he saw it—a small form wedged between two posts.

He stopped breathing and clenched his fists. He felt sick, and his blood roared in his head. "Dear God—no," he moaned as he forced his leaden legs to move. He waded into the waves, oblivious to the cold. Slowly at first, then more quickly, he stumbled toward the piling. As he approached Iya's limp and lifeless body, her arms floated aimlessly in the rhythmic surf. He knew his greatest fear had come true, and he sobbed as he gently lifted her from the icy water and clasped her tiny body to his. Her lips looked blue and her skin felt ice cold. Frantically he searched for signs of life—but there were no breaths, no flutter of eyelids. Iya was dead.

Erik clutched her to his chest and buried his face in her hair. "Dear God! No! Not this! Not Iya!" Standing knee-deep in the bay, he clung to the still, little girl and sobbed.

Clasping her tightly, he turned toward shore and carried her from the sea's cold grasp. Once on the beach, he stumbled and fell to his knees.

People began to gather. Cries of alarm and sorrow rose from those who knew Erik and Iya. "Can I help?" asked a kind voice. Erik didn't hear. He only knew his little Iya was gone. He struggled back to his feet and plodded up the beach.

Anna didn't know what drew her to the wharf, but with deep trepidation, she knew it was there she would find what she searched for. Cold fear washed over her in waves. When she heard a cry coming from the beach, she hurried her steps. Then she saw him. Erik stood on the sand with a small body in his arms. His tormented face was empty. She stifled a cry and held her arms stiffly at her sides as she waited for him.

He looked up, knowing instinctively Anna would be there. Their eyes met. Anna was afraid to look at the form in his arms, but when Erik looked at the lifeless bundle, Anna followed his gaze. Like a sleepwalker, she moved stiffly toward Erik, her eyes clinging to the limp child in her husband's arms.

She stared down into Iya's sweet face, gently lifted a strand of wet black hair and brushed it back, then caressed the little girl's cheek. Silent tears slipped from her eyes, then, unable to restrain her torment any longer, she allowed her head to fall across the little girl's chest and a wail rose from her throat, followed by another and another. She and Erik fell to their knees, leaning against one another, with Iya's body cradled between them.

They rocked slowly back and forth as a chant of death rose from Anna's mouth—a lament from her people, one she had sung long ago when it had been only her and Iya.

The song slowly died away, and Anna took Iya into her arms and knelt on the sand. "Iya, oh Iya," she sobbed. "Please come back," she pleaded, knowing it was an impossible request. She tore her eyes from her sister's lifeless body and, with tears streaming down her cheeks, looked at Erik, seeking an answer to this unbelievable tragedy.

With pain-filled eyes, Erik could only stare back.

Anna gazed at the ocean. In a still, empty voice, she said, "I no longer love the sea. It has taken everything from me."

Erik looked back toward the town of Juneau, his jaws tightened, and his eyes turned hard. "Jarvis," he muttered. "It was Jarvis." Abruptly he stood up and took a step toward town. "I'll kill him."

Clutching Iya to her, Anna cried, "Erik, no! That will not bring her back. This must be left to God. Please, Erik, I cannot lose you too."

"He will pay for this," is all Erik said.

Anna set Iya gently on the ground, stood up, and grabbed Erik's arm. "Erik, look at me."

With angry, cold eyes, Erik stared down at Anna.

Anna shuddered. She had never seen Erik like this. She swallowed and tried to think. Slowly and deliberately she said, "Erik, you cannot do this. Iya is gone. There is nothing we can do to bring her back." She glanced down at her sister lying so still on the sand, her wide, bright smile forever extinguished, and Anna's eyes filled with fresh tears. She looked back at Erik. "Let God take care of this," she pleaded.

Anna could see Erik's torment. "Anna, I have to. Please try to understand. This man has to be stopped. I can't let him get away with it. If I'd done something sooner . . ."

"Let the law take care of this."

"The law?" Erik asked contemptuously. "What law? They won't do anything! What do you think they will do about a white man killing a native?" He knelt next to Iya again and caressed her arm. "I have to do it for her," he choked. Abruptly he stood up and searched Anna's eyes for a moment. "Please understand," he begged as he held her. "I don't have any other choice."

Anna knew there was nothing more she could say. "Be careful . . . I love you," she whispered.

Erik stood back from her and, with one more glance at Iya, stumbled up the beach toward town.

Anna watched him go. "God, help him. Give him peace." She prayed and felt an unusual sense of quiet fall over her. Amid the most horrible of circumstances, she suddenly felt blanketed in God's love.

She sat down in the sand next to Iya and lifted the young girl's head and shoulders into her lap. She studied her sister, knowing it would be the last time she would look upon her. She seemed so peaceful. Her dark lashes rested against round ashen cheeks, and Anna tried to remember how she had looked when she had headed for town earlier. She had worn a broad smile and walked with a swaggering step of confidence. Tears slipped down her cheeks. She couldn't believe Iya was gone.

"Anna," came a soft voice.

Anna looked up into Millie's gentle eyes. "Oh, Millie . . ." The woman dropped to her knees and wrapped Anna in her arms.

Both women cried softly. "I am so sorry," Millie said. She cradled Anna for several minutes.

"Why, Millie? Why?"

"I wish I knew, but there are some things in life we can't explain or understand." She lifted Anna's chin and looked straight into her eyes. "One thing you can know is that Iya is with Jesus now."

"Millie, I want her here with me."

"I know. Me too," is all Millie could say.

Chapter 23

Jarvis wrenched the bureau drawer open and began shoving his clothes into a knapsack. When the drawer was empty, he swept his few personal belongings from the top of the dresser into the pack. *I'd better get out of here before people put two and two together,* he thought as he went to the wardrobe and yanked his coat off its hook. He stuffed it into the pack, then took a lighter weight jacket and slipped it on. He scanned the room for anything he might have missed. "Looks like I got everything. Time to hit the road. Dang that girl!" he nearly shouted.

As he headed for the door, it suddenly opened, and Joe stood blocking his way. The big Indian studied Jarvis, a look of contempt on his face. He stepped into the room and closed the door behind him. He took in the disheveled bureau and empty closet before looking at Jarvis again.

"You going somewhere?" he asked.

Jarvis met his gaze. "Yeah, I'm leavin'. Nothin' left for me here."

"Maybe a hangman's rope?" Joe asked flatly as he crossed to the closet and ran his hand over the top shelf. He turned and looked squarely at Jarvis. "Where is the money?"

Jarvis licked his lips nervously but didn't answer.

"Where is the money?" Joe repeated, this time more loudly.

"What money you talking about?"

Through clenched teeth, Joe said, "You know what money."

Conceding the fact that there had been some stash, Jarvis said, "I might have packed it by mistake." He made a show of looking through his pack. "No not here. You must have taken it and don't remember," he said, recinching the bag.

"Let me take a look," Joe said as he ripped the pack out of Jarvis's hands. He pulled it open and rifled through it. With a sardonic smile, he pulled out a pouch and asked, "What's this?"

"Well, will you look at that," Jarvis smirked. "I guess I took it after all."

Joe doubled up his fists and glared at Jarvis.

"I was going to leave you half," Jarvis lied.

"Oh? Pretty interesting way of going about it," Joe said and dumped the contents onto the worn spring bed. Coins and banknotes fell into a pile on the wool blanket. Joe quickly divided the money and stuffed Jarvis's share back in the leather pouch. "Here, this is your half," he said as he threw the bag toward Jarvis. It landed at the man's feet.

Jarvis slowly bent to pick it up. "Thanks," he said scornfully.

"That little girl's father came looking for her—and you."

"Yeah. What did you tell him?"

"Not much. I did not know where you were."

"Good." Jarvis said as he tied the pouch to his belt. He glanced back at Joe who was still staring at him. "I don't know where she is. Last I saw of her she was hightailing it down the street."

"So, where have you been?"

Jarvis glanced out the window. "What business is it of yours?" he growled. "I don't have to answer to you. I'll go where I please when I please."

"Looks like you are doing just that."

"I'm sick of this place. It's gone stale. And I don't need you no more, either."

"I don't know why I stayed with you. I guess I was stupider than I thought."

"You needed me, that's why. You were nothin' without me. I'm the one who knows how to handle the cards."

Joe glared at him then scooped up the remaining bills and coins and clenched them in his fist. "You better go far," he threatened. "I hope I never see you again."

"Fine by me. I've got things to do, and they don't include you," Jarvis retaliated.

"If that girl's father finds you, I will not help you. You're on your own on this one." He stuffed the money into his pocket. "From the look of him, you're a dead man if he gets his hands on you," he added with a grin. "I told him you were after her, last I saw you."

"You what?"

Joe grinned.

Nervously Jarvis hefted his pack onto his shoulder and readjusted its fit. "He doesn't scare me," he lied. "I've got plans. He'll never find me. He can look all he wants." Jarvis stepped to the door and, with his hand on the knob, stopped and looked at Joe. A momentary sense of regret washed over him. Joe had been the closest thing Jarvis had ever had to a friend. Tempted to say farewell, Jarvis quickly squelched the impulse and pulled the door open. *I don't need him. I don't need nobody,* he told himself as he slammed the door and stormed down the dimly lit corridor.

He fought a growing sense of panic. He knew Erik's anger would be too much for him if he ran into him. *I'd better get out of here before that Injun lover finds me,* he thought and hurried his steps. He hesitated in the hallway before cautiously entering the lobby, making certain Erik and his friends weren't waiting for him. Finding it empty, he marched out the door without a glance back.

Mentally he checked off the tasks he needed to accomplish before he could be on his way. *First, supplies. I'll need some staples if I'm going to stay out of the way for a good while.* As he strode down the street, his money pouch slapped against his hip with each step. It felt good and gave him a sense of security. *I'll need a horse if I'm going to make good time. If Joe had just been two minutes later, I'd have had all the money,* he lamented. *More than enough to buy a horse and still have plenty to get me on a ship out of here when the time comes.*

At the livery he picked out a lanky blue roan and a saddle. As he led the animal out of the stables and mounted him, he planned his escape. Staying on the back streets, he headed for the mercantile farthest from the center of town, always watching for Erik. Once he made it to the store, he dismounted and tied his mount at the back. Taking long, hasty strides, he went inside, swiftly made his purchases, and loaded them on his horse.

Panic drove him out of town, and he kicked his horse into a lope as he headed south. He'd seen an abandoned shack on an earlier trip into the hills surrounding Juneau and figured no one would find him there until things settled down. Before winter set in, he figured on taking a ship south. "I've had enough of the cold, wet weather. It's California sun for me," he muttered to himself as he urged his mount on.

It was nearly dark as he started up the steep path that lead into the heavy timber. His stomach quaked as he looked at the sharp drop beside the path. "You'd better keep your footing old man," he told his horse, hoping the sound of his voice would chase away his fear. "I'll put a plug through your brain if you dump me," he added, his voice shaking as he tried not to look down the steep embankment.

His horse proved to be surefooted, and they moved on easily, but when the trail grew narrower Jarvis realized he would have to dismount and lead the animal. Glancing down at the steep precipice below him, he carefully swung his leg over the horse's side and gingerly lowered himself down, squeezing between the bank and the lathered flanks of the animal. Sweating profusely, he took the reins and carefully inched forward, never taking his eyes from the ledge. Once in front of his mount, he leaned against the rock wall and looked up the narrow trail. It seemed to stretch on forever. He wiped the sweat from his brow. Tired and angry, he cursed as he slapped his hat against his leg. His horse shied away and yanked on the reins, nearly backing off the ledge. Jarvis grabbed hold of the animal's halter and yanked him back. "Stupid nag," he said as he planted his hat back on his head and headed up the rocky path. "I'd better find a place to camp soon."

When Jarvis finally crested the bluff, the sun had set behind the horizon. Thankful for even ground, he sighed with relief and sat on a large boulder to rest. Taking out his tobacco pouch and papers, he rolled a cigarette and lit it, inhaling deeply as he surveyed the valley below him. Juneau looked small against the backdrop of mountains, forests, and sea. He wondered how much gold was still waiting to be found. Unreasonable anger rose within him as he remembered Joe's promise to help him find gold. "He never did nothin' he said he would. The liar," he griped as he blew smoke out in small puffs.

His mind returned to Iya, and as he remembered watching her thrash in the bay, he set his jaw. *There was nothin' I could do,* he told himself. *I couldn't jump in. I'd drown.* "Stupid girl. It's her own fault for not staying out of my business. I warned her," he reasoned aloud. "She should have listened," he said into the wind as a raven swept past him and settled on a nearby spruce branch. Jarvis studied the bird. "You're s'posed to be a sign of good luck," he said.

The black-feathered creature squawked at him, then took to the air and dove into the valley.

Jarvis drew on his cigarette, slowly letting the smoke slither from his lips and drift away on the breeze. He stood up, flicked the remaining butt over the embankment, and led his horse to a nearby stand of trees.

The wind began to blow as darkness settled over the land. *Looks like as good a place as any,* Jarvis thought as he pulled his jacket up tightly under his chin, wishing he'd worn his warmer coat but too lazy to get it out of his pack.

A marten suddenly broke free of the bushes and darted in front of his horse and across the clearing, disappearing into the underbrush. Jarvis's mount shrieked in terror and reared back. Jarvis yanked on the reins, but the horse, fighting the tautness, struck Jarvis in the chest with his hoof and knocked him to the ground. With the wind knocked out of him, Jarvis could only watch as the frightened animal loped off the way they had come.

A string of oaths flew from his mouth. "Come back here, you hack." But the horse ignored him and kept on running. Incredulous, Jarvis sat where he was for a moment before gingerly pushing himself up from the ground and dusting off his backside. "Now what am I gonna do? Everything I had was on that good-for-nothing animal."

He searched his pockets to see what he had on him, but all he found were his knife, cigarettes, and a few matches. He examined his pistol, making certain it hadn't been damaged. His money still hung from his belt. He patted it. "A lot of good it'll do me now," he complained. With a heavy sigh, he sat on a log and took out his crumpled cigarettes and matches. They were nearly gone. "Better save them," he said testily and shoved them back in his pocket.

He glanced around at the darkening forest. "I'd like to get my hands on that rodent. I'd have me some roasted marten for supper. I'm so hungry even that would taste good," he added as his stomach rumbled. "Food or not, I'll need a fire," he said as he glanced at the sky. Wisps of clouds blotted out the first stars. "It'll be cold."

He gathered enough kindling for the evening, then took his knife and cut stout limbs from the trees. "This is not what I had in mind," he grumbled, thinking of the comfortable cabin and hot meal he'd planned on.

After he had cut several limbs, he piled the dry twigs and grasses into a mound and knelt next to it. Cupping his hand around the tinder, he waited for the breeze to quiet and lit a match, holding it to the dry grass. A sudden gust of wind extinguished the flame before it could light, and he had to try again. This time, the pile quickly ignited, and he gradually added larger pieces of wood. Only after he had a good fire going did he sit back and rest, pulling his lightweight jacket closer. He shivered. Even with the blaze, he could feel the autumn chill. He thought of his warm coat and blankets still strapped to his horse. "They're probably back in Juneau by now," he muttered. His stomach grumbled and he wished he had a rabbit roasting over the fire. "And a drink wouldn't hurt either," he said as he stared at the leaping flames.

The night closed in around him, and he huddled closer to the fire as he contemplated what he would do. *I'll have to go back. I can't make it without supplies.* He cursed, and kicked at a rock.

A faint sound came from the trees, and Jarvis held still as he listened. He slowed his breathing and waited. It came again, but Jarvis still couldn't tell what it was. His heart pounded, and goose bumps raised on his arms. "Ah, it's just the wind in the trees," he told himself, but he pulled his revolver from its holster anyway. He peered beyond the light of the fire, trying to penetrate the darkness. A low growl came from the bushes, and the hairs on Jarvis's neck bristled.

For a long while, he heard nothing and slowly began to relax. *Whatever it was, it must have moved on,* he told himself as he lay back and tried to get comfortable on the hard ground. He shivered against the cold and thought of California and its sunny, warm days. *Yep, I'll head south. Maybe when I go on down to Juneau for supplies, there won't be much of a ruckus. She was just an Injun. Maybe I can head for California right away.*

A snarl came from the forest, only this time it was somewhere behind him. He jumped to his feet and gripped his gun between shaking hands. All he could hear was the blood pounding in his head. "All right, where are you?" he yelled into the blackness, then tossed a large stone in the direction of the sound.

As if in answer to Jarvis's question, a honey-colored brown bear broke free of the trees into the light of the fire. His small black eyes sought out Jarvis. He rose to his hind legs and sniffed, his mouth agape and claws pawing the air, threatening the interloper who had dared to set foot in his domain.

Fear strangled Jarvis as he crouched, ready to flee. He fired at the animal but missed. He fired again and again, emptying his weapon. His mouth dry and his stomach churning in fear, Jarvis stood defenseless against the enraged monarch of the forest.

The bear blustered and snorted as he threw his huge head back and forth.

Keeping his eyes on the bear, Jarvis tossed his useless gun aside, slowly squatted, and reached for a piece of burning wood. With an unexpected burst of energy, the beast dropped to his feet and rushed at Jarvis.

Jarvis leaped back and cowered behind a tree. The bear veered off. His heart beating wildly, Jarvis leaned his head against the rough bark of the pine and thought he might be sick. Taking rapid, deep breaths, he peered into the darkness where the bear had disappeared. He could not see or hear anything, but he knew the bear was there. Fearing he had circled around behind him, Jarvis whirled around, but all he saw was empty blackness.

Panting now and with sweat dripping from his brow, he whispered, "You're out there. I know you're there." Then he heard it. Bushes and twigs crackled and broke as the beast stormed toward him through the underbrush. Jarvis felt as if his heart stopped. Quaking, he pulled his knife from his belt and stood ready to sink it into the animal, but just as the bear was upon him, he veered off, once more.

Knowing only terror now, Jarvis blindly scrambled through bushes and trees. Limbs ripped at his face, and logs reached out and tripped him. "God, help me!" he screamed as he stumbled and plunged to the earth. "Help me!"

But God was silent.

Jarvis could hear the bear approaching. The animal's snarling rage sent spikes of fear through him. He pushed himself to his feet and ran desperately into the blackness. The sound of tearing brush followed close behind, and he knew the animal was near. He felt the beast's hot breath on his back, but forced his legs to move—one step—another—then he felt searing pain as the animal sank his teeth into his shoulder. The bear yanked Jarvis off his feet, then suddenly released him and Jarvis fell to the ground. Fear flooded him with adrenaline, and he scrambled to his knees, oblivious to his pain as he fought his way through berry bushes and brush, wishing he could find a place to burrow, safe from the attack. But the bear pursued and, once again, Jarvis felt the agony of the animal's teeth. The brute lifted him into the air and shook him like a rag doll, pouring all his fury into the destruction of this man. Jarvis wished it would end, longed for the blessed blackness of unconsciousness, but it was not to be—he remained aware, knowing his own death.

This is it—the end. His mind reeled. *I'm going to end up in the belly of a bear.* Unexpectedly the animal let him loose and trotted away, leaving Jarvis bleeding and dying.

For a long time he lay in the darkness, unable to move, knowing his life seeped from him with each beat of his heart. He listened for the bear's return, unaware of the passage of time. He remembered hearing the screech of an owl and something scurrying in the brush—and a tiny shriek as the owl found its prey.

Then the scent of bear filled his nostrils, and he was suddenly alert and helpless as he tried to sink into the earth. Fear welled up within him, and he broke into a sweat as he lay in the dark, shaking with terror. He fought the desire to scream as he waited for the end.

He felt the sharp pressure of the bear's teeth against his scalp. It was the last thing Jarvis knew before the bear's massive jaws crushed out his life.

Chapter 24

As Anna cleared away the morning dishes, she watched Luba with concern. Once again, the little girl had refused to eat and stood staring out the window and up the trail, as if waiting for Iya to return. Anna set the dishes down and joined her. Together they watched the bare trees bend beneath a blast of cold wind and listened to it howl as it whipped under the eaves and around the house.

The dismal weather seemed fitting to Anna. Nothing had been the same since Iya's death. The house felt too large, and their lives felt empty. Luba had taken it the hardest. It had been a month, and the little girl still rarely spoke and looked lost much of the time.

Anna wrapped her arm around Luba's shoulders and felt her tense beneath her touch, then relax and shudder slightly as she struggled not to cry.

"Luba, how can I help?" Anna asked gently.

With tears slipping from her eyes, Luba bit into her lip and shook her head. Anna pulled her close, knowing there were no words that could ease her daughter's pain. It was too great a sorrow.

Despite the weather, the boys spent hours outdoors, expending their grief in a physical way while Erik poured himself into mining. Anna was glad he had his work. *It will help him if he keeps busy,* she thought.

The day he found Iya, Erik had searched for Jarvis, but his enemy had managed to slip away. Anna was thankful. Erik had been so enraged that she knew he would have killed the man if he had found him. *Even if Jarvis deserved death, Erik should not carry the shame,* Anna thought and thanked God for sparing him from his own impulsive rage. No one had seen Jarvis since that horrible day, and Anna hoped they never would again.

"God must deal with him," she had explained to Erik, while

struggling against her own need for revenge. Together, they spent hours seeking God and his comfort, their only solace. He alone offered peace. Slowly their anger and hatred ebbed, leaving behind a pain to be healed. Anna struggled to not let bitterness hold her in its deadly grasp. She knew it would take time yet longed for freedom from the inner turmoil and grief that blanketed her.

She gave Luba a squeeze. "Why don't you go out for a while today?"

Luba didn't look at her but continued to stare out the window. "Why should I?" she asked flatly.

"The fresh air will make you feel better."

"I don't want fresh air," Luba cried. "I want Iya." Sobs rose up and choked off her words.

Anna felt her own tears begin, and her throat tightened as she knelt and hugged Luba. "We all want that." She hesitated before continuing. "But it is not possible. Iya cannot come back."

Even as she said the words, Anna couldn't believe she was saying them. It didn't seem possible that her sister was gone. She had always been so vibrant with so much to give. She had loved life. How was it that she was the one whose life had been taken? *God, it's not fair,* Anna lamented. She squeezed Luba tighter. Fresh pain washed over her with its too familiar ache. She fought her tears, but they spilled down her cheeks, and with them, life seemed to seep from her.

She watched as the wind swept the autumn leaves across the dry earth. A lone osprey swooped over the river and a moment later rose with the wind, its talons empty. She listened as its sharp cry carried across the forest, sounding lonely and wretched.

I cannot bear this, Anna thought. *It is too much.* Then she remembered Millie's words. "We do not say good-bye forever. Iya still lives, only in heaven now. At this very moment, she is basking in God's love and light. Her departure from us is only temporary. One day we will join her." The words soothed and comforted her, and as Anna thought of Iya in God's presence, she smiled softly.

She took a deep breath and wiped away her tears, then knelt in front of Luba. Resting her hands on the little girl's shoulders, she said gently, "Luba, Iya is not dead. She is in heaven where she lives with Jesus. It is a good place, and she is very happy. One day we will go there too."

Tears cascaded down Luba's cheeks and dripped off her quivering chin. "But I miss her. She has always been here. How will I live without her?"

Anna swallowed hard, struggling to keep her own emotions under control. "Luba, do you believe God loves us?"

Luba nodded.

"If that is so, then we must trust him. Nothing touches us that he does not allow. He will help you live without Iya." She wiped a tear from Luba's cheek and brushed a strand of hair off her face. "You will always have her here," she said as she pressed her hand against Luba's chest. "She will always be a part of us."

Luba looked at Anna. "Sometimes I do not want to remember," she said quietly.

"I know. It is hard now, but one day when you think of her you will feel joy." She paused. "There was a time when I thought I could not live without those I loved. I felt lonely and wanted to die. Remember when I told you of the great wave that took my people? Iya and I were the only ones left. I longed for death, but Erik came to help us. He told me of the one true God who loves us. In time, I found happiness again."

"I don't think I can."

"You will, I promise," Anna said and stroked the little girl's hair.

"What if we forget Iya?"

"We will never forget. But soon it won't hurt so much," Anna reassured Luba as she pulled the little girl close and hugged her tight. As lightheartedly as she could, she said, "Now, you go out and play."

Luba looked at her, her eyes still haunted with sorrow.

"Iya would feel sad if she knew you wouldn't play anymore," Anna prodded.

Luba nodded, and her mouth turned up in a quivering smile. "Iya loved the creek," she said as she turned and took her coat from its hook. "I will go there," she added as she glanced back at Anna and stepped outside.

Anna watched from the window. Luba huddled in her coat and carefully stepped off the porch. She looked up at the sky and, with a whimsical look, closed her eyes. Anna's eyes burned with tears as she watched a smile emerge on her daughter's face. Her step a little lighter, Luba walked toward the path that led to the creek.

Anna sighed as she turned and faced the empty room. She shivered. The fire had died down, and the room felt cold. She added more wood and returned to her chores. As she worked, she began to hum an ancient tune her mother had taught her years before. She and Iya had sung it many times, but it had been a long while since they had shared the song. She remembered how it had lifted their spirits when she, Iya, and Erik had traveled to this new land in the umiak. It seemed so long ago . . . and like yesterday. She hugged herself. "Oh, Iya, I miss you," she whispered.

A knock at the door disrupted her thoughts, and Anna went to answer it. As she opened it, a rush of emotions swept through her. First shock, then anger, and finally curiosity. Why would Jarvis's partner visit her?

For a long moment, she said nothing. Trying to control her storming emotions, she studied the man.

Joe was unable to meet Anna's stare and looked down at the wooden planking under his feet. Finally breaking the silence, he said, "I, uh . . . wanted to talk to you."

How can I speak to this man? His partner killed our Iya. Everything within Anna screamed for her to spew her anger and hatred upon him, then slam the door, shutting him out of their lives, but instead she heard herself say, "Please come in," and opened the door a little wider.

The big man stepped inside.

Uncertain whether she could trust him, Anna glanced beyond him to see if the children were in sight, but there was no one. She felt a prickle of fear as she realized what this man might be capable of. But as she studied him, she detected no threat, only . . . she didn't know—meekness?

She closed the door and crossed to the kitchen. "Please sit. I will pour us some coffee."

Joe glanced around the room. "This is nice," he said as he sat down at the table and folded his hands in front of him.

Anna noticed he was unusually graceful for such a big man.

He kept his eyes on his hands, afraid to look at Anna. "I know this must seem odd, my coming here," he mumbled. "I would understand if you wanted to throw me out."

Anna set a cup of coffee in front of him. "I thought of it," she answered warily and took a seat across from him. "Why are you here?"

Joe looked at Anna. "I do not even know exactly. I thought on it all the way over here. Ever since that day . . . " he paused and wrung his hands. "I have wanted to talk to you, but I could not bring myself to. I feel real bad about what happened and wanted you to understand that. I know it does not change anything, but I just needed you to know . . . " He stopped and took a deep breath. "I'm sorry about the little girl."

"She was my only sister," Anna said shortly.

Joe nodded and sipped his coffee.

Anna studied hers, but left it on the table, cupped between her hands as she waited for him to continue. *I wish he would leave,* she thought. *I do not want to talk of this. I do not wish to soothe his conscience.*

"I didn't see what happened," Joe went on, "but Jarvis was real mad when he took out after your sister . . ."

"Iya," Anna supplied.

Joe glanced up at her then back at his hands. "I should have gone after them. Maybe I could have done something. I don't know. But I'm real sorry."

Anna could feel the man's remorse, his guilt—maybe even repentance? Her anger began to fade. She tried to hang on to it, but as she looked at the broken man sitting across from her, all she could see was his pain and self-loathing. She flinched at his torment.

Her next words shocked even her. "It is not your fault," she said gently.

"I never meant for anything like this to happen. I knew Jarvis had a mean streak, but this? I did not know." His eyes brimmed with unexpected tears. "If I had known, I could have stopped it. I feel like it is my fault. Please forgive me."

Anna's anger melted away. She reached out, touched Joe's hand, and looked into his tortured eyes. "I do not hate you," she said quietly. "I forgive you, but you must take this to Jesus. He is the one who forgives all sin."

Joe took a ragged breath and, with a puzzled look, stared into Anna's eyes. "Your sister is dead. How can you forgive me?"

It was then that Anna realized the enormity of what was happening, and joy welled up within her. "It is not me, but God in me," she answered.

Joe only looked at her.

"I wanted to hate you, but God would not allow it." Her eyes brimmed, and the muscles in her throat tightened as she continued. "Years ago, I learned of a God of love who sacrificed his Son for me. When I understood, I put my trust in that Son, Jesus, and he has lived within me ever since. Because of him I live and grow stronger each day. I see the world through new eyes. I have learned to trust him no matter what, and he comforts and helps me to love when I am unable, to forgive when it is impossible, and to follow him through the darkest times. It is not me who forgives you, but God in me."

Joe looked at his hands again. "I have heard of this Jesus. The God of the white man. But I never believed it."

"Once I hated him."

"You are not like most people," Joe said hesitantly. "I wish I could be like you, but I am nothing. My life is vile. How could God ever forgive me?"

Anna smiled. "He forgives because he is God. If you seek his truth, he will give it. Believe that his Son, Jesus Christ, died for you, that he took all your sin upon himself, and you will be clean, free of sin."

"I don't know," Joe said, shaking his head. "Why would he do that?"

Anna waited until Joe looked at her, then answered evenly, "Because he loves you, Joe."

His voice tight with emotion, Joe said, "It is hard to believe anyone could love me."

"God loves everyone," Anna said as she got up from the table. "I would like to read something to you," she added as she walked to the bookshelf and reached for her Bible. She set it on the table and sat down, then flipped through the pages. When she found what she was looking for, she stopped.

"In the book of John, the fifth chapter, it says, *'Most assuredly, I say to you, he who hears My word and believes in Him who sent Me has everlasting life, and shall not come into judgment, but has passed from death into life.'*"

Joe thought a moment, then asked, "What does it mean 'passed from death into life'?"

"If we do not trust in God's Son for our salvation, we will spend eternity without him—in hell. A living death. But if we trust in him and accept his gift of salvation, we will live in heaven with him forever—a place where there is no darkness, only light, a home without suffering, only joy."

Joe glanced out the window, then back at Anna. "I know you believe what you're saying. I see it in your eyes and in your life." He paused. "I will think on what you have said." Joe pushed himself up from the table and walked to the door. He looked less battered. "Thank you."

"Joe, what is your last name?" Anna asked as she followed him to the door.

"Nikolie," Joe answered.

"I'm glad to know you, Joe Nikolie," she said and grasped his hand and shook it.

Joe nodded slightly as he opened the door and quickly stepped outside, closing it behind him.

Calm settled over Anna as she watched the big Indian leave. "Thank you, Father," she said as she went back to the table, sat down, and began to read her Bible. She felt at peace, the kind of peace only God can give.

After dinner that evening, when the children had gone to their beds, Erik sat in his chair reading the Bible while Anna sat across from him, putting the finishing touches on a quilt.

"I had a visitor today," she said quietly.

Erik looked up. "Who?"

"Joe Nikolie."

"Who's that?"

"You know, Jarvis's partner," Anna said warily, uncertain of Erik's reaction.

Erik's expression turned angry. "What did he want?"

"He came to apologize. He feels it is his fault that Iya . . ." Anna couldn't finish the sentence.

Erik didn't say anything, but stared into the fire.

Anna could see his jaw twitching in anger. "Erik, I told him about Jesus. I think he might believe."

Erik didn't look up.

"Erik, I don't hate him anymore. God helped me to see the real Joe and what he feels. He helped me to forgive. I want Joe to have a place in heaven too. And I know that is God's will."

Erik looked at Anna through tear-filled eyes. "I know you're right. It's just so hard. I've prayed and prayed, but I can't forgive him."

Anna crossed the room, sat at Erik's feet, and rested her head in his lap. "God will take care of it. Allow him to change your heart. When the time is right, it will happen."

"Sometimes it seems she's still here," Erik said, his voice catching.

"I found something today," Anna said as she pushed herself up and walked across to their room. A moment later, she returned with a small bundle in her hand. "I found it when I was cleaning," she said as she held out the doll Erik had fashioned for Iya their first winter together. "I was going to store it, but I think we should keep it out where we can see it. That way she will always be here." Anna caressed the toy. "She loved this doll more than all her others, I think, because it's the one you made for her."

Erik took the crude toy from Anna. "I remember. It was her first Christmas," he choked.

Anna leaned against him as they stared at the gift, remembering that first year.

A deep sense of loss settled over Anna. "Erik, Iya and I were the last people from the beach. When I am gone, there will be no one."

Erik stood up and placed his hands on Anna's shoulders and turned her toward him. "You and Iya weren't the only ones who left that beach."

Anna puzzled over his words.

"Luba was with you too. Remember? She already lived within you."

Anna smiled softly. "Yes, there is Luba."

"Anna, all your children are a part of your people. Each of them is from you. And their children and their children's children . . . forever. Your people will continue."

Anna took a deep breath as she tried to comprehend the promise of future generations. "I must tell them. They need to know where they come from. They must never forget."

She went to the trunk where she stored her most precious possessions. Slowly she opened the lid and carefully sorted through the items. When her hands found a small box resting near the bottom, she stood up. "I put this away many years ago," she explained as she returned to Erik. "I think it is time to take it out." She opened the box and lifted out the walrus tooth necklace Erik had found on a shattered beach so many years before.

"I will wear it again. It will remind me of where I come from and who I am." She slipped it over her head, allowing the glossy ornament to rest against her skin. "When Luba is grown, it will be hers. And she will remember. We will continue."

Erik pulled Anna into his arms. "One day we will *all* be reunited for eternity. And there will be no more good-byes."

Anna smiled and sighed, the agony of her loss fading in the light of God's eternal promise.

About the Author

*M*uch of Bonnie Leon's adult life has been spent as a homemaker and mother. She's dabbled in writing for years, but never set it in a place of priority in her life until an accident in 1991 left her unable to work. Little did she know at the time how important writing would become for her. Bonnie has never regretted the change in her life and thanks God for her family, who has supported her through the difficult but exciting new direction her life has taken.

Bonnie and her husband, Greg, live in the small rural community of Glide, Oregon, with their three children—Paul, eighteen; Kristi, seventeen; and Sarah, fourteen.

Although Bonnie spent her childhood in Washington State, her ancestors originated on the Aleutian Islands of Alaska. She grew up listening to fascinating and inspiring stories about Alaska and its people. Bonnie's mother, grandmother, and great-grandmother lived amid poverty and prejudice. But with the help of a loving God they grew up without the bitterness those conditions can bring. The story of Alaska's early peoples is Bonnie's heritage—a heritage she wishes to pass on to others through her writing.

In the Land of White Nights follows Bonnie's first book, *The Journey of Eleven Moons*.

An excerpt from *Return to the Misty Shore,*
Book 3 in the Northern Lights Series:

*W*hat *if Nicholas has already left?* Luba worried
as she hurried into town. She searched the streets and shops. *I must
find him,* she anguished. Just when she was ready to concede he'd
left Juneau without her, she saw him.

Nicholas stepped out of the mercantile, and seeing Luba, he
nonchalantly leaned against the front of the store and waited for her.

As Luba approached, he made no move of welcome, only
watched her with a guarded expression.

He's angry, Luba thought, her heart thudding against her chest.
"Hello, Nicholas," she said hesitantly.

Nicholas didn't move. "Hello," he answered almost indifferently.

"I . . . I thought about what you said."

Nicholas squared his jaw without comment.

"You were right. I'm not a little girl anymore, and it is time I
made my own decisions."

Again, Nicholas made no response.

"Please, say something."

"What is there to say?"

Luba swallowed hard. "Nicholas, I need you."

"Do you?"

"Yes. And it *is* time I grew up. I love you and want to marry you."
She took her bag from her shoulder and held it out to the unyielding,
young native man. "I'm ready to go with you."

"What about your parents?" Nicholas asked.

Meeting his gaze, Luba replied, "You are more important."

Nicholas finally smiled and pulled Luba to him. He held her
tightly and smoothed her hair. "I knew you would come," he said
quietly.

"I have been a longtime advocate of the pioneering research of Daniel Amen. I believe this book may be his best ever as it distills much of his previous work coupled with some of the newest research into a comprehensive, but clearly stated lifestyle program. The science behind the program is complex, but its execution is easy to follow if you truly want to separate biological age from chronological age."

—Barry Sears, Ph.D., author of *The Zone*

"*Use Your Brain to Change Your Age* is inspiring and practical. Its case studies make this book powerfully impactful, both for adults and young adults in schools. I can't think of a single reader who won't find himself or herself represented in the stories of women and men who have used Dr. Amen's wisdom and research to live healthy lives. This is a must-read for anyone interested in the human brain and the body that shelters it."

—Michael Gurian, author of *Leadership and the Sexes* and *Boys and Girls Learn Differently*

"Thorough, practical, and inspiring, this is an essential guide to reclaiming your brain—and your life! It's never too late to start . . . or too early. I recommend it to anyone with a brain."

—Hyla Cass, M.D., author of *8 Weeks to Vibrant Health*

"Your brain health is intimately tied to your physical health, and in this revolutionary and life-transforming book you will learn to help the organ that the majority of the medical, psychiatric, and psychological healthcare professionals neglect—the brain! Whether you are a first-time reader of Dr. Amen or someone like me who has read all of his books, you will learn new insights and will feel motivated to make the changes in your life to become a younger, better-looking you. If you change your brain you will not only change your life, you will improve the quality and length of your life!"

—Earl R. Henslin, Psy.D., author of *This Is Your Brain on Joy*

"I couldn't stop reading Dr. Amen's new book until I was finished. As a holistic neurosurgeon, I found it to be the best user's guide to optimal brain function I have ever read. His incredible storytelling skill combined with practical information will change your life."

—Joseph C. Maroon, M.D., professor and vice chairman of the Department of Neurosurgery, University of Pittsburgh Medical Center, and team neurosurgeon, Pittsburgh Steelers

"This book is so engaging that I almost burned my dinner while reading it. . . . The overarching message is hope and motivation. As Dr. Amen proposes, the fountain of youth is between your ears."

—Ingrid Kohlstadt, M.D., Ph.D., *Townsend Letter*

"Obesity, depression, and Alzheimer's disease are current epidemics that are predicted to get worse. If you want to avoid them and improve your physical and mental health, read Dr. Amen's books."

—Stephen R. Covey, author of *The 7 Habits of Highly Effective People* and *The Leader in Me*

"*Use Your Brain to Change Your Age* provides outstanding and practical advice based on what we know about how the brain and our body work. The information in this book is tremendously important for anyone wanting to stay young and keep their body and brain as young and healthy as possible. Important for everyone whether you are older and want to grow younger or younger and want to get a head start on living a long and vigorous life."

—Andrew Newberg, M.D., coauthor of *How God Changes Your Brain* and director of the Myrna Brind Center of Integrative Medicine, Thomas Jefferson University

"If you want to think smarter, you need to have a healthier brain. This is another incredibly helpful book from Dr. Daniel Amen for anyone who wants to increase their brain capacity. I want to stay sharp, and that's why I read everything Dr. Amen writes—and you should too!"

—Dr. Rick Warren, author of *The Purpose Driven Life*

"Sign me up for a better brain. We are all getting older. But if you want to do it feeling younger and able to remember where you put your glasses, read Dr. Amen's new book. It is filled with great stories and inspiration to take care of the most important part of you."　　　　—Bill Cosby